Benjamin's Crossing

Jay Parini has written four books of poetry and five novels, including *Anthracite Country*, *The Patch Boys*, *Town Life* and *The Last Station*. He has also written a biography of John Steinbeck and a critical study of Theodore Roethke. He teaches at Middlebury College, in Vermont, where he lives with his wife and three sons.

D1341381

A NOVEL

BENJAMIN'S CROSSING

Jay Parini

TRANSWORLD PUBLISHERS LTD
61–63 Uxbridge Road, London W5 5SA

TRANSWORLD PUBLISHERS (AUSTRALIA) PTY LTD
15–25 Helles Avenue, Moorebank, NSW 2170

TRANSWORLD PUBLISHERS (NZ) LTD
3 William Pickering Drive, Albany, Auckland

Published 1998 by Anchor – a division of Transworld Publishers Ltd.

Copyright © 1997 by Jay Parini

A catalogue record for this book is available from the British Library.

ISBN 1862 30039 9

Typeset in Adobe Caslon by Phoenix Typesetting, West Yorkshire.
Printed by Mackays of Chatham plc, Chatham, Kent.

For Devon, every word of it

BENJAMIN'S
CROSSING

I came into this world under the sign of Saturn – star of the slowest revolution, planet of detours and delays.

1 GERSHOM SCHOLEM

Port-Bou, Spain: 1950. Here I stand, a man who did not even weep at the death of his own parents, weeping for Walter Benjamin, my dear lost friend. The graveyard has a vertical pitch, suspended over a green-gold sea in the shadow of the Pyrenees.

A decade or more has passed, but I still hear his voice shunting the dry grass, curling with the wind, caught in the boom and tingle of the surf. 'If I were to join you in Palestine,' he said, 'it is entirely possible that my situation would improve. Then again, who can say? I tend, as you see, to pause at the fork in every road, shifting my weight from foot to foot.' He wrote that in 1931, when the opportunity was still there. He could have come, you know, to Jerusalem, where he would have lived among like-minded people. There was no need for this destruction. I would eventually have found him a position in the university – or in a school, perhaps. Teachers are always in demand. Or a library. He would have made an excellent curator of manuscripts and objets d'art. Who knew more than Walter Benjamin?

He never guessed the extreme turn things would take in Europe: Benjamin was simply not that sort of man. It is fair to say that he understood little about real life; he was – dare I say it? – an ignoramus when it came to politics. But what a literary mind! He could enter the labyrinth of a text and, like Theseus, unspool a thread from his heart that he could follow back to the light, having gone down so deep, having stood face-to-face with the Minotaur itself and slain it.

The European mind has lost its champion, its dauphin, its sweetest prince, though nobody really knows it. Would they care if they knew? I doubt the world can produce another quite like Benjamin. Even if it does, the soil of this continent is no longer right for such a mind. It could never thrive in this befouled and selfish, soulless climate. I should don sackcloth, hike into the desert, mourn. I should cry out with Jeremiah: 'And I brought you into a plentiful country, to eat the fruit thereof and the goodness thereof, but when ye entered, ye defiled my land, and made mine heritage an abomination.'

But here I stand, on the Spanish border, where he died ten years ago. He was my friend, and I had to see this grave for myself. To visualize and confirm everything. And to see exactly what happened and where it happened, this tragedy that can still bring a good night's sleep skidding to a halt.

The surf breaks on rocky shingle below me, and bladder wrack lies exposed like intestines among driftwood and boulders, the anemones pulsing in little rock pools like yellow hearts, as if trying to keep the great beast of the sea alive. There is such struggle for life everywhere. But the entropic nature of the universe cannot be denied. Things fall apart, and that's that.

This is the place where Eva Ruiz, a French-born woman who runs the only hotel in the village, tells me he is buried, but I'm not sure which grave is his.

'He was a polite man, your friend,' she said this morning, serving me coffee in the terraced garden behind her pink-faced hotel, which is perched on a cliff overlooking the sea. 'I liked him very much.'

'That was a long time ago. You must have had so many guests,' I said. Her hands fluttered in her lap like a pair of white moths.

'Oh no,' she insisted. 'I remember him well, your Dr Benjamin. A small and very sensitive man, and a Jew, as I recall. He had a bushy mustache and wore thick glasses and was kind to my daughter, you see. A mother remembers that sort of thing. Suzanne still refers to him.'

'May I speak with your daughter?'

'That is impossible, I'm afraid. She has been sent away to school, in Nice.' Her face grew rigid, and the mothlike hands flew to her neck, as if she might strangle herself before my very eyes.

'The way he died,' she said, 'it was too sad, really, and so ill-considered.'

'Pardon?'

'From my viewpoint, of course. Given my situation, you see. I am a widow. One has to take many things into account.'

'I'm afraid you confuse me, madame,' I said.

'Do I?' She leapt to her feet and looked out the window. 'I have no gift for words, I'm afraid. I say the wrong things. It used to exasperate my husband, who was an officer . . . under General Franco. He met the general on two or three occasions.'

I realized there was no point in interrogating her further, but it interested me that Benjamin had made such an impression on her. She could not have known him well. If my calculations are correct, he was only here in Port-Bou for a day or so, in early October 1940 – the last day of his life. Nevertheless, Madame Ruiz had been able to shed impressive tears on his behalf when I first mentioned that he was my friend; mascara streaked her powdery cheeks, making black lines that followed and deepened the heavy creases in her skin. Her broad forehead was a plinth for the tall black statue of her hair. I supposed that in her youth she would have been a formidable beauty, but now she was appalling.

'He had several friends with him, as I recall. They were all quite pleasant. A middle-aged woman and her son. And another man, I think. A Belgian teacher or accountant – I forget which. They had come a great distance on foot, over the mountains! The poor things were exhausted!'

'It was a common route for Jews, was it not?'

'For Jews, yes. And others. I did my best to make it easy for them, but it was never easy, you see. The border guards were vigilant, and the local police . . . you could never trust them.' She whispered under her breath that General Franco was not especially sympathetic to the Jews. This hardly surprised me. The history of the Jews in Spain has been an anguished one, going back to Isabella and Ferdinand, who did their best to scatter us to the ends of the earth. The fires of pogroms licked the night skies as shiploads of Jews cast off for Africa or the Middle East.

'You are yourself a Jew?' she asked.

'Yes.'

'I see from your passport that you live in Jerusalem.'

'I do.'

'It must be a lovely city,' she said. 'One of my sisters married a Jew. A large fellow, with a purple birthmark on his forehead. He's in the fur trade. Bernard Cohen, his name is.' She looked at me as if I should somehow know him.

I chose not to interpret her remarks but accept them as a piece of unmediated personal history. Whether or not this Madame Ruiz approved of her sister's marriage was not my business. That she was probably an anti-Semite was clear enough.

She introduced me to a diminutive, wrinkled man called Pablo. In rapid Catalan, she explained to him what I wanted, and he seemed to understand. He led me to an unmarked grave – one of a dozen or so unmarked graves at the end of an allée of cedars. Wisteria, succulent and purple, dangled in the sea breeze from a stone wall. This was, I thought at once, an appropriate sort of place for one's bones to meld into dirt: a little squint of heaven on earth.

Pablo smelled of wine, and I did not trust him. Like Madame Ruiz, he did not look at me as we spoke.

'Are you sure this is it?' I asked, testing my Spanish. The stone marker was pocked and mottled, with no initials on it, no date, nothing. It seemed much older than a decade.

Pablo shrugged. 'I buried him myself,' he said, or seemed to say, in Catalan. Though I am a linguist by training, Catalan defeats me.

I did not believe him but tipped him anyway, indicating I would like to be alone at my friend's grave, or supposed grave, under a hard, blue Spanish sky, rocking back and forth in prayer as a rabbi might have done that terrible day in 1940, had there been a rabbi. I wanted somehow to complete a circle I had begun to draw so many years before, and to make amends for something that can never be amended.

Our correspondence of three decades ended abruptly in the late spring of 1940, and it was some time before I heard that he had died – by his own hand, apparently. For many reasons, this information did not surprise me. It would have surprised me more if he had actually made it to New York or Cuba or Casablanca; it would have suggested resources not obviously within his grasp.

I first caught a glimpse of Benjamin in 1913, at the Café Tiergarten in Berlin. Those smoky establishments along the Kurfürstendamm have long passed out of existence, but in those days there was nothing like them, with their cool marble floors and high ceilings and potted plants that dangled and drooped like creatures from another world. One could sit and chatter about politics, philosophy, and literature until the morning star rose over Berlin without having to buy more than one cup of thick Turkish coffee. Young Berliners hoping to fashion themselves as intellectuals or artists flocked from all parts of the city, testing the quality of their minds and hearts on one another.

Benjamin had not yet awakened to a sense of his own Jewishness then, in those innocent years before the Great War. He was a votary of Gustav Wyneken, that Pied Piper for rebellious sons of the haute bourgeoisie, who had been his schoolmaster at Haubinda, an elegant country boarding school in Thüringen, which two of my cousins also attended at roughly the same time. The bond between Benjamin and his teacher was famous in certain circles.

I will not pretend otherwise: Benjamin and I were both well off, and perhaps a little spoiled by our circumstances; we had grown used to ridiculous luxury, a life cushioned by the labor of countless servants, to well-appointed houses or apartments crammed with handsome (if rather heavy and ornate) furniture. Our walls were hung with dreary landscape oils by minor Bavarian artists of the mid-nineteenth century, and our floors covered by Persian carpets. The truth is we both disliked, even resented, our circumstances; the sheer lack of spiritual or (as he would say) 'dialectical' interest shown by our parents and their friends appalled us. 'Their life is so thin,' Benjamin would say. 'I pity them, and their souls.'

It happened that Benjamin was making a well-publicized speech that evening in the Tiergarten, which is the reason I had come. An acquaintance had said to me, 'Walter Benjamin is the new Kant,' thus enraging me. I wondered why on earth people said such things. Still, my curiosity was piqued, and I determined to see this 'new Kant' for myself.

There were two rival groups of students in Berlin at the time: the Wyneken band, who formed the Youth Movement and deployed rather pseudopatriotic arguments for the preservation and promotion of Germanic culture, and the Zionist group to which I belonged, known as the Jung Juda. My group understood only too well that Germany was no place for Jews, no matter how comfortable Jewish life in Berlin had grown. I don't think Wyneken's little friends even noticed they were Jewish, though most of them were. If they did, it meant nothing to them. You might ask them directly, 'Are you Jewish?' and they would answer, 'I am German. My family is Jewish by tradition, but I do not practice any faith.'

Because of his reputation for uncompromising brilliance, Benjamin had been chosen by Wyneken to represent the Youth Movement that night. Eighty or so of us gathered in a large room over the main café: young men mostly, with a few women. Everyone was smoking and drinking coffee, misting the room with their presence; I can still hear the crackle of cups and laughter and loud debate typical of those gatherings.

Of course, a hush fell as Wyneken himself stood to introduce Benjamin, whom he called 'a young philosopher, poet, and literary scholar known to many of you already.' It was peculiar to hear a young man who had published nothing described in those exalted terms. I began to understand what everyone saw in Wyneken: He was a flatterer.

Even Benjamin seemed embarrassed by his teacher's epithets as he listened to the introduction. He crushed his cigarette into an ashtray on the table beside him, then rose slowly. He began with a quotation from Hegel clearly designed to frighten off the wrong sort of people. Much to my surprise, I saw that Benjamin was not the sort of man to make concessions to an audience. He did not even bother to mention which of Hegel's works he was citing, assuming that his listeners would know it. If they didn't, well – that was too bad. You shouldn't be there if you didn't know your Hegel.

The speech itself was tortuous but – I had to admit it – brilliant. Benjamin's voice had a strange but melodious quality: a subtonic aura, familiar in its way but still idiosyncratic. I later thought of it as a well-seasoned viola, though on rare occasions it squeaked like a cheap fiddle. The real melody was in the argument itself. It would have sounded reasonable if overheard through a wall so thick that the words themselves could not be made out, only the tune.

Zionism, he proclaimed, had its merits, but educational reform was the most pressing issue before German-Jewish youth of the day. This raised my hackles, and I sat up tall, feeling my pulse quicken. I began to tap my fingers on my knees as Benjamin's voice rose and fell, pulling the audience forward in their seats (especially when the sound level dropped to the merest whisper). As he talked, he kept his eyes fastened on the far left corner of the ceiling, as if there were something he strained to see. Only once, when he seemed to be struggling to regain his thoughts, did he interrupt this stare to face his listeners directly, and it was disconcerting – as if for the first time he realized other people were in the room! He recovered, however, locating his beloved corner of the ceiling once again. It was impressively odd.

The talk finished, he did not even nod toward his audience (who clapped politely, some of them with real enthusiasm) but, improbably, left the room altogether. I somehow imagined there would be questions, but he walked straight up the central aisle, peering at the floor ahead through the gold rims of thick glasses. He gave the clear impression of a man who did not care what anyone thought about his speech – an attitude I grudgingly admired. Why answer all of these dolts? Moreover, there was something sublime, even otherworldly, about his self-absorption. One could easily imagine him as an old man drowsing over the Talmud, in some remote yeshiva.

I noticed in passing that his black shoes were highly polished – an attempt at conformity, perhaps – but he had smeared the wax onto his white socks, and the results were ludicrous; his tie was food-stained, and his shirt needed pressing. In all, he was short, thin-boned, extremely dark in complexion, with masses of wiry black hair that looked more like a fur hat than real hair. He walked with the sideways shuffle typical of myopics, his peripheral vision poor or nonexistent. In later years, when I saw him coming toward me in the distance, I often thought of Charlie Chaplin, and once or twice I called him Herr Chaplin to his face – a joke that seemed not to register.

My first personal encounter with Benjamin came two years later, when he was twenty-three and I seventeen. It was 1915, a year into the Great War, and a singularly hot and melancholy summer had consumed Berlin. The streets teemed with eager young soldiers who did not quite realize the devastation that lay ahead of them, although one sensed from all the wild merrymaking that many could feel death coming on, could even smell it rising in their nostrils. Army vehicles appeared in the streets, rattling down the broad vistas and beside the parks, some of them already scorched and pocked from battle; the Kaiser's face blazoned from posters in shop windows. Flags multiplied and fluttered from every balcony in the city. I remember seeing a phalanx of equestrian warriors riding grandly through the streets – an absurdity in the age of machine guns and gas warfare, but typical of Germanic sentimentality. The myth of Teutonic invincibility would take decades to shatter.

I ignored the war as best I could. I was in the habit of attending lectures now and then, and one evening I chanced upon an address by a popular (and now deservedly forgotten) figure called Kurt Hiller, who had just published a book about the wisdom of boredom. His remarks went down very well with everyone but me. As I recall, he attempted to argue that history was complete nonsense, that we are born into one generation and this remains our reality. Whatever happened before us must be erased, forgotten. Since history cannot be fathomed or described, there is no point to worrying over it. And so on. A disgraceful performance.

I interrupted him rudely at one point, objecting to some particularly weak link in his argument and adopting, I fear, a pompous tone. Though a teenager yet, I had confidence in my own powers of intellect, and I did not suffer fools gladly. Benjamin, who was sitting in the row ahead of me, turned and smiled when he caught my eye. I believe I winked at him, involuntarily, then rued my peculiar gesture. What would he think of me?

As was the custom of this group, a discussion of Hiller's lecture was held the next week in Charlottenburg in a student residence hall, and Benjamin – as I had dared to hope – was present. He wore a baggy suit with a waistcoat, and a gold watch chain draped in a semi-circle across his belly, which bulged slightly: a hint of the portly middle-age that as yet lay sleeping in the cave of his youth. The seat beside him was empty, but I shifted for a while at the back of the room, wondering if I dared sit next to him. Several people came in, and my heart thumped: I wanted someone else to sit there, to relieve me of having to do so. But no one did. I steeled myself and sat down firmly beside him, nodding politely when he looked up to see who I was.

In the ten minutes or so before the discussion began, I tried several times to get up sufficient courage to speak to him. Werner, my brother, had put the fear of God into me about Benjamin, and I preferred not to make a fool of myself. Once the meeting got under way, however, I found myself speaking volubly, challenging nearly everyone who made a significant point. For his part, Benjamin said little, sitting beside me like a sphinx, his eyes fixed ahead of him. What he did say, however, contradicted me, though not explicitly. In retrospect, I can see the crude beginnings of his vexed posture toward history in his remarks that night, but these were sufficiently inchoate then; one could not have pinned him down, I suspect.

At one point I contradicted him sharply, and I felt weak and silly as I left the room, thinking I would never see him again. Already I had lost two friends, old schoolmates, in the war, and sometimes it seemed that everyone I knew would eventually be sucked into that whirling vortex, swallowed whole by the History that people like Kurt Hiller so readily mocked.

Life grew less comfortable at this time, even for people like my parents. Mysteriously, servants disappeared; meals became less bountiful, and certain foodstuffs disappeared from shops. Meat, for example, became almost too expensive to buy, and fruit became scarce. Veal, which had been a staple of our prewar diet, seemed to vanish. 'The troops are eating well,' my father would say, with only a touch of irony.

One day, perhaps a fortnight after the discussion in Charlottenburg, I was in the catalog room of the university library, sitting at a long table with a lacquered top, when Benjamin suddenly appeared. His jacket was covered with a snowy lint of dandruff, and he leaned harshly to one side, as if the ship's deck of the room had shifted in a great swell. He came right up to me, splay-footed, his face bobbing on his neck, and stopped within a foot of my face. He did not say a word as he surveyed my presence from shoe to scalp. Impassive myself, I tried to meet his gaze, my heart pounding. Then he turned and rushed from the room. Not a minute later, however, he was back. This time he strode right up to me, as if emboldened.

'I believe you are the gentleman who had much to say about history the other night?' he said. It was impossible to determine his tone. Was he accusing me of something? (Later, I would come to understand his peculiar way of speaking, which was curiously inward and indirect, as if the world were far too difficult to interpret up close.)

I confessed I was, indeed, the gentleman in question.

'In that case,' he said, 'you must give me your address and telephone number. We should have a talk.'

I scribbled the details on a slip of paper, which he stuffed into the pocket of his jacket. I imagined it jostling there with laundry slips, tobacco crumbs, and random notes on the philosophy of

Schopenhauer. Here was a man who did not compartmentalize like the rest of us, nor did he compromise with everyday life. His mind was ablaze with ideas, and their concrete embodiments in the world seemed only to puzzle him, to disrupt the pure serenity of mind. It would seem, as I came to know him, that the details of living actually hurt him; he did not want, could hardly stand, the necessary interruptions that human life entails.

Before taking his leave, he bowed with exaggerated courtesy. 'Thank you very much, sir,' he said.

Not three days later a note arrived for me at home: 'Dear Sir – I should like you to visit me this Thursday at around five-thirty.'

No sooner had I opened the note, however, than the telephone rang. It was Benjamin.

'I wonder, Herr Scholem, if you might come on Wednesday instead? Or perhaps Tuesday? Tuesday is perhaps a better day for me.'

'So I will come on Tuesday,' I said.

'No, I think Wednesday is better. Do you like Wednesday?'

'Wednesday has always been a particular favorite of mine, Herr Benjamin,' I said.

There was a gap as he tried to process my tone.

'Are you there, Herr Benjamin?' I asked.

'This line is not good,' he said. 'Wartime conditions, I suppose.'

'I hear you quite well.'

'Ah, good! Very good. Is Wednesday all right, then?' He was now shouting into the phone, distorting the sound.

'Yes, I am free on Wednesday.'

'Marvelous. I will see you on Wednesday, if you're quite certain.'

It was a maddening trait of his, this indecisiveness, which in his case was complicated by his extreme politeness. He hovered ceaselessly between this and that opinion or idea, terrified to put his money down. When it came to women, he was also hopeless in making decisions; no woman was ever quite right, unless she was living with somebody else or found him unattractive. In smaller ways, too, this lack of firmness arose only to confound him; in a restaurant, for example, he would order the fish, then call the waiter to change his mind several times; in the end, it was the fish he ate, all the while coveting whatever morsels appeared on the plates of others. Once I said, 'All right, Walter, I shall switch plates with you. It ruins the meal for me to watch you stare at my food.' But even then, with the plates switched, he sighed, 'I was right the first time around, wasn't I? Yours is not so good.'

Benjamin lived at that time with his parents in the Grunewald section of Berlin, at 23 Delbrückstrasse, just around the corner from the broad, tree-lined Jagostrasse, near the famous park. A dark, oak-paneled elevator took one to their apartment on the top floor, where an elderly maid in a navy blue dress with a lace collar let one in. It was all quite proper, as one might expect of a wealthy household in the western section of Berlin in those days.

'We have been expecting you, Herr Scholem,' said the maid.

I was led to Benjamin's room down a long corridor from which I could glimpse the opulence of the apartment itself. The 1870s (Grunderzeit) furniture cried out to the onlooker: 'Be careful what you say in my presence!' In the main sitting room, the sofas were covered with a mauve velvet; the curtains were a thick silvery brocade. I noticed a particularly nice Aubusson tapestry hanging on one wall: a hunting scene with several rapacious Dutchmen attacking a hapless wolf. There were purple and red rugs on the floor, like islands of color in a sea of honey-brown wood. Burnt-orange flowers drooped from Chinese vases, redolently oppressive. It was all quite grand, though something of an haute bourgeois cliché.

The walls along the corridor boasted depressing landscapes in oil by minor Parisian and Bavarian artists; they had presumably been acquired by Benjamin's father, Emil, who was rumored to have made a killing in the field of art. Indeed, my father had recently bought a painting at Lepke's, the auction house on Koch Street that Emil ran, so I had heard a good deal about the elder Benjamin, who was also involved in the wine and building trades. 'Herr Benjamin,' my father pronounced last night over dinner, 'has a finger in every pie.' He liked very much that I should be friendly with the son of this respectable man of business.

'Ah, Scholem, it's you!' Benjamin said, opening the door of his bedroom. 'I am pleased to see you, Herr Scholem.'

A slightly younger fellow sat beside him, elegantly dressed in a brown suit, quite unlike Benjamin in appearance but unmistakably a brother; they had the same dark eyes and ever so vaguely hooked noses.

'Let me introduce Georg Benjamin, my brother,' he said.

I shook hands with Georg, who began to chatter about a party he attended the night before, a bash held in honor of friends soon to be sent to the front. There was much drinking and dancing, and the girls were loose. I pretended to listen, forcing the occasional grin. I could see that Georg's performance displeased his older brother, who stared out the window with a serious frown.

The objects in the room held my attention, the way everything tumbled on itself. Old and new books lined every wall and formed precarious stacks in two corners. I happened to see Nattlau's biography of Bakunin lying open on a narrow bed, its margins crammed with notes. I could just make out the word 'NONSENSE!' in capital letters beside one paragraph and cringed. One always regrets these youthful ejaculations in later years. The *Aufruf zum Sozialismus* of Gustav Landauer lay on the floor, facedown – a second-rate but dangerous book pleading the case for socialism. A novel by Balzac could also be seen, open, near the table by his bed, although I could not read the title.

Benjamin seemed to ignore me while Georg blathered on. It was quite a surprise when, unexpectedly, he belted out, 'Georg, please! You will drive us mad!'

Georg caught himself midsentence, as if hung up and dangling on barbed wire.

'You must not rattle on like this,' Benjamin added. 'Herr Scholem has come here to discuss a lecture that we both attended.'

'I see,' he said. He took out a pipe and began to play with lighting it. 'So, discuss.'

'It was very kind of you to invite me around,' I said, trying to shift the conversation into its proper channel.

'My dear Scholem, you must never apologize for yourself. It does not become you.'

'I'm sorry.'

'Sit down, please. We were going to talk about history, I believe. The Hiller lecture got us thinking didn't it?'

'Yes,' I said. 'I've been thinking about history – not any specific history, but the notion of the past, and the ways we try to represent it.'

I saw Georg wince. He was not used to thinking about these things, or thinking at all.

I was settled now in a large leather chair, the arms of which overwhelmed me. Benjamin sat opposite, cross-legged, on the bed. Georg stood in the corner, with his pipe, now disgorging blue rings into the air.

'You must explain why you reacted as you did to what Herr Hiller was saying the other night,' Benjamin said. 'I disliked it, too, but perhaps for different reasons . . . and not so intensely as you.'

'Only an idiot would believe that history is of no consequence,' I said. 'The man has obviously been reading Nietzsche.'

'You dislike Nietzsche?'

'He is a dangerous influence. We Jews, you know, have a vested interest in history. People who forget their past may wish, perhaps unconsciously, to destroy their future. They have the stink of death about them. What they really hope is to destroy every trace that leads to their loathsome present.'

'Bravo!' cried Georg. 'You have a wonderful manner of speaking, Herr Scholem. A real Demosthenes!'

Benjamin rolled a cigarette on his lap, ignoring his brother. 'I am largely in agreement with your point of view,' he said, speaking very slowly. 'You see, my work here, such as it is, concerns the nature of history, the historical process. There is no such thing as history, you see. It's a grand fiction, a layering of points of view.' He paused for quite some time. 'History is a kind of myth,' he added. 'It's a dream, perhaps even the dream of a dream. All very subjective – I suppose that is what I'm saying.'

'I cannot agree, Herr Benjamin,' I said.

'Nor I,' said Georg. 'It was my worst subject in school. I nearly failed my exams last year because of history.'

'So what *is* history?' I asked Georg.

'It's what has happened.'

Benjamin was smiling hugely, his crooked, tobacco-stained teeth like an ill-conceived fence around his gums. 'So how would you describe the current war, Georg? What has really happened?'

'We have had to defend ourselves against a vicious enemy.'

'I see.'

'You make everything so complicated,' Georg added. 'There is no need to dismantle every incident, to tear apart every text, limb from limb. Life is too short for that.'

'Some lives are shorter than they need be,' I said, although the implications of my remark appeared not to register.

Now Benjamin weighed in at some length, talking about what he called 'the fragile text of history,' which he said 'we revise over and over.' It was clear he'd read a good deal of Hegel and was fond of what he called dialectical thinking. Quite naturally, we moved on to discuss socialism, which was in the air now and on the tip of every tongue in the more interesting cafés. I had myself been reading Fourier with some distaste.

'Socialism is simply jealousy,' said Georg. 'Quite naturally, the poor would like what the rich possess. If they can't get it any other way, they will legislate it into their pockets.'

I could not disagree. 'You would detest my brother, Werner,' I said. 'A rabid socialist, but he doesn't think his ideas through. He's something of a gadfly.' I went on to describe my own interest in anarchism, having recently read the Russian anarchist Kropotkin.

'Ah, Kropotkin,' Benjamin sighed. 'A dear soul but no thinker. An enthusiast, really. It is the problem with most dialectical thinkers: They see too little at one time. The *form* of the argument controls its content.'

'Socialism is a kind of secular religion, is it not?'

One hates saying the obvious, but I don't think Benjamin noticed. Because of his myopia, he was peculiarly unresponsive to the mood of anyone around him.

'You are a Jew, of course,' I said, 'and, as such, you must see things from a certain angle. I do.'

'I am a Jew, I suppose. I do myself like to visit synagogues, don't you? They are beautiful museums of a lost culture.'

It startled me to realize that here was a man afraid of his own heritage. Like most assimilated Jews, he preferred to keep the subject of Judaism at bay.

'A Jew is by definition an outsider,' I said, 'especially in Germany. Which is why Zionism seems to me a natural response to a specific historical circumstance.'

Georg Benjamin blundered in: 'The Germans have been good to Jews. There are no real Germans anyway: The country is a recent invention, composed of many different races. The Jews make up one little piece of the large mosaic that is modern Germany.'

Benjamin nodded as if he agreed with him, although I later discovered one could not rely on these ordinary signals of human discourse. There was something oddly disjunctive about him; he did not telegraph his intentions, like most of us do. There was an invisible wall between himself and the real world, but it was solid; his friends were constantly rebuffed and stunned by its solidity and omnipresence.

'Socialism is at heart a messianic creed, however secular,' I continued. 'This is perhaps too obvious to need stating. My own feeling is that spiritual feelings – a vision of justice – should arise from reading the Torah. I am, after all, a Jew.'

You would never know this, of course, if you merely observed my parents from a distance. Like Benjamin's parents, they had lost touch with their roots; they were branches swaying in thin soil, ready to be toppled by a culture they adored but which despised and reviled them. Hindsight is perfect sight, but even then I could envision only too crisply the fate of Jews in Europe. The self-deception practiced by Jews everywhere around me was sickening, and I vowed to persuade Benjamin of the importance of Zionism before it was too late.

'In wartime, we are all Germans,' said Georg.

'A Jew should not fight in this war,' I insisted. 'There is no good reason to support this fabricated nation with our lives. The Germans will never thank us. They will kill us, eventually.'

Georg seemed to scoff but said nothing.

'My brother is a simple patriot,' Benjamin said. 'He actually believes that war will have a purifying effect on people.'

'Have you been called up?'

'Soon I shall be, as will you.' His eyes glittered with mischief. 'Can you see me with a rifle in my hands?'

'You would shoot yourself in the foot,' Georg said, laughing. 'If the enemy knew enough, they would beg Germany to enlist you, Walter.'

Benjamin himself chortled now, an odd laugh to which I grew accustomed in years to come. 'It amuses me to hear you speak of "the enemy," Georg. The enemy!' His laughter grew shrill, even offensive.

'So you imagine we have no enemy?'

'I refuse to imagine nonsense. The politicians do that for us.'

Benjamin, in later years, was rarely so explicit. He simply withdrew from the world of everyday politics, retreating into himself: into a world of ideas, a heavenly conversation in which Plato, Kant, Nietzsche, Heine, Baudelaire, Mendelssohn, and a dozen others sat in glory above the fray, on an alabaster cloud.

Georg left the room now, shaking his head.

That afternoon, Benjamin and I began to think of ways to avoid conscription. However different our views of history, we shared a belief in the disastrous nature of this particular war. If ever any conflict was pointless, this was it. What could Germany possibly hope to gain from it? How could one justify the millions of young men gassed, bayoneted, shredded by machine guns – or pushed beyond despair into nihilism by the absurdity of it all? This was a war without spoils, and without honor – a point that would grow even clearer in the years to come.

When I think of him, a peculiar, almost inexpressible pity overwhelms me. The death of Benjamin was, for me, the death of the European mind, the end of a way of life. If only he had come to Jerusalem, this final disaster might have been averted. But his stubbornness killed him, and his impossible vacillation. He waited too long for everything, my dear Walter. Far too long. It was perhaps inevitable that it should come to this: an unmarked grave in Port-Bou, and the wasted, sad years without him stretching before me like a desert.

WALTER BENJAMIN

*A person listening to a story is in the company of the storyteller; even some-
body reading a story aloud shares this companionship. The reader of a
novel, however, is isolated, more so than any other reader. In this
solitude, readers of novels seize upon their material more jealously than
anyone else. They are ready to make it completely their own, to devour it,
as it were. Indeed, they destroy and swallow up the material presented
to them as a fire devours logs in a fireplace. The suspense that permeates
a good novel is akin to the draft that fans the flame in a fireplace and
enlivens its play.*

Walter Benjamin to Dora Benjamin

Paris

9 June 1940

My Dearest Dora,

I sit, as usual, in the library, at the same table where I've sat for the past decade, working on the book. *The book*: Dare I call it so, these thousand pages that have become my life? I have been absorbed by these pages; they have soaked me up, blotted out my life.

I could have had a life, a 'real' life, something other than this. A life with you and our dear son, my darling Stefan. Could have, should have, might have . . . I lose myself in the tenses.

What a ridiculous man you married, Dora. Not a man at all: a locus for meaning, however temporary. Words gather around me, shift through me. My apartment, as you know, is nothing but a room of books, of clippings from journals, of pages that swirl in the air like crisp October leaves caught in an updraft. Neitzsche insists that God is dead, by which he suggests that all forms of centralized or centralizing meaning have been called into question. You could say I am the embodiment of this death, this loss of determined meaning. I no longer believe in it myself, or wish for it nostalgically.

The Nazis are coming, bringing their own kind of determined meaning, their hatred of all ambiguity. They have gobbled up so much: Austria and Poland, Holland and Belgium. It gives me some relief that you and Stefan are safe in London. If I can, I will send the promised money soon. I have little at present: Teddy Adorno seems to have forgotten our arrangement, and the post contains no checks, rarely even a good word. I must not, however, complain about the Institute. They have made it possible for me to live by writing and research this past decade. Their stipend has allowed a meager living.

I wish I could place a few reviews and articles in the French papers, but this will not happen. I have had to sell everything, even the edition of Heine that I bought in Munich, with you, soon after we were married. Do you recall it, with the gold flowers splayed on a maroon buckram cover? We read the poems aloud to each other through much of the night, then made love by a wood fire, in the apartment overlooking the park that Ernst let us borrow while he was in Italy. You see, I remember these things. Does it surprise you?

You underestimate me, Dora, you really do. Just because I could not make my feelings plain to you, you assumed I did not have feelings. It was my fault, of course, for expressing so little. I never knew quite what to say.

My sister and I will stay here as long as we can. I cannot believe that Paris will fall to the Germans, no matter what the papers say. Everyone is so pessimistic. But in case I must go, I have been making arrangements for exit visas. I will go to Portugal, or perhaps to Casablanca. One can get to New York from Marseilles, so I'm told. It is difficult to verify anything.

I will visit you both in London when the war ends; it cannot last long, you know. Hitler is already overextended, pressing forward on too many fronts. There is considerable opposition among the people he wishes to colonize, as you may have heard. In France, for example, one rarely meets people sympathetic to the Nazis.

I realize that, because we have been living apart for so long, we are nearly strangers, but I would like to visit you again. Each time we meet, the spark between us seems to rekindle, does it not? And Dora, you must believe that I want very badly to be a father to my son. A boy in his teenage years needs a father. You have said as much in your letters, and I agree with you.

Perhaps with cause, you do not trust me. Often I do not trust myself. I wander the blazing streets of Paris at night, and I see the giddy, terrified, motley crowds moving together – this mass of humanity – but I do not feel connected. I do not know how to acknowledge my part in their vast company.

Last night, in the theatre in Montmartre, they showed several of my favorite Chaplins. I do love the sweet small man, his wide-eyed wonder at the world, that hapless shuffle. I laughed and wept so hard: for you, for me, for all the comical, unhappy lives whirled around us like scraps of newspaper. The pages are torn and scattered, and the whole paper can never be reassembled.

Have you heard anything from Scholem? I often wish I had followed him to Palestine, and taken you and Stefan there as well. We might have found an apartment overlooking the Old City. Your father, I know, would have liked that. But here we are, with the Channel between us, and all borders closed. I would make the crossing if I could. I would come immediately.

Please give Stefan my love, and tell him to behave in ways that would make me proud. It is so important, you see, to choose the right path, and to follow it consistently. That I have failed to do so myself is of course of genuine pain to me, as you will understand.

I hope you can find it somewhere in your heart to forgive me, Dora. I have been unfaithful to you, but also to myself. Yet I can change. I can do so, now that the book is finished. If I may boast, I will say that it is good. If there is any reason for my brief residence on this planet, it's in these pages.

Please write to me when you can. We are not leaving Paris soon, not if we can help it.

With much affection,

Walter

Gershom Scholem to Dora Benjamin

Jerusalem

15 September 1940

Dear Dora,

I seem to have lost track of Walter. Do you know his whereabouts? His last letter seemed to trail off in midsentence. I imagine if anyone knows where he might be, you do. He always loved you, as I'm sure you know.

It didn't surprise me that you could not live together in peace. He is a difficult man, though a great one. Yes, I will use that improbable word: *great*. I do so in full awareness of his limitations. He happens to possess the most subtle mind of our generation. It is fair to say that he has never, not once, compromised this brilliance – something one can say about so few of us. His mind burns up whatever text or image comes before it. It dissolves meaning, then reconstitutes it, making it present to itself. Only the greatest critical thinkers can do this.

Had he been more disciplined (and, my dear, we all know his distracted manner), he might have walked the corridors of eternity with Plato and Moses Mendelssohn. He would still make a welcome guest at their table, would he not? Even if, as usual, he said almost nothing, they would find his aura – the gnomic stare and occasional wisecrack – interesting. And then, suddenly, the way his conversation will lift off vertically, move into strange, unearthly regions . . .

Has it really been two decades or more since our time together in Switzerland? We very nearly reached a point of perfect intellectual congress, as if the normal barriers of skin and skull did not inhibit the fluid transfer of ideas. Words somehow did not come between us, as they do now, hopelessly tainting clear thought and lucid expression. We seemed in those days to move beyond language, but *through* language. I still don't know what happened, or how the enterprise collapsed on us. It was never the same again after that.

I loved him, Dora, as did you. But he could not love either of us fully – not in the way we loved him. He could not release some part of himself. Was it selfishness? I don't think so (though you might well disagree). Something like the emotional equivalent of myopia. And yet, when he saw, he saw completely; he could read a person the way he did a text, entering that labyrinth boldly, going into the deepest recesses. I felt plumbed by him, interrogated and discovered.

But I fear for him now. He has stayed too long in Paris, Dora. The Nazis are winning this war. They may well consume Europe and destroy whatever we thought we meant by the term *civilization*. I swear, if they damage one hair on Walter's head, I will curse them forever. He represents, in a curious way, everything they oppose. He is so open to everything: the contrarieties, the absurdities. He will face death, I know, with a rueful wince, then a dark chuckle that will boom through heaven.

If you hear of his whereabouts, write to me at once. I will try to contact him. Meanwhile, if you and Stefan are in need of anything, please do let me know.

With my regards,

Gerhard

Walter Benjamin to Asja Lacis

Paris

12 June 1940

My dearest Asja,

No word of you, not for two years. I have almost given up hope, but I write just in case what everyone says is wrong. The rumors are terrible, Asja. If there is any truth to them, you will never see these words, never know that I am thinking of you.

I did try to suggest that you leave the Soviet state to its own machinations. I will say nothing more on this matter. It is not my place to make judgments for other people. As you know, I have only admired your political constancy and idealism, so hugely greater than my own. I often recall that winter in Moscow, when I came because I loved you. I knew I could only be happy in your love, folded into your life. The idea of existing outside the glow of your being seemed unthinkable. You said it was nonsense, that I would certainly find someone else and be just as happy. But you were wrong. I have found no-one. I have not found anything that resembles love in these fifteen or sixteen years.

I have been living with Dora, my sister. You have never met her. She is a peculiar woman, deeply inward, hugely bored by life. She has read nothing and has thought about nothing. In this, I suppose, she resembles most people one might encounter on the street. In a way, I find this easier than living with the other Dora, my former wife. She had indeed read everything and was full of ideas. Like you. Only we fought for every inch of intellectual ground, and my life became exhausting. If only we had never had a child . . .

Oh, Asja, what is the point? I keep writing and writing, hearing nothing and fearing the worst. Should I resign myself to your perpetual absence from my life? Should I put my pen in a drawer and shut it tight?

I will talk to you, darling, if only in prayer. If only to myself, whispering in the night, conjuring your presence as one summons the dead. There is some comfort there.

From the day we first met, on Capri, I have had no image dearer to me than your face. Sometimes it appears in the dark, glimmering above me, its candle-yellow glow and kindling stare. I talk to this vision, earnestly, but there is no answer, no counter-love, no response. I am alone, Asja. I know it. You often said I was the loneliest man you knew, and I protested. In this, you were correct. The loneliness only grows, I'm afraid. And the worse for lack of you.

Your own, always loving,

W. B.

Now I am on the last half-emptied case of books, unpacking my library in the quiet hours past midnight. Other thoughts fill me besides the ones I have mentioned – images more than thoughts, memories. I remember so vividly the cities where I found certain books: Riga, Naples, Munich, Danzig, Moscow, Florence, Basel, Paris. I recall Rosenthal's sumptuous apartment in Munich, and the Danzig Stockturm where the late Hans Rhaue lived, and Süssengut's musty book cellar in North Berlin. I recall the exact rooms where these books were stored, and my own unkempt rooms as a student in Munich. My apartment in Bern comes to mind, and my solitude on the Lake of Brienz. Finally, I recall my boyhood bedroom, where only four or five of the thousands of books piled up around me now once lived. Oh, the collector's bliss! The bliss of a man of leisure!

2

Benjamin would not leave Paris, that much was clear. There was no point. First of all, the Germans would never make it so far; they would be stopped at the Belgian frontier. René Gautier, writing in *Le Monde*, had been quite specific about this. 'Hitler's army,' he wrote, only yesterday, 'is inherently weak, in morale and physical strength.' He also noted that 'Hitler is no fool, and will never push beyond the limits of obvious power.' Even in Germany itself, so he heard, the opposition was gaining ground each day.

He had been sitting alone by a bright window in the Café des Deux Magots for some hours, nursing a single demitasse of espresso. His last pack of cigarettes – a cheap Turkish brand called Salomé that he loathed anyway – was gone, and the prospects for buying another today were nil. The waiter, who had come to know his strange but courteous customer, had left a basket of rolls on the table, without charge, and all but one had been gratefully eaten. (Benjamin did not want to appear greedy, especially in the eyes of the super-cilious maître d', who stood in a black tie by the front entrance, as if vetting customers.)

The motley street life along the Saint Germain des Prés did not interest him as much as his open notebook. Even a chilling parade of army tanks seemingly in a hurry did not hold his attention; the war, in his mind, was still metaphorical. It was something Dora, his frightened sister, nagged him about every night. 'We must leave Paris while the going is good,' she kept saying. 'The going will never be good,' he would reply. In the course of nearly five decades on this benighted planet, the going for him had never been anything but difficult.

This morning, in the café, Benjamin hit upon the idea of diagramming his life, and his preferred spatial model was unquestionably the labyrinth. His pencil circumnavigated the page, swirling inward; his labyrinth soon began to look more like a reverse, impacted spiral. 'Enough!' he shouted, to no one in particular, causing eyebrows to be raised around the room and attracting the waiter's attention.

'Another coffee, monsieur?'

Benjamin looked up from his notebooks, wearily; he was exhausted now, mentally and physically. Sometimes it was painfully awkward to fight through the scrim of thoughts that he had drawn, meticulously, around his consciousness over the past decade. All gestures from the outside world felt like incursions, and were unwelcome. 'Coffee?'

'Would you like another cup of coffee?'

'Ah, coffee!'

The waiter shifted from foot to foot, trying to fathom what Benjamin had meant; then he left. He had, by now, grown accustomed to this customer's odd ways.

Benjamin tapped his fingers on the tablecloth. It had been several weeks since he sent his essay on Baudelaire to New York. He hoped his friend Max Horkheimer would soon get back to him, perhaps with good news, although it worried him that Max had showed an edge of coolness in his letters for several years now. Benjamin himself considered it harder to reject than to be rejected, so he appreciated Max's situation, which he interpreted as the necessary coolness of all editors. Nevertheless, the essay was brilliant. He knew it was brilliant, and it was distressing that Max had not responded quickly.

If the article was accepted, a little money might be forthcoming – something beyond the pitiful stipend that had sustained him, more or less, for some years. His situation had never been so precarious, not even during those first years in Paris, when he lived on next to nothing. Had he not borrowed a sum of money last month from Julie

Farendot, he wasn't sure where he would be. Julie's loan had made it possible for him to eat at all, and now that money was gone, too.

He gazed out the window as a large military truck scattered a bank of pigeons, which ascended in a cloud and settled among the pearl-and-black frieze of a building, blending in perfectly; when several of them fluttered in the air, it seemed as if part of the facade were flaking into wings. This image, or series of images, brought to Benjamin's mind the philosophy of Heraclitus, who believed all nature was flux. Everything changes, so there is no point in resting one's hope on any given moment; there were no good and bad times, only changing times. He admonished himself for his own reluctance to admit change, for the way he clung to whatever in life happened to seem familiar and comforting at any given moment.

The linden trees along the curbside were beginning to turn pale yellow, riffling like pages in the wind. The air itself was cold today, unseasonable. It was June, after all – a time for blowzy winds and languorous hours, with no hint of metamorphosis. A time for disguise and false hope. Benjamin would have liked even a little false hope. The knife-edged breezes of autumn should still be gathering far away, on the Russian steppes, far from the long slow burn of a Parisian summer.

But everything was different these days, ominous and out of sorts. You could trust nothing and no one. 'There are German spies everywhere,' Dora warned him. 'You must be careful!' But what was he supposed to do about these spies? Stab them? Turn them over to the authorities? Pursue them down blank alleyways like a character in some film noir thriller? The peculiar melodrama of this moment in history bored him to death. His attraction to Marxist dialectics notwithstanding, he longed for the stasis of some *ancien régime*, a world of predictable circumstances and reassuring conventions.

All eyes swung to the entrance, where a tall, rather imposingly handsome military policeman appeared with several underlings in tow. He wore black leather gloves, which he meticulously removed while scanning the room, as if looking for someone. Benjamin knew that 'aliens' like himself were being rounded up and sent to 'relocation centers,' supposedly for their own protection, and he dipped his eyes to the floor. Under no circumstances would he consent to this kind of relocation.

He fumbled to close his notebook, as if he had written something illicit. The maître d' seemed quite dizzy with excitement, motioning to the waiter who had served Benjamin. They exchanged whispers, and then the waiter came to Benjamin's table.

'I am terribly sorry, but we need this table,' he said.

'Ah, yes,' Benjamin said. 'I understand.' But he did not understand. In the past decade of his life in Paris, he had never been dislodged from a café table. It just didn't happen.

As he left, Benjamin caught the officer's eyes; they were strangely remote, as if without pupils. He had once read a cheap French novel about a race of aliens who invaded the world; their only distinguishing nonhuman characteristic was their eyes, which had no pupils.

Benjamin put his head down and stepped outside, into the cool air. A hollowness filled his chest, and he noticed – much to his horror – that his hands were shaking visibly. What was wrong with him these days? Was forty-eight such a vast age that he should tremble and quake like an elderly gentleman? In the evenings, he could actually feel the energy dribbling through his mesh of consciousness, draining him of motivation. His heart was very bad, he knew; he could not walk ten minutes without gasping, and even the three flights of steps leading to his flat at the end of the rue Dombasle had become an obstacle. If he could afford it, he would see a doctor soon. There was a man in the rue de Payenne who specialized in heart patients, and he would go to see him as soon as a check came from New York.

His apartment was bare, unpleasantly so. Indeed, its single adornment was a chipped mahogany desk with a leather top, which once belonged to his father, Emil Benjamin. His brother, Georg, had managed to ship it from Berlin just before the Nazis took him under 'protective custody' in 1933. Five years later, Benjamin had written sadly to Gretel Adorno: 'My brother has been transferred to the penitentiary at Wilsnak, where he is forced to work at building roads. I believe life there remains bearable. The great threat for people in his situation is, I'm told by German friends, the concentration camp, which is where they take long-term prisoners. It is most distressing, although perhaps Georg is safer in these camps than on the front.' It was distressing that Georg could not write to him and he could not write to Georg. He had tried many times, but the letters were mostly returned, and there was no reason to believe that the few that had not been returned had gotten through.

Walking the streets on the Left Bank this morning, Benjamin noticed the tension in the faces that passed him; he heard the mad blowing of horns in the streets and the intemperate shouts of passersby. All night, sirens blew at the city's distant periphery. *Perhaps I am wrong*, Benjamin said to himself. *Perhaps the Germans really are coming?* He wondered how he could have done this to Dora, who counted on him. His sister-in-law, Hilde, had written urging him to leave, and Scholem, in Jerusalem, had warned him many times. 'Get out while you can,' he wrote only last month. Adorno, Horkheimer, and even Brecht had tried to get him out of Paris. 'Go to America! Go to Portugal! Go to Cuba!' they screamed in their letters. But who can leave Paris so easily? If Adorno and Horkheimer had been serious, why had they not sent money, and why not several years ago, when it would have been easy to leave France?

Of course, he would have left only with profound reluctance. Paris was the universal library, a vast reading room, and a boudoir so cruelly seductive that it had trapped him and nearly everyone who came under its spell. At night, sleepless, he imagined himself in its arms as a fire burned in the cracked marble fireplace at the far end of his bedroom. He dreamed of being surrounded by swelling cushions, sleek skins, and knickknacks of tinted glass and china – rather like Balzac in his private chambers. A silver vase on the mantel sprouted the ten lilies of the city's coat-of-arms, and there were books, sets of books everywhere in elegant buckram covers, row upon gold-lettered row.

Paris was also a particular library, one that he knew like a blind man knows his own house. For much of the past decade he had sat in the same chair at the same polished table in the Bibliothèque Nationale, in the brilliant shelter of its famous reading room, which had been designed by Henri Labrouste, libertine and architect laureate of the Second Empire. Its nine domes, colorful enameled tiles, and cast-iron columns emulated the chambers of the ideal mind, the mind in glorious contemplation of eternity. For a decade he had worked there, reading and writing, often in an attitude akin to prayer; he had waited, with infinite patience, as if a voice might speak to him as light flooded in overhead, huge pillaring beams that caught a billion dust motes in their bright atomic dance.

One reason he especially liked the reading room was that it recalled the ornate synagogue on Oranienburger Strasse in Berlin. He would go there for refuge as a teenager, not to worship but to sit and think. Built in the mid nineteenth century, it was a place removed from the chaos of his life; a place where the holy lingered, undogmatic, even unassertive. Its vast Oriental dome had been the wonder of European Jewry. This temple of tolerance proclaimed to all the world: Yes, the Jews of Germany are acceptable people after all! The neo-Gothic facade seemed to swear the allegiance of Germany and Judaism.

Berlin was, after all, the city where Moses Mendelssohn and Gothold Lessing had strolled arm in arm together in their long cashmere coats through the manicured, well-ordered parks, discussing metaphysics and aesthetics. Think of what German culture owed to Heine and Börne, to Egon Friedell and dozens of other playwrights, composers, poets, and painters! All were Jews, and all were Germans.

It had been a melancholy day when Benjamin's cousin Hannah wrote to him in the autumn of 1938 to say that the synagogue had been destroyed, burned to the ground by crazed nationalists who did not understand that Germany had room enough for all. 'There is no hope for us now,' Hannah had written, much to Benjamin's despair and disbelief, 'none whatsoever.'

Benjamin blended into the Parisian crowd, anxious and alert as more army vehicles passed in the streets, making the ground shudder. Indeed, a terrifying phalanx of soldiers crossed the Pont Neuf, and Benjamin paused to listen to their boots drumming, drumming. An elderly woman in a black shawl stood beside the bridge, weeping, and he went up to her.

'Is there anything I can do, madame?'

She looked at him curiously. 'What is that?'

'May I assist you in some way?'

The woman stared at him, uncomprehending, and Benjamin merely tipped his hat and withdrew. He realized that he did not understand the French as a people, though he had been living in Paris for more than a decade; perhaps he would never understand them.

Now he rushed toward a stalled trolley, with its antennae poised awkwardly above its black-and-white exoskeleton. As he got within several yards, it sped away. 'Stop!' he cried feebly, then bent forward to catch his breath. His heart seemed abruptly huge and violent, ripping through his chest, and pains rippled down his forearms. He noticed three small boys nearby, laughing at him, their cheeks smudged and pinched. One of them, whose features gathered on his face like fungus, stuck out his tongue, and Benjamin noticed with horror that it was covered with dark splotches. Was this whole nation suddenly diseased? Were even the children tainted?

Julie Farendot lived nearby, on the rue de Buci, and he decided to visit her before going home. It was like this in Paris: You set off in one direction and found yourself moving in another. Impossible to decide on a course of action. Everything in Paris caught the eye, beckoned, enticed with options. It would take the mind of Descartes, with its steely focus, to plunge forward unabashed amid such plenitude; or the heart of Balzac, which could take in everything and give it back in kind. Benjamin was neither Descartes nor Balzac, though he could once in a great while understand what lay behind these different kinds of genius. He had those unusual powers of empathy afforded only the rarest of critics, and he knew it. What he needed now was time to finish his masterwork and to assemble a collection of his best essays on literary and cultural topics. There was so much good work ahead of him: on Baudelaire, on Brecht. But where would he get the time, now that everyone seemed intent upon pushing him away from the library, and Paris?

Even today, in turmoil, Paris beckoned enticingly. It was somehow above and beyond the pettiness of war. It was the city of arcades, that dazzling consumer invention which had been the subject of his research for over a decade. He recalled his original enthusiasm for the arcades project, recorded in a letter to Scholem. The arcades, he said, were 'the embodiment of the collective dream of French society.' And this dream would necessarily be unsatisfying. The desires and longings of human society may have found expression in this materialistic glitter, but they had done so in such a repressed, censored, and displaced way that it could never have been satisfying for anyone. This kind of involuntary, collective dreamwork kept the nation, as a whole, from waking to its fullest expression. It left it prey to spiritual aliens, who would trample on their dreams.

Asja Lacis – the only woman he had ever loved so intensely – would say to him, liltingly, 'My dear Walter, a classless society is the ideal. A society where justice prevails. You know that very well. I don't know why you fuss so.' It was just like her, to dwell on his fussing. He was, at heart, convinced that the economy should not rule, or consume, people's lives. A line from Max Horkheimer kept returning to him: 'The blind sentence passed by the economy, that mightier social power which condemns the greater part of mankind to senseless wretchedness and crushes countless human talents, is accepted as inevitable and recognized in practice in the conduct of men.'

'You are an artist, Walter,' Asja would say to him. 'You, unlike the rest of us, are free.'

But Horkheimer was right on this, too: 'Individuality, the true factor in artistic creation and judgment, consists not in idiosyncrasies and crotchets but in the power to withstand the plastic surgery of the prevailing economic system which carves all men to one pattern.'

'You stand alone, Walter,' Asja would flatter.

'I wish it were so,' he would say. 'But I do not have the strength of a major artist. I am not a poet. My stories are incomplete, a maze of false starts. Even my essays are unfinished.'

Benjamin had visited her in Moscow in the winter of 1926, hoping to ignite their romance, to come to permanent rest in her love. He wanted a lover who shared his political ideals and who understood his spiritual project. But a peculiar distance seemed to grow between them whenever they discussed serious matters. Her Marxism was oddly unfocused, uncomplicated. She just bought the Party line, which he inevitably found embarrassing. Indeed, he could not help smirking when she introduced him to her Soviet friends as Comrade Benjamin.

His old friend Scholem had his own ready answer to the question of what fullest expression might be. 'The restoration of a messianic kingdom – *tikkun*,' he would say. It was a lovely concept, *tikkun*. But what Gerhard (who now called himself Gershom) Scholem meant by restoration was so filtered through a library of arcane works on Kabbalah that Benjamin could not approach it without a feeling of unease. It would take Scholem a lifetime to understand the concept himself, so what chance was there that he, Benjamin, could glean its essence? Perhaps if he learned Hebrew and settled down to a proper course of study, these hesitations would vanish . . . But that dream, like many others, had dissipated. He would never learn Hebrew and would never, in fact, see Jerusalem. Worse yet, he doubted that the world would ever be repaired in his lifetime.

Benjamin fought his way through vendors and pushed open the iron gate at 17 rue de Buci, turning in to a damp courtyard that smelled of laundry and stale garbage. He stepped over a broken tricycle and climbed several flights of dark stairs to Julie Farendot's flat.

He recalled that day, perhaps five years before, when he was introduced to Julie in the Café Dôme by Hans Fittko and his wife, Lisa. The Fittkos were omnipresent in left intellectual circles in the late thirties in Paris; they had ludicrous energy and were perpetually organizing protests against Hitler or gathering money to be sent to undercover anti-fascist groups in Austria or Germany. Julie and Lisa had worked closely on a pamphlet urging the French to organize against Hitler before it was too late – an essay that Benjamin had read (and dismissed as impracticable) even before he met Julie.

Only a week or so after their meeting in the Dôme, he saw her in the library. She was doing research, she said, for an article on the French Revolution as a subject for historical writing. She began talking immediately about Carlyle's history of the Revolution and his peculiar but compelling version of those shattering years. 'I adore Carlyle,' she insisted, 'even when he is wrong. He is so fierce. I love fierceness.'

Benjamin, who was never himself fierce, objected. 'Carlyle was the worst sort of Englishman – dogmatic, rude, and megalomaniac. The London clubs are full of such people.'

This mild opposition was apparently enough to win her heart. She invited him back to her flat that afternoon, and he had no sooner closed the door behind them than he found himself unbuttoning her blouse. She was thirty-one, with tight little breasts like Asja's, and slim hips. Her blond hair spilled in ringlets over her collar. She had the same gray-green eyes and straight teeth. She had everything that Asja had except, alas, a cold, merciless heart, and he missed that. Julie was soft inside, and therefore uninteresting except in the most superficial ways.

He knocked softly on the oak door, sighing. The climb to her flat had been difficult for him, and he felt his heart banging in his throat. He could scarcely breathe.

Julie peered through a crack in the door, keeping the chain latched. In these days, there was no telling who might come.

'Julie?'

'Walter!'

'Am I so frightful?'

'Come in, Walter. I was not expecting you.'

As she opened the door, he tipped his hat and bowed.

'You must be the last Jew in Paris!'

'Please,' he said. 'May I come in? I would like to sit down.'

Julie closed the door and put her arms around him. She kissed him gently on the forehead. Although their romantic affiliations had ended, they maintained a small ritual of intimacy on these occasions. Once, only the year before, this ritual had led to sexual intercourse, quite unexpectedly, but that was the exception.

'Have you eaten?'

'A little, in the café. But I am still hungry.'

'Then you will join me,' she said, with the firm expectation of obedience typical of a good headmistress. 'I hate to eat alone.' Within a few minutes, she put down before him a large bowl of broth thickened with onions, carrots, and bits of pale yellow celery; fragments of chicken floated to the surface when he stirred. An open bottle of Bordeaux sat on the table, and Julie expected him to help himself.

'Paris is not itself,' he said, swirling the wine in his glass. 'Everywhere, the people seem restless.'

'Haven't you seen the placards?' Julie asked. 'You don't look around you, do you? For you, politics is theoretical.'

'But not history,' said Benjamin, between slurps. 'History is real enough.' He turned to the soup again. 'You must excuse my etiquette,' he said. 'My mother used to scold me about bad manners. One never outgrows these habits.'

'There are placards everywhere,' Julie said. 'All *ressortissants allemands* must report to the military for transportation to special camps. It's what they call protective custody. If you choose to disobey, you will find yourself in prison. They are not joking, Walter.'

Benjamin's face registered no impression. 'I am not a German citizen,' he said, 'as you well know. I'm a refugee in flight, an anti-Nazi. What could they possibly want with someone like me? If they arrest me, they will have to feed me. I will be a drain on their economy.'

'Even the Austrians, the ones who fled the Anschluss, must report,' she said. 'They aren't picking and choosing. Everybody with the slightest connection to the Reich . . .' Her voice trailed off into a vapor of hopelessness, a kind of breathless sigh. She knew there was no point in talking to him about this. Benjamin would do as he pleased. 'To the French,' she explained, 'all German-speaking émigrés are the enemy, *les sales boches*. They despise the German accent, so anyone with the slightest trace of it must be a spy.'

Benjamin said in a high, thin voice: 'I have a hard time believing the same nation that produced Voltaire and Montaigne could be overrun by such pettiness and . . . stupidity.' He tipped his chair back, precariously, as if daring fate to hurl him to the floor and break his neck.

'Philosophy aside, you will have to report,' she said. 'But they will sort out the good Germans from the Reichsdeutsche pretty quickly. You had best go along with them.' She reached across the table to touch his hand. 'Don't let them think you are hiding something.'

Benjamin gazed into her eyes, chewing slowly, almost gingerly, as if the food contained hard foreign objects; he sipped the wine and let a whole mouthful seep into his gums before swallowing. 'It's all quite insane,' he said. 'Preposterous! Let them come for me, if that is their wish. I will not condone their paranoia.'

Julie swept her hair to one side, and he saw again how lovely her face was, with a straight, small nose, her lips pale and pink. Her eyes burned distantly, like moons on early winter mornings. Unexpectedly, he wanted to make love to her again, to feel the length of her beneath him, and her heels digging into his back. He reached for her leg under the table, and she let him slide his hand up to her panties.

'It would be far worse if the Germans got you,' she said, touching his face as if it were a piece of Limoges. 'You know what they are like. You grew up among them.'

'Let them take me to prison,' he said. 'It will be their punishment. Also, I'm quite heavy, as you know. Hard to carry.' He pulled close to her and began to nibble her ear.

'Most of the men have already gone,' Julie said. 'It's a little crazy that you should be here. I don't see how you've survived this long. You remember Hans Fittko – the man who introduced us?'

Benjamin nodded. The Fittkos had been on the periphery of his consciousness for several years, and he had once visited them at their small flat in Montmartre, at the intersection of the rue Norvins, the rue des Saules, and the rue St-Rustique: a crossroads painted several times by Utrillo. Benjamin admired the paintings more than the actual site. It was curious, he thought, how one loved reality in reflection more than in its unmediated form. Life without art would be too bare, too unadorned.

'I saw Lisa yesterday,' Julie continued. 'Apparently Hans has been taken to a camp in the south. She is to report to the Vélodrome d'Hiver, for relocation.'

'Impossible!'

'My dear Walter, you don't read the newspapers, do you?'

'The news is far too depressing, and in any case I prefer Baudelaire.'

Julie stood to allow him to unlatch her belt, and her skirt fell to her ankles. Benjamin slipped her panties down as well.

'I find Baudelaire just as depressing,' she said, letting him kiss her stomach. 'The Germans are on the outskirts of Paris, you know. Thousands of troops. I heard the artillery fire last night. If they get their hands on you . . . well, who knows? I cannot imagine you in those camps, Walter.'

Benjamin stood to embrace her. He kissed her lips, then paused. 'They will murder me, I suspect. It is part of their program, and I don't really object.'

'How can you say that?'

'They have already murdered thousands of Jews. The whole world knows this. My sister-in-law, Hilde, has written to me about these things. And my brother, Georg . . . is missing.'

'Is he alive?'

He shrugged. His expression, for the first time, betrayed a feeling of hopelessness, a sense of ruin. He already considered himself among the names of the lost. 'The situation has become impossible.'

'Nonsense,' she said, opening her mouth to his deep kisses.

They fell back onto the purple couch, and Benjamin made love to her quickly. He was always like that: pouncing, never lingering. When he was finished, he quickly pulled on his trousers and sat beside her. She lay back, naked, watching him coolly. A cigarette dangled from her lips.

Benjamin lit the cigarette, then took one for himself from her pack.

'I will miss you, Walter,' she said, exhaling the smoke.

Benjamin leaned forward and touched her cheek. 'The sad thing is I have not finished my work here. I had so many plans.' His eyebrows twitched in a way that told his excitement. 'May I read you something? I think it will interest you.'

Julie sat back with her arms folded, her back stiff: a rather masculine posture that reminded him of Asja. He used to read to her in the evenings on Capri, and she would sit with her arms crossed like that, in passive judgment.

'I have this marvelous picture in my flat,' Benjamin said. 'You remember it?'

'The Klee?'

'Yes.'

'It's a peculiar image,' she said. 'One doesn't forget it so easily.'

He dug a manuscript from his briefcase and sat beside her, close. He bent near the page to discern his tiny handwriting, which transversed the page in a crabwise scrawl. 'A Klee painting called "Angelus Novus,"' he read, slowly but distinctly, 'shows an angel looking as if he were about to move away from something he is gazing at with steady concentration. His eyes stare ahead, his mouth hangs open, his wings are outstretched. This is how one might visualize the angel of history. His face is fixed on the past, and where we may see a chain of events, he perceives a single catastrophe that continually heaps wreckage upon wreckage, and that hurls this wreckage at his feet. The angel may wish to stay, to waken the dead, to restore what has been ruined. But a gale is blowing in from Paradise; it has caught its wings so violently that the angel can no longer fold them. The gale sucks him backward into the future, the wreckage still piling skyward before his eyes. This gale is called progress.'

After a long pause, Julie said, 'That is very sad, Walter, but quite beautiful.'

'History has failed us,' Benjamin said. 'But I was unrealistic, I suppose. I thought everything would happen differently.'

Julie watched him intently. She could only just comprehend that such a creature lived and breathed, so eccentric and lovable.

Benjamin continued: 'You remember what Kafka said. "Yes, there is hope, lots of hope. But not for us."'

Julie stroked his hair now, but Benjamin seemed not to notice. His mind plowed itself up, churning in the moment's mud. Suddenly, he began to cry. She had never before seen him cry.

'Are you all right, Walter?'

'I must go home,' he said. He began to button his shirt now and to search for his tie. 'My sister is waiting for me. She will be worried.'

'You have probably frightened her to death, making her stay in Paris. Take her away quickly.'

Benjamin still did not, or could not, hear this. 'Where could we go?' he said. 'I have only my flat, a few belongings. But everything I love is here.'

'Get to Marseilles – before it's closed. There are ships leaving every day, but not for long.'

'I don't want to leave France.'

'But you must!'

Benjamin sighed. 'Everything is ruined,' he said. 'I don't see the point.'

'You must not talk like that. The Americans will join the war. It'll be over in a few months, but you must not do anything stupid in the meantime.'

He smiled. 'This will be difficult for me, as you know.' He rose slowly to put on the rest of his clothes, and Julie put on a bathrobe. In moments, he was standing in the doorway, his tie in place, his briefcase suspended from one hand. He felt like a stray bird in a windstorm, blown from limb to limb. There was nowhere to rest for long, and no comfort in the world.

'Have you had enough to eat?' Julie wondered. 'You never finished your soup.'

'You are better than soup,' he said.

She put her arms around his neck, close enough to smell his breath. 'I will miss you,' she whispered, letting her chin rest on his shoulder.

'You are very dear, Julie, and kind as well.'

'Write to me, Walter. Wherever you go.'

She went to a drawer and took out an envelope of money, and she tucked a wad of bills into Benjamin's pocket.

'You've already given me so much,' he said, scarcely protesting. 'I don't feel that I can take this.'

'Don't even think about it.'

'Are you sure?'

She nodded, letting him kiss her formally on either cheek. In her heart of hearts, she believed she would never see him again, not in this life, and she needed every ounce of energy not to break into loud sobs. He would have hated sobs.

Benjamin pushed blindly onto the dark landing, his steps uncertain, his head throbbing from the wine, the exertion of sex. As he climbed down the staircase, he could feel himself falling into a pit. The ground – terra firma, the literal and unimagined world – seemed impossible and far away, a point in space and time he could never reach, not in a million years. He would get to the bottom of this winding stair only to find himself face to face with the Minotaur, who would devour him.

WALTER BENJAMIN

The people cooped up in Germany today can no longer see the contours of the human personality. Every free man strikes them as an eccentric. Imagine for a moment the peaks of the high Alps silhouetted not against the bright sky but against folds of dark drapery. The mighty forms would show up only dimly. In exactly this way a heavy curtain shuts off the sky in this abominable country, and we can no longer see profiles of even the greatest men.

3   LISA FITTKO

Dear Hans,

I miss you, darling, wherever you are. As I write, I am hoping you are alive. I know you are. You are not the sort they can kill so easily.

I'm writing from Gurs. You know Gurs, near Oloron, where we sent letters to friends in the Brigade? Didn't Lars used to call it 'the Gurs Inferno'? He liked to exaggerate, of course, to make things sound more dangerous, more exotic. I've been here for several weeks, and it's nothing like Dante. More like Hell in that painting you once showed me, 'A Garden of Earthly Delights.' What was the painter's name? Since coming here, my memory has played dreadful tricks. I can barely recall my own name some days.

It's part of their strategy, perhaps. To try to make you forget the past. To become a number, not a name. It's much easier to manage people who do not know themselves or their past. History does not exist here. There is only the moment, which dangles like a lightbulb from a fraying cord, unshielded and ugly. There is no hint of a future here, either: that glint of hope pulling us forward in time. The word *tomorrow* has dropped from our vocabulary. We live in the present, which surrounds us like a gun-metal tube, with no light at either end.

Let me try to reassemble what happened, for myself as much as you. Getting the words down will clarify something.

Not long after they took you away, the women were herded into the Vélodrome d'Hiver. The police took into custody virtually anyone with a German name or passport or even the slightest connection to the Reich. Blond hair and blue eyes and a straight back would do it! Woe to those of us with an accent!

Paulette and I decided to report together, and we stood in line for almost five hours outside the stadium, waiting to be 'processed,' while the guards stared at us like we were diseased cattle.

Some of the women were hysterical and had wild excuses. Such imagination on display! None of us lacked an absolutely irrefutable reason why it was utterly absurd and impossible that she could be under suspicion of any kind.

'I'm a Pole,' one said. 'They'll never intern a Pole! Poland is the enemy of Germany! This doesn't make any sense!'

'I've got a bad heart,' said another. 'Feel my pulse! Have you ever felt such a pulse? And my liver is shot. I drink, you see. I've been drinking for twenty years! Gin and vodka, the worst stuff in the world. My doctor gives me not months to live, but weeks! Do you hear me, weeks!'

'Look at my swollen ankles,' cried a minuscule woman in a red dress to nobody in particular. 'How can they put a woman with ankles like this behind bars?'

'They will never put us in prison,' said another, a woman with hair like a white dandelion puff, her voice quavering with the faint hope of the damned. 'There must be ten thousand women here. What jail in Paris could hold so many people? They will let us go. All of us. This whole exercise is pointless – typical French bureaucratic madness.'

These women didn't seem to understand that each individual case is just one small part of the greater case called History. We are all the daughters of Ruth, aliens in time.

The *criblage*, as they called it, was being done by this garlicky police commissioner, who interviewed me with Paulette, assuming we were sisters. I am my own worst enemy sometimes, Hans, as you have noticed more than once. I said to the man, 'You asshole, I'm not a German! Look at my papers! Do these look like the papers of a German?'

This wasn't clever of me, but I knew they were interning the lot of us anyway, so it hardly mattered what I said. It was important to let off steam.

'I decide who is a German and who is not,' he said, grunting with a short cigar pinched between his lips, the tobacco juice drooling onto his chin. Of course, he didn't even glance at my papers. I was a wiseguy, so dangerous. A white-haired guard with bad lungs took me away, wheezing through a cough; he was a good fellow and said it would 'all be over soon enough.' For him, I suspect, it will be.

You know, Hans, it still amazes me how many of the people I thought were friends have proven fickle. Is it just human nature? You remember Mme. Girard, with the frizzy hair and blue shadow on her cheeks? The bearded landlady? I ran into her in the street, only a day or so before leaving Paris, and she pretended she didn't even know me! As if I hadn't taken her mother to the hospital in a taxi only a month before! I was shocked, but I guess it was silly of me. I keep wanting to believe the human race is finer, more altruistic and generous, than it really is.

The scene in the Vél d'Hiv, Hans . . . How to describe it? You could easily think you were listening to the cries of a slaughterhouse behind the black iron gates at the west end of the stadium, where most of the older women had been led to a glass-roofed section by the time night fell. I was glad to sleep out under the stars, where I felt free and happy. But those poor women . . . Nobody laid a hand on them, but suddenly the weight of their situation became clear; the reality hit them in the face. They were not ready. Who can be?

Paulette, bless her, had come prepared. You know Paulette. Toothbrush, a pot with a handle for cooking, two spoons, lipstick, and razors. (The razors were our safety net, in case there was no other way out.) We slept on loose tufts of hay provided, so the rumors went, 'by the Americans.' What Americans? Why do they get all the credit these days, when they do nothing but sit on their isolationist asses, as usual? Paulette swore the hay came from a Jewish relief organization run by a friend of hers, but I didn't believe that, either. There is no way of separating truth from untruth in times of war:

Rumors are everything, and you cling to them for consolation and for hope. They are like small footbridges that span the moments; without them, we would all be lost.

Paulette is such a schoolgirl, laughing at everything, even snickering. That pug nose of hers, and the freckles, and the way she shakes her hair into place – all so adolescent. Perhaps because I've known her for so long, I no longer even notice the eccentricities. Friendship is like that: You ignore those excesses of character that a stranger might find disagreeable.

The absurdity of life in the Vél d'Hiv might have amused us for several days, but the air-raid alarms sounded day and night, and so our sleep was miserably broken. (You know what I'm like when I haven't had my rest!) And the drone of bombers overhead sent our pulses racing – such an eerie sound, the way it seems to come from nowhere. I hate those planes – malevolent wild birds swooping up from hell to blacken our skies.

Newspapers were scarce, but we got our hands on the odd page, ripped off and smuggled around. The stories often seemed contradictory, but one thing was certain: The Germans were coming, and fast. They had smashed through the northern border, their tanks rolling over wheatfields, vineyards, orchards. Rumors circulated to the effect that whole villages had been burned and pillaged, that women had been raped, children abducted, and thousands of able-bodied men shot to prevent them from becoming enemy soldiers. If the German troops caught up to us, we were finished. Nobody doubted it.

Two weeks in the Vél d'Hiv was enough for anyone. Paulette and I were already planning our escape (it would not have been hard, I think) when orders came for evacuation. It was horrible, because Paulette and I were to be separated. Her husband, you know, has joined the Foreign Legion, and the wives of soldiers were bundled together. I was set to be squeezed into a military bus with the hoi polloi.

Paulette's reaction surprised me. She began to weep these huge wet tears, and her lips quivered. I don't know what got into her.

'You mustn't let them take me,' she said. She clung to me like a small child.

'Don't rattle yourself. You're making *me* frightened!'

I adopted a stern, don't-give-me-trouble attitude – you will know exactly what I mean, Hans! – and it worked. Paulette grew calm, then annoyed. But anger is better than fear, so I had done my duty.

'You're impossible!' she cried.

'So are you,' I said.

'You've got no feelings!'

'And you're unreliable. Imagine what will happen to you if the going gets rough!'

'This *is* rough, damn it!'

'Nonsense. This is kindergarten. Just wait for what's coming.'

We continued for several minutes with our hackneyed, school-girlish bickering, amusing a young guard, who smoked a hand-rolled cigarette and watched us with a faint, superior smile. At one point, he said, 'Easy, girls, easy.'

The buses were ugly green beasts, and dozens of them stood hip to hip like rhinos, their engines throbbing. They belched a black smoke that seemed to strip the air of anything breathable. A crudely painted sign on each of them read: RÉFUGIÉS DE LA ZONE INTER-DITE. So that was it, I thought. I was a refugee from a restricted zone! The windows were darkened, as if to hide our shame or protect the public from seeing us huddled together. Nobody said a word, we were all so terrified, and because none of us had bathed in two weeks, we smelled like barn animals. I put a woolen sweater to my nose to filter the smell, but it was quite impossible.

I don't know exactly where they unloaded us, but it wasn't far away. Probably the Gare d'Austerlitz. The Germans were coming from the north, so we would head south. This was confirmed when, several hours later, we stopped briefly in the station in Tours. A smallish crowd milled on the opposite platform, and – much to my amazement – they jeered us and threw rocks at the train. I'd never before seen such hatred in human faces. I had to close my eyes.

We rode endlessly into the blackness, the train swallowing the rails whole, swaying, whistling through tiny stations so quickly you couldn't read the names. I don't know how many days and nights we rode. Two or three? Even the days seemed dark. And there was scarcely enough food; we would pass around a tin of pâté, a crust of bread, a cup of bad water. The toilets in the train were locked except for a brief period at night and in the morning for an hour or so. People were shitting in their underpants, pissing between cars. One old woman moaned continuously, something about her son, who apparently had some position of authority. 'He will murder you!' she sobbed. 'He is a high official. He will murder all of you!' Once a soldier brought around a pot of hot food. 'What is it?' the woman beside me asked, as if it mattered. '*Du singe*,' he said. Monkey meat. They call any kind of meat *singe*.

It felt like we had crossed a continent, and we all wondered where on earth they could possibly be taking us. None of the soldiers would dare to say a word. Then one morning soon after dawn I felt the train slowing; in the middle distance, the faint outline of a small city could be seen. The brakes began to squeal, and the train rocked from side to side. I can't say how, exactly, but I knew it was Gurs. The camp had been built rather hastily for refugees from the civil war, I believe. In any case, I remembered the stories Lars told us about Gurs, and I shuddered.

Over a narrow footbridge, through a barbed-wire fence, we trickled in a stream, entering the camp through a gate in the snaggle of barbed wire surrounding it. The female guards acted like little Nazis, yelling 'One-two, one-two, quickly, girls! Step quickly!' We were 'processed' at the so-called Reception Center, a low-roofed block building whose architect could not have entertained the slightest notion of aesthetics, then funneled into one of the dozens of barracks laid out in precise rows.

I hated my barracks immediately. The roof is tin, without virtue except in a rainstorm, when it makes the most wonderful, continuous hum. One bare lightbulb, a pathetic object suffocating from a lack of voltage, casts a pale glow over three dozen straw pallets pushed close together along each wall. They lay on the clay floor, damp and moldy as old cheese, riddled with mice and bugs. I don't know why, but I cried for the first time when I saw the pallets, just lying there on the floor, without cots. I had somehow expected cots.

It's best to get on with things, as you always say, so I slung my rucksack onto one of the pallets and was about to plop myself down when a fierce-looking young woman with snarled red hair screamed, 'That's mine, you bitch!' Temper, temper, I thought, taking my few belongings elsewhere. I don't think she is in her right mind, the poor thing.

I was glad that several of the others in my barracks were acquaintances, if not friends. Remember Anni? She and I found pallets together, and it was like old times. We quickly forgot how awful everything was, for a little while. Hans, I was so, so tired. Even the bedbugs could hardly penetrate my consciousness. It was like falling into a deep, even bottomless, well; whatever nonsense went on above ground hardly mattered as I toppled, end over end, through the endless dark. The world might have been coming to an end, and it wouldn't have mattered.

The guards – most of them women in the barracks – are generally unsympathetic, I must say. Hitler will love these natural-born fascists, though it perhaps dignifies them to ascribe an ideology to their behaviour; they know nothing but power. 'Do what I command or I'll make your life miserable,' they seem to be saying, even when they don't speak. 'Out of bed, ladies!' they shout at seven. 'Line up!' 'Clean up!' 'Stand up!' 'Shut up!' Everything up, up, up! The only thing to raise my spirits are the hills, the Pyrenees, a luminous blue line in the middle distance that spells one word in my heart: *freedom*. Spain beckons, so beautiful and beyond human foible. At least that is how it looks from behind these bars.

Let me get back to the bedbugs, which have become a major topic of conversation. We've had plenty of bugs together, Hans, have we not? If I remember right, you were the one who hated insects, like that time you got covered in bird lice, those little creatures more like white dust than members of the insect kingdom. You shrieked and danced! The doctor sprayed us with noxious chemicals at the hospital – it's a wonder he didn't kill us. Well, our pallets were so infested, so thick with maggoty things that swarmed and crawled and snapped, that I enclosed a dead one in an envelope and tried to convince our guard – a fairly decent woman, as prison guards go – to pass it along to the commandant. She opened it and said, 'If you don't like French bedbugs, maybe you will prefer those of the Nazi persuasion.'

If we were brought here for our own protection, why do they treat us like criminals? Is there something wrong with the so-called French mind? I questioned one of the guards, a fairly innocuous woman named Nicole, about his incarceration, and she said blithely that the camp was indeed full of Nazis: Reichsdeutsche. Spies. This is silly, of course. Only one woman in our barracks could be described as a genuine Nazi, and she actually worked for the German government in Paris as some vaguely official representative. But how do you reason with blockheads?

We began to communicate among ourselves, and this brought an immediate sense of hope. Our courage grew. One day we decided to organize a committee, and this committee would demand a meeting with the commandant. Nicole, the 'good guard,' as we called her, took a petition to his office on our behalf, and he proved more reasonable than you would suppose. We were allowed to elect a leader from each barracks, and the group of leaders formed a kind of unofficial parliament. Suddenly, the guards began to treat us like human beings. All it took was a little gumption.

You remember Sala, don't you? From Berlin, with the crooked nose? She is here and feisty as ever, forever holding meetings. The irony of her situation kills her, she says. Here she is, imprisoned by the enemies of Germany for distributing anti-German propaganda! We have put her in charge of everything, and that makes life easier for me. I feel like I can rest, knowing somebody is doing something to enhance my living conditions all the time! Praise Allah for Sala!

Some of the things here would amuse you, darling. The absurdities, I mean. The women rise early, in the thumbnail light of dawn, shivering, and begin putting on their makeup. Even Anni, who is not a beauty, as you may recall, pencils her eyebrows and rolls her hair! One of the women here, Louise, was a hairdresser in Paris, and she comes around every day and, for a cigarette, will comb your hair.

You should see them all, strutting and preening. At noon they gather outside in the yard to wave at a yellow biplane that flies low over the camp almost every day. The helmeted airman (who has perhaps been airborne since the last war) waves back at them gallantly, and sometimes tips his wing, ever so slightly, for their titillation. 'He saw me! He saw me!' they yell, dancing like schoolgirls. This is what passes for a sex life in Gurs.

A lot of what I see is sad. There is one strange girl, Gisela, who sleeps on the floor near me, on a pallet so thin it can offer no comfort. She apparently saw the Nazis beat her father with a rifle butt till his head burst; he died on the floor in his wife's arms. Her mother came here at the tail end of a long fight with cancer, her skin high yellow like an octoroon's, her eyes sunk deep in her skull like old nails. The unfortunate woman would go outside on wobbly knees every afternoon to lie on a rough wool blanket that Gisela would spread out in the dirt. In the evenings, she would sing her mother to sleep in a soft, hollow voice, singing folk songs I had never heard before. What surprised me was the lack of conversation between them; they seemed content to sit in each other's presence. Perhaps there was just too much to say to make the attempt at speech worthwhile? Or maybe the opposite was true. That such terrible things had happened to them and continued happening to them was perhaps beyond the claims of language. In any case, the mother died a few days ago. I was right there, beside her, and I saw her crumble like a burnt-out coal: the shape intact for a while, then imploding, then nothing but ash to scatter in the wind.

Gisela did not cry or even speak when they took her mother away. She was expressionless, tearless, drowned in an ocean of grief, I suppose. She has been sitting on her pallet all day today, the husk of her. The blue circles under her eyes have deepened, and she rarely opens her eyes. I tried to talk to her this morning, and offered a cigarette, but she didn't even respond. Not even a nod of the head or a grunt. I'm a little afraid for her, I think. One can stand only so much.

A pompous but amusing woman called Ili sleeps on a pallet across the room from me. I don't think you knew her, but she was always around in Paris – a friend of Julie Farendot, I think. I used to see her across the room at big parties, so eye-catching in her furs and jewelry; she was perpetually smoking cigarettes through a long ivory holder, and blowing smoke rings. She used to annoy me, but not now. I rather like her gumption and bravura. We need more like her to get through this war.

She told me that when the Nazis swept through Vienna, they dragged Jewish women into the streets and made them clean sidewalks on their knees. Ili stormed onto the pavement in her furs and jewels and shouted at the bastards, 'Give me a broom! I insist!' They said, 'Please, madame, we don't want you. Go back inside.' 'I am a Jew!' she cried. 'Give me a broom or I'll complain to your superiors!' They slunk off meekly. Don't you love it? They are cowards, you know, these goose-steppers. They are just hiding in those uniforms.

Ili brought a paint set with her: oils, brushes, even some rolled canvas, which she stretches on frames supplied by the guards, who seem only too eager to oblige her. (If you ask for a slice of bread, they spit at you, but if you want a frame for a canvas painting, that's apparently more like it!) On our second day in Gurs, she set up her studio outside on the lawn and began to paint. It was rather dramatic, as a gesture, and people gathered around her to watch, baffled but intrigued. And now she is giving lessons! I suppose there is no point in trying to tell her you cannot live by art alone . . .

You certainly can't live on the food. Chickpeas every day, then more chickpeas. They come like little pebbles, dry and tasteless, and you have to soak them overnight in rusty water, then cook them for an hour. You get maybe a dozen or fifteen peas in all, nasty pellets that you mouth slowly till they form a tasteless mash you can swallow. The guards come around in the morning with a cup of fake coffee that's so bad you want to puke after the first sip.

Sometimes we get a rubbery carrot or clump of stale cabbage. The potatoes are moldy and black. Loaves of bread are divided with the kind of stinginess you would imagine, one loaf among half a dozen women. You get your portion in the morning, then you have to gauge how much to eat at once. I try to hold off, letting my hunger build to the point where it hurts and I can't stand it; then I force myself beyond that point, eating only when the hunger subsides. That seems to work best, though I don't understand it.

The only chance we get to wash is in the morning, when it's so cold you don't want to do it anyway. A long and muddy trough runs along the barbed-wire fence behind the barracks, with a pipe running parallel to the fence and spigots poking out like teats along it. The hardy souls who decide to clean themselves that day line up, naked, and race through the cold water, which sometimes dribbles and sometimes gushes. Like everyone else, I try to wash my clothes while I'm there, but it's not easy. Soap is impossible to come by, though I did remember to bring some with me. When it's gone, I'll have to rely on elbow grease like the rest – or be content to smell.

The soldiers who guard the outposts and checkpoints like to stare at the women when they bathe, and this panics some of the younger ones. There is a particularly prudish girl, about seventeen, who refuses to take off her underwear at all. It's the age, I suppose: the fear that every lid is the top of Pandora's box. I must say, I really don't give a damn. Let them see me. Who cares?

I'm a little more hesitant about performing private acts in public when it comes to the latrines, which are dazzling constructions, reminiscent of a gallows. One looms behind us, not a few steps from the barracks. You climb a rickety ladder to a wooden platform perched on stilts; they've cut round holes in the floor and put metal tanks below to collect the shit and piss as it falls. These are emptied every morning, much to my relief (since I sleep by a window that opens right onto it!).

These French troops are Germanic in their efficiency, which scares me. I fear the worst when the full Occupation comes. Imagine: They have laid narrow-gauge tracks along the back fence; it runs by each of the latrines on a regular schedule. The Spaniards hired to do the dirty work come every morning on flatbed cars to empty the tanks on their miniature train – we call it the Gold Express – which rumbles from latrine to latrine, driven by an impassive old gentleman with long white hair and ice-blue eyes. If you happen to be doing your duty when the Express comes, you just hold your nose and gaze to the fields beyond the fence, where dandelions ready to be blown to smithereens by the slightest winds blanket a gentle slope.

I'm writing to keep my sanity, Hans. There is something gloriously essential about getting this language onto the page, about making the translation (however crude) from feelings into words. Does this make sense to you, darling?

My dear, it is so hard being separated from you, even though I believe, I *know*, you are all right. You are always all right. That is, if anyone is, you will be. I fell in love with you because I sensed, I understood in my bones, that you were indestructible. When I look into your eyes, I see it: diamondlike, immortal. The body may fail, but your spirit won't. It simply can't, any more than Plato can fall from the Western intellectual sky. Some things will not change.

It's terribly important, in Gurs, to count one's blessings. Lucky for me I've not been dumped in the barracks reserved for 'undesirables.' These women have been here much longer than the rest of us, and I pity them, even though some are indeed Nazis. Most seem to be anti-fascists of one kind or another, and a few are well known in these circles. They somehow ran afoul of the Deuxième Bureau, that gang of thugs hiding behind their fancy desks and nameplates on the doors.

These women are starving to death, so we hear. I've organized a group to smuggle bread to them through the double barbed-wire fence. It's a little dangerous, but the truth is I enjoy this smuggling. It takes one's mind off the cruder details of everyday life and makes one feel so curiously alive. Remember how it was in Prague, with the two of us sneaking around the city at night, meeting with different cells, trying to keep Masaryk's boys from discovering what we were doing? And in Switzerland, setting up the network? I still can't believe you talked me into slipping over the German border for those meetings in Baden and Württemberg. What if they'd caught me?

We were crazy, Hans. Crazy for a cause, I suppose. For freedom. Neither you nor I can bear injustice when it hits us in the face. This drives us forward, doesn't it? But it's a good drive, the need to feel alive and free, to know you are doing something to preserve human dignity. God knows, there is little enough left in the world.

I will write again, Hans. An underground post is just beginning, and I'm in touch with people who will smuggle this to you. If you're alive, you'll get it. If you are not alive, then I am not alive either, and so none of this matters.

With all my love to you, darling.

Lisa

WALTER BENJAMIN

History is the subject of a structure whose site is not homogeneous, empty time, but time filled by the presence of the Eternal Now. Thus, to Robespierre, ancient Rome was a past infused with the time of the Now, which he blasted out of the continuum of history. The French Revolution viewed itself as Rome reincarnate. It evoked ancient Rome the way fashion evokes costumes of the past. Fashion has a flair for the topical, no matter where it stirs in the thickets of long ago; it is a tiger's leap into the past. This jump, however, takes place in an arena where the ruling class gives the commands. The same leap into the open air of history is the dialectical one, which is how Marx understood the Revolution.

Lighting a cigarette, Benjamin wondered when they would come for him, and how it would happen. He had heard chilling stories, about a man wakened in the night by a policeman, then led to a waiting van while his wife and children stood by. Another had been snatched from a restaurant, not a minute after his meal had arrived. He knew personally of a man who was seized while playing chess in a park at midday – whisked into a van without his belongings, the last moves in the game all left to his opponent.

Benjamin's own health was so precarious that he wondered if he could survive a shock like that. His heart would probably stop dead on the spot if he were apprehended without warning. He would collapse into their military arms, an instant corpse, and they would have to waste a couple of good hours burying him, and it would serve them right.

The chairs in the reading room of the Bibliothèque Nationale had been emptying over the past month. His own table was now like a mouth with missing teeth. A goodly number of scholarly Jews had made a home of this celestial room, with its vaulting domes; these faithful readers could be found in place most days, plowing through massive tomes on Roman history, aerodynamics, modern linguistics, whatever. Solomon Weisel, Joseph Wertheimer, Salman Polotsky, Jacob Spiegel, a dozen others. Benjamin knew them all well; they formed a silent family, each with a private candle burning in the altar of his mind. Every one of them had made astounding sacrifices to keep that candle burning.

This was the sort of thing the secular world did not understand. What was it that could drive a man to sit for nine hours a day in a library chair, exploring byways of human knowledge? What form of ambition led to the sacrifice of family, friendship, worldly possessions, even communal esteem? For the most part, there was no gold medal from the academy to adorn the scholar's neck at the end of his road. There was no public acclaim. Most of the books composed in this room would never find a publisher; if they did, the readership for each book would be minuscule. So what accounted for this vigilance?

Benjamin was perhaps the most vigilant of all, sitting day after day in the same chair, willfully blocking out whatever seemed irrelevant to his project, including the Nazis. He had been researching and writing his book since the late twenties, when it began in notes and aphorisms. A thick wad of material accumulated in brown folders. He kept wishing he had not left behind so many notebooks at Brecht's house in Denmark, where he had been a summer guest two years before. The prospects of returning to Denmark grew slimmer and slimmer, and he could not rely on Brecht to send the material on to Teddy Adorno. Brecht was lazy and indifferent. 'He is a scoundrel, but a holy scoundrel in his way,' Benjamin said to his sister, Dora, who would reply, invariably, 'They all take advantage, Walter. Every one of them takes advantage.'

Although he never would have said such a thing, even to himself, Benjamin felt sure that his encyclopedic study of the Parisian arcades, now all but done, would help to justify his existence, which otherwise amounted to fits and starts, a thousand insights fluttering like crisp leaves on an autumn tree before being wasted by the proverbial four winds. It had, at first, jostled for room amid other projects, always on the back burner; Benjamin reserved the white flame of the front burner for immediate work: a critical essay, a review that was due the following week, a story, or, occasionally, a poem. The arcades project moved toward the full heat of his attention during the bitter winter of 1934, when he was staying at a cheap *pensione* in San Remo, in a bare, whitewashed room overlooking the gray-green sea. By this time Germany had become uninhabitable for a Jew or, for that matter, any person of conscience.

In Benjamin's mind, he was a defender of the Enlightenment. This was his private work against fascism. In his journal he admonished himself to 'clear fields where until now only madness has been seen, to forge ahead with the sharp ax of reason, looking neither left nor right in order to protect myself from the madness beckoning from the primeval forest.' With a rare ferocity, he wrote: 'All ground must occasionally be broken by reason, made arable, cleared of the messy undergrowth of delusion and myth.'

Delusion and myth ruled the world that Benjamin knew. Paris, as both capital of the nineteenth century and the unholy womb that had delivered into being this rough beast of the present, was therefore an appropriate focus for his research. The consumerism on display everywhere, the thirst for acquisition, distressed him, and this madness was uncannily represented by the arcades, which in French and German were called passages, emphasizing their spatial aspect. These lurid, glittering paths were, quite literally, passageways; the glass-covered tunnels became a showroom for every product of modern capitalism.

The arcades turned the otherwise rational structure of the city into an irrational maze, a nightmare of connecting tunnels, an inward spiral culminating in a kind of spiritual implosion. The streets of Paris, with their symmetrical houses and perfectly ordered parks, all meant to mirror Reason, now foundered in the dream-architecture of the ancients: the figure of the labyrinth. As Benjamin said, 'What generates the mythic dimension of all labyrinthine structures is their downward pull; once inside, the spectator is seized, drawn into a convoluted world with no visible or predictable existence.' The labyrinth is both interior and exterior: street and house, mask and voice speaking through the mask. Weather does not intrude upon the glassy corridors of the arcade labyrinth; even the light of the sun is filtered and distorted, caught in the enameled squares of floor tile, in the polished metal facades and glaucous mirrors that everywhere double reality and turn it in upon itself, in the eyes that swarm, dissatisfied, searching for some bright thing to land on, to consume.

Benjamin mused on the symbol of the labyrinth in history:

> In ancient Greece, one pointed out places that led down into the underworld. Our waking existence, too, is a land where hidden places lead into the underworld, full of inconspicuous sites where dreams trickle out. In the daytime we pass them by unwittingly, but once sleep comes we swiftly claw our way back to them and lose ourselves in the dark passageways. The city's labyrinth of houses, by day, is like consciousness; the arcades (those galleries that lead into its past existence) trickle unnoticed into the streets. But at night, beneath the somber mass of houses, their more compact darkness gushes out frighteningly.

Benjamin saw the world as many-layered but, like the Greeks, he believed in a deep substructure, a mythic or spiritual dimension on which the present rested as on some invisible yet sturdy foundation. He savored the daily shunting back and forth between night and day, between sleep and waking, mirrored by the mind as it moves between conscious and unconscious realms. Dreams, for him, were real. 'We pull the material of our dreams back with us into the world of wakefulness,' he said. 'It is all part of our journey.'

But the journey cuts through hell, through the purgatory of consumerism. 'The modern age,' he said, 'is the age of hell. Our punishment is the latest thing available at the time.' And the 'latest' is always 'the same thing through and through. This constitutes the eternity of hell and the sadist's mania for novelty.' Thus fashion fills every shop window, consumes all our conversation and thought, becomes a regressive phenomenon, a form of compulsive repetition in the mask of novelty.

Thus the nightmare of history returns: liberated, vengeful,

unyielding, uprooting. This is what Sigmund Freud meant when he referred menacingly to the 'return of the repressed.' It is the Minotaur that must be slain, that lies half asleep at the bottom of the labyrinth. It glimmers in the unnatural light of consumerism, which is merely an aberrant extension of our normal appetites for food, for shelter and clothing, for personal objects that endear us to the world and, unfortunately, to ourselves.

What nettled Benjamin was the alienation from history produced by this cycle of unwanted recurrence, an alienation that he himself experienced, and that restrained his ability to gaze, clearly, on the present. The past now became a substratum of nightmare and irrationality, of ancient fury cloaked in the forms of myth. Progress was the flight from this bad dream, made swifter by current technologies; the past had never seemed more distant. Yet distance was simply a spatial metaphor. 'We have been schooled in the romantic gaze into history,' he said. Hence, Walter Scott, Stendhal, the fetishing of medieval iconography, the worship of ruins, the reverence for dark mythologies as in Wagner. What could save us, he said, was nearness; 'history recovered, dissolved'; propinquity was all.

But how to accomplish this? Aren't those who have gone before us irretrievably lodged in a far, impossible country? Who can wake the dead? Benjamin believed that the equivalent of a Copernican revolution in thinking must occur. Fiction would replace history, or become history. The past, 'what has been,' had previously been accepted as the starting point; history stumbled toward the dimly lit present through the corridors of time. Now the process must be reversed; 'the true method,' said Benjamin, 'was to imagine the characters of the past in our space, not us in theirs. We do not transpose ourselves into them: They step into our life.' One does not proceed by seeking empathy with the past: *Einfühlung*. This was historicism of the old mentality. Instead, he argued for what he called *Vergegenwärtigung*: 'making things present.'

History, as such, was the dream from which we must awaken, and to understand culture as the dream of history was to understand time as postponement, as that which stands between us and the realization of an eternal kingdom. The task of the anti-historian, as Benjamin saw it, was to render visible the utopian element in the present, working backward toward the past. 'Literary montage,' in his phrase, was 'the instrument of this dialectic, the act of placing moments of history in apt juxtaposition.' This was what he had tried, in the arcades project, to accomplish: to create the ultimate montage, to recover and dissolve history in one bold stroke.

They came for him, not in the middle of the night as he expected, but at noon. It was a Tuesday, and he had quite by chance decided to work at home instead of the library. He was writing at the three-legged oak table in the alcove off his sitting room, cutting a picture from a fashion magazine: an advertisement for toothpaste, with three beautiful women holding brushes and smiling like the three Graces of mythology. He had, only a few moments before, copied out an apposite passage from a favorite book about Paris: *Le Paysan de Paris* by Louis Aragon. Walking through the streets of the capital, Aragon had contemplated the faces that flickered by:

> It became clear to me that humankind is full of gods, like a sponge immersed in the open sky. These gods live, attain the height of their power, then die, leaving to other gods their perfumed altars. They are the very principles of any total transformation. They are the necessity of movement. I was, then, strolling with intoxication among thousands of divine concretions. I began to conceive a mythology in motion. It rightly merited the name of modern mythology. I imagined it by this name.

One of these concretions – in the shape of a military policeman – was now standing in the doorway of Benjamin's flat on the rue Dombasle; he wore a uniform that Benjamin did not recognize. The jacket was belted, with tarnished silver buttons and expansive epaulets, the sort of thing a soldier in a music-hall comedy might wear. The fellow's capacious silver mustache pushed out ahead of his face like the cow-catcher on a steam engine.

To Benjamin's relief, the man was French and therefore not German. A German soldier would have been devastating.

'I'm looking for Monsieur Walter Benjamin,' he said. 'Are you, in fact, this gentleman?'

'Yes,' he said. 'I am Dr Benjamin.' Perhaps because the official was polite and well-mannered, Benjamin did not feel afraid. It also helped that the man was not young; the young, Benjamin decided, are more frightening in the guise of power. They are not aware of the dangers to themselves as well as others. Silly, tragic things can happen too easily when inexperience is a factor.

Benjamin continued, 'What may I do for you, sir?'

'It has come to our attention that you are an illegal alien from Germany.'

'I am a Jew.'

The man looked over Benjamin's shoulder. 'I'm afraid you must come with me, monsieur. You may carry one bag – a small one, if you will. I would definitely recommend a small bag . . . for your convenience.'

'I am working on a book, you see. I would need to bring a brief-case. It is not especially large.'

'As you like,' the man said, nodding, then stepping back, as if not to intrude on the last moments of Benjamin's privacy.

'You will give me a few minutes?'

'I shall wait for you in the hall,' he said.

'Thank you.'

Dora hovered in the bedroom, afraid to come out. She had thus far eluded the authorities and would not present herself to any public official voluntarily, no matter what the papers said. When her brother hurried into the bedroom to pack, she whispered, 'Please, Walter, you must escape the back way! The stairs to the basement! Go!'

'It is quite all right, Dora. They will not hurt me. The officer is French.'

She scoffed. 'I know the French as well as you do. They will cut your throat, given the chance.'

Benjamin studied his sister's round, even puffy, face; her big eyes – like the eyes of an ox – stared at the world dumbfoundedly. He could not understand her distrust of the French people, who had sheltered them so hospitably. He himself admired the French unreservedly, with their fierce intellectual tradition, their literature and architecture, their sense of morality and love of justice. The French were among the most remarkable of civilizations. He had said that often, in public, much to the despair of his (mostly) French friends, who never tired of deriding their own kind.

Dora was sobbing now, a small-boned woman in a rumpled, gray dress. Her mascara ran, making black splotches on her cheeks.

Benjamin drew close to Dora. 'I shall write to you at once. You'll know exactly where I am, and you must not worry,' he said. 'They are protecting us, Dora. You must understand this. If you would only . . .'

'Never!' she said, in a loud voice.

Benjamin looked over his shoulder nervously, hoping her shout had not carried.

'I will stay here until I die,' she said. 'If they want me, they can wring my neck, like a chicken.'

'You are a stubborn woman,' he said. 'You are like our mother.'

'And you are like our father: stupid. What you know about politics could be written on the back of a postage stamp.' She grabbed his shirt, popping several buttons. 'There is a war on, Walter. They are killing Jews. They are murdering Jews!'

Benjamin sighed. He had not, in his last minutes with his sister, wanted to quarrel. 'Be careful, Dora,' he said. 'If you need help, get in touch with Julie. Georges Bataille will be useful, too.' He scribbled a phone number on a slip of paper. 'Call him at once if you find yourself in difficulty. His brother has a position in the finance ministry, and he can pull strings if the situation becomes tricky.'

'You think this isn't tricky?' Dora said, shaking her head. 'I suppose, for you, this is a picnic?'

'I cannot argue. Not now, Dora . . .'

'You put too much faith in your friends. But ask yourself this, Walter. Has it ever done you any good? Why didn't Scholem find you a job in Palestine? It's a disgrace, that's my opinion. We could be living off the fat of the land by now, in Jerusalem.'

Benjamin tried to shush her. He heard the soldier knocking at the front door, and he began to cram a few necessities into his bag. There was no point in going over this ground again with Dora: Scholem was a difficult friend, at best. He had a consuming ego, and somewhere along the way Benjamin had trampled on it; he had not acquiesced in Scholem's point of view on everything, so he was being punished. No matter now. When the war was over, he would visit Jerusalem and make amends. Although he and Scholem had fallen out frequently in the past, each time the dispute had led to periods of greater understanding.

Teddy Adorno – that was a different story. Benjamin had felt keenly the fragmentation of that friendship. Adorno had meant so much to him; they knew each other so well that even their dream life had been shared. But something had occurred along the way; Benjamin had not simply bought into the dialectics of the Frankfurt School or subscribed uncritically to the politics of the Institute. He could never quite subscribe to any dogma, except partially. It was his nature, as a critic, to complicate issues and to dissent. His natural skepticism was, in part, a legacy from the Enlightenment, and one he was loath to relinquish.

Benjamin kissed Dora, who had managed to control her sobbing, and joined the soldier in the dark hallway. The man looked sympathetically at Benjamin, who said, 'I am ready.' A small suitcase hung from one hand, a briefcase in the other.

'Can I help?' the man asked, reaching for the suitcase.

Benjamin refused. It was too absurd.

They climbed down the staircase, slowly; Benjamin was obviously having difficulty in seeing the stairs, with his nearsightedness. Now his chest began to squeeze, and pain rose in his throat and traveled down his arms to his fingertips. He had seen Dr Dausse, a fellow refugee and friend, only a few weeks before about these recurring chest pains, and today he wondered if the ordeal that lay ahead of him would be too arduous for a man in his condition. The phrase *congestive heart failure* had been offered, somewhat lamely, by the doctor, who added: 'With the heart, one is rarely confident of a proper diagnosis. You might live for twenty years or twenty minutes.'

Benjamin wished he had asked Dr Dausse for a medical excuse. What could the French authorities want with somebody too ill to cross the street without experiencing palpitations and weak spells? He could no longer walk more than twenty or thirty steps without having to stop for a rest. He would be worse than useless to the French army. But there was no way to argue the case; this was the problem with a large bureaucracy. Kafka understood this perfectly. Anonymity was the enemy, reducing everyone to an integer on a piece of paper. The artist's job was to overcome this blankness by naming things. Like Adam in Eden, he must find names for every object, animate and inanimate. He must invent a language full of racy particulars, finding the identities of everything. This was the imagination's endless and desperately important work.

Benjamin bent over, exhaling slowly.

'You are having difficulty breathing, is that it?' the Frenchman asked. 'Are you in pain?'

'What a kind man you are,' Benjamin said, straightening himself out.

'We can sit down if you like, on the steps. There is no rush.'

'I'm all right,' he insisted, swallowing hearty gulps of air. An impish smile came to his lips. 'We had better hurry. The war will be over soon, and we'll have missed it.'

He was taken by military train to a collection point near the Camp des Travailleurs Volontaires at Clos St-Joseph Nevers. The first night was spent, not unpleasantly, in a small boardinghouse with pink shutters and wrought-iron balconies, where he shared a double bed with a pleasant man called Heymann Stein, whom he had met in Paris some years before.

Stein was a well-known journalist and, like himself, a bookish fellow. He had lived in Vienna after the Great War and had moved to Paris during the early thirties after a period as a schoolmaster in Bern. Having studied philosophy at Mainz, he tried to keep up with the subject in case he should one day go to America, where he had been told positions were easily available in the major universities. He carried with him a volume by Martin Heidegger, a fact that Benjamin did not hold against him (however much he despised Heidegger not only for his writing but for the way he had mesmerized and seduced his young relative, a philosophy student called Hannah Arendt). In time, he would set Heymann Stein (and Hannah) straight on Heidegger, whose fraudulent appropriation of Kant and Hegel had irritated him ever since he read 'The Problem of Historical Time,' Heidegger's inaugural lecture, delivered in Freiburg in the spring of 1916, and later published in the *Zeitschrift für Philosophie und philosophische Kritik*.

The sergeant in charge of the 'volunteers' woke everyone at six-thirty, allowing them just half an hour to get dressed and swill a cup of coffee and a bit of stale bread with jam before they were to leave for the camp. 'Eat up, boys!' he shouted. 'This is the last of the good food.'

Stein was annoyed. 'Get up, lie down, eat up, sit down,' he said. His white hair stuck out, as if electrified. He had a big nose with a dark nubble of a wart on the left side. An open collar was always his trademark, his sign of identification with the working classes. 'There will be a lot of shouting, you can tell. They love it, this ordering around.'

'I don't mind,' said Benjamin. 'It makes life very simple. You do what you're told. Like school.'

Stein was not convinced.

'I knew your brother, Leon,' said Benjamin.

'Leon the bookseller.'

Benjamin had indeed bought many books from Leon Stein, whose little shop on the rue du Vieux Colombier had become a refuge for German expatriates in the past decade; more important,

Leon had bought many books from Benjamin when he was frantic for cash, often paying more than they were really worth.

'What's the point of putting men like us into a camp?' Benjamin wondered.

'Even an old horse can plow a field. They can't afford to pay real workers, so they steal labor where they can.'

'You're a cynic, Heymann.'

'So wait and see. We're prisoners of the French army, nothing more, nothing less. Why dignify the arrangement?'

Benjamin dressed quickly, putting on his baggy brown suit, worn threadbare at the elbows, his rumpled white shirt, long since permanently stained beneath the armpits, and the red polka-dot tie that had been his father's. He was worried about the weight of his black leather briefcase, which contained not only a vast manuscript of material for his arcades project but the final draft of his latest essay, 'On Some Motifs in Baudelaire,' as well as some books. He could not travel without books.

But he had not counted on the fact that they would be marched to Nevers, en masse: thirty-seven men herded like cattle along a dirt road for a dozen or so miles, with a drill sergeant screaming at the side of the phalanx, more a sheepdog than a man. 'They ought to muzzle that dog,' Stein said. 'He's probably rabid.'

Three times Benjamin collapsed, falling on the gravel-and-tar road. The first two times he managed to struggle back to his feet; the last, he was put onto a stretcher and carried straight to the camp infirmary, his briefcase and suitcase on his stomach like paperweights.

'You will not be allowed to work,' the camp physician, Dr Guilmoto, told him. 'This is not a concentration camp like in Germany. We are not intent upon killing you.'

'So why not send me home? Let the Nazis take me away. It will be easier on everyone.'

'You are making a joke?' the doctor asked. His eyebrows lifted like quotation marks. 'Yes, you are. I enjoy a sense of humor.'

Benjamin said, 'This is so absurd.'

The doctor smiled, rather patronizingly. 'We want to be sure the Nazis do not take you away. That is the whole point, Dr Benjamin.'

'But you think some of us are spies . . .'

The doctor studied his own hands, avoiding Benjamin's gaze.

'You are afraid of us, in other words,' he continued.

'I agree, there are those who worry about such things. Part of our job here is to weed out those who might cause trouble, should the Nazis invade. One cannot tell what will happen.'

'The Nazis have already invaded.'

The doctor listened to Benjamin's heart with a stethoscope, then said, 'What are we going to do with you, Dr Benjamin? You are unfit to work.'

'I'm lazy by nature, you see. I will spend my days reading and writing. If only there were access to a library . . .'

The doctor laughed. 'Would you like a secretary as well? I will speak to my superior. We appreciate intellectuals in France, as you know. The word *intellectual* is a French invention.'

Benjamin understood only too well the vexed origins of this word in France. During the Dreyfus scandal, those brave men and women (led by Zola) who spoke up for reason and enlightened values in order to defend an unfortunate Jew were called intellectuals by an outraged press. It remained a term of opprobrium in the popular mind, especially in England. (Benjamin had received mournful letters from Dora, his ex-wife, who detested the English for their snobbishness and refusal to think about serious topics. According to Adorno, the situation was even worse in America, where cultivated and intelligent people had to feign dullness and ignorance just to make a living.)

After two days of rest in a whitewashed clinic with acceptable food, Benjamin joined Heymann Stein and twenty-eight others in a tin-roofed building that had once served as a slaughterhouse for poultry. The men slept on rotting canvas cots without mattresses; each volunteer was issued a single woolen blanket, and most were so moth-eaten you could hold them up to the moon and see an imitation Milky Way poking through. Meals were taken outdoors in what was grandly called the 'dining hall,' though it amounted to no more than a platform with a tattered covering of oil-slicked canvas; long makeshift tables had been fashioned from scraps of pine and rusty metal drums.

Most of the work of the camp consisted of latrine duty and cooking. The food, though fetid, was available in sufficient quantities to fuel the activity of the camp at a fairly low level. As it had been raining ever since Benjamin arrived in Nevers, nobody had begun to work very hard. The guards were themselves unwilling to stand in the rain and supervise. The rains, which virtually everyone regarded as a godsend, continued through the first three weeks of Benjamin's internment: a steely drizzle that made September feel like December.

Like nearly everyone else in the camp, Benjamin could not get warm, no matter how hard he tried. The meager blanket covering him at night only made things worse, since it reminded him of what such coverings were supposed to do. He slept, rather badly, in the fetal position, blowing into his closed fists for warmth. In the morning he felt as though his joints had rusted in place. It hurt simply to stand or bend over.

Benjamin insisted on referring to his fellow detainees as colleagues, and not inappropriately; many were voracious readers, and several had managed to bring into captivity some classics of literature and philosophy. One particularly cold night, a young man from Bavaria acquired a bundle of dry sticks from a sympathetic guard, and a fire was lit in the stove squatting in one icy corner of the barracks. The men gathered around to plot their survival.

Heymann Stein said, 'You know, we should consider ourselves lucky.'

'How is that, Stein? a cocky younger man asked. 'I would like to know about my good luck. Maybe I've been misreading the situation.'

'We have in our midst a brilliant writer and philosopher – Dr Benjamin.'

This lavish if somewhat unctuous compliment embarrassed

Benjamin, in part because he did not regard himself as a brilliant anything. Perhaps when the arcades project was published, he might be worthy of notice, but not at present. When several of the men began clapping, it shocked him. Were they simply going along with Heymann Stein?

'Good friends,' Benjamin said, under his breath. 'I'm very grateful.'

'So why don't you lecture, Dr Benjamin?' asked Stein. 'We can turn a bad situation into a better one. You can teach us something – philosophy, perhaps. We can turn Nevers into a little university!' He swept his hand around as if onstage. It was quite a performance, Benjamin decided. Stein stared at Benjamin, as if to convince him. 'You must do this, for the sake of everyone here.'

Benjamin thanked Stein but demurred. He was not nearly so accomplished as Stein pretended. Furthermore, it had been a long time since he had seen the inside of a classroom. Even after he got his doctorate, he had never done much teaching.

'I, too, would like to hear some lectures,' said a white-bearded man called Meir Winklemann, who had studied to become a rabbi in Odessa before the Great War. 'Something with a religious theme would be especially good,' he added. An unfortunate marriage had apparently scuttled Winklemann's promising career, and he had since made his living as a salesman, crossing borders so blithely that he no longer believed in the existence of separate countries.

Others chimed in, including Hans Fittko, who had just arrived in this camp from another. He was among the handful of familiar faces in the room, and his presence was reassuring to Benjamin. Something about Fittko made everyone feel confident that the situation was, ultimately, under control. 'We should make the best use of our time here,' said Fittko. 'Herr Stein is right about this.' He went on to explain how, during the Spanish Civil War, Loyalist prisoners of war had famously put their captivity to good use, holding poetry readings and philosophical lectures in camps where living conditions were notoriously inhuman.

A man called Kommerell, a former teacher in Leipzig who had

spent several years in an English university, produced from his rucksack a copy of Plato's *Dialogues*, in an English translation by Benjamin Jowett of Oxford. Someone else had works by Rousseau and Kant. Stein himself had carried a dog-eared book by Martin Buber, with so many passages underlined that you could not easily read many pages. Benjamin had brought with him a selection of essays by Montaigne, whose work had long been a source of comfort. He also had in hand Mendelssohn's beautiful (if somewhat decorously old-fashioned) translation of the Torah.

'So we've got a library!' said Hans Fittko. 'What else do we need?'

'What do you say, Dr Benjamin?' Stein prodded.

'He will do this, of course,' said Fittko confidently. 'I heard him lecture in Paris. He is very good.'

Benjamin wiped his forehead, suddenly thick with perspiration. 'If you all wish, I will do as you like,' he said. His attention was tugged into the room's far left corner as he contemplated the prospect of lecturing on philosophy under these conditions. After a pause, to demonstrate his gratitude for their interest, he said, 'I'm quite happy to conduct some philosophical discussions . . . if that will help to pass the time. But you must bear with me. I am not a teacher, nor a philosopher.'

The next morning, soon after breakfast, with the rain still thundering on the roof and the camp guards reluctant to drive anyone to work, Benjamin began to lecture on Greek metaphysics, reading aloud from Plato (but translating from Jowett's Victorian English into German by sight). He explained from the outset that his real interest was as much in Kant as in Plato, but he considered the two thinkers so linked in their approach to the world that it was necessary to begin with the great Athenian. 'It is often said that Western philosophy consists of footnotes to Plato,' he said. 'If this is the case, Kant's footnotes must be considered the most elaborate and original.' He paused, then began again, in a small voice: 'It seems clear to me that in the framework of philosophy and hence of the doctrinal field to which philosophy belongs, there can never be a shattering, a collapse, of the Kantian – and thus Platonic – system. One can only imagine a revising and expanding of Kant and Plato, their philosophies ripening into doctrine, which is not necessarily a good thing.'

He was intrigued by Plato's 'invention' of Socrates. 'He is both real and unreal, both historical and ahistorical,' Benjamin explained. He noted that any philosophical system began with an attitude, an approach, to history, and that Plato's understanding of how one could grant eternal life to a figure such as Socrates was utterly ingenious. It was not a question of mere appropriation. 'We've seen what happens when a writer overwhelms his subject, as with Max Brod and Kafka,' he said. 'Brod did not respect the aura of the individual genius; he did not proclaim Kafka's separateness from himself, and so his biography of his friend is horribly flawed.' He explained to them that the figure of Socrates in Plato's dialogues was 'made up' in the sense that Plato had transposed the man he once knew into intellectual and moral situations he had never, in life, encountered. But Plato knew the spirit of Socrates so intimately he could give him a life ancillary to the one he 'really' had. Plato could, in other words, be trusted with Socrates; the fiction was real.

Heymann Stein leapt to his feet when Benjamin drew the allusive quotation marks around the term *really* with fingers in the air. 'Surely,' Stein argued, 'one *has* a life. One does not "have" a life.'

Benjamin said, 'I am sorry, Herr Stein. I should have made myself clearer. It is our tendency as moderns to cast everything we say in ironic light. This is a mistake, of course.' He began to pace, as if thinking intensely, trying to work out something fresh. 'Language brings reality into being; it is, as it were, a bridge between what happens in the mind and what occurs in the world. Perhaps I will try to put this more boldly: Unless one frames reality in words, the reality does not exist. This theory of language plays havoc with conventional notions of time, and that is a problem; on the other hand, I do not believe in time. That is, I can't believe in unimagined, linear time. To put something between brackets is to expose its linguistic element, its dependency on invented time, its mystery, its final unreality.'

He noticed that Heymann was staring at him, rapt, and he smiled slightly. Perhaps he was a good lecturer, after all? 'We are working,' he said, 'here and always, to achieve a reality that is not so terribly contingent on mere expression.'

He paused long enough to notice puzzlement on some of the other faces in the audience. Perhaps what he said was not clear? Perhaps he did not himself understand exactly what he was saying? It was frustrating. He wanted to talk about history as catastrophe, about revolution as the only legitimate way out of the nightmare of history, but that would have to wait for another day. He must stay, for the moment, with Plato. But even as he spoke, he was aware of the final goal of all philosophy; in his 'Theses on the Philosophy of History' he had put it well: 'The messianic world is the world of all-sided and integral immediacy. Only there is universal history possible.'

One did not have newspapers in this so-called *camp des travailleurs volontaires*, so gossip abounded. 'The Germans have overrun Paris, and they will be here any moment,' Stein whispered to Benjamin. 'I have this from a guard, who would not lie.' But there was no artillery fire in the distance, and the guards did not seem especially nervous. Surely if the Germans were really coming, the camp would have devolved into chaos?

Benjamin felt detached from camp life, as if somehow floating above it. The physical discomfort was curiously bearable, and even the worst things felt oddly acceptable: the bitter nights under the single blanket or the agony of a weekly sprinkle under a cold spigot. The dinners of lukewarm broth, with a chunk of gristle lurking at the bottom of the bowl like a creature from the deep sea, were demoralizing but not devastating. Even the humiliation of shitting in a putrid shed with a dozen other men could be borne. Perhaps the finite amount of reading material was the worst thing to suffer, but even this he could tolerate.

It was harder when the boy who slept in the cot next to him developed a terrible pain in his side one night and died a few days later from a ruptured appendix. Young Efraim Wolff – he was not yet twenty-three – had come to France only recently from Lublin, where he had taught in a school for young boys. He was already ailing when he arrived, and the guard would do nothing to help him, even though he begged to see a doctor. 'Stop the nonsense. You have indigestion,' said the guard. 'Who wouldn't have indigestion, given the food in this place?'

Efraim Wolff lay in agony for three nights, groaning; he subsided to a whimper on the fourth day, and he died, in silence, on the fifth, with Benjamin applying wet towels to his forehead and whispering lies into his ear about how the indigestion would soon pass. The body was interred on the sixth day, on the edge of a hazel wood half a mile or so from the gates of the camp, with a dozen men saying Kaddish above the grave. Benjamin, for the first time in many years, wept as he rocked back and forth on his heels.

In the third month of his captivity, a *commission de triage* informed Benjamin that he would soon be released. His sister Dora wrote to explain that this good fortune was due in part to the intervention of Adrienne Monnier and Jules Romains, who had circulated a petition on his behalf among the right people. 'The God of the Jews is with you,' she had said, though it was most unlike her.

The reaction in the camp was mixed. On the one hand, people were glad enough to see one of their number freed. It was a propitious sign; if Benjamin had been released, perhaps everyone would be sent home soon. Perhaps even the war itself was nearing an end? On the other, a beloved figure in their little society was to be withdrawn, and his lectures – which had proved entertaining even to those who could not really understand a word of what he was saying – would come to an end.

'So I'm left here to rot like a squirrel while you do the cancan in Paris?' Heymann Stein said on the night before Benjamin's release. 'I see you've left all the hard work for me, the lectures on Neitzsche,' he added. 'I hope you sleep very badly, thinking about what I'm going to say.'

'Neitzsche we don't need,' said Meir Winklemann. 'Not today. Hitler will have us all reading Nietzsche next week.' He stood close to Benjamin, studied him as if he were a piece of sculpture, then kissed him on either cheek. 'Go with God,' he said.

Hans Fittko, too, with his strong masculine face and dark hair pushed back like a film star's, kissed Benjamin. 'We'll meet again soon,' he said, squeezing his hands. 'If you see Lisa, tell her I'm well.'

'But you're still a *schmuck*,' Stein insisted, and everyone laughed.

That night he fell into a woolly sleep and had a dream in which he was led by his friend, Dr Dausse, into a steep underworld: a version of Hades, a labyrinthine tunnel. There were many chambers in this tunnel, and beds were pushed to the walls at either side. Men and women – some of them friends, some acquaintances or strangers – lay on the beds or sat up, a few of them smoking cigarettes. In one vast candlelit chamber full of golden stalactites, Benjamin noticed a blond woman with short hair lying on her bed with her legs slightly parted. He came close to her and saw she was beautiful. Upon hearing him approach, she opened her eyes, and their green lightning dazzled him. The blanket covering her seemed to hold in its luminous pattern an intricate design much like one that Benjamin had once described to Dr Dausse: a kind of spiraling blue line. 'A spiral,' he said to himself, 'is a circle released from space.' He suddenly realized that the woman had lifted the blanket to one side to show him the design, which seemed to offer some kind of spiritual key, a way out of the labyrinth into which he found himself burrowing. He must reverse himself now. He must seek the light.

Her eyes were glittering, and her white thighs. Her small breasts lifted with each breath. It was all so heartbreaking, so beautiful. But did he know this woman? Would she speak to him? Was she, indeed, alive or dead?

Benjamin wakened to find himself staring at the ceiling of the barrack, which was crossed by rotting beams; through his narrow window he could see a million stars pricking little points of light in the black sky. Galaxies seemed to be exploding, spreading great concentric rings of fire. He realized that he would never be able to go back to sleep. The dream burned like coals after a hot fire, and it warmed his whole body. For once he felt no compulsion to interpret the dream; there would be plenty of time for that in days to come. Just now, as he lay there, he felt something strangely akin to bliss.

WALTER BENJAMIN

The growing proletarianization of modern man and the increasing formation of masses are two sides of the same coin. Fascism tries to organize the newly created masses without affecting the underlying property structure . . . Fascism sees its salvation in giving these masses not their right, but a chance to express themselves. The masses have a right to change property relations, but fascism seeks to give them an expression while preserving property. The logical result of fascism is the introduction of aesthetics into political life . . .

All efforts to render politics aesthetic culminate in one thing: war. War and war only can set a goal for mass movements on the largest scale while respecting the traditional property system. This is the political formula for the situation. The technological formula may be stated as follows: Only war makes it possible to mobilize all of today's technical resources while maintaining the property system.

5 SCHOLEM

It was never easy, getting and holding Benjamin's attention. He was self-absorbed, even selfish; his work came first, to a point where one never believed he really heard what one said. Often I wanted to shake him, to say, 'Walter, listen to me! I am talking to you!' His wife, Dora, would say, 'I must get a hand grenade. I could scream, "Walter, I've just pulled the pin. Wake up!"' Then again, even that might not work. The whole house could crash around his ears and he wouldn't notice.

One thing that did lure him into the open was sex. He was, at various times in his life, a visitor of brothels, although he complained that sex lost some of its excitement when one had to pay. 'Perhaps it's the miser in me,' he would say. 'I can always hear the coins dropping in the till.' His eyes were always darting about, and his hands; more than once a firm slap on the cheek had been required to subdue him.

Friendship, I'm afraid, came third in his life, after books and sex. I did not like being third. The possibility for perfect intellectual and spiritual friendship had loomed before us: a piece of ripe fruit hanging from a bough just beyond reach. More than anything, I wanted a friend who understood my deepest concerns, whose language and knowledge were in every way equal to my own. I had given up hope for such a thing, and then I met Benjamin, although our encounters over many years were often disappointing. It is not easy to know a man who does not know himself.

Three or four times he tried to take his own life, usually in despair over some woman. It seemed inevitable that he would succeed one day, perhaps by accident. Once, in Berlin, not long after we became good friends, he said, 'Life is not something we can control, but death we can. It may be the last option, but it's an option.'

I tried to explain to him that suicide was not an option. If one believes, as I do, in a single, all-knowing, and all-powerful God, there can be no justifiable reason for total self-destruction. Suicide is always a spiteful act, a fist raised in the face of the Almighty. It is unethical, too, because it cuts against the grain of nature, confounding the logic of organismal development, which is God's invention. All living things break into being, are nourished, grow and flourish, then fade and die; the rhythm is essential, and it remains the only hope for man: Everywhere in the universe one sees rebirth. No energy is lost. Not a single drop of rain is wasted.

Of course I do not expect to return to earth as myself, as Gershom (Gerhard) Scholem, scholar of Jewish mysticism. But my energies will somehow manage to reassemble. If life comes with so many surprises, imagine what death must offer! I do not actually want to come back as Scholem. I want to be sky: a wide-awake mind over-arching the world, weeping with the clouds, shimmering with the sun, throwing Jove-like bolts of black lightning at whatever angers me, laughing like an earthquake when the folly of man amuses me. When the core of the earth rumbles, they will say, 'Scholem is stirring again. Beware!'

I suspect the idea of suicide was planted in Benjamin's mind back in 1914, when his beloved friend, Fritz Heinle, killed himself at the outbreak of war. Heinle was a brilliant poet, with tangled red hair and the whitest skin, and Benjamin loved him. 'I am not sure which I loved more,' Benjamin said to me, 'the man or his words.' Heinle would sit in cafés until well past midnight, reading his poems aloud to anyone who would listen. He had to fight his way through a stutter, but it was Demosthenes speaking with a mouthful of pebbles; the effect was thrilling.

Heinle and his girlfriend, Rika Seligson (a Germanic beauty with long legs and blond hair) entered a suicide pact; they did so, or so they said in a note, because they did not want to live in a world where human beings destroyed other human beings in the name of morality. 'The immorality of this war will infect the entire country,' they wrote, defending their self-destruction. This double suicide disturbed our cozy little circle in Berlin.

Benjamin had hoped to stand in solidarity with German youth in support of the war, and only days before Heinle's death he had volunteered for service, reporting to the cavalry barracks on Bellalliance Street. That very night he learned of Heinle's death; in an instant, everything changed. He realized that war was no answer to whatever vague questions might be hanging in the air. When he was notified that volunteers were to report for a physical examination the following week, he presented himself as a palsy victim. He had rehearsed with great care the trembling associated with those who bear that disease, and he succeeded in fooling the army doctors. He was told to report back in a year for reexamination.

The next year he followed a procedure meant to induce palsy that was adopted by many in our circle at the time; it involved drinking poisonously strong, black coffee for days on end. Benjamin did so in the Neu Café des Westerns on Kurfürstendamm while playing cards (a variant of Sixty-six, a popular game among our crowd). The coffee brought on shortness of breath and red eyes, and it made one's hands tremble and one's vision double. Speech usually became slurred. I sat up with Benjamin all night before the exam, and he was suitably crimson-eyed and shaking by the time he saw the doctors, who gave him another reprieve. I worried, in fact, that he had overdone it: His heart was racing, and he could scarcely talk. Shortly after failing the exam, on the way home, he collapsed on the trolley, and it took several days for him to feel well again.

Those were peculiar times for all of us. The war rolled on, and schoolmates – some of them good friends – went off in waves to the front, where most of them appeared on casualty lists within a month. My neighbour and boyhood best friend, Fritz Meinke, was cut to ribbons by machine guns in France, and even though we hadn't been close in years, I spent several days alone in my room, gazing out the window at an impossibly dull winter sky. The utterly pointless killing of young men in the millions was too hard to understand.

Having spoken to no one for days, I went to see Benjamin at his apartment. He behaved in an unsettling way.

'What did you expect?' he asked. 'When there is a war, men die.'

'Fritz was a boy,' I said.

'It is inhuman, I agree. One does not like to see children murdered. But you must not sentimentalize war. It is a construct of the human mind, like everything else, one cannot alter it.'

'We must oppose the war.'

'No. We must not participate in the war, but opposing it would be useless and silly. History is a machine, and if you withdraw the fuel, eventually it will run down.'

Our conversation turned to the Youth Movement. We both agreed that the original ideas of Gustav Wyneken had been betrayed by Wyneken himself when he decided it was proper for German youth to get involved in this war. I maintained – I still do – it is never *dulce et decorum pro patria mori*. War represents a complete disfigurement of the human psyche, a perversion of ethical principles. After wavering briefly, Benjamin came around to my viewpoint, although one could never really tell. There was always something noncommittal about him, something oblique.

I was pleased, however, when on March 9, 1915, he wrote a blistering letter to Wyneken in which he dissociated himself permanently from the Youth Movement; he even accused Wyneken of 'sacrificing young people to the state.' In spite of this, Benjamin thanked him for being 'the first person who introduced me to the life of the spirit,' and he promised to be true to that spirit forever. Wyneken had represented, for Benjamin, an escape from the bourgeois mentality of his parents and their friends. The ideals of freedom and self-determination lay at the heart of the Youth Movement, which had taken up school reform as one of its main tasks. At first, I quite sympathized with their program, which began as an attempt to critique the imperial tradition of German education, founded on a vision of Greek culture that put a good deal of emphasis on 'harmonies' and 'heroism.'

In his pro-Wyneken days, Benjamin wrote a fascinating essay called 'Teaching and Valuing' in which he decried the Old Athenian model of education and its emulation of 'the misogynist and homo-erotic Greek culture of Pericles, which was aristocratic and based on slavery.' He railed against 'the dark myths of Aeschylus.' The problem was that Wyneken himself seemed devoted to an autocratic form of leadership, arguing boldly for 'free commitment to the self-chosen leader.' He was himself, of course, the leader he had in mind.

Benjamin was repelled by strong leaders and preferred to live in the margins, beyond the influence of power brokers. In an article called 'Dialogue on Religious Feeling Today,' he called for 'a new religion,' one that would 'emanate from the enslaved.' He placed writers among those groups of slaves who would eventually be responsible for creating the conditions of freedom for humankind. A writer, he said, is 'always a kind of Jew, an outsider. But our future salvation is dependent on this man.'

I was not convinced. Benjamin was curiously out of touch with reality, especially when it came to politics and women. His ignorance of the former is what killed him in the end – his refusal to face history in any form unmediated by language; the latter just made his life miserable, although it was not unrelated to his view of history. He could never meet a woman face-to-face; his affairs of the heart were often conducted in the safe realm of memory or imagination; embodiment, for him, was always a disappointment. (With Asja Lacis, for example. She blazed at the back of his mind like an altar. The few occasions when she actually slept with him were disastrous. 'Only Zeus can rape the world with impunity,' he once said. 'The rest of us must tell our parents what we've done.')

I will never forget that afternoon when I met him on Unter den Linden with a dark-eyed, vaguely rotund young woman called Grete Radt. She had unusually bad teeth, and when she smiled, one instinctively turned one's gaze away. I had noticed at once that she wore an engagement ring but was truly stunned when Benjamin referred to her as his fiancée.

'What?' I said, in a loud voice that seemed to panic both of them. 'You are getting married?'

'That is the whole point of an engagement,' said Benjamin, coolly, while Grete looked around as if terrified somebody might overhear us.

Many years later, in Paris, Benjamin explained to me how that engagement had come about.

He had become friendly with Grete sometime during the war, and she seemed to enjoy chatting with him about philosophy. He had planned a little holiday (financed by his father) in the Bavarian Alps, and when he told Grete about his trip, she somehow mistook this for an invitation. 'Yes, I would love to go with you to the Alps, Walter,' she said, in a highly formalized manner that made his skin crawl. 'I have always enjoyed the mountains – their height and so forth. They are very high, the Alps.' Benjamin acknowledged their massive height and was stuck.

A few days later, rather stupidly, he told his father that a woman was going with him on this holiday. This was not, he assured him, a 'romantic affiliation.' Nevertheless, unmarried couples simply did not travel together in those days, and Herr Benjamin could not approve. He grumbled something about appearances, but he did not cut off funds, which his son unwisely regarded as a kind of tacit support.

While he was walking in the Alps with Grete, he received a post-card from his father which said, simply and enigmatically: 'Sapienti sat.' *A word to the wise*. Assuming this was a note of encouragement, if not a mandate, from his father, he proposed to Grete at once, and she accepted the offer with some befuddlement. It seemed odd that a man who had never kissed her, never even struck a romantic note, should make such a move.

The immediate consequence of the proposal, according to Benjamin, was that Grete allowed him to come straight into bed with her that night. It was his 'first time,' he told me. 'I was dizzy with erotic desire, and I made love to her for three days straight. We hardly stopped for meals, and she was scarcely able to walk at the end of our holidays.' He continued, in his usual blunt way on this subject, to recount their various postures during intercourse, and her animal responses. It was always odd, listening to Benjamin on this subject; he became clinical, exasperatingly honest. (I am not prudish, mind you. I simply do not kiss and tell. A gentleman does not discuss his sexual activity as though it were a behavioral science).

Benjamin later discovered, much to his chagrin, that his father had simply been trying to advise his son – in cryptic language that would evade the censors – to remain on neutral territory, in Switzerland, until the war had passed. In the latter years of the war, only the paralyzed could actually count on avoiding conscription.

It took Benjamin two full years to extricate himself from this engagement. The crowbar separating them at last was the aggressive Dora Pollak, who later became Benjamin's wife and the mother of his only child, Stefan. Dora was lovely to behold: beautiful, quick-witted, worldly. She was taller than Benjamin by four inches, with cascading blond hair and gray-blue eyes. Her full breasts and large hips were in those years nicely contained, even explosively so, though discerning eyes could see a tendency toward the Junoesque. She was passionate, with a quick temper, and her tongue could sting.

Her father was Professor Leon Kellner, an early Zionist and Shakespeare scholar. He was later famous for his edition of the diaries and letters of his Zionist friend, Theodor Herzl. Perhaps I was more impressed by her pedigree than Benjamin, whose attention was almost wholly directed toward her breasts, which he once described as 'hanging like exotic fruit from the tree of her body.' He said this in front of her parents, much to my terror and amazement. It was just like him to say the most embarrassing things in public, though in general he was reticent about his feelings.

Benjamin met Dora in Munich, where he had gone after managing ingeniously to fail another physical exam. For many years he had known of her existence, even before her marriage to Max Pollak, a rich financier. She was active in the Youth Movement in

Berlin before the war, and she often attended Zionist lectures. I myself had admired her from a distance many times and was eager to make her acquaintance, if only to gain access to her father.

I visited Benjamin several times in Munich, where he lived in a smoky basement flat across from the Holtz gardens. I was there, in fact, in November of 1917, when Franz Kafka was reading to a literary society. The poster announcing his appearance said he would read a story called 'In the Penal Colony.' Kafka was never much in the public eye, so this was a rare occasion, but neither I nor Benjamin could attend that night. Given Benjamin's later obsession with Kafka's fiction, I've often wondered what might have happened had the two actually met. Probably nothing of course: Both were extremely shy. Men of genius are like massive continents – wholly bounded by water, and discreet. They have very little to say to one another, and it is usually a mistake to bring them together.

The war was going badly for Germany, as everyone except the government seemed to know. Millions had been slaughtered by January 1918, when Benjamin received in the mail a call-up order. He was suddenly reclassified as 'fit for light field duty,' which meant he was fit to be lined up before enemy guns without further ado. My own situation was not much different: I had been repeatedly hauled in for reexamination. In those years I suffered from a nervous condition that the military doctors had diagnosed as dementia praecox; this lovely disease meant I could not possibly be subjected to violence on the battlefield, and I was classified as unfit for duty. As one might have expected, my physical condition did not improve, so I never had to lay my body on the line in aid of German nationalism.

As in the past, I spent the night before his latest physical exam with Benjamin, dining with him and his family. We were served, as usual, by servants in black dresses with white lace collars, and we dined on veal and cabbage (even during the war one could, for a price, obtain decent food). Herr Benjamin produced an elegant bottle of Hoch, and cigars were passed around to the men. It pleased me that Herr Benjamin believed that neither I nor his sons should fight in this war.

'It is one thing to lose a war,' he said, 'but another to lose a son.'

It always puzzled me that Benjamin himself did not understand his father's sympathies. I, for example, would have been pleased if my father remotely understood my position on the war, but I was broadly considered a traitor and coward in my own house.

Benjamin and I talked until dawn in the living room, which featured a large Christmas tree decorated with sweets and candles. It was disconcerting to see this blatantly Christian symbol in a Jewish household, but the Benjamin family was no different from most liberal Jewish families in Berlin at this time. When I expressed my feelings on this subject to Benjamin, he chimed in with his father: 'Christmas is a national festivity. It is not a religious holiday anymore.' Imagine such nonsense filling the mouths of intelligent men, and Jews!

Much to our horror, Benjamin passed the exam, which took place on a Friday morning, and was ordered to report for duty the following Monday. From what I later discovered, he spent the weekend in seclusion with Dora, who used hypnosis to produce sciaticalike symptoms. A doctor was called in, and he wrote a detailed report saying that his patient had suffered a relapse of an old back ailment and could not possibly be moved without risk of severe injury. A flurry of letters was exchanged, and the army medical board eventually acquiesced; the invalid was given a few months' reprieve.

Wisely, Benjamin slipped over the border into Switzerland not a week later, and Dora followed. I was at this time studying philosophy and mathematics at the university in Jena, and Benjamin had decided to enroll at the university in Bern for doctoral work. I thought about my friend every day. It was as if an inexplicable force drew me toward him, and I kept wanting to drop everything and cross the border. I wanted his attention and advice, but especially his conversation.

Benjamin invited me to Bern that summer of 1918, just a few months before the Great War ended so ignominiously for Germany, which deserved everything it got. I joined him and Dora for a sojourn that lasted well into the next year. What should have been an idyll of companionship turned rather nastily into something else, although I am still not sure what went wrong. It was not simply a case of my not wanting Dora to come between Benjamin and myself. My brother kept saying this was so, but he knew nothing of the situation. In truth, I came to understand Benjamin much better through his wife. She was a prism, and my friend's soul-light was all the more radiant when refracted through her. They were married, but still a good deal of courting went on between them – and this included a kind of emotional tug-of-war that looked, from the outside, like hell.

We lived minutes apart by foot in separate apartments on the outskirts of Bern; the village was called Muri – a delightful little place, with a few shops and a school for young children. Chalets dotted the hillside, and the tinkle of goat bells could usually be heard. My bedroom had a big desk in front of the window, and I looked out across a meadow, with snowy peaks in the distance. The sky was invariably blue, or so it seemed. (Memory is a thick gauze that filters out whatever information does not fit, is it not?)

Our arrangement in Muri was potentially cozy for everyone. We would write and read in the mornings, pursuing our various projects; in the afternoons we would meet for chess or walks in the deep pine wood behind the village; in the evenings we would dine together. I loved to cook in those days, and I prepared some of the best meals of my life for them: an array of Mediterranean and Middle Eastern dishes. I had recently increased my vocabulary of kosher dishes, too, and I tried several of them on my supposedly Jewish friends, who made jokes about my 'shtetl kitchen.'

Benjamin and I were not especially similar in temperament, despite our shared intellectual concerns. I was, and remain, fairly high-strung, nervous. I work to the point of exhaustion, then collapse until my energy gathers slowly, then I attack my work again. Benjamin worked steadily, was quite relaxed in general; he could digest terrifying quantities of material, but there was invariably a block when it came to writing. 'Leaping the gap from silence into language is so intimidating,' he would say. 'Just get it down,' I would tell him. 'You can worry about revising later.'

We were both academic renegades in those days, drifting hopefully from one university to another, always looking for the right mentor. It was not easy. German and Swiss universities were spilling over with pompous bores who knew how to strangle the life from any subject, however interesting in itself. I was at dreadfully loose ends, trying to decide whether or not to pursue doctoral studies in the philosophy of mathematics at Jena under Paul Linke, who had been a pupil of Husserl's.

For his part, Benjamin had used the influence of his father-in-law to enroll at Bern for doctoral work under Richard Herbertz, a colorless and narrow man, but his prospects there did not look good – at least not to me. 'One must be practical about these things,' or so Benjamin, the least practical of all men, told me. 'Herbertz may be dull, but he is not capricious or evil, so he won't plot against me. I can do whatever I want, and he will ignore it. In the end, I will get my degree, which is all that matters.'

It amused me to see Benjamin in this mode of worldly wisdom, but it also annoyed me a little. I looked to him for spiritual guidance, not cynicism. No man was ever by nature more ethical, but he could say the most awful things; it was as if, being extraordinarily moral by instinct, he had to counterbalance this with a vein of crude expediency. The awkward question of money, for example, arose one night soon after my arrival, and it kindled our first real argument. I had mentioned that I felt guilty living so well on what was, after all, my father's money.

Benjamin listened impatiently, drawing slowly on a hand-rolled cigarette. After a lengthy pause, he said, 'I am living off my father, too. He bought this very chicken we are now so greedily consuming. He paid for this excellent wine as well. Let's drink to him!' He and Dora grinned and clinked glasses.

When I refused to participate in their little joke, he scowled at me, saying, 'Oh, dear Gerhard. You are suffering from scruples again! It is always a bad sign in people.'

Dora saw my ears go crimson but could not resist fueling the fire. 'He is still terribly young,' she said to him. 'And idealistic, too.'

'I do not understand,' I said, trying to remain cool. 'You are so eager to live like the bourgeoisie, whom you despise. You talk about morality, but look at you . . .'

'Look at *you*,' said Dora, turning on me with those diamond-hard eyes of hers, which I had come to fear. 'You spend your father's money just as we do, but somehow you imagine that because it troubles you, you occupy some high moral plane. That's not only outrageous, it's conceited.'

'At least I am honest.'

'Nonsense!' Benjamin cried. It was a rare outburst for him, and it quite surprised me. 'I'm unhappy to hear such a ridiculous sentence on your lips. You are an intellectual. We are all intellectuals. Our obligation is therefore only to the world of ideas. The money be damned!'

'I'm afraid that's hypocritical,' I said quietly, 'unless I'm mistaken.'

'Then so be it. I feel no need to make my ideas and my life conform to some external law. I am not a rabbi, thank goodness.'

'You make me strangely uncomfortable, Walter,' I said.

He stood, rather grandly. 'That is because you are a small boy in your heart, and not a man. When you grow up, you will see that one does what is necessary. The work matters, and nothing else: politics, family, love. You must become ruthless, amoral.'

He was angry now, and perhaps a little drunk. A trifle uncertainly, he poured another glass of wine for himself, swirled it in his glass, sniffed the bouquet, then gulped it down. After smacking his lips, he left the room, tripping as he crossed the threshold.

'He is drunk,' I said to Dora, 'and irrational.'

She lowered her eyes rather seductively. 'Don't take his little poses too seriously,' she said. 'He should have joined the Yiddish theater.' Her fingers picked at my sleeve – a gesture of intimacy that I thoroughly disliked. 'Have another drink with me.'

Reluctantly, I accepted a glass of brandy. They had very good brandy.

Dora suddenly came around behind me to massage my shoulders. 'Relax,' she said. 'Why are you so stiff?'

I tried to relax, but she was making it impossible. I took several deep breaths.

'You are very sexy when you get angry,' she whispered in my ear. 'Have you ever been with a woman, Gerhard?'

'Yes, of course,' I said.

'I don't believe you.'

'Your belief or disbelief is quite irrelevant,' I said.

Now her hands moved through my hair, and – unwittingly – I began to get an erection.

Suddenly Benjamin called for her. 'Dora!' he shrieked. 'I am in bed, and naked.'

'You see what a pig he is,' she said. 'It's not all Kant and Hegel around here.'

I stood, brushing her aside. This situation made me hideously uncomfortable, and it was not untypical. 'I'm afraid I must go, Dora.' I swilled the brandy.

'What, you don't want to join us?' She gave me a teasing look, then flicked her own glass against the stucco wall so that it shattered on the tile floor. I realized how drunk she really was.

'What are you doing out there?' Benjamin cried. 'I am waiting for you!'

Dora was busy pouring herself another drink and lighting a cigarette. But before she could say another word, I had slipped outside, into the clear, cold night.

The next day, at lunch, nothing of what had transpired the night before was mentioned. It was like this between us. We would say rude things, part company, then pretend that nothing hurtful had ever been uttered. Once or twice I had stumbled in upon Dora and Benjamin at the wrong moment – when they were in the act of sexual intercourse, in fact – and even this was never mentioned. I don't think either would have minded if I'd sat at the edge of the bed to watch them fornicate!

It was obvious now that Benjamin was unhappy in his marriage to Dora. They would shout at each other in front of me, as if unaware of my presence, occasionally saying things too cruel to believe. It unnerved me to see a man whom I admired so profoundly, even revered, acting like an ordinary, run-of-the-mill jackass. Dora would call him names, deride his vanity, and bemoan his lack of attention to her, tossing various small, hard objects in his direction: a book, a cup, a piece of bric-a-brac. Once she actually shattered a china plate on his forehead. He looked up, virtually unfazed, and said: 'Why do the English make the best china? Has it anything to do with the fragility of their empire? It is built on sand, you know. They do not have the necessary temper.'

One night, in the midst of dinner, he and Dora began arguing about something trivial. Benjamin suddenly dismissed her concerns as too boring to discuss, and Dora rushed off to the bedroom in tears; rightly sensing that he had gone too far in humiliating her, he followed her, and I was left to finish the meal alone.

Later that night, close to midnight, there was a knock at my door. Since Benjamin almost never came to my apartment, I was quite surprised to see him standing in my doorway, nervous as a child who has done something wrong. The whites of his eyes were speckled with red, and his hair was disheveled.

I brought him inside and tucked a snifter of brandy between his icy hands.

'Thank you so much,' he said, shuddering. He brought the golden brown liquor close to his face, inhaled deeply, then drank. The relief on his face was palpable.

'You were so agitated tonight,' I said. 'Can this marriage possibly work, Walter?'

'My dear friend, you are young. You don't understand about love. There is always difficulty, even real pain, but it doesn't matter. What you can't see very well from where you stand is that I do love Dora.'

'What I see is a man in distress. You fight with her about every-thing. Not one little thing appears to satisfy either of you.'

Benjamin made an odd face, taking another long sip, which he held in his mouth for a full minute before swallowing. 'We have not made you happy, Gerhard,' he said at last. 'I hope you have not regretted coming to Bern.'

'I'm learning a great deal,' I said.

'About love?' he asked, laughing.

'Love of the kind that you and Dora must endure does not interest me. It might as well be called war.'

His remote little grin tumbled quickly into a frown. 'Love is war, perhaps.' He paused, hunching forward in his chair, holding the brandy up to the candlelight as if to inspect it for impurities. 'One day you will understand.'

'You are patronizing me,' I said.

'I'm sorry. You are right.' He leaned toward me, as if searching for something. 'What I like about you is your directness. You say exactly what you think. It's what drew me toward you in the first place.'

Whenever his attention locked onto me like this, my heart raced. Although I considered us equals in most regards, he was also my teacher, and there is no holier connection between two people than teacher and pupil. Indeed, the word *torah* simply means 'instruction,' though not as the mere transmission of information, as in school. What Benjamin taught, by example, was a way of regarding everything in the world as a text that, with sufficient intellectual pressure, one could interpret.

'You must know that I want nothing but your friendship,' I said.

This awkwardly formulaic fragment pleased him, and he said, 'Tomorrow we shall begin reading Kant together, as we planned. You would like that?'

'Yes, that would be good,' I said, tentatively, not wishing to appear overly eager. I had indeed just finished Hermann Cohen's insipid but fashionable book on Kant's theory of experience, and I was full of questions, guesses, inklings. As usual, Benjamin had been able to anticipate my intellectual growth, and he would lead me forward. Even if he didn't, I knew there could be no better way to spend one's days than reading Kant with Benjamin.

'Will Dora participate?' I asked, nervously.

'Just you and me,' he said.

'Ah,' I said. It would have been unkind to say more, to put into words a feeling that was better left unexpressed. Sometimes, in friendship, it is important to know what not to say. And sometimes only the stout of heart are willing to say nothing.

WALTER BENJAMIN

Of all the ways of acquiring books, writing them oneself is often regarded as the most praiseworthy method . . . Writers are merely people who write books, not because they are poor and cannot afford them, but because they are dissatisfied with the volumes they could buy in a bookstore.

6 LISA FITTKO

It was late June 1940, in the camp in Gurs. I remember waking up one morning convinced that Paulette and I must flee that day or be captured by the Nazis. There was no doubt about it: The Germans were coming. One did not know where they were exactly, but they were close. You could see them coming, their boots and buttons flashing, in the eyes of the French guards, who had been languid for days, hesitant to command; the stuff that makes a person willing to give an order and stand behind it had been drained from them. They were dummies filled with straw.

'We're going today,' I whispered to Paulette.

'How can you say that?'

'Going,' I said.

'Going where?'

'South. As far south as we can get.' I knew that south was the only possible direction.

I had managed to steal release certificates from the commandant's office, and I gave one to Paulette. We wrote our names on them and forged the commandant's signature: These might come in handy one day for purposes of identification. I doubted that we could really use them today.

'How did you get these?' Paulette asked.

'Nosy people don't survive in times of war,' I said. 'Ask fewer questions.' I don't know what came over me, but I was no longer in a mood to let events dominate me. I was also a little frustrated by Paulette, who seemed to lack initiative. She wanted to pretend that a war wasn't really on.

'What are you girls doing?' the guard asked, watching us from a distance of fifty yards.

'I'm writing a dirty novel,' I said. 'Do you want to read it, Jacques?' His name was not Jacques, but he looked to me like a Jacques, so I called him that. It seemed to annoy him, which made me that much happier to have found the name.

He just scoffed, turning his back to light a cigarette. I don't think he had any notion of what to make of us. We were all, in his mind, deeply peculiar.

'I'm not sure about this,' said Paulette. 'The Germans are every-where. That's what the radio says. Even in the south.'

'You can't trust the radio,' I said. 'It's propaganda, whatever they say.' I put a hand on her shoulder. 'Look,' I said, 'if we stay here, we're finished. At least in the countryside we have a chance. We can hide. It's easy!'

'I want to find Otto,' she said.

'And I want Hans. But we're not going to find them here. Not in Gurs. If the Germans capture us, we'll be shipped back to the Fatherland. We'll be shot in a ditch. Tortured first, then shot in a ditch, and you know it.'

The rumors from Germany, Poland, and Belgium had been drifting through the air like poison, and we all knew that some of them must be true. The Germans were committing atrocities on a scale new to modern history.

Paulette, who was usually quite composed, suddenly began to tremble. Her lips were blue and tightly drawn. Tears glistened on her cheeks. 'I can't go with you,' she said. 'I'll stay behind.'

I don't know why I did this, but I slapped her. 'You mustn't lose your nerve, not now!' I whispered loudly. 'If you want to see Otto again, you have got to hold steady.'

It was quite unlike me, but I put my arms around her. Paulette was still a child, really. She required comfort, and clear boundaries. I must use whatever authority I had; Paulette needed that. She needed me to remain strong.

'You're so kind to me, Lisa,' she said, her head on my shoulder.

'We're friends, aren't we?' I patted her back lightly.

Jacques, meanwhile, stared at us from his end of the barracks, smoking. I simply stared back, and that was enough to get him to avert his eyes.

That morning the commandant himself came to visit with us; it was the first time anybody had ever seen him here, in a barracks. The women swarmed around him, shouting, 'What's going to happen to us, monsieur commandant? What's the plan?'

The plan: a comic notion. Everybody wants to believe that somebody is in charge and has a program. This is doubtless why religion is so popular, especially among the masses, who have no sense of being able to control their own fate.

'Where are the Germans?' one of the women shouted above the others. 'Tell us the truth!'

'The situation is under control,' he said.

'They say we are losing the war! Is this so?' another woman asked.

He waved at her to dismiss the allegation. 'Don't believe these things you hear,' he said. 'There is too much wagging of tongues.'

'The Germans have taken Paris, and they'll soon be here!' the same woman maintained.

'It's all rumor, nothing more,' he said with a firmness that revealed a lack of hard information. Like an aging, third-rate actor's, his chest swelled and his voice grew comically rotund. 'You must not panic, ladies. The French government assumes full responsibility for your protection.'

It has always amazed me how platitudinous and empty people in official positions can sound. Having purposefully donned the mask of their function, they quickly lose touch with anything resembling a human voice.

'They will kill us!' the woman shrieked.

The commandant pointed a chubby finger at her. 'You must not listen to those who try to frighten you,' he said. 'If everybody stays put, there will be less trouble. We will guarantee your safety.'

I whispered into Paulette's ear: 'We're getting out of here!'

By now, she understood that we had no choice. The Germans would eat this petty commandant for lunch and the rest of us for dessert.

At midday, a shiny black Hispano appeared at the gate of the camp: the kind of car only a high-ranking officer would use. Several men rushed out to greet the gentleman, who despite his polished brass and crisp uniform looked quite desperate; his eyes had the wild look of the hunted, and he was hunched and squinting. He was accompanied by two obsequious underlings and a driver.

There was general confusion in the courtyard, with soldiers leaving their posts and rushing about. A current of panic spread among the detainees, with shouts and cries, and the guards, for the first time, seemed not to care. Many appeared to have gone back to their own quarters, perhaps to pack their belongings.

I knew in my gut that the Germans were close and that we must leave at once. 'Stay right beside me,' I told Paulette. 'When the guard asks where we are going, flash your certificate. Don't tell him anything, even if he asks.'

'We're going to do this, aren't we?'

I nodded, then grinned.

Fortunately, Paulette went along with me. I had not so much convinced her as not allowed her the possibility of opposing me. The idea that she might remain behind, without me, was on another level quite unthinkable. Paulette and I were, for the time being, a couple.

A dozen or so women had gathered in the courtyard, arguing among themselves about the progress of the Germans, while only two guards chatted to each other by the front gate. Dogs were barking, and a few chickens squawked. I remember seeing a red shift flap in the breeze on a makeshift clothesline. An occasional plane zoomed over. I had not had the foresight to pack my things the night before but, like Paulette, managed to stuff what I really needed into a rucksack.

With studied nonchalance, we strode toward the gate.

'Hey, where are you girls going?' one guard asked us. His voice did not register great concern, however, and he was almost at once distracted by some shouting elsewhere in the camp.

'I have a pass,' I said, waving my certificate. 'So does she.' I nodded in Paulette's direction. 'Ask the commandant if you want – he has released us.'

The young man looked temporarily confused, but we didn't wait for more questions. We just walked out of Gurs, not looking back.

It's odd how easy the impossible tasks in life can seem, and how difficult the simple ones. The notion of merely walking out of Gurs had never struck me before this morning. But there we were, free and strolling under sunny skies. Not even our shadows followed us.

At last, I could not resist playing Lot's wife and looking back: The guard was now preoccupied with someone else. Other women were obviously trying the same thing. I could see that nobody was going to come after us, and I made a slight leap in the air. A thrill like I'd not felt in years – part fear, part exhilaration – coursed through my body.

We just kept walking, steadily, heads slightly down, at a fair pace. We walked down a dirt road lined with plane trees. In an hour or so, Gurs had disappeared behind us: a blur of bad memories. We had no food, no money, nothing, but it hardly mattered. For the moment, we were free.

Then I heard a vehicle closing in behind us, and I thought all was lost, especially when this drab military car stopped only a few paces ahead of us. A young officer rolled down the window to greet us in passing. He had sharp blue eyes and yellow hair, parted neatly in the middle. His teeth were ridiculously straight and white. 'Hey, girls! Want a lift?' he said.

It was obvious from his tone that he was not taking us back to Gurs, so I got in. It was important to put as much distance as possible between ourselves and Gurs. Paulette, though hesitant, followed me.

'Where are you girls coming from?' he asked.

'We're Belgians,' I said, making sure to catch Paulette's eye. She nodded, assuring me that she understood.

The officer grunted, as if my remark explained everything. He soon launched into a monologue about a summer holiday that he had spent, years ago, in Belgium. In time of war, people become obsessed with their own past, with the story of their lives; they begin to live everything all over again, sifting for evidence of a kind that cannot be found.

I was by now exhausted, and nodded off in the back seat, leaving Paulette to listen and respond to our driver, whose name was Lieutenant Ratié. The snatches of talk I overheard did not inspire my confidence in the leadership of the French army.

By the time we pulled into Pontacq, a rural village with long sloping hills rising just beyond it, I was refreshed and wide-eyed. The adrenaline surged as we stopped directly in front of police head-quarters, a stone building with shuttered windows. Paulette reached for my hand like a frightened child.

'You girls wait here,' the lieutenant said, and went inside.

Paulette's instinct was to flee, but I trusted our rambling officer who emerged from the building with two overweight policemen at either elbow. 'These women are Belgian refugees,' he explained. 'The Gestapo wants to kill them. I will hold you personally responsible for their safety.' For the first time, his manner seemed plausible.

Inside the station, we showed our false certificates of release. (I held in reserve my old Czech passport, which would have compli-cated our already complex story.) I had become Lise Duchamps. My companion was Paulette Perrier. Nice names, I thought. I should have been a novelist.

The constable in charge assured us that we'd be looked after, and we were. They drove us to a farm at the edge of town, where the elderly farmer's wife, Madame Derauges, welcomed us with feigned enthusiasm, anticipating a nice subsidy from the police. We were given beds in a rough wooden bunkhouse beside the garden; it had high rafters, a hayloft, and cracked windows, but it was private and not uncomfortable. That night we ate our first decent meal in months: thick bacon slices, fresh bread and salt, turnips, dandelion salad. There was even a carafe of syrupy local wine.

'There's a village pump at the end of the road,' Madame Derauges said. 'Wash yourselves and your clothes there. And don't forget to close the gate! We keep hens, you see. If they get loose, it's impossible to find them.'

She pointed to the outhouse that she and her husband used. 'Just ignore the outhouse,' she said. 'That belongs to us. Use the garden. It's good for the plants.'

When the police left, the old woman began talking more freely. 'Nobody knows where the Germans are,' she said. 'There are rumors. I have no idea how safe you are here. How safe am I?' She cocked her head to one side, almost threateningly. 'I may not be able to lie to protect you,' she said. 'This farm . . . it's all we have in the world. I can't risk it, you see.' Her husband was not to be seen, though she referred to 'we' on every possible occasion. Apparently the old man was living with their daughter in a nearby town, having quarreled with his wife very badly just a few days before we arrived.

For most of the week, we stayed put. After Gurs, it was agreeable to return to a semblance of normalcy. We washed our clothes at the pump, helped the old woman around the farm with various chores, did a lot of cooking. In the second week, toward evening, we drifted into the village to sit under a huge linden tree on a bench and chat with locals. Refugees would stagger by, often moving in small clusters like ghosts, and we'd question them about the progress of the war. Several of the women from Gurs passed through, and we heard from them that soon after we escaped the entire camp was broken up. The women were scattered like chicken feed into the countryside. Once, a motley group of soldiers came through the village, but even they seemed ignorant of what was really going on. One of them actually assured me that the war was over! 'I am going back to Paris,' he said. 'My mother will be so pleased.'

One night a motorcycle pulled up to the bench where Paulette and I were sitting, and we couldn't believe our eyes. It was Alfred Sevensky, a Pole whom we had both known in Paris. When the war broke out, he joined the Polish Legion and they had fought the Germans on their march toward Paris. He told us they had been thoroughly routed near the Somme; those who were not killed, injured, or captured were on the run, like himself. For the time being, Alfred would come to stay with us. It was oddly comforting to be with someone whom one knew, however slightly, from an earlier, easier time.

One day in the late afternoon the bus from Pau, a neighboring village, stopped in the square at Pontacq, and a small group of refugees got off. Although the chances of knowing any of them were slender, one nevertheless grew attentive. These were people like oneself, after all. My gaze was drawn to a perilously thin old man with long white hair and yellowish eyes; he leaned on a cane as he approached. Paulette suddenly grabbed my arm tightly.

'What is it?' I asked.

'I am seeing things!'

'What are you talking about?'

'My father!'

The old man was indeed her father. Der Alte, as we called him, the Old One. He had made his way to Gurs in search of his daughter, and he had just kept going. It was a miracle that he had found her.

This was obviously a moment of tremendous feeling for both of them, but what surprised me was the casualness of the encounter, the way they suppressed strong emotions. The two walked in slow motion into each other's arms, and they remained for some time quite still. I could see der Alte's eyes, their yellowness like the late-afternoon sky, dusty and worn, with a touch of wildness in it, as in a lion's eyes.

'Come,' I said at last. 'Let's bring der Alte home. He looks hungry.'

'Please,' he said. 'We must go quickly to Lourdes. The Germans will be here in a day or two.'

'We can hide in the forest,' I said. 'They'll never find us.'

Der Alte shook his head. It was quite possible that Paulette and I could blend with the French people, but there was no way to hide him. He was a German Jew: There could be no doubt about his origins.

'It is not safe here,' he said. 'Ask the women who were on the bus.'

Paulette did her best to reassure him, and (reluctantly) he agreed to come back to the farm with us. The lure of a good meal and a bunk was not easily resisted. He had been traveling for days on end without sufficient food or rest; indeed, he was on the brink of collapse when he found us.

One of the other refugees from the same bus was Joseph Kaminski, another Pole. He bore horrifying tales of his escape from a camp that was overrun by the Germans. That night, he joined us as well, and we made a campfire and fried bacon and potatoes. Much to my amazement and joy, he said he had seen Hans, and it thrilled me to have confirmed what I already knew in my heart: Hans was alive.

I gave him a letter for Hans, with my address. It was written in code, of course, with a false name that he would recognize. A lot of letters were being passed among the refugee community this way, and it proved an efficient system. I sent messages to a dozen people over the next day or so, and before long I received another confirmation that Hans was alive.

The note came from my brother, himself a refugee, within a matter of days. 'Your husband was seen on a bicycle between Limoges and Montauban,' he wrote in his straight up-and-down hand. It was enough.

The decision now rested on when, not if, we should move, and in what direction. A trickle of refugees had started in early summer and swollen to a great river by mid-July, yet before we actually joined this conduit of human misery and fear, we thought it wise to test the waters. One morning Paulette and I hitched a ride into the country-side with two young men who were driving a military supply truck. They quizzed us about our origins.

'So you're from the north?' the driver asked.

'From Belgium,' I said.

'Where in Belgium? My cousin lives there.'

He knew we were lying, but I decided to play along. I mentioned a town, trying to seem casual about it.

'Ah, that's where my cousin lives. Do you know the gas station across from the town hall?' His friend grinned ear to ear. They were cleverly attempting to catch us out.

'You are not very nice to us,' I said, with a scolding air whose underside was coyness. 'Is this any way to treat the wives of prisoners of war?'

To my surprise, this little ploy worked; their grins evaporated, and the conversation ended. We continued on in what felt like embarrassed silence, but this was preferable to talking with these louts.

It was a dewy morning, with sunlight glazing the hay, the long fields rich and deep in grain. Drab tents were pitched in the fields, and cots were lined up in rows outside them. Most of the soldiers slept out under the stars, by preference. There was maybe something comforting about the stars, whose pinpoint legends never change, despite the vagaries of life on earth. Alfred had talked a lot about the comforts of nature in time of war, and I understood this now. So much is already given, and it cannot be taken away.

We got out at Tarbes, near a crossroad that had become a meeting place for refugees and so a good place to find out about our husbands. I milled about, trying to discover if anyone had seen or heard anything about Hans. I was by now desperate for each morsel, which I devoured greedily. We heard fresh reports of the exodus from Paris, of millions caught in the stream of history and swept southward, with human rivulets cutting into the landscape. Everyone was trying to get out of France, but there were few escape routes left. No one doubted that even these would close soon.

I struck up a conversation with a dashing French officer who was standing by an expensive Italian car. He seemed to like me, so I asked for a lift.

With an easy smile, he said, 'Come on, both of you.'

We set off from Tarbes in high style, Paulette and I luxuriating in the red leather seats. It seemed utterly safe to be riding with an officer in such a fine car. The refugees trudging along the road looked at us anxiously as we passed, and one or two of them waved mechanically. In well-bred people, the social forms will survive long after their content has been drained of meaning. On the other hand, it was smart to wave at everyone, friend or enemy. Hedging one's bet was a good habit to acquire in wartime.

We came to a bridge not three miles from the city, and my stomach clenched when I saw a military blockade. This is it, I said to myself. We stopped, and the guard came over and asked for the officer's papers.

'You must turn back, sir,' the guard said, having examined the papers. 'We have strict orders. No one may pass.'

'I am passing,' the officer said.

'Please, sir. I have my orders.' He glanced warily at the two of us in the back seat. 'I have orders to shoot,' he added, lowering his rifle in a threatening way.

The officer suddenly drew a revolver and pointed it straight at the guard. 'I will cross the bridge,' he said.

The guard stepped back slightly, and our car zoomed forward.

Half expecting shots to be fired into the back windshield, I ducked my head. But no, we were going to be all right, once again. Another miracle had saved us.

Some miles from Pontacq the officer dropped us off when the road divided. 'Please, ladies,' he said, 'all you need do is cut through that field. You'll arrive in Pontacq within the hour.'

We thanked him and began our walk through a field of corn-flowers. Bees zummed by our ears and butterflies scattered in our wake. At the edge of a pond, where we stopped to drink, a woman about my age was sitting beneath a large oak, reading a book in German. When my eyes adjusted to the light, I saw it was Hannah Arendt, whom I'd met several times before in Paris. She had studied in Germany at several universities and was said to be brilliant.

After hearing a brief account of her wanderings over the past few months, I invited her to come back to Pontacq with us.

'I think it's safer to travel alone,' she said. 'In any case, I prefer it.'

I tried to persuade her to join us, but she was adamant. So we left her there, reading in the shade of that spreading oak, her face dappled by shadows. It was one of those peculiar meetings that stays with you in memory.

Der Alte's frantic desire to go to Lourdes swayed us, and we decided to accompany him. As Arendt said, it was less conspicuous to travel singly or in pairs, so Paulette and I decided to hang back for a few days. We would meet der Alte and Alfred in the city's main square at a prearranged time. Staying in Pontacq, however comfortable, was not a permanent solution, since the Germans were definitely coming. Nobody doubted this now.

We entered Lourdes on the handlebars of two bicycles, having been picked up on the outskirts of the city by two benevolent soldiers, who claimed we were their girlfriends. This helped whenever we encountered a checkpoint: They waved us through with a wink. Any touch of romance was welcome in these dismal days.

The city itself teemed with refugees, lost soldiers, men and women given up for dead by relatives in distant places. Paulette and I strolled arm in arm along a wide boulevard thick with people, stopping now and then to press our noses against the windows of a pastry shop.

Every major city in France had opened a Centre d'Accueil to welcome refugees, but we had been warned to stay away from them; people without valid passports were being arrested and thrown into holding camps. The lucky ones were merely turned away, homeless, without provisions.

As planned, we met up with Alfred, who had found a hotel room for us by tricking the authorities into giving him billeting slips. I congratulated him on his deceptiveness. We had all become such fast talkers that we thought we could get anything from anybody! If the Germans caught me, I planned to tell them I was Hitler's cousin from Austria. I had the whole family tree outlined in my head. Why not? Who would risk killing Hitler's cousin? Or even someone who might be Hitler's cousin if she wasn't lying? Was that a risk anybody in his right mind would take?

The hotel room was glorious, with faucets that worked, a full-length mirror with a chipped but gilded frame, a bidet with a curtain around it. The beds were made up with crisp, clean linens that smelled wonderfully of soap, and there were fresh towels for everyone. One could even manage to draw a trickle of warm water from the tap!

Luck was definitely with us, since we managed the same day to find der Alte. When he saw the hotel room, he beamed. 'You see, you listen to your father,' he said, 'I told you Lourdes was the place for us! I am very happy here.'

It was all splendid, though we knew it was temporary. Even in Lourdes, one could not escape the Germans forever.

Meanwhile, I called at the post office each day to inquire if any mail had come for Lise Duchamps, the name I'd given to Hans for such purposes. This paid off one Saturday afternoon. A telegram had arrived, saying Hans awaited me at Montauban. It was signed with a false name and addressed to General Delivery.

My sense was that now we must get to Marseilles as soon as possible. This was the only place where one could hope to find passage to America or Cuba or somewhere far from the black dogs of Europe barking at our heels. I wrote explaining this to Hans, and set about getting us railway tickets to Marseilles. I told him to meet us in Toulouse, though such a rendezvous was predicated on our having acquired a certificate of safe conduct. These were currently available, I was told, from the Commandant Spécial Militaire de la Gare de Lourdes, so I set off immediately to find him.

He was a small man, clean shaven, smelling of hair tonic. Paulette and I presented ourselves, as usual, as Belgians.

'May I see your papers, please?' he asked, adding, 'I would be much obliged.' The politeness was noticeable and rare. The war had a way of stripping away the niceties, leaving a kind of jungle talk: 'Give me this! Don't take that!'

I said, 'I'm afraid they were lost in flight.'

He looked at me with sympathy. 'Have you got anything I can see?'

I handed over our moldy certificates of release from the camp at Gurs and der Alte's dog-eared *carte d'identité*.

He looked at us with genuine sadness. 'I'm terribly sorry,' he said. 'I wish I could help. You see, I'm in charge of military transportation, nothing more.'

Something in his voice, his hesitancy, encouraged me to press on. 'Listen, *mon capitaine*,' I said. 'You must help us. I will tell you the truth: We are running from the Nazis. We were forced to flee our homeland, and we came to France because it has always welcomed political exiles. Hitler is our enemy as much as yours.'

The man wearily drew a stamp from his drawer and marked our papers one by one. He wrote POUR MARSEILLES in large blue letters on each page and signed his name. 'This may work, but on the other hand it may not. I can't say. In any case, you must try. Good luck to you.'

I began to thank him, but he waved me off. 'You must not insult me with your thanks. I am a citizen of France and an officer in its army. We've behaved so badly in this war. In fact, it is I who am in your debt.'

I will never forget this lovely man. He was a real Frenchman, not a traitorous swine like Pétain or Weygand or Laval. He gave me courage.

That evening I wrote to Hans to explain our plans, and we left several days later on the train for Marseilles, stopping in Toulouse well before lunch; the idea was that Hans should join us there. To my horror, he was not at the station as planned.

I told Paulette, Alfred, and der Alte that I was not going anywhere without Hans, and they knew I meant it. They agreed to wait at the station while I made my way by train to Montauban, which was close by.

'If you aren't back in time for the last train,' Paulette said, 'should we assume you're not coming?' The poor girl wrung her hands.

'Assume I'm dead,' I said, keeping a straight face.

In Montauban, an hour or so later, I ran into an old acquaintance, the brother of a friend, who told me that Hans was living in a half-built villa in the hills to the west of the town. I set off on foot, intermittently running and walking. In my head, I kept rehearsing what might happen. It was a scene I had already played a thousand times in the theater of my mind, with a thousand different scripts.

I turned a corner to see the villa in the near distance, a structure that recalled a Greek ruin. The owner had apparently begun the project with grandiose plans, laying out elaborate gardens and creating a paved courtyard, but the war had frightened him, or bankrupted him, and he'd run away. Hans stood on the front steps, his arms crossed, the walls of the villa roofless but brilliant.

The reunion plays itself out in memory like a series of time-lapse photographs: Lisa running knees high, head back, tense. Hans, eyes fixed, white eyes, burning. Sun-glazed walls, long cypress trees. Lisa's head on his chest, crying. Hans folding arms around Lisa. Big hands on shoulder blades. Big hands on sides of face. Lisa and Hans, kissing. Lisa crying. Hans laughing, looking over her shoulder at the camera.

A long time passed before I remembered how angry I was. 'Why didn't you meet us as planned? We all could be in Marseilles by now!'

He had a good explanation, of course. I'd almost forgotten how nimble he was with words. He needed a few more days to acquire a safe-conduct pass, and in any case, he wasn't at all sure that going to Marseilles was the right plan. Everyone was going to Marseilles, even the Germans. Shouldn't we lose ourselves in the countryside? France was a big country, and the French peasants were hiding refugees rather well in lofts, in cellars. One could also disappear into the woods and live like primitives: eating roots, hunting small animals, drinking rainwater. Notions tumbled from his lips, played off the cracked smile.

'Why didn't you write to me with your objections?' I asked. 'This is holding everybody up.'

'There wasn't time.' He stood back, offended. 'You're so bossy, Lisa. You just issued a command for me to appear in Toulouse. It's not so easy.'

I should have guessed that Hans would not be told what to do. It wasn't his way. You would think I hadn't lived with him long enough to know this.

It also must be said that Hans had a good point. Rumor had it they were arresting people right off the train in Marseilles. Without the right papers, they would simply turn us over.

I saw at once that we must stop Paulette, Alfred, and der Alte, who would be boarding the last train for Marseilles at five P.M. It was already three-thirty, so we didn't have time to chat. 'Let's go!' I shrieked, grabbing his arm.

'Where?'

'Don't ask questions! Hurry!'

After a breakneck journey, we arrived in Toulouse with ten minutes to spare.

'Get on the train, anywhere!' Paulette shouted, her head sticking out the window. 'It leaves any moment!'

I explained quickly that we must not go to Marseilles.

'If I believed every rumor I heard, I'd do nothing. I would die on the spot,' said der Alte. 'I am going to Marseilles.' Despite this declaration of independence, he stayed with us. At this point in the war, he'd had enough of striking out by himself.

We went straight back to Montauban, to the villa. It was idyllic there: a camp with nobody to bother us. We got provisions from the town, and the weather was perfect: warm but not sweltering, rainless. I didn't mind sleeping out under the stars, and there were flowers blooming everywhere. The natural world seemed wonderfully ignorant of the war.

A week later, news spread that the inspection of trains coming into Marseilles had become lax again, so we decided to move while movement was possible. Hans, in particular, was eager to get back in touch with the anti-fascist elements of the emigration. And der Alte was champing at the bit, sure that the Nazis were just over the hilltop behind the villa. 'If we sit here, we are dead, kaput,' he said. 'They will shoot us on sight.' Alfred, too, was afraid to stay any longer. Only Paulette seemed reluctant to risk the venture. 'It is so quiet here, so peaceful,' she said wistfully. 'I don't want to go anywhere, not again. I want to stay.'

'You can't stay,' I said. 'They will kill you if you do.'

Paulette sighed. 'I wish, Lisa, you were not always so goddamned *reasonable*. It is boring.'

The journey into Marseilles was uneventful, but as the train approached the station everyone grew tense and silent. We had agreed beforehand to separate upon disembarkation, so as not to draw attention to ourselves.

'Let me go first,' said Hans.

'No, I will go first,' der Alte insisted, pulling his suitcase from the luggage rack overhead. 'Old men are perfectly useless.'

We knew there was no point in arguing with him – that would only attract stares. Nervously, we followed him with our eyes as he stepped onto the platform, adjusted his tie, and began to walk toward the gate. Within moments, he was approached by two policemen, who asked him to produce his papers.

'*Nix comprend, nix parle!*' he shouted.

He was arrested on the spot, but with amazing presence of mind he did not look over his shoulder as they led him away.

Paulette settled back into her seat, trembling. She was convinced that she would never see der Alte again, but Hans and Alfred reassured her. 'They will take him to the station, then to a staging point for refugees. I will get him back,' Hans said with his usual authority. One simply believed him when he said these things, and it certainly reassured Paulette.

Der Alte had, in effect, created a distraction. The rest of us passed through the station as if invisible. Aware that hotel rooms were impossible to find, we went straight to Belle de Mai, a school where refugees were encamped in the high-ceilinged auditorium. There, no papers were required, no questions asked. It was unspeakable in every other way, however, with few sanitary facilities, no fresh drinking water.

'The good side is there are no rats,' I said to Hans, who had insisted we come here.

'Even rats have a little dignity,' Hans replied.

Everyone at Belle de Mai had the same wish: to get out of Marseilles as soon as possible – to Portugal, Casablanca, Cuba, Santo Domingo, even China. One heard outlandish stories of escape, a fair portion of which I dismissed as dangerous fiction. I consistently argued that we must bide our time and await the right opportunity.

The days grew steadily hotter and more miserable. Hans and Alfred searched, without luck, for der Alte. Paulette fretted, making us all frantic, while I stood in line at the Spanish embassy, hoping to acquire exit visas from France. Rumors of a German invasion of Marseilles spread like a late-summer grass fire among the refugees, putting even more pressure on everyone to get out.

My brother's wife, Eva, was taking her small daughter to Montpellier, near Port-Vendres, a small seaport close to the Spanish border, and Hans thought it best that I join them. 'You could take them over the border,' he said. 'Get them safely to Portugal.' In the meanwhile, he would help the others in their search for exit visas while Paulette continued to search for her father.

'But Hans,' I said, 'this is ridiculous.' It was just too awful to think of leaving him now.

'It's really better this way,' he said, 'and safer. We'll meet in Cuba or Portugal, somewhere.'

'But when? How?'

'Soon,' he said, kissing me on the forehead. 'It won't be a problem. We'll stay in contact.'

I don't know why I always believed him, but I did. Hans Fittko was like that.

WALTER BENJAMIN

Marseilles — the yellow-speckled maw of a seal with brine dripping between its teeth. When its gullet opens to snag the brown and black bodies thrown to it by ship's companies according to their timetables, it exhales a stink of oil, urine, and printer's ink. This comes from the tartar baking hard on its massive teeth: newspaper kiosks, lavatories, oyster stalls.

The harbor people are a bacillus culture, the porters and prostitutes issuing from the city's continuous decomposition with a resemblance to human beings. But the palette itself is pink, which is the color of shame here in Marseilles, and of poverty. Hunchbacks wear pink, as do female beggars. And the filthy women who cruise along the rue Bouterie take their only tint from the sole pieces of clothing they wear: pale-pink shifts.

Benjamin returned to Paris in November, finding his sister, Dora, alone in semi-hiding at his apartment on the rue Dombasle. She did not, at first, answer the door. Only repeated shouting through the keyhole convinced her to open it for her brother.

'Walter! You're alive?'

'Look at me,' he said, standing in the doorway. 'You call this alive?'

He had lost a great deal of weight in the camp at Nevers, and his arms and legs were ghostly, insubstantial. His eyes had been swallowed by craters of skin. The only thing that remained unchanged was the paunch, which he carried like an unwanted fetus; his belly jutted forward, an inorganic bulge above spindly legs.

'You are sick, Walter. Look at you.' Her fingers quivered as she touched his unshaven, bluish cheek.

'Everyone is sick.'

She gave him a bowl of watery soup with a few egg noodles floating amid scraps of fatty chicken. He devoured a stale loaf of bread all by himself.

'I'm so glad to find you,' he said. 'You see, I thought you might do something silly.'

'Do what? Leave? Where would I go?'

Benjamin wiped his mouth with a yellowing linen napkin, one brought from his parents' house in Berlin. 'We must leave at once,' he said. 'I saw Jules Romains at the station, and he said there were boats leaving from Marseilles to Cuba, freighters with plenty of room for passengers. They are apparently quite comfortable.'

'It's hot in Cuba,' she said, 'and there are flying insects, poisonous snakes. What do you want with Cuba?'

'I will get us tickets.'

'I don't want tickets to Cuba.'

He raised himself up on both fists: 'Then I will go without you, Dora!'

When the moment of anger passed, he looked at her sadly, and he knew of course that he would not go to Cuba without her; he also knew he was not himself going to Cuba. He was only talking, and Dora quite rightly saw through his theatrics. His fondest hope now was to live in New York, the capital of the next half of this century. Two years before, visiting Brecht in his house in Denmark, he had gone into the bedroom of the playwright's son and seen a map of Manhattan pasted to the wall. He had studied the map carefully, scanning the formidable grid of numbered streets, noting the blue swirl of water that buoyed it up. His eyes had fixed on Central Park: that floating island of green amid so much gray civilization. He could see himself sitting in this park, reading a book, even writing with his journal on his lap. He had heard from Teddy Adorno about Central Park, and he loved it without seeing it.

'The war will be over in a month or so,' he told Dora, without conviction. 'Wait and see. There is no need for all this fretting.' He looked up at Dora and felt sorry for her. She was dumpy and weak, without the means to negotiate for herself in this terrible world. He wished he could help her, but he now understood the impossibility of this; she was an adult, and he was not her father. It occurred to him that she might well not survive this war.

'What are you going to do, Walter?'

'About what?'

'Here, now that you're back.'

'My research,' he said. 'I see no reason to stop now. The project is almost finished. I have most of a manuscript completed, you see.' He looked toward the door, where his swollen briefcase slept against the wall like a small, pregnant animal.

'All you think about is yourself,' she said. 'This was always the case. Mother said so. "As long as he gets what he wants," she said, "he's happy."'

Benjamin ignored his sister, much as he had ignored his mother – when he could. The two of them were alike: relentlessly chattering, making pointless remarks, criticizing. His mother had talked so much, so aimlessly, that he had learned at an early age to develop a strong inner life and to live in his imagination. It was still the best place to go, especially when the world pressed in, pulled, picked.

'You're not listening to me, Walter,' Dora said.

'I am,' he said.

'You ignore me. You've always ignored me.'

Benjamin did not respond.

That night he was relieved to sleep in his own bed again, however narrow and uncomfortable it might be. Though exhausted, he read for comfort from Proust for an hour or so before dozing off, the bare light bulb above his bed burning through the night.

The next morning, instead of beginning work immediately at the library, he wandered the city to feast on familiar sights. On the heights of Sacré-Coeur, which he climbed for the view, he thought of a passage from Daudet's *Paris vécu*: 'One gazes from on high at this city of palaces, monuments, houses, and hovels, which seems to have been assembled with an eye to some cataclysm, or several cataclysms.' At noon, with a croissant and piece of ham for a meal, he sat on a bench in the Luxembourg Gardens and read, contentedly, from Baudelaire.

That afternoon a doctor examined him, and the results were not good. His heart had been weak to start with, and those unsparing months in Nevers had done further damage. Benjamin would have to treat himself like an invalid now, taking frequent rests, walking no farther than was absolutely necessary. He must stop smoking, too. The doctor insisted on this.

But he could not stop smoking, and he would certainly continue to walk the streets of Paris as long as he lived in Paris. What else were the streets for? As if to defy his doctor, he roamed the quays throughout the next weeks, stopping to admire his favorite buildings, such as the Hôtel de Ville – the historic, emotional seat of government. It was the natural place for revolt to gravitate, as it had done in 1357, when the rich draper turned revolutionary, Étienne Marcel, had stormed the town hall in an attempt to arouse peasants all over France against their despotic king, Charles V. Again in 1789, after the fall of the Bastille, rioters had flooded the hall, and throughout the Revolution it was in the hands of the Commune. It was here that Robespierre had been shot in the jaw by one of his enemies the day before he was guillotined in the frenzied summer of 1794. This noble building had played host to the new emperor, Napoleon, in 1851. And it would someday, perhaps, play host to another new emperor, Adolf Hitler.

Benjamin knew that Paris would fall, but he could not imagine it; that is, he could not translate this abstract knowledge into images that might compel action. Friends urged him to flee, of course; it had become a routine conversation, and each time, he tried to explain that he must first complete his research on the arcades. He had received his new library card for the Bibliothèque Nationale on January 11, 1940, and it was with extreme lightness of heart that he entered that great building, sat under the splendid, colorful dome, and resumed work in his usual place at the long table overshadowed by a verdant fresco by Desgoffes.

Light flooded through the north windows, pooling on his notes. He had several projects in need of completion. Foremost was the book on the arcades, which still needed work; nevertheless, it felt like a miracle that he had come so far. Another year or so of hard work and it could be done. The study of Baudelaire was gathering weight in his notebooks, though it still seemed sketchy; he had begun with a portrait of Paris during the Second Empire and hoped to proceed to a detailed survey of the poetry in light of the poet's experience of high capitalism. Questions about the fate of poetry suddenly occurred to him as he sat there. How could this exquisite, fragile art compete with modern technology or with the high technologies of art? Was poetry doomed to marginalization, like so many other things he loved?

He turned a page and saw a sketch he had done: the angel of history, based on the Klee print. Why did that picture obsess him? Unexpectedly, urgently, almost against his will, he found himself writing an essay on the philosophy of history at the end of his notebook, covering pages from back to front. He always worked best like this: in the margins, prompted by an urge, an image, a strange tingling that he must satisfy with exact language, with a swirl of letters on a page. His strength as a critic lay in fugitive blasts of insight, not in systematic, massively planned and executed arguments, so the essay was naturally his best form.

His view of history seemed to be shifting under him. He could no longer believe in 'the conception of progress as such.' Indeed, the last few years felt distinctly more like regress, and grand speculations like those of Marx had come to feel less and less relevant. It didn't take a prophet to see that both capitalist and socialist economies were utterly selfish and founded on the exploitation of nature. Technology had grown to a point where nature could be mastered, or nearly mastered, and only an equally fierce technology of social power could restrain it, but with this latter technology would come the danger of totalitarian rigidity. No control or total control: The alternatives were equally demoralizing.

The one hope he could envision lay in humanizing work, work that 'far from exploiting nature is capable of bringing forth the creative potential now dormant within her.' But only in the context of a genuine revolution could such work exist, a revolution constituting a 'leap into the open air of history.' This urge to revolution was 'the grasping of the emergency brake by the human race as it travels on the doomed train of world history.' But what would such a revolution really look like? The Nazis had their own version, of course; the Stalinists had another. Each was horrific. How could one prevent any revolution from turning into a nightmare?

Benjamin felt as if bright lights burned outside of his ken; he could feel the heat but not see the light. Truth seemed only to recede, further and further, as he circled each formulation. As always, he revised compulsively, hoping to bring himself closer with each version to expression identical with truth. But it was hard. At times the ontological status of language seemed itself the problem; it was not reality. Words and things embraced on rare occasions, but often without comfort. And what was history but words, an imperfect string of vocables designed to stand in for something supposedly more real? As often happened these days, Benjamin found himself weeping as he wrote, struggling with his own limitations as a thinker, as a human being.

One of these limitations was his overwhelming attraction to erotic imagery. He could not think straight if he was sexually frustrated or aroused. A young woman from the Sorbonne had recently established herself at a neighbouring table in the Labrouste room, and it had become a problem. She had short, blond hair like Asja Lacis's, and the same green eyes. Her teeth were like ice, glittering and straight. Her long arms, when bare, had an alabaster glow, with the hairs as soft as cornsilk. Her fingernails were dangerously unpainted. And when she laughed, she cocked her head to the side, again like Asja. Benjamin feasted on her with his gaze, studying her every expression as she read or scribbled. But he never spoke to her, and whenever her head rose, he averted his eyes, pretending to stare into the distance.

Added to this, the frustrations of his work seemed debilitating, and he would stagger back to the rue Dombasle convinced that the strain provoked his shortness of breath and caused his chest to tighten. The pain often stirred in the pit of his stomach, rose stealthily along the rib cage, and surrounded his heart like a troop of devils, jabbing forks into the beleaguered organ. Every breath would hurt, and he felt dizzy and weak in the knees. His wrists tingled. Sometimes his vision blurred. It was as if his body were exerting a pressure against the brutality of the outside world, an equalizing force from within that countered the brutality from without.

He stopped reading the papers, even stopped paying attention to the rumors. He was sick of being told that the Germans were coming. But on the night of June 15, it became clear to him that he had to go. Even Dora wanted to go now. 'What are we doing here?' she asked, as if suddenly waking to reality.

Georges Bataille had promised to look after the research materials Benjamin had gathered for the arcades project, and this eased his mind somewhat. The latest draft – the only full draft of his work – would stay in his briefcase, however tedious it might be to lug it around the world, to Cuba or Buenos Aires or the South Pole. He could almost imagine himself happiest there, in Antarctica, snow-bound, glacierbound. It was relaxing to contemplate the end of organismal life, to imagine stasis, now that every growth seemed malignant. Even the Desgoffes frescoes in the reading room had become, in his mind, a nightmare of overripeness, an example of rampant cellular multiplication and unchecked growth. He must go away, as far as possible.

Dora's mind was working obsessively on the matter of where to go, now that they *must* go somewhere. 'My friends have all gone to Lourdes. It's very pleasant, I hear,' she said.

Benjamin did not point out that, in fact, she had only one friend, Emma Cohn, who had been at school with her in Berlin. She had written to say the place was 'pleasant enough, compared to many places.'

The idea of Lourdes attracted Benjamin, too. Lourdes was a place of hope. Indeed, generations of ailing men and women had gone to Lourdes for healing, and it had become a haven for refugees. The good people of Lourdes apparently liked pilgrims; in any case they fed and housed them. It was their lot in life to play host and to heal. It was Benjamin's lot, or so he mused, to play guest and suffer. He was the perpetual visitor, the eternal transient. Dare he say it? The Wandering Jew. 'In hard times,' he wrote to Max Horkheimer in New York, 'we fall upon our essential selves. The lineaments of the soul emerge, like bones sticking through shrunken skin.'

Horkheimer and Adorno were supposedly working on an exit visa for him from the U.S. consulate, a little bit of official paper that would liberate him from this misery. He sent an urgent note to them: *A letter from the consulate certifying that I could expect my visa with virtually no delay would be of primary importance to me.* Did they not understand the absolute quality of his necessity?

He could not fathom the unreceptiveness of his friends in New York. They had seemed, only a few years ago, so encouraging; indeed, a small stipend from the Institute for Social Research, which they controlled entirely, had sustained him through difficult times. But times were more difficult, and his savings nonexistent. According to Horkheimer, the Institute itself was in financial trouble. If this was so, there was no hope for more money. In fact, he had not had a check from New York for eight months, although Teddy Adorno had promised that, at the very least, he would be paid for the Baudelaire essay. But when? And now that he must leave Paris, how would the money find him?

'Teddy is using you, as always,' Dora said.

'This is inappropriate, Dora. How is he "using" me?' he asked, his voice rising. 'I would not have been able to live these past years without the Institute.'

'He manipulates you. Everyone says that. You think I made it up?'

'What people say does not concern me.'

Benjamin hated the way gossip distorted things. He had actually stood his ground against all attempts by Adorno to reshape his ideas. He had also welcomed many of his suggestions. It was not terribly wrong to say that Adorno had brought his thinking forward into realms he never would have ventured toward if left to himself. He had been indispensable, as adviser and friend, as reader. And the money, however paltry, had kept him going for some years. But the money was gone, and Benjamin was forced to borrow a considerable sum from Adrienne Monnier on the night before he left Paris with Dora amid the blue-gray smoke of dusk.

Adrienne had proved a reliable friend. Indeed, her letter had convinced the authorities to release him from the camp in Nevers. Now she even volunteered to send money to Benjamin's wife and son in London, and he – with humility and gratitude – supplied their address. It would have been too selfish of him not to accept Adrienne's charity.

It was comforting to think that Dora and Stefan had managed to land on their feet, having escaped from Vienna in the spring of 1938. They were staying with friends in Islington, where Stefan had enrolled in school. But it also hurt him to know his son had grown into a young man without him, and that he had not been a decent father. Indeed, he barely knew the boy anymore – except in dreams, where he and Stefan were friends.

Now he and his sister made their way through darkened streets to the station, their heads down, hurrying. Like most people in their situation, they simply abandoned their worldly goods, hoping that after the war they might retrieve them. Tonight, it was enough to carry a few small bags – and Benjamin's manuscript, although Dora couldn't see why he had to bring it. 'Give it to Monnier, let her look after it. Or somebody else! It's safer here than on the road!'

'You don't understand,' he said.

'It's a bag of bricks. It is slowing us down!'

As they pulled away from the dimly lit station, which smelled of oil and dust, the Eiffel Tower shone above the city in garish moonlight: the world's most preposterous radio transmitter, and Benjamin imagined it calling invisible cries of desperation across the dark Atlantic to anyone who might be listening. It is often like this with technologies, he thought. Function follows form.

The tower itself, he recalled, had been erected whimsically, a monument to the sheer magniloquence of steel. Three hundred skyjacks had sunk two and a half million rivets to create what seemed, at first, like a three-hundred-meter flagpole. It had been a mere fancy, a piece of artifice, an unnatural wonder of the world that tourists might gawk at for generations; then came radio, and in 1916 the edifice suddenly acquired a meaning. Benjamin took a notebook from his briefcase and wrote: 'Meaning as after-echo. The point of apparently pointless events, too, becomes clear long after. This is the end of history: the post hoc accumulation of significance for random, inarticulate events, beautiful or cruel.'

'What are you writing, Walter?' asked Dora, sitting beside him. 'You're not listening to a word I'm saying.'

'Nothing,' he said.

'What does that mean? Nothing! Talk to me.'

'I have nothing to say, that's what I mean,' he said, a trifle angry. He did not want his thoughts interrupted.

'You seem so sad,' she said.

'I am not sad,' he insisted.

'You are.'

He yawned. It was exhausting to deal with Dora.

'Ever since you were a little boy, I could tell when you were sad,' she continued.

Benjamin closed his notebooks and wanly said, 'You are quite wrong, Dora. The truth is I may even be a little happy.'

They traveled through the night, sleeping fitfully in the crowded railway car. He watched Dora as she dozed, her head sloping to her chest and a double chin forming. It reminded him, again, of his mother, who had grown pudgy in middle age. And himself, for that. A family replicated the production of the world, the organic historical growth of objects in time: He and Dora were still connected in the most literal sense to his parents, Émile and Pauline. He withdrew from his wallet a yellowed photograph of his family, an instant locked in the glacier of memory that preserves such images. There he sits, bald, in a long white gown with ruffled collar, on his mother's lap, his right hand raised slightly, a look of concentrated attention on his face; he is perhaps five months old. Georg holds his left hand, protective, loving. Already a lostness narrows his gaze, a bewilderment born of credulousness. His black hair is ruffled, and his dark eyes burn holes in the picture. Pauline sits primly, the billowing sleeves of her dress a sign of affluence and ease. There is a firm aura of control in her expression, in the way her right hand balances her child so effortlessly. But there is fear on her face as well. Her confidence has been shaken, and she does not know if she will find herself capable of summoning Motherhood on such a scale. This self-doubting is visible in the arch of her back, the way she leans forward ever so slightly, as if afraid she might slump and then crumble. Only

Émile shows total confidence; he stands a full foot above everyone, or more; he is centered in the photograph: *paterfamilias*, provider, benevolent source of life. His vast, meticulously sculpted mustache is much in contrast to Benjamin's, which is stubby and thick, unkempt.

Dora began to snore heavily, embarrassing him. He wished he could simply get off at the next station and leave his sister forever. He wanted to separate from the Benjamins of Berlin, from his inherited place in the continuum of pain and responsibility. He wanted the experience of total freedom, that free fall beyond time and place. But he knew better, and he stood and wrapped a blanket around Dora's shoulders and was relieved when she did not waken.

From the inside pocket of his coat he took a weary letter from Grete Steffin, Brecht's lover. He and Grete shared an affection for Brecht that was unbroken despite the fact that he had treated them both with contempt. Brecht treated everyone horribly – everyone except those who promised to get him something: money, sex, fame. He was a disturbing man. A little boy, really. All he wanted was adulation, gratification. He pretended to be a Communist and attended every world conference on literature sponsored by Stalin, feigning a profound social conscience, but Benjamin felt that Brecht was in some ways a fake, a brilliant fake. It was the underside of his genius.

They had met in Capri that fateful summer of 1924, the same time he met Asja Lacis, who had simultaneously ruined his life and given him the one important thing he had ever had: the experience of deep, erotic love. But this particular love had brought desire, and desire had consumed him. He had never been free again. Sometimes he could think about nothing but Asja's green eyes, the faint, alluring smell of her breath, the way her hair fell lankily across her forehead. Often, in the sixteen years since he met her, he lay in bed all night thinking of her, unable to waste himself, to drain himself, to exhaust this terrible need.

He was dreaming of Asja when the train pulled into the station at Lourdes in the bluish pink of dawn. He and Dora found a room in the boardinghouse where Emma Cohn was staying on the rue de la Cité; it was a modest room, but it overlooked a garden full of lemon trees and hibiscus. They each had a bed, and there was a bathroom down the hall shared by a dozen or so others, mostly refugees from Belgium. It pleased Benjamin that Dora had a friend here, as he did not relish spending too much time with her.

When, in mid-July, the opportunity arose for Dora to accompany Emma to a town in the south of France where refugees were apparently making their way into Spain quite easily, he encouraged her to go.

'It's your chance,' he said. 'You must take it, Dora. We can meet in New York, in a few months.'

'I'm afraid, Walter.'

'If you stay, there is no hope. Horkheimer and Adorno are sending me a visa. Not two visas, but one. And passage on a ship to New York. I am expecting this.'

'You should come with me.'

'Why are you always like this, Dora?'

'Like what?'

'Insisting, resisting . . .'

'You treat me like a child, Walter.'

'This is a ridiculous conversation.'

'Emma says there is room. You could join us. What if they don't send you a visa or get you a berth?'

'I will take my chances.'

'You are being stubborn. Look where it's got you.'

He was getting angry now. 'What are you talking about?'

'You expect everyone to take care of you. You expect miracles.'

'I don't have to listen to this.'

'You are worse than Georg.'

'Please, enough of Georg. Enough of this chatter.'

'I will go alone, with Emma.'

'Good.'

'You are a disappointment to me,' she added. 'Mother was always right about you.'

Benjamin chose not to answer. His sister made him furious. She was perpetually opening old wounds. She could not let any dog lie buried.

'I will never see you again,' she said, and began to cry.

He drew her near. 'Dora, you exaggerate everything. You worry all the time. Mama used to say, "Dora, you fret too much." Remember?' He took a handkerchief to her eyes. 'She was right about you.'

'I will go to New York,' she said.

'That's good,' he said. 'You always wanted to go to America, didn't you?'

'No,' she said, 'that was you.'

'Ah,' he said. 'I will give you Teddy Adorno's address. You must write to Teddy. He will know my whereabouts.'

'Come with me, Walter.'

'No,' he said. 'I will go to Marseilles, then to Cuba.'

'You will hate Cuba.'

'Or Buenos Aires.'

'That is worse.'

'Or Antarctica.'

They both started laughing. It was a relief to have this conversation behind them. Later that day he took her and Emma to the train station, and he gave Dora enough money to last three months: exactly half of the money Adrienne Monnier had given him. 'And remember what I told you,' he said. 'I will see you soon, believe me. A few months, no more.'

'I believe you, Walter,' she said, her expression betraying her actual words. She did not believe him. Indeed, disbelief flooded her last looks, dampening the tiny fans of wrinkles that widened from the corners of her eyes. Benjamin watched the train pull out, with its breath of ashes. He understood perfectly that he would never see Dora again.

The heat of July nearly exhausted him, and he lay in bed most of the day, reading and writing letters: to Grete Steffin, to Adorno, to his ex-wife, Dora. Near the end of July he wrote to his cousin, Hannah Arendt, explaining his situation: 'Hideous and stifling weather reinforces my need to maintain the life of both body and spirit in a state of suspension. I cloak myself in reading: I've just finished the last volume of the *Thibaults* and *The Red and the Black*. My extreme anguish at the thought of what is going to happen to my manuscripts is now doubly painful.' He sent the letter to the last address he had for Hannah, in Paris, although he could not imagine it would find her. The mail was so fickle now. You dropped a letter into a mailbox without the slightest sense that it was going anywhere, although some letters, amazingly, seemed to get through. Since many of his correspondents were in flux, or flight, there was no telling where they might be. Letters occasionally came back marked UNDELIVERABLE AT THIS ADDRESS. Most of them dropped, like feathers, into the well of history.

Alone in the boardinghouse in Lourdes, he felt unbelievably lazy, but he did not mind. A sentence from La Rochefoucauld returned to give comfort: 'His laziness supported him in glory for many years in the obscurity of an errant and hidden life.' He considered himself a deeply lazy man, and his life had certainly been obscure. Many of the people he knew, especially the writers, loathed any form of sloth, but he did not. He had tried for many years to cultivate leisure, to let happen what happened, to allow his imagination room to graze, always searching for that distant valley where larks rise on strings of sound all day and the sun is steady in the sky.

He believed in chance, in lazy luck, and the benefits of serendipity. It had never let him down, and he had stumbled upon so many treasures in nearly five decades of living; these formed his secret hoard. The fact that he had never written a whole book, a 'real' book, apart from the *Habilitation* on German tragic drama, bothered him, but only a little. If the war ended soon, he would publish the arcades book, and that would be his magnum opus. The work on Baudelaire would follow, a brilliant adornment. And a neat, pocket-size selection of his best essays and aphorisms would be lovely, and perhaps a posthumous book would appear. He had, after all, scattered countless fugitive pieces in old publications in different countries. Surely one could assemble miscellaneous collections from these, and they would make for good reading. (Indeed, he had once published a collection of random jottings called *One-Way Street*, and it had found its way into many appreciative hands.)

An aphorism stuck in his head: *Scripta manent, verba volent:* Writing stays, but talk flies away. Was that Martial or Juvenal? Either way, he knew it was true. But he loved conversation as much, even more, than written words. He had loved the long hours with Gerhard Scholem, the late-night talks with Brecht, the prolonged, even timeless café mornings in Paris with Bataille and Klossowski. In the few times when he and Asja Lacis had been alone, they had often talked through the night instead of making love. Now he had nobody to talk to, so he was dependent on letters: writing even more than receiving them. He found himself in his letters, pulling from peculiar depths an energy that was then shaped by the expectations of a particular, well-imagined reader.

My selves are many, he thought. One by one they emerge in my letters. They are all true, even when contradictory. I embrace them all.

If he regretted anything in his life it was the way he allowed himself to disappear in the presence of strong personalities, like Scholem or Brecht. Scholem was somewhat easier to deal with: The man was a scholar to his fingertips, and he understood the vulnerabilities of a scholar, the dependence on the text, the material at hand; he was acquainted with the need to lose oneself in digging, in rooting for truth; he also knew that one must invent the truth over and over, never forgetting that life is a process of continual revision in the interest of greater understanding. But Brecht . . . My God, what a difficult man! What an impossible friend!

Brecht abused his friends and used his enemies. He was ruthless with women, lying to them constantly about his affections, pretending to be faithful when no man was ever less faithful. He had nearly ruined Elisabeth Hauptmann, who wrote portions of *The Threepenny Opera* in exchange for affection. And he had worn out poor, dear Grete Steffin: She was a bag of skin now, her lungs as fragile as flypaper; she coughed up blood each day and was light-headed, weak. But she loved Brecht. She would do anything for him, swallow any lie, do any cruel deed for a smile from him, a wink, a gesture of acknowledgement.

The sad letters poured in from Grete: Not even the war could stop them. Sad news travels well, it seems. Benjamin wanted to take her by the hand and lead her to freedom, but he was not free himself when it came to Brecht. He considered Brecht – for all his reliance on the women in his life as editors, even co-writers – a genius. It was unmistakable. The fact that others contributed to his works did not matter; he gathered their language into his own groundswell; he transmogrified everything.

That last summer in Denmark with Brecht had been equally exhausting and exhilarating. Brecht was ailing, and he lay in bed most of the time, demanding constant attention. Night after night, Benjamin sat beside him and listened. Occasionally he would offer a response, or an objection, and Brecht would flare into anger: 'How can you say such a thing, Walter?' or 'You are too intellectual, Walter. You do not understand the real world.' He was, like Gramsci, a pessimistic Marxist. Fascism had definitely taken over the world, or would soon rule everything and everyone. But the future, said Brecht, is always a place of hope. One must never give up hope.

Brecht had taught Benjamin what he liked to refer to as *plumpes Denken*, or 'crude thinking.' All useful thought must be simple, crys-talline, and fresh. The elaborate metaphysical turns that had become second nature to him through long years of philosophical study must be sacrificed now. He was going to write the most straightforward sentences he could imagine. To make himself crude, peasantlike, and useful. His essays would become tools, picks and shovels, and he would put them into the hands of ordinary people. Here was the hope he kept alive in his heart: a dream of future writing.

Almost in defiance of the historical moment, he maintained a small flame of hope as he boarded the train for Marseilles. He decided that the only plausible way out of this beleaguered country, for him, was by ship. One heard fantastic stories of eccentric captains taking shiploads of refugees to strange (and mythical) islands. Benjamin discounted most of these tales, but he felt sure that plenty of ships left Marseilles every day: merchant marine ships, cargo ships, passenger liners of one kind or another. He had been told it was quite easy to get false papers, and that Cuba was wide open. It would make a fine temporary layover. And when the war ended, he would go straight to New York to found the firm of Adorno, Horkheimer, and Benjamin, Ltd. It sounded like a company of haberdashers, but he and his friends would sell ideas to the world instead of clothes. 'It is astonishing how a few men with the right ideas can shift the world,' Adorno had written to him only the year before. 'We must become these men.'

It was maddeningly hot and humid in the train, and Benjamin was forced to stand in a vestibule beside the toilet all the way to Marseilles. He spent three agonizing days in search of a place to stay, sleeping at night in parks with his head on his briefcase. (He checked his bag at the station, aware that he was too weak to cart it around; the briefcase was another matter, since it contained his manuscript. One could not risk leaving it unaccompanied.) His chest pains, which had eased somewhat in the healing air of Lourdes, returned with a vengeance in Marseilles, and he frequently had to stand still for twenty minutes, frozen in place by pain that radiated, like filaments, down his arms to the tips of his fingers.

Life would have been difficult had he actually found a place to sleep, but it seemed impossible in these conditions; exposed to the elements, trudging from one makeshift bed to another, he wondered if he might die in Marseilles, a city that felt like the eye of a storm; strangely lit, awkwardly peaceful, with occasional swirls of wind reminding him that war was everywhere but here. One could see any number of uniformed men in the streets: fragments of the scattered French army, delinquent members of the Foreign Legion, military policemen on loud, brawny motorcycles. Whole convoys of troops occasionally moved through the city streets, as if randomly searching for the war. Lumpish cargo planes flew overhead, as did bi-winged trainers. But the war never actually erupted on this particular spot.

On Benjamin's third night in Marseilles, as black rain fell, he was forced to take shelter beneath a sandstone bridge with an old and toothless woman. Zigzag lightning ripped the nearby grass, and thunder boomed. The woman suddenly began to sob.

'Are you afraid of thunder, madame?' he asked her, reaching for her hand.

'I don't want to die,' she said.

'How old are you?'

'Seventy-three,' she said.

'That isn't old,' he said. 'My grandmother lived to be eighty-seven.'

Somehow, his tone of voice soothed her, even though what he said might not, under normal circumstances, have given much comfort. She was grateful, however, for his attentions and asked if he might stay with her for a few days. He declined, of course, explaining that he must try to find a berth on a ship as soon as possible.

'You see,' he told her, 'I am a Jew.'

She nodded slowly, thinking, then spoke: 'You must go then. This is no place for Jews.' To his amazement, she took some money from a rumpled purse that she used for a pillow. 'It's all I have,' she said. 'But you must take it, sir.'

He smiled and took her hand. 'I have just enough for my ticket to Cuba,' he said. 'But I thank you, madame. You are very kind.'

The next morning, quite by chance, he ran into Hans Fittko in the street. He had not seen Fittko since leaving the camp in Nevers.

Fittko recognized him first, and said, 'Dr Benjamin, what a surprise! Are you well?'

'Nobody is well, I think,' he said. 'But it is always good to see a familiar face.'

Hans bought him a cup of coffee in a local bar, and he wrote Lisa's address in Port-Vendres on a small scrap of paper. 'You must go to her,' he said. 'She will take you out of France.'

Benjamin explained that he was waiting for a visa.

'This is mad,' Fittko said. 'You will never get a visa. Anyway, the ships are full.' He lit a cigarette and sucked on it hard, as if it were a straw. 'Do you smoke?'

'Yes,' said Benjamin, taking a cigarette. It was the first cigarette he'd had in several days, and it filled him with hope. As long as one could smoke one more cigarette, the world was not over.

'Where would you go, if you could?'

'I have friends in New York,' Benjamin said. 'But I really must get a berth – it doesn't matter where.'

'They will be closing the port of Marseilles any day now.'

Benjamin listened, growing steadily more anxious, as Hans outlined the hard reality of the situation. The prospects for each of them grew bleaker every day. Hans was himself going to abandon Marseilles in a week or so. 'The only way out is over the Pyrenees,' he said.

Benjamin thanked Hans for the coffee, the cigarette, the good company, and most of all, for Lisa's address in the south of France.

That same day, in the afternoon, he saw Fritz Frankel sitting in a sidewalk café. Dr Frankel had been a famous doctor in Berlin in the twenties; he had been in Paris for much of the past decade and was respected among the émigrés, who sought him out eagerly for his expertise in nervous disorders. Benjamin himself had once consulted Dr Frankel, at Dora's insistence.

The doctor noticed that Benjamin was staring at him, and he stood. 'Benjamin!' he cried. 'Come and sit down! Let me buy you a drink.'

Benjamin bowed politely and accepted the invitation.

'So what brings you to Marseilles?' the doctor wondered.

It was just like Frankel to ask a dumb question, thought Benjamin. What was any Jew doing in Marseilles right now? 'I'm here for the Olympic tryouts,' he said. 'Did you forget I was a pole vaulter?'

'Listen, you stick to me, and we'll both get out of here,' Dr Frankel said. He explained that it was impossible to get a berth on a ship in the usual ways. Every berth had been sold long ago, and the authorities were cracking down on exit visas. Nobody could leave France now except by hook or by crook. Excitedly he explained that he had discovered a way out that had already worked for dozens of people he knew. You dressed up as a sailor and were taken aboard a merchant ship heading for Ceylon. The other sailors, for a small fee, were more than willing to smuggle you aboard. If Benjamin had any money, there was no doubt they could both make it to Ceylon in a month.

'What do you do once you get to Ceylon?' Benjamin asked.

'It is British,' Dr Frankel explained. 'The Germans can't touch you out there. And I hear it's quite pleasant, with tea plantations and lots of fruit. You like fruit, don't you?'

Benjamin looked at the old man's shaggy, long white hair and fragile body and wondered to himself if Dr Frankel could really pass himself off as a sailor. Perhaps money talked louder than he had previously imagined.

'You are apparently skeptical, sir,' Dr Frankel said.

Benjamin shrugged. At this point, it was worth a try. One heard of more fantastic escapes every day. Indeed, an eighty-five-year-old Jew from Odessa had apparently escaped into Spain in a helium balloon. Given his fear of heights, Benjamin was much happier to go by sea, even if he had to pose as a deck swab. As for the money, what did it matter?

Dr Frankel took Benjamin back to his boardinghouse, inviting him to sleep on the floor.

'I'll make a bed for you,' he said. 'There is a sofa in the hallway. I'll get the cushions.'

'Please, just a blanket. At least you have a roof.'

'Make yourself at home,' the doctor said.

There was a comfortable chair by the window, and Benjamin settled in for the afternoon. The doctor had a volume of essays by Karl Kraus, and Benjamin was delighted to spend an afternoon in such company.

'Will you be all right, Benjamin?'

'Yes, thank you.'

The doctor said he had some urgent business and left Benjamin alone. Early that evening, he returned with a sailor's costume for each of them. They were mildly absurd: rough wool uniforms with baggy trousers, berets.

'You've just been drafted into the merchant navy,' he said. 'You look like a sailor, did you know that? Try it on.'

'The trousers are too small. I can tell by looking.'

'Maybe you are too big,' the doctor said. 'Look, we're not going on a fashion show. We're going to Ceylon, where Jews are safe. Wear what is to wear.'

That night, as Benjamin lay on the floor on lumpy cushions beneath a moth-eaten blanket, Dr Frankel described Ceylon in colorful detail. It was a marvelous place of small brown people and large gray elephants, a land of cardamom, cinnamon, saffron, paprika, breadfruit. The luscious names filled Benjamin's heart with desire. All night he dreamed of bare sandy beaches, with an orange moon hanging between big-finned palms. There would of course be no books, no libraries, no European newspapers, and their absence was a definite problem, but he had enough material in his briefcase to keep him busy for a year or two. Perhaps he would even write stories, or maybe even poems!

The next morning he and Dr Frankel crept from the boarding-house in their ill-fitting uniforms. Benjamin left his suitcase in the station; it would be unwise to take it with him, and it contained nothing he really cared about. He carried his briefcase and a small satchel with a change of clothes. Aware that he was going to sea, where dampness is often a problem, he carefully wrapped the manuscript in waxy paper that he bought from a fishmonger by the docks. Dr Frankel's small and tattered suitcase was strapped to his back.

They took a trolley to the waterfront, where they stopped at a bar for a cup of *café crème* and a hot croissant, consuming them greedily at a table that had a wide-angle view of the bay. The prodigal sun had tossed a million gold coins on the water, which was so bright one could scarcely see the dozens of ships coming in and out of the old harbor. The tangerine sky was streaked with clouds, and gulls swooped to feed on garbage. Indeed, there was garbage everywhere.

'Even the people are garbage,' said Dr Frankel, referring to the riffraff that gathers in ports of call. 'Whores, pimps, winos, bums, pickpockets, swindlers, Gypsies,' Dr Frankel mumbled.

'And Jews,' said Benjamin.

Dr Frankel looked at him curiously. 'You are a strange fellow, Dr Benjamin.'

'I have heard this before,' he said.

Because he was leaving France this morning, perhaps forever, everything that touched his senses was bathed in nostalgia. He even decided that he loved Marseilles – its thronged, tree-lined avenues as well as its putrid smells, the grating noise of engines, the clanking of chains, the lurid calls of women who loitered, even at this hour, along the docks in search of custom. He twisted his neck to see, through the dazzling light, a heavily laden freighter ply its awkward way into the harbor with its whistle gasping, dwindling into echoes, ghosts of steam.

'Have you ever visited a brothel, Benjamin?' asked Dr Frankel.

'Many times, when I was younger. Mostly in Berlin,' he said. 'But also in Munich. Once or twice in Naples, I think.'

'You *think*? You don't remember?'

Benjamin wished he had said nothing. 'I have never been to a brothel in Paris,' he said. 'I don't know why. Age, perhaps. I was never a young man in Paris.'

Dr Frankel raised his eyebrows. 'You are *still* a young man, dear fellow. Forty-eight years old! I am sixty-three!'

Benjamin was surprised that Dr Frankel was only sixty-three, especially since he looked well over seventy. It was the war, of course. It put a decade on everyone.

A tall gendarme suddenly passed them, and they grew still. This was no time to have to produce their papers, and increasingly the police were demanding identification. They knew that before long the Nazis would swoop into Marseilles, and that those who lacked a proper attitude would suffer. Lenience would not be tolerated.

After breakfast, they made their way to the Italian freighter, the S.S. *Genovese*, which would carry them to Ceylon. It was a long, hulking freighter with a rusty bow and portholes like bloodshot eyes. Oil spilled into the water around it, forming a thin blue skirt on the water. There was considerable activity, with men loading huge barrels into the hold; the grinding sound of winches forced them to raise their voices when they spoke.

'Are you certain they will take us?' asked Benjamin as they approached the gangway.

'Of course. My contact is called Patrice. He is in charge of all deckhands.' After a pause, he added: 'We are deckhands, you see.'

Sure enough, a dark-skinned man called Patrice welcomed them aboard: he was about forty, with thick eyebrows, a curly beard, and a large belly that bulged the dark blue horizontal stripes of his shirt. He accepted the roll of bills from Dr Frankel without bothering to count, as if nobody in these circumstances would dare to cheat him.

'You must hide below,' he said. 'I will show you where.' They followed him down into the dim, smelly bunkroom. 'Don't even show your ugly faces till I say so.'

'I can hardly thank you enough for this,' Benjamin whispered to Dr Frankel when they were alone.

'Please, enough,' he said, beaming. 'For a start, it's your money. Second, you will do me a favor one day. Life is like that. It's called tit for tat.'

Benjamin lay back on his bunk in the sweltering room. 'My wife and son are in England you know,' he said. 'Sometimes I miss them both, even though I'm divorced.'

'Ah,' said Dr Frankel. 'Someday I will tell you what happened to my wife and my son. It is not a pretty story.'

They lay quietly on the bunks provided by Patrice, and it was thrilling to hear the clanking of chains as the anchors lifted at around seven; the huge engine, not fifty feet from the bunkroom, chittered and whined, and the ship began to tremble. At some barely discernible point, it was obvious that they were moving. The engine began to purr, and the ship rocked gently forward and backward, parting the slight waves. It was a pity, thought Benjamin, that they did not have a porthole.

Suddenly, a gruff man appeared in the doorway, shouting, 'All hands on deck!' He paused beside Benjamin and Dr Frankel. 'You, too!' he shouted. 'Both of you! On deck! Now!'

Benjamin reached for his briefcase. He was not going anywhere, even on deck, without his manuscript.

'Come, Walter,' said Dr Frankel. 'We must do what they say. This is only routine.'

Benjamin scrambled up the narrow ladder behind the doctor, his heart pounding in his temples; halfway up the ladder, he had to pause for two or three minutes. An invisible fist seemed to press into his solar plexus, and he could hardly breathe.

'Are you all right, Walter?' Dr Frankel cried, peering back down the ladder behind him.

'Give me another minute, please,' Benjamin said. 'I am not used to ladders.'

'On deck! Quickly!' shouted the sailor, snapping at Benjamin's heels. 'Get your fat ass up that ladder!'

Somehow, he dragged himself into the blazing light, onto the broad deck, where an officer of some kind was haranguing the deckhands like children. He spoke in argot, not easily understood. Benjamin guessed he was from Nice, with Italian roots. You could tell from his eyes, and the sneering grin, that he was not a pleasant man.

Patrice stood beside him, gesticulating weirdly, pointing to Benjamin and Dr Frankel, who stood side by side with the other deckhands, who were mostly in their late teens or early twenties. They were Italian or Greek, Benjamin guessed, with Mediterranean skin. Even the youngest of them looked wizened, even prunelike.

The officer lurched toward Benjamin and stood over him, smelling of brandy. 'Give me your papers,' he said.

Benjamin produced a number of faded documents from his briefcase, including an old library card from the Bibliothèque Nationale. He could see from the look in the eyes of Patrice that this was a mistake.

Dr Frankel was clearly distressed, shifting from foot to foot. He said, in hideously mangled French, 'We have worked on many merchant freighters. We are very good sailors, I swear. Give us a chance, sir, please!'

The officer seemed amused, and grinned. His teeth were like iron nails driven into his gums. 'May I have the names of several ships you have worked on before? Perhaps we have worked together?'

Dr Frankel showed considerable invention, although none of the freighters he mentioned seemed to ring any bells.

'How old are you?' he asked Dr Frankel.

'Forty,' he said.

'Ah, you are well preserved,' he said.

To Benjamin: 'You are nineteen, I suppose?'

'I am thirty-one, sir,' Benjamin said.

'Ah, a truthful man!'

Benjamin stared ahead, trying to give away nothing with his expression. Any flicker of distress or failure of nerve could be disastrous.

'Can you swim, sailor?'

'I am a good swimmer,' said Benjamin. Weren't all sailors?

'And you?' The officer glared at Dr Frankel.

'Me, too,' the doctor said. 'I swim very well . . . for my age.' He looked at his feet. 'I require, perhaps, a little practice.'

'That's quite easy,' the man said, trying to restrain a laugh. 'Overboard with them!' he shouted.

The other deckhands looked nervously at their superior. Was he kidding?

'Are you deaf? I said, overboard with them!'

Two husky seamen seized Benjamin and Dr Frankel by the arms.

'What does this mean?' Dr Frankel asked in a loud voice, almost threateningly. He turned to Patrice. 'We have paid good money!'

Patrice looked anxiously toward the deck.

The officer said, 'What this means is that you will have an opportunity to practice your swimming.'

Benjamin could hardly focus on what was happening. All he could think about was the briefcase, which he clung to fiercely, even as the officer's henchmen tossed him over the railing. He felt himself dropping swiftly, turning head over heels. The sensation of hitting the water was surprisingly transitory, and the first thing he knew, he was underwater, still holding the briefcase, still dropping, taking for granted the fact of his death. It was simply not possible to survive this, the plunge, the infinite amounts of water, the vacuum that seemed to suck him downward, down and around, the spiral to oblivion.

Suddenly, his head broke the water, though he could see nothing.

'Benjamin!' cried Dr Frankel. 'Over here!'

A young man in a rowboat had pulled Dr Frankel into his small craft.

Benjamin, of course, could not move. It amazed him that he was floating.

'Give me your briefcase,' the doctor cried, reaching down for it.

Benjamin relinquished it and soon felt the upward pull, the astonishing and unexpected lift to safety.

As he shivered in the boat, unable to see through watery lenses, Benjamin half wished he were still tumbling in those unimaginable depths where fish are blind and black rocks huddle for shelter from the faint light that filters down. How he had managed to get from the water into this rowboat was beyond guessing, another miracle – a major miracle, this time. He knew for certain this morning in the harbor in Marseilles that God existed, for in a Godless universe he would certainly have lost everything by now.

Streetcar travel in Moscow is a supremely tactile experience. Here, the newcomer soon learns to adjust to the odd tempo of the city and the ancient rhythm of its peasant population. A total interpenetration of technological and primitive modes occurs here, in this brave historical experiment – the new Russia. A ride in any streetcar will illustrate my point. The female conductors hover in fur coats at their stations like Samoyed women on a sleigh. A vigorous shoving and lunging during the boarding of a car already loaded to the point of bursting happens without the slightest murmur of objection, and with immense cordiality. (I have never heard an angry word uttered on these occasions.) Once everybody is inside, the journey begins in earnest. Through the ice-glazed windows, you can never quite discover where the car has stopped. If you do find out, it hardly matters, since the way to the exit is blocked by a human wedge. Because you must board at the rear but exit from the front of the vehicle, you are forced to thread your way through the human mass. Fortunately, people travel in bunches, so at all important stops the car is virtually emptied.

The traffic in Moscow is to a large degree a mass phenomenon. Thus one finds whole caravans of sleighs blocking the streets in a long row because loads that demand a truck are being piled on five or six sleighs. The sleighs, of course, must first take the horse into consideration, then the passengers. These animals do not understand the excess: a feeding sack for the nag, a blanket for the passenger – that should be enough. In any case, there is only room for two on the narrow bench, and since it has no back-rest (unless you are willing to call the low rail such a thing), you must keep a good balance on sharp corners. Everything is based on the assumption of the highest speed; long journeys in the cold are difficult to bear and distances in this city immeasurable. The izvozshchik *drives his sleigh close to the sidewalk. The passenger is not enthroned high up but looks out on the same level as everyone else and brushes the passersby with his sleeve: an incomparable experience for those delighted by the sense of touch.*

Where Europeans, on their high-speed journeys, enjoy a feeling of superiority, of dominance over the masses, the Muscovite in the little sleigh is closely mingled with people and objects. If he has a box, a child, or a basket to take with him — for all this the sleigh is the cheapest means of transport — he is merged into the street bustle: no condescending gaze but a tender, swift brushing along stones, people, horses. You feel like a child gliding through the house on the sleigh's little chair.

Walter was odd, but I loved him. Perhaps love isn't the right word, but I can't think of a better one. He was terribly, terribly important in my life. He drove me mad, but I needed him, too. I adored his conversation. He amused me, flattered me, teased me, scolded me. Every conversation was an act of attention, and I have not found another like him in the whole world.

We met in 1924, just off the piazza in Capri. It was an exhaustingly hot day in midsummer, and I was trying to buy some almonds. Sometimes one simply wants almonds. But, for the life of me, I couldn't recall the Italian word for that delectable nut. The grocer gestured wildly, spouting a dialect I could not fathom. He kept handing me things that were not almonds. Exasperated, I was about to leave without the almonds when I noticed a short, bespectacled man in a white suit. He stood right beside me, breathing heavily through his mouth, staring through thick glasses.

'May I help you, please, dear lady?' he asked, bowing in a courtly manner and tipping his white straw hat. I took him at once for a Berliner.

'Do you know the Italian word for almonds?'

He began to sputter a peculiar dialect, and suddenly a large bag of almonds was in my possession. I did not even have to pay for it.

'I can't thank you enough, sir,' I said. 'I adore almonds.'

'May I accompany you?'

'If you like,' I said. It was a peculiar request, but I have entertained worse. 'I must be getting back to the hotel. My husband is waiting.' I was not married, but I felt like saying that, as a precaution. With men, one can never be sure about their intentions.

He took the bag of almonds from me, as if they were terribly heavy.

'There is no need,' I said. 'I am quite strong.' I flexed my muscles.

'Please, dear lady. I must carry the almonds. They are the product of my tongue, after all.'

It was quite ludicrous, but I didn't mind. I was bored on Capri, where the light is blinding. Who wants to live at the center of a diamond chip? After a certain point, even leisure becomes tedious, and I was eager to return to Berlin.

As we passed through the piazza, Walter volunteered to buy me a drink at a café with huge green awnings, and I accepted. I was thirsty, and my feet were killing me.

'Allow me to introduce myself,' he said, stirring countless lumps of sugar into his coffee like an Arab and lighting a cigarette. 'I am Dr Walter Benjamin.'

'And I am Dr Asja Lacis,' I said.

He looked at me skeptically. I was not a doctor, but I could not resist the temptation to tease him. I have never liked this Germanic obsession with titles. Herr Doctor this, Herr Professor that.

We had a pleasant, if somewhat indirect, chat, and he insisted on following me back to the little hotel where Bernhard and I were staying. We had left our friend Brecht in Positano and had come out here to be alone, but we seemed to quarrel as soon as we stepped off the ferry.

Walter Benjamin went out of my thoughts as soon as we said goodbye at the gate to my hotel, but a day or so later, he entered a café where I was sitting with Bernhard and a German theatrical agent named Willie Manheim, whom we had met on the ferry. Walter found a small, marble table by the door and began scribbling in a notebook. Every now and then he looked up, looking in my direction with that peculiar intensity one associates with myopia. He would nod gravely, then resume writing. Each time, I met his gaze directly and nodded back.

To end this silly game, I went to his table and invited him to join us, as both Bernhard and Willie seemed eager to meet another literate German. To everyone's delight, he talked knowledgeably about the Deutsches Theatre in Berlin, which Bernhard administered, giving the impression that he had seen every major production in the past ten years.

'He is a learned gentleman,' Bernhard later said. 'I've read a few of his reviews. We actually met once or twice, in passing, at one of those big parties in Berlin that Benno Reifenberg used to throw.'

'Ah, Reifenberg,' said Willie. He was always keen to associate with the right literary editors, and Reifenberg ruled one of the better roosts in Germany, the *Frankfurter Zeitung*.

'Isn't he a homosexual?' I asked, quite innocently. But my question seemed to freeze both Willie and Bernhard, who found such topics unacceptable.

'He is a very gifted and unusual man,' said Willie. 'Quite unusual, in fact.'

Walter somehow lingered in my mind, and I felt certain that we'd see a lot of each other in the coming years. I'm a bit of a clairvoyant when it comes to relationships, and it struck me from the beginning that he found me attractive, though I found him mildly repulsive. There was something about his smell that put me off. Worse, his stumbling and periphrastic manner was irritating. I like people who approach a subject directly, forthrightly. There is no need for circumlocution, for beating around every bush.

My hotel overlooked the sea, as most of the good ones do in Capri, so the view was dazzling. I liked our room, too, with its white, pasty walls, the vaulted ceiling, and brightly painted tile on the floors: one stepped through Venetian doors onto a *terrazzo* for breakfast under a broad canvas flap. Elegant cypress trees rose up like needles in the garden just below, aromatic in the soft breeze. In the early evenings I would sit alone there and read as the sun dropped behind the limestone cliffs; the air grew chill, and swallows dipped and veered, making passes at the fountain below. I was enchanted by the island, which like Prospero's cell entertained so many lively spirits, some of them at odds.

I thought frequently of Ariel and Caliban, the opposing creatures of Shakespeare's play, and could feel their clash in the island air: the fluting voice of the sprite above the gurgle and belch of the monster. Earth, air, fire, water were all present here like primary colors, transmutable substances. Earth and water belonged to Caliban, whereas fire and air were Ariel's. I began to write a poem about this, but as usual it unraveled in my hands. I am not a poet.

But I love poets. I loved Bernhard, who was a poet of the theater. And I loved Brecht, the greatest poet of them all. I began to think of him as Prospero's evil brother. It was clear to me that he hoped to rule over my kingdom, wanted to make me another of his many pagan brides. But I was not so foolish. Not like the others, all fawning and frightened. They somehow imagined that the oxygen would be withdrawn from their world if Brecht ceased to meet them once or twice a month for a night of passion. What held them so? His snaggletoothed smile never appealed to me in that way. His eyes were cold as mine. We would have frozen the universe together.

It is not that I'm cold inside. I'm perhaps a little too hot at times. When I crave a man, it is impossible to think of anything else, or to dampen the flames. What's the line from Racine? 'I burn for Hippolyte'? That sings to me. When I first met Bernhard, I knew a part of me was finished. Here was destiny, the snake that eats its own tail. I had borne a child already, had moved through several lovers. But Bernhard, with his dark glances and insouciant smiles, lit a rare fire. I took him away from the woman he was soon to marry, and I left my child for him. I surrounded him, became a whirligig of attention. My focus never wavered. I became irresistible.

Like most women, I wanted, I needed love: the erotic love that makes a night blaze in memory like a torched stubble-field; I would walk the cindery, sparking ground in a daze the next morning, and for weeks afterward. It was always painful, beautiful, and fraught.

Sometimes I think I sought these memories more than the

experiences themselves, the afterglow rather than the burn. But with Bernhard, it was the nights themselves, the fire licking the ceiling of his bedroom, the walls flickering and the twinning shadows of our nakedness.

I was, at heart, a woman of the theater, and this was all part of my attraction to Bernhard. Ever since my days as a schoolgirl in Riga, I was drawn to the stage. Not always as an actor, but as a spectator. I prefer life transformed, perfected, by art. But I insist that art be revolutionary, too: It must address the demands of the present, transmit a feeling of urgency to the people.

It is too reductive merely to assert that economics rules the world – the basic Marxian presupposition – but there is some obvious truth in it. The material world is all we have and the only world we will ever know. I do not understand religious people. They have been sidetracked, hoodwinked, hounded into adopting preposterous notions. There is a God, but He is the world: rocks, streams, clouds, people. Every man and every woman is a little god. If anything, I preach the religion of man, the divinity of man, the sacredness of daily life. The hierarchies must go: man over woman, king over subject, rich over poor. The ideals of the French Revolution still strike me as the correct goals – liberty, equality, fraternity. Perhaps not in that order. Equality precedes liberty: We cannot be free until we are all equal, materially if not socially. As long as one man is begging for bread in the streets of the capital, there is no equality among men, and there can be no freedom or brotherhood.

My dear Walter Benjamin was no Marxist, though he was apparently moved by my arguments that summer in Capri, and he dutifully worked his way through *Kapital*, my very own copy, which he borrowed and did not return. I also gave him my copy of *History and Class Consciousness* by Georg Lukács, a book he had already read but not properly.

It was there, in Lukács, that Walter found his own thoughts about the degeneration of German society confirmed and elevated to a system that was, as I think he put it, 'coherent and epistemologically consistent.' Lukács examined in his rigorous style the spiritual crisis of the West. Walter had himself experienced this crisis, and it had driven him in esoteric directions, toward mysticism – a sure sign of dissolution. It seemed important to him that Lukács was able to rescue the spiritual tradition of the West and turn it to better use, suggesting ways to harness these same energies and transform them into instruments of social progress. Walter began, for the first time, to understand that without radical change in Europe, there was no hope at all.

He gulped down the books I gave him, and I was awed by his mental powers. Bernhard and I were both struck by his way of speaking slowly in complete and beautifully structured paragraphs. He had a philosophical turn of mind and had been trained in the Germanic tradition; Hegel (whom I had never read carefully) was second nature to him, which made Marx and Lukács appear quite simple. I became, simultaneously, his teacher and his pupil.

Walter leapt ahead of me, intellectually, in no time. He quickly understood the finer aspects of dialectical materialism better than I did. But he was not, and would never be, a committed revolutionary. He was intractably, incorrigibly bourgeois, a Berliner of the old school, a man of the burgher class. No matter how much he claimed to reject his background, it was always there, undermining his revolutionary zeal. He was, at base, a collector, a connoisseur, a mystic. I don't think he ever committed himself to revolution except in the most abstract and cerebral ways. In fact, he was downright pathetic when it came to revolutionary zeal. His skeptical nature made him the most improbable of would-be Marxists, and it quite irritated me when he feigned commitment. It was all humbug.

We met several times in the same café in the piazza, and he drew me out patiently, asking questions that grew increasingly personal.

'You will forgive me, fräulein,' he said, 'but I want to know everything about it. It is like that when I first make someone's acquaintance.'

'You must be very busy,' I said.

'I mean, when I make the acquaintance of someone terribly special . . . a friend of the future.'

He seemed idiotic but also compelling. I generally like intelligent men who present a complex argument based on concrete knowledge of the world. Walter, of course, had read everything, most of it twice. He was a walking, breathing encyclopedia, almost to the point of caricature, with this insane, compulsive, inhuman desire to know everything about everything that could be found in books.

It is not that I dislike reading; novels especially, and books on history, are part of my life. I was reading Tacitus and Suetonius at the time, both of whom told appalling yet wonderful stories about the Emperor Tiberius on Capri. What a monster he was! A pure fantasist and libertine, self-indulgent to a sublime degree. He reminded me, in a perverse way, of Brecht.

The café with the green awnings faced the cathedral, and we usually met after lunch. By midafternoon a blunt perpendicular light splashed over the adjacent stone stairway, although the steps themselves were obscured by flowers in vases. At one side of the piazza was a terrace surrounded by tall white columns; a black-and-white sign pointed to the funicular, which carried one to the sea. Above, an old bell tower boomed the hour, its clock face made of blue tile, which it wore like a monocle. It sported a Bourbon crest, the mark of some previous era of colonization. What I liked about Capri was its feeling of survival; many conquerors had come and gone, but the island itself remained – a glittering rock of freedom in the bright green sea. It was timeless and equal to anything that history could give it.

The piazza was crowded with elderly gentlemen in waistcoats, with leathery-faced fishermen, chattering housewives, children, and tourists from around the globe. It was all teeming, tumultuous, squawking. White, yellow, and pink facades squinted in the sun, and red peppers hung from a long beam behind our seats. A distant smell of onion, olive oil, and garlic touched our nostrils: part of the ongoing, obsessive task of meal preparation that is Italy's only religion.

One day Walter leaned over and said, 'Will you come to the cave with me? Tomorrow?'

This was uttered sotto voce, like a proposition. After some hesitation and polite questioning, I agreed to follow him the next morning to some legendary cave. How could one turn down such a proposal? Bernhard was preoccupied that morning, and he did not think of Walter Benjamin as a potential rival in matters of the heart, so I was quite free to explore the island with him. 'Just make sure he doesn't fall into the sea,' Bernhard said.

We met at nine in the piazza and proceeded on foot along the Via Croce: a steep, narrow path with thickly planted gardens in a string on one side and a nearly vertical descent to the sea on the other. Walter huffed and puffed like a steam engine, and I made fun of him. 'You are out of shape!' I said. 'Look at that potbelly! How old are you, sixty-five?' He just squinted and smiled, accepting my ridicule as a form of intimacy.

We came to a crossroad at the end of our climb, and from there could see the Tuaro Hills and a panoramic view of the sea, with its mass of dark shadows and, in the near distance, the Faraglioni – tall standing rocks that jut from the water like spires. Sorrento glimmered in the distance, a white coin in the red of the rocks. It was almost too beautiful.

I followed Walter into the woods, then up another steeply banked path through a patch of olive trees, arriving suddenly at the mouth of a large cave called the Matermania. It burrowed into the sheer sides of a limestone cliff, surrounded by myrtle bushes and mastics. Close by stood a patch of elegant sea pines, pungent with their ooze of pitch. Seagulls hung in the air, white-winged, like angels.

Unfortunately, I am by nature claustrophobic and detest small spaces, which means that a cave – however spectacular – is my worst nightmare. I have dreamed of caves all my life: winding caves with no end, with no possibility of a return to the light. Labyrinthine caves.

Walter beckoned from the shadows.

'I'm sorry, Walter,' I said. 'But I can't do it. I have this fear. You must forgive me.'

'Please, Asja,' he said. 'Come!' There was something a little frantic about his plea.

'It would kill me,' I said. 'It really would.'

He began laughing. 'You are neurotic. Of all people! Who would guess?'

'You may insult me all morning,' I said, 'but it will not persuade me to get into that cave.'

Walter changed his tactic, still hoping to persuade me. 'In fact, it is beautiful inside. I have come twice already, you see. This is my third visit.' As he spoke, he reached out and took my left hand, then gently, almost imperceptibly, led me into the cave, which rose gradually into a dark recess. 'You must not be frightened,' he said in a kind of stage whisper.

'Why are you whispering?'

'Caves are full of spirits,' he said. 'Some perhaps more dangerous than others. And then, there is the Minotaur at the bottom. It is best to let him sleep.'

My back was suddenly pressed against the wet, cool wall. I could see nothing but felt Walter close to me. And he was hard, his groin against me, his head on my shoulder. It was more peculiar than erotic, although I confess I did not find it unpleasant in any way. Men are men, and one must not expect otherwise.

It was certainly never my intention to get involved with Walter Benjamin. Not in a romantic way. Indeed, I was never in love with him. Never dreamed about him, not in the way one dreams about a lover. But I found his needs overpowering, and his attention – his guileless, relentless attention – was compelling. He fixed me with his eyes, and like an insect caught in his web I was stung into submission, or near submission. The truth is, I never gave myself wholly to him. Never let myself go. I never truly became, in any meaningful sense of the term, his lover.

That time in the Matermania was our first 'exchange,' as he called it. And it was typical. A bizarre pattern of titillation and frustrated expectation was established, one that he would retrace compulsively for many years.

He pressed against me, and eventually his lips moved toward mine. I let him kiss me, although I did not eagerly kiss him back. I was passive, and he invaded me.

I could feel his hand moving my hand toward him, toward the hardness that pressed against my stomach. He had by now unbuttoned his trousers, which had fallen about his knees. I liked the hot flesh in my hand, its curling hardness; he came, it seemed, within seconds, and he said, 'I love you, Asja. I love you.' It was disconcerting.

I did not respond, as perhaps I should have, but it was not possible under those circumstances. Over the next month, we met several times for 'exchanges,' but they were all like the one in the cave: slantwise, cryptic, somewhat less than visible. We never commented afterward on what happened between us, as if we had done something so terrible that it must never be mentioned. I don't, to this day, understand why I permitted it to go on.

The truth is that Walter was not a physical man. To begin with, he was so myopic that he never looked at anything like the rest of us do. Everything was quickly abstracted into language, framed, hung on the broad wall of his mind. Even the erotic aspects of life were well removed from the normal levels of physicality, although the embers of eros were often fanned by my resistance. It is like this with many men: They want passionately whatever they cannot have. If you give it to them, they disdain it. If you refuse they drive you mad with begging for it.

Near the end of the summer, my relations with Bernhard had degenerated, and I was ready to abandon him altogether. In a foolish moment, I said to Walter, 'All right, you may return to Riga with me. We can live together in a house owned by my cousin. It is a wooden house, with a tile roof that shimmers in the rain. You will like it.'

A dark shadow crossed his face, and then he looked at me with a sadness he had by this time in his life perfected, accompanied by a melancholic plunge of the eyebrows; the spirit of the man absconded through the eyes, so that he became the husk of Walter Benjamin. The expression frightened me.

'What's wrong?' I asked. 'Isn't this what you want?'

'I am in love with another woman,' he said. 'Her name is Jula, Jula Cohn.'

This took me by surprise. 'What about your wife, Dora?' I asked. 'And your son? Do they matter so little?'

'I have been in flight.'

'Ah, flight,' I said, unable to suppress an ironic twang. It was bad enough that he was married with a child, but he had a mistress, too. I was merely another mistress: a lady-in-waiting to his throne.

'I am sorry,' he said. 'Did I hurt your feelings? If so, I apologize.'

'Don't feel too bad, I wasn't going to ask you for your hand.'

'It is not that, it's just . . .'

'Please, Walter. It doesn't matter. Not at all. Life is complicated. I understand.'

'It *does* matter.' He brought a closed fist to his forehead, a remarkable gesture for him.

'It doesn't,' I said. 'We all make mistakes.'

I felt ridiculous, having to utter such banal nonsense. It's what happens to people in these situations. Even intelligent people with brilliant philosophical minds talk to one another like morons when it comes to love. When I left the next day for Riga, via Naples, Rome, and Florence, I knew that Walter was not going to let it go at that. And somehow I did not believe his story about Jula Cohn. It was a ruse, a way of not committing himself to a course of action.

Jula Cohn was a sculptress, or so everyone said. (I never saw any piece by her in the Berlin galleries.) She was apparently passive, almost plantlike, and it was later pointed out to me by Brecht that Walter's best single essay, on Goethe's *Elective Affinities*, was written in response to a crisis over Cohn. She was Goethe's Ottilie – the erotic ideal which can never be fully humanized. 'Great writing,' said Brecht, 'is always a response to pain.' This may or may not be true, but Walter was clearly in agony when he wrote that essay. It saturates every turn of phrase.

Jula had actually predated Dora by several years. She and Walter had met in Berlin before the war, and he pursued her in his paradoxically fitful but obsessive manner for years. Even after he married Dora in 1917, he continued to see Jula and write to her. In Heidelberg after the war, she knew everyone in the arts. In fact, her name was mentioned a few times by Bernhard and his friends, who regarded her as a hanger-on, a member of the self-important fringe that grows concentric rings around most artistic circles.

Fringes never interested me, that feeling of hanging around the edges. A Communist wants power: The power to feed those who are hungry, to give shelter to those who need it. The power to break down walls between classes and eventually to eliminate classes altogether. You cannot achieve these things by standing on the fringe. Marginality appeals only to the bourgeois sensibility. It allows the bourgeoisie to justify their own ineptitude. It is a good place to hide, to feel safe and satisfied.

I moved to Moscow precisely because it was the center of the people's revolution. I was eager to experience genuine power, and so was Bernhard; he intended to make a name for himself in the theater there and possibly at Gosfilm, where the Soviet film industry had lately blossomed. The Moscow horizon, for both of us, appeared endless. Indeed, I quickly established ties with an organization devoted to bringing out the hidden creative forces in the proletariat, called Proletarskaia Kultura. (Walter showed not the slightest interest in this movement: another sign of his doggedly bourgeois sensibility.)

Walter had a way of appearing in my life like an electrical storm that blows up from nowhere, booms and flashes, tingles the air, then slips over the horizon, leaving behind his after echo and days of rain. Having first refused my invitation to Riga, he came uninvited a few months later, taking a room in a fleabag hotel without even saying he'd come. He began walking the streets, hoping for a glimpse of me. In a fragment called 'Stereoscope,' he wrote:

> I appeared in Riga to see a woman. Her house, the city,
> the language were unfamiliar to me. Nobody was waiting
> for my arrival, and nobody knew me. For a couple of hours

I wandered the streets alone. It was the only time they were ever so empty. From each gate a flame shot, each cornerstone spraying sparks, and each streetcar raced toward me like a fire engine. Somehow, it was important that, of the two of us, I be the one who saw the other first. She could torch me with her eyes, which were matches. Had she touched me first, I'd have exploded.

It was agony to deal with a man in this state. Like an idiot, I let him stay in my house for two weeks. Crazier yet, I let him seduce me one night, after many drinks. He said, 'My dear, you look painfully stiff. Let me give you a massage.' Before I knew what was going on, his hand was between my legs. One thing led to another, then his body lowered itself upon me, from behind. I was immobile, and I could not resist, although the next day I said to him: 'We must never do that again. I do not want to have sex with you. Bernhard is my lover.' I asked him to be my friend, a real friend. 'Friends are more important than lovers, you know,' I said. He seemed hurt by this and left Riga in a bitter mood.

In the winter of 1926 he appeared, again without warning, in Moscow. I had been living in a sanatorium, recovering from a break-down. The doctors all agreed that years of straining for professional success in the theater combined with political activism had taken a harsh toll on my nerves; I was not by nature a strong person, though I pretended to be tough. My relations with Bernhard, to start with, were unsatisfactory. He played games with me, showing approbation only to undercut what he said with smirks and subtle digs. He was, I think, used to having actresses jump through whatever little hoops he put before them. I found this intolerable and would scream, 'You are not my director!' But it was hopeless. Bernhard's personality was set in concrete.

I had no wish to see Walter just now, but there he was beside my bed, fidgeting and smoking one cigarette after another; he begged me with those dark, sad eyes to abandon Bernhard, to become his lover. What an absurdity! He telegraphed his arrival, asking poor

Bernhard to pick him up at the Belorussian-Baltic station. (Bernhard, of course, agreed; he considered Walter 'a dear old thing.') They came straight to my room – Bernhard puzzled, Walter breathless with the kind of expectation one can only frustrate. He presented me with *One-Way Street*, his manic little book of fragments. It was dedicated to me: 'This street is named Asja Lacis street, after the engineer who laid it through the author.' Bernhard, when he saw this dedication, looked at Walter in amazement. There was no jealousy in him, thank goodness. It was not in his nature. Privately, he said, 'You mustn't lead him on, Asja. The man is obviously mad about you.' But I was not leading him on. I wasn't leading him anywhere!

What exactly did he expect to gain from this visit? I was not going to let him leap into my sickbed: One can only do so much for the People, and Walter was already wavering in his political commitment. He had seemed, in his letters, on the verge of joining the Party, but now, having arrived at the center of the revolution, he resisted. 'I am not sure about Bolshevism,' he would say, 'yet I believe in the principles of socialism. It's just that I cannot see how, in practice, this ideology will be productive. There are many things I must settle with myself before I join.' On and on, indecisively, he prattled.

I explained to him that if he wished to stay in Moscow and get ahead in the literary world there, he must join the Party. Contacts would soon occur, and these would lead to assignments. He could review plays or write articles for the *New Soviet Encyclopedia*. There was plenty of money available for the right cultural products. The Soviets were especially eager to improve relations with Germany, and they needed advocates in the press, native speakers. Who better than Walter Benjamin, who already reviewed for several important papers in Berlin and Frankfurt? 'Play your cards right,' I told him, 'and you'll make out big. They'll hire you in the Kremlin!'

As usual, Walter nodded vaguely. He was always nodding vaguely.

I suspect the Ernst Toller affair turned him against the Soviet State. Toller was by far the most influential socialist playwright of the day, a member of the short-lived Bavarian Soviet Republic. His plays, in translation, were produced in Russia before huge audiences. Now his arrival in the capital had been loudly trumpeted: Posters appeared everywhere, plastered to walls and fences, on the sides of trolleys, in the railway stations. He was scheduled to give a lecture at the Kameneva Institute, and hundreds turned up to hear him. Alas, he was attacked just before his arrival by an enemy, Paul Werner, who argued that Toller's work was counterrevolutionary. *Pravda* unexpectedly sided with Werner, and when Toller appeared to give his lecture, the doors to the Institute were locked.

'This is outrageous,' Walter kept saying. 'Imagine turning on Toller like that, forbidding him to lecture. He is a very great man!'

I tried to explain to him that in Russia many conflicting ideas were in circulation, and received opinion shifted constantly. Toller's star in the theatrical firmament would rise again if he proved himself a valuable member of the Party.

'Who cares if he belongs to the Party or doesn't?' Walter asked, a little too loudly, as he sat beside my bed. Some of the attendants in the sanatorium were already suspicious, having overheard us talking facetiously about one thing or another.

'We must pull together,' I said. 'One Party is all we can afford. There may be differences of opinion within the Party, of course. There ought to be. But the forces of reaction will kill us if we show too much division among ourselves.'

Bernhard would sit behind Walter, rolling his eyes; he did everything he could for him, even introducing him to the editor of the *New Soviet Encyclopedia*, who commissioned an article on Goethe. One might have expected gratitude from Walter, but no. His mind was elsewhere, on me.

I can still see him sitting there, sighing, staring into my eyes like a dying man afraid of darkness. He would appear at my bedside every afternoon, his arms laden with flowers, sweets, honeycakes, fresh cream. He talked fantastically about our future: 'We must return to Capri,' he kept saying. 'To the Matermania Cave.' Once or twice, when Bernhard was absent, he lunged at me, and I had to play a cool game, running my fingers through his hair but not giving too much. I became quite frightened once, when he began to weep, telling me that if I could not return his love he would surely die, perhaps on the floor beside my bed.

'Do you love me, Asja? Please tell me the truth!'

'Yes,' I said. 'But I love you more as a friend.'

'More as a friend than what?'

'Than a lover . . .'

This produced sobbing and remonstrations. He was so childish about everything . . .

'Look,' I said, in desperation, 'I will come and visit you in Berlin, soon. We must sort this out.' I begged him, however, to restrain himself in front of Bernhard, explaining that most men in Bernhard's position would have murdered him by now. I also tried to point out that I myself was not a well person.

'You will visit me in Berlin?' he asked, his eyes innocently wide.

'Yes, I promise.'

'Without Bernhard?'

'By myself, alone.'

I knew that if I did not promise something along these lines, he would stay in Moscow forever, hoping eventually to seduce me. I could see that Bernhard was losing patience with him; indeed, one night in my room, he urged Walter to leave Russia as soon as possible. 'You will never be able to live by your pen here, Walter,' he said.

'You are quite right,' Walter said, much to my surprise. 'I will go home.' He reached for Bernhard's hand, which he grasped. 'Thank you for being frank with me.'

Bernhard was also frank with Walter about his work, often shockingly so. 'A good writer does not always write beautiful, dense, and memorable sentences,' he said to Walter one afternoon, referring to *One-Way Street*. 'The ratio of splendid sentences to mediocre ones is about one to thirty in Tolstoy or Gogol. But in your prose, every other sentence is dense and memorable. There is finally too much to remember. There is no forward tilt.'

On hearing this, Walter seemed quite upset at first; then he said, 'You are exactly right, I'm afraid. I will never find an audience.'

'Not unless you change your style,' Bernhard said.

'I cannot do that,' he replied. 'That would be immoral, would it not?'

This was perhaps the turning point of the Moscow visit. The next day he began to make his preparations to leave.

I was feeling well enough the next week to accompany Walter to the station myself. It was early February, but a thaw had set in; the snow was all slush at the sides of the broad Tverskaia, and one had to step around the puddles and steaming manure piles. Walter held my hand tightly as we walked, saying nothing. Twice he stopped, looked intently into my eyes, and sighed.

As he boarded the railway car, he turned and stared at me pitifully.

I said, 'Are you going to be all right, Walter? Really?'

'I would give anything for your love,' he said.

'I know, I know.'

'Is there any hope?'

'There is always hope,' I said. 'What is life without hope? But you must not dwell on this.'

Walter bit his lip severely. Then he began to speak, his lips moving distinctly, though no words came out.

Much to my relief, the conductor blew his whistle, and the train sighed as the brakes released.

'You must find your seat,' I said.

'I can think of nothing but you.'

'Please,' I said, 'there are better subjects. Think about Goethe.'

'You are more important.'

It is so tedious when a man loves you more than you love him. And heartbreaking. I tried to wave to him as his train pulled away from the platform, but he would not look out the window. He had his face buried in his hands, and his shoulders were hunched forward. Maybe it was just the light, but his hair seemed white as frost, a ghostly puff around his head. I suspect he was weeping. What a great bloody bore, I thought. A great bloody bore.

WALTER BENJAMIN

The déjà vu effect has been described quite often. Nonetheless, I wonder if the term is well chosen, and whether the more appropriate metaphor should not be taken from the realm of acoustics. One might do better to speak of events reaching us like an echo awakened by a call, a sound that seems to have been heard somewhere in the darkness of our past life. Accordingly, if we are not mistaken, the shock with which moments enter consciousness as if already experienced in some previous life usually strikes us acoustically, in the form of a sound. A word, tapping, or a rustling noise is somehow endowed with the magical power to transport us into the cool tomb of long ago, from the vault of which the present seems to return only as an echo.

9   LISA FITTKO

Hans was still trying to get himself aboard a ship to Casablanca, and so was my brother. His wife, Eva, and their little girl, Titi, were entrusted to me. According to our plan, we would make our way over the border into Spain; the route along the sea was apparently wide open, and it was an easy hike. From Spain, one could cross into Portugal, which was deemed a more suitable place than Morocco for sitting out the war. Portugal would certainly remain a neutral zone, and the standard of living there was reasonably high. It was assumed that, somehow, we'd all meet up when the Nazi winter ended, however long that might take.

Eva and Titi had been living temporarily in Montpellier, with friends, and they were to board my train en route to the Spanish border. I had cabled them with my exact times, but I am always nervous about connections; they are so unpredictable.

The train pulled into the station, and as feared, I saw no Eva, no Titi. The conductor shouted, 'All aboard!' The whistle blew, a sharp blast.

I rushed to the conductor. 'I'm expecting some relatives,' I said. 'They were to meet me.'

'I'm sorry, madame,' he said.

I knew that by hanging off the steps of my car, I could delay the train, and I did so.

'Please, madame! Step inside! We have a schedule!' the conductor said.

I dangled from the steps, pretending not to hear a word.

A minute passed that felt like ten, then came the welcome shriek: 'Auntie Lili! Auntie Lili!' Eva was behind her, racing to keep up.

I had saved a place for them in my compartment, much to the annoyance of the other passengers. One beastly old woman in makeup like a death mask had said, 'You can't reserve seats! It's not allowed in France!' But I stood my ground. 'It's allowed,' I said, letting my voice slide a few registers. Even the conductor had been unable to dispute my assertion. 'I would have to look this up,' he said, when questioned.

No sooner had we sat down than Titi cried, 'Have you got a piece of cake or some chocolate, Aunt Lili? Mama thought you would.'

'I'm sorry, Titi, I've got nothing for you.'

'Here is some bread,' said her mother. She fetched a small loaf from her bag and broke off a piece for Titi. '*Du pain*,' she said.

The child grabbed the morsel. 'In German, we say *Brot*. Do you say *Brot* or *du pain*, Aunt Lili?'

Her mother and I froze. If we were taken for Germans, there was no telling what might happen.

'I haven't seen you in such a long time!' I said loudly, sweeping the child into my lap. 'You are such a beautiful little thing!' I patted her blond curls to distract her.

Eva sat with jaw quivering. Fortunately, none of the others in the car – most of them were soldiers – noticed what the child had said. Adults don't often hear children when they speak; their chatter is like background music, a kind of vaguely annoying or sometimes charming prattle that does not translate into sense unless one happens to be the mother or father.

Port-Vendres, a coastal town right on the Spanish border, was the last stop for most émigrés in flight. We arrived in the late afternoon, and as I stepped from the train, my eyes filled with tears. I had forgotten it would be so beautiful: the ragged line of blue hills in the near distance, the meadows beside the tracks now deep in hay, and the sloping village that wore the Mediterranean like a bright turquoise bib. The sky was orange in the cool of early evening, with puffy clouds making fantastic, whimsical shapes across a windbreak of cedars. The little houses tumbled on each other, pink and blue and white, like children rushing toward the sea. A nervous peace hung in the air, so unlike the mad clatter of Toulouse or Marseilles.

Nature is always with us, I thought. It is wild and regenerative. It lifts us up or tears us down, always to rebuild, so fresh, so infinitely deep, perfectly calm but savage as well, and sweetly ignorant of human misery and greed and sorrow. One can never be sad for long or afraid in nature's presence. What could the Germans do to me? I thought. They might kill me or even torture me. But nothing they did would last for long. I would soon enough reconnect to the earth, the rocks and rills, the mountains and trees. That was my real kingdom, and it could not be taken away from me.

Hans gave me the name of Jean-Luc Ferrier, who apparently knew a great deal about escaping over the border, and we went to visit him after settling into the apartment my sister-in-law had found.

He was avuncular and gave us hot chocolate to drink. 'Dozens of refugees are currently hiding in Port-Vendres,' he said, his white eyebrows going up and down as he spoke. Like most of the men in French villages, he was quite elderly. The young men were either fighting or hiding in the mountains, where Resistance units were already forming.

Whole families clustered in damp basements or dark attics, and the braver ones walked the streets, heads down, trying to attract as little attention as possible. For the most part, the villagers of Port-Vendres were sympathetic to the refugees, who were all waiting for the right moment to make their crossing into Spain.

For several months now, refugees had been pouring steadily into Spain via Cerbere, hiking the bright coastal path for five or six hours – a day's journey, in effect. The border guards had been lax until the week before, when orders came down from the German Kundt Commission (a Gestapo agency that was operating in unoccupied France) that all refugee traffic must be stopped immediately. Nazi sympathizers emerged within the ranks of the border guards like poisonous flowers fed by the black soil of this dark time; perhaps in anticipation of the total occupation, the entire *garde mobile* became fantastically zealous. Trainloads of refugees were already moving north, bound for 'repatriation,' which meant they would be shipped promptly to German concentration camps.

Banyuls-sur-Mer was another town on the border, a bit farther to the west; its mayor was a portly gentleman called Monsieur Azéma. He was an avid socialist, according to Monsieur Ferrier, and this meant he would help anyone in flight from the Nazis. I went to see him a day or two after settling in, eager to find out more about a secret route into Spain that Ferrier said was still passable. It was called *la route Lister*, after General Lister, the Republican hero of the Spanish Civil War who had used this route to smuggle men out of Spain.

Azéma lived in a stone house – more of a hut than a house – on the edge of a steep, thistle-strewn path. I knocked at his door firmly. He opened it and stared at me, squinting in the sun.

'Are you Monsieur Azéma?'

'May I help you?'

'Monsieur Ferrier sent me. I'm a German socialist, and I must get to Spain.'

'Ah Monsieur Ferrier – a marvelous man!' He lifted his eyes in a most disconcerting way, revealing their whites. 'Come inside, madame.'

It made me anxious to place my fate so directly in this man's hands. Who could tell friend from foe in these times? But a point comes when one must simply trust, and there was something in this man's voice that led me to trust him.

We sat at his kitchen table, and he listened to my story intently. His face was amazingly open, rather mild in aspect. I realized that my first impression was quite wrong. I had nothing to fear from him.

'I will help you,' he said, 'but you must assist me, too. You see, there are many people in your situation. They are desperate to flee.' He began to tap his fingers on the table. 'I can tell by looking into your eyes that you are a strong woman, with experience.

Unfortunately, *la route Lister* is a difficult one – very dangerous. On the other hand, it may soon be the only way out of France.'

I said I would do whatever I could to help, so he went on to describe the route in detail, drawing a map for me on a piece of yellow notepaper. 'You must go yourself, alone. Memorize the path, so you can then teach it to others. I may not be here next month, next week . . . There are people watching me, you see. It's not safe for me to take anyone into Spain.'

'I will do what I can,' I said, aware of how little that might be.

The old mayor kissed me on the forehead, the coarse brown skin around his lips wrinkling, prunelike. 'My dear madame, God has sent you.' His eyes were watery now. 'I am so grateful, you see. I embarrass myself.'

What else could I do? You simply do not say no in these situations. I resolved to remain in Banyuls or Port-Vendres for a discreet period, before escaping to Spain myself. *La route Lister* must remain an avenue of escape as long as possible. Of course I would see to it that Eva and Titi were among the first to cross the mountains: There was no telling how long it would take for the border guards to catch on, and I wanted my brother's family to arrive safely in Portugal as soon as possible.

Azéma handed me a large bag filled with vegetables and tins of milk. 'You must give this milk to the child,' he said. 'And this bottle of wine is for you. Do you like wine?'

I was glad for the wine and the other goods, though the heavy bag made my hike back into Port-Vendres more burdensome. Still, I could hardly not enjoy the zigzag journey along the cliff wall. Somehow I had not looked at the landscape properly on my way into Banyuls-sur-Mer that morning, my mind being preoccupied with Azéma. But I felt calm now, having established this link with the mayor. I could look around at the world more calmly.

The sea glimmered in the distance, while moss, scrub oaks, and furled cedars clung to the foothills rising to one side. Vineyards sloped into the valley on the other side, rich and hazy, with cadres of women working among them: small women, quite elderly and sun-dried, a small part of that veritable army of wizened and black-hooded widows who populate the Mediterranean basin. The sky was bluer than the sea, and deeper, and I stood for a long while in the late-morning sun and watched a gull hang on the edge of a cloud. There was no way to describe adequately what this felt like to me. You had to be there to understand.

A day or so later, as I was resting in my room in Port-Vendres, a knock came at the door. A very faint, limp-wristed knock that I half mistook for a distant shutter banging loose. Gradually, I understood that somebody was at my door. I don't know why it annoys me when people are so unassertive, but it does. I said, too loudly, 'Who is there?'

There was no answer.

Puzzled, a little frightened, I opened the door to find a small, middle-aged and potbellied man in a crumpled woolen suit and thick glasses.

'You will please excuse my intrusion, Frau Fittko,' he said, fumbling for words, bowing and shifting from foot to foot. 'It is my hope that I have not come at an inconvenient moment.' He had a bushy, dark mustache that rose and fell oddly when he spoke. He smelled strongly of dry sweat and tobacco.

It took at least a minute to recognize Walter Benjamin, who seemed to have aged a decade in the past year. I noticed his brightly polished, black leather shoes, his out-of-fashion tie, gone shiny with age, which seemed to be strangling him. The sleeves of his jacket, like the cuffs of his trousers, were badly frayed.

He did not look at me as he spoke but seemed to focus above me, behind me. 'I have recently seen your husband, Herr Fittko, and he suggested I might contact you here. You will excuse the presumption, but he said that you might kindly take me over the border into Spain. I would go myself but, you see, I am unfamiliar with the region.'

It was just like Hans to assume I could do anything, and of course, he was right. I could do most things pretty damn well. Nevertheless, there was a certain presumption on his part.

'Please, Dr Benjamin,' I said, 'will you not come in?'

He shook his head, reluctant to enter the room (probably because I was a woman and alone), so I agreed to walk with him into the village. We found a small outdoor café with a view of the sea, and we took care that nobody should overhear our conversation. Though we sat facing each other, his eyes avoided meeting mine. It was awkward, but I understood that here was a Berliner of the old school. I have never liked false manners, but his were merely formal and not false. He reminded me of my grandfather, who used to tip his hat to everyone on the street.

I had seen Dr Benjamin at parties and knew him glancingly. Our circle in Paris was, of course, quite small, and Dr Benjamin had established a reputation among the émigré community as an intellectual. Hans occasionally referred to him as 'the man who sits in the Bibliothèque Nationale and produces nothing.'

Herr Benjamin (or Old Benjamin, as I took to calling him in my head) had not been as unproductive as Hans imagined. He kept beside him at all times a decrepit leather briefcase containing a huge masterwork. 'Everything I know is in these pages,' he said, showing me the manuscript, 'and this is the only copy.'

'What you need is a roomful of monks,' I said.

He looked at me queerly.

'To copy the book.'

'Ah, scribes,' he said, smiling gravely. Though devoid of rollicking humor, he was subject to slight rumbling chuckles, often accompanied by a strange breath, as though he were sucking the joke into his lungs. I guessed that very little in his life had been conducive to humor. Indeed, he had recently been flung into the sea in Marseilles, and it was only the chance passing of a rowboat that saved him and his manuscript from watery oblivion.

'Please, would you have a cigarette?' he asked.

'No, thanks.'

He lit one himself, meticulously placing it between his lips and then cupping his hands so his match would not falter in the stiff breeze coming off the sea.

After taking a long puff, he said, 'I will go to Madrid first, and then perhaps to Tangiers, where I am assured of safe passage to Cuba – should that seem appropriate. After the war, I expect to live in New York.'

'New York is apparently quite beautiful,' I said.

'So I'm told. I have friends there, you see.' A glaze came over his eyes. 'The truth is, I know several people in New York quite well.' The wistfulness of his tone, and the way his voice trailed off at the end of each phrase, told me he did not believe for a second that he would ever get to Cuba or New York. He may have even doubted the friendships. He was letting this rhetoric out, like a balloon on a string; it bobbed in the breeze, colorful. But it was just that, a balloon. Any sharp attention to its meaning might well prick and destroy it.

In Marseilles, Old Benjamin had befriended a middle-aged woman by the name of Henny Gurland. She and her teenage son, José, were also frantic to get out of France, having been denied (like the rest of us) an exit visa in Marseilles. Her husband, Herr Gurland, had been killed earlier in the summer while escaping from a military prison near Tours, where he was being held for 'repatriation' to Germany. Old Benjamin wanted the Gurlands to come with us over the Pyrenees.

'So you will take us into Spain, Frau Fittko? I am right in assuming so?'

'I will, if I can.'

'Surely you can,' he said. 'I feel terribly confident about this.'

I explained that, so far, I had not had a chance to test the route myself. Indeed, I had nothing to go on but the rough sketch given to me by Azéma, and he had, after all, drawn that map from memory. One knows how unreliable this can be, especially when recalling turns in a path. And there were several crucial landmarks that one must not miss: a mountain hut that one must keep on one's left, a high plateau with seven pine trees that must be kept on one's right; apparently a vineyard appeared at one point near the crest, and if one threaded it properly, one came to the appropriate crest. Steep ravines fell off to one side of the path, which became very narrow in places, while loose rocks and gravel slides only made the crossing that much more treacherous. It was not, as Azéma emphasized, an easy climb.

'This crossing is not without risks,' I said, rather understating the situation, since there was no point in spooking him. 'And you are obviously not in perfect health.' He had already told me more about his health than I really wanted to know, and it was not good news. His heart and lungs were weak, and he could not rely on his stamina. Even now, his hands trembled like those of an elderly man.

'The real risk, I'm afraid, would be to stay put,' he said. 'There is no alternative, is there?'

No sane person would argue with him. The real questions I had now concerned the accuracy of Azéma's map and, indeed, whether or not Old Benjamin could possibly survive this crossing.

We met the next morning, as planned. The idea was that we should first speak to Mayor Azéma, who would again describe the route to both of us; this way, it would be impressed on two minds. I told Eva to hang back for a week or so: I would take her and Titi on my second crossing, when I could be sure of the route.

My inner alarm bells began to sound as soon as we set off for Banyuls-sur-Mer. Old Benjamin was limping, and he seemed terribly short of breath, insisting – over my vehement objection – that he carry his briefcase.

'I'm afraid I don't trust the landlord,' he said. 'There have been several incidents lately.'

I didn't press him about these incidents. It was clear to me that Benjamin and his manuscript were inseparable.

By the time we reached the mayor's house, Benjamin was – quite literally – livid: the blood had drained from his cheeks, which shone with a sickly white pallor. He sucked in deep breaths, as if frantically trying to feed his lungs. His lips were bluish pale.

'Are you all right?' I asked. 'I could find a doctor in Banyuls, with the mayor's help – if it's necessary.'

He held up a hand. 'I am perfectly well, thank you,' he said, huffing. 'Just a little out of breath. I am not used to walking great distances, you see.'

I don't know why I simply accepted his word on this. He was deeply unwell, but there was no way of breaking through the iron lace of courtesy that he draped over everything. To question his response would be indecorous.

The mayor greeted us with enthusiasm, taking a carafe of red wine from his cupboard. We sat on his terrace and drank several glasses of the wine, which had a tangy flavor, and listened carefully to his description of the route. He pointed to the high Pyrenees, mauve in the distance.

'Those mountains, the ones near the top,' I said, 'they seem rather formidable.'

Mayor Azéma did not comfort us. 'They are steep, but that's where Spain lies: on the other side.' As if to comfort me, he said, 'The steepness is good, you know. It will protect you and your friends.'

Old Benjamin said, 'Have you ever read *Don Quixote*?'

The mayor beamed. '*Bien sûr*, my friend. I have a copy in my bedroom!'

'Then you will understand my quest for Spanish soil. I shall ride into Spain on Rocinante.'

I began to think, Yes, indeed, Old Benjamin, you have cottage cheese for a brain. Your invisible horse, Rocinante, may be just what is needed.

The mayor leaned toward us, his broad red face and massive head wobbling on his neck. 'You must go now – along the lower part of the trail, before *la route Lister* actually begins; it is deceptive, and one can make a wrong turn quite suddenly. It is best understood in daylight.' He leaned forward over his map. 'Go as far as this clearing.' He referred to a point on his sketch, marked X. 'Then come back, and we will confer again.'

'Is it a long walk to the clearing?' Old Benjamin queried.

'You will arrive there in maybe an hour or two. A pleasant walk, I assure you.'

'You are very kind to us, sir,' Old Benjamin said, filling his mouth with wine, which he held for a long time before gulping.

The mayor explained that the border guards had already expanded their numbers in the Banyuls-sur-Mer region, and they were constantly on patrol. 'Day and night, I'm told,' he said. 'Of course, you understand the consequences. I don't have to explain.'

'It is always good to be warned,' I said, making sure Old Benjamin heard me. I had this eerie feeling that he was not sufficiently frightened and, therefore, might do something a little foolish.

I can still hear Old Benjamin taking leave of the mayor, bowing steeply: 'I give you a thousand thanks, *monsieur le maire.*'

The Gurlands were staying in Banyuls, at a small boardinghouse, so there would be no problem with logistics. We would scout the lower path this afternoon and leave for Spain the following morning, at four sharp.

We set off immediately after lunch. I was relieved by the apparent vigor of the Gurlands, although I quickly saw that José was remote and troubled – more so than most boys of his age – and hoped this would not interfere with the crossing. Frau Gurland was a broad-hipped, blond woman in her late forties, although she seemed younger. José was fifteen and very strong, with hard, blue eyes and corkscrew-curly hair – blond hair over dark olive skin, a peculiar combination.

'We will have such a nice walk this afternoon!' Old Benjamin said.

José looked at him with pity.

'Why don't you wait here?' I suggested. 'Better to save your energy for tomorrow, no?'

'I feel very well today,' he said. 'I want to go with you, to get a sense of it. One tends to worry until the reality is underfoot, you see.' His cheeks were flushed, but he seemed remarkably eager and fresh. One could obviously not dissuade him.

'You will let me carry the briefcase for you,' said José, who seemed fond of Old Benjamin.

'If I feel tired, I will hand it over,' he said, 'but for the time being,

I am quite happy with it. I have so many good years packed inside, you see.'

We set off in cold sunlight that clarified and examined everything it touched, as if preparing for the kill of winter meticulously, callously. A scrawny hare scurried into a deep hole. Blackbirds gathered on a broken limb. There was a sliding breeze off the sea, and it rushed into our faces, making it difficult to press forward. Old Benjamin, in his suit and city shoes, his wrinkled white shirt and food-speckled tie, seemed ludicrously out of place as we tilted into the breeze. I could more easily imagine him on the Paris métro.

Gulls swooped overhead, some grazing in the stubble-fields on the immediate outskirts of Banyuls-sur-Mer. Bales of hay were pitched here and there, like tamed lightning. The colors in the landscape shone with the vividness of late September: blues like in oil paintings, glossy and slightly green, and browns bordering on russet. 'We are walking on the world,' I said, to nobody in particular. And it was like that: as if we had acquired some elevation. I felt light, at ease, and happy. At least for now, I was not worried about the border guards.

Each of us drifted in our own balloon of consciousness, avoiding conversation. Old Benjamin seemed much livelier than earlier, on the walk from Port-Vendres, when he had to stop every ten or fifteen minutes for a breath. At one point, much to my surprise, he was actually singing something under his breath, in German. Something from Wagner's *Tristan*? It seemed unlikely that he would favor an anti-Semite like Wagner, but one never knows. Intellectuals have their own reasons. In any case it was hardly prudent to be singing in German just now. I said nothing only because there was nobody near us, and the wind was strong enough to muffle the words.

I studied Mayor Azéma's sketch as we proceeded, taking careful note of each landmark. The first leg of the journey, on this early scouting mission, was not going to be the hour or two of pleasant walking that the mayor had imagined. We encountered a severe upward turning in the path only forty minutes after setting off, with perhaps three or four hours of walking ahead of us. Old Benjamin gratefully passed the briefcase to José Gurland as the path inclined, and I could see from his color that he was having a difficult time. Every quarter hour or so he would stop to rest for a moment, sucking in his cheeks as he inhaled, then blowing out with a whistle of phlegm.

In the second hour, Benjamin seemed overwhelmed, and I suggested that he go back with José. Henny Gurland and I would push ahead by ourselves.

'I am perfectly well,' he said, adamant. 'You must let me have a little breather now and then. It is normal for a man of my age.'

What was I to do?

Fortunately, the path soon leveled. At last, we came to a ruined stable: our first major landmark. Beyond that, we found the clearing the mayor had mentioned. Resting there, I produced bread and cheese for everyone from my rucksack. Henny Gurland had a bottle of water in hers, which we duly passed around. José had squirreled away some chocolate, which he also shared.

'Picnics are wonderful occasions,' Old Benjamin said.

Suddenly a patrol appeared in the distance: four or five soldiers in a file, their black shadows tilting ahead of them, clearing a way.

'Into the stable!' I whispered, ducking. My heart jabbed in my neck, in my temples, as we scrambled toward it, keeping as low to the ground as possible.

We waited for an hour, crouching in the stale hay. The border patrol had obviously not seen us.

'Are they *everywhere*?' Henny Gurland asked.

'These mountains are too big for that,' I said, improvising. 'They probably send out dozens of small patrols, but the chances of being intercepted by any one of them is slight, especially as one gets higher. The foothills are riskier. We should probably have come at dusk.' Privately, I began to doubt the wisdom of Mayor Azéma, who had recommended broad daylight for scouting purposes.

'We're sitting ducks,' said Old Benjamin, his eyes bulging behind his glasses. It amused me to see a man of his capacities uttering a line from a third-rate detective film.

We stepped outside and could see just ahead the huge boulder that Azéma had mentioned, a great bulbous mass like a bald pate surrounded by a fringe of grass and thistle.

'What a monstrous thing, that rock,' Old Benjamin said. 'Like Balzac's forehead.'

'Like what?' asked Henny Gurland.

'Balzac,' he said, 'the novelist.'

Frau Gurland sighed. It could test one's patience to listen to a man like this. Everything reminded him of a book, a character in a book, or the author of a book. On his deathbed he would shout, 'I remember a scene in a book where it happens like this!' Only when he was dead would the references cease, the allusions to other points in time and history, and it would come as a relief, probably to him as well as everyone else. At some point, the moment itself matters and does not connect to other moments in time. The time of one's death is like this. One is always a virgin at death.

'The clearing!' cried José.

Henny Gurland was unnerved by the shout, and I thought, for a horrid moment, that she would slap him, but fortunately that moment passed in the excitement of arrival.

Indeed, a circle of grass in the high brush caught the afternoon light and shone like a massive coin about a hundred yards in the distance. It was definitely the one marked firmly on Azéma's map.

Old Benjamin began to walk more quickly. 'Let's go,' he said, the first and only time I heard those words come from him. White-faced, his mouth open to gulp breath, he rushed toward it, dragging the ball-and-chain of his briefcase beside him. At one point he even broke into a peculiar, listing run. Upon reaching the clearing, he simply collapsed, sprawling in the grass with his face down.

José rushed to his side, asking if Old Benjamin had hurt himself.

'But I am wonderful, wonderful!' he said, rolling onto his back. 'This clearing . . . it does one a lot of good sometimes, just a circle in the woods. The light, you know, surprises me. It is quite beautiful here, I think.' He quoted a line from Verlaine.

Poor José did not understand this babble, but he revered the old man for reasons he could only intuit. For me, Benjamin was the European Mind writ large. Indeed, as I later realized, Old Benjamin was everything the Nazi monsters wanted most to obliterate: that aura of tolerance and perspective that comes from having seen many things from many angles. Even that rueful laugh of his was part of the aura. Here before us was the last laughing man, I thought. The last man to laugh the laugh of the ages. From now on, history would be tears, and the work of intellectuals would be the work of grieving.

We lay together in the grass now with the sun sliding down the western sky, cold at our backs; we had a good view of the dark valley below. A faint moon had already pricked through the firmament, with a silvery haze around it. It would soon be dusk.

I said, 'We must get back now, to the village. We begin again before dawn, so we'll need our sleep.'

José immediately jumped to his feet and began to brush the grass from his trousers.

'Not me,' said Old Benjamin. There was an eerie firmness in his voice.

'What are you talking about?' I asked.

'I cannot walk another step today, I'm afraid. My legs are gone.'

It was impossible, exasperating. How was I going to get this man over the Pyrenees?

'You must not look so mournful, Frau Fittko,' he said. 'I am perfectly capable of sleeping here tonight. The grass is quite comfortable. Indeed, I will be quite happy here, and by tomorrow I will have gathered my energy for the climb. It will give me the boost I need to make it over.'

'Indeed,' I said. No point would be served in arguing with him, that much was clear.

'You will freeze,' said Henny Gurland.

'Here,' said José. 'Take my pullover, doctor.' He immediately stripped and gave Old Benjamin his sweater. 'I will bring your suit-case, tomorrow.'

'Thank you, José,' he said, accepting the sweater gratefully. 'You are so thoughtful. And with your sweater, I shall be toasty all night and sleep like a newborn.'

'Newborns don't sleep,' I said. 'They feed every two or three hours.'

'Then I shall feed on the stars, on the moon,' he said. He quoted some appropriate lines from Heine on the subject, which none of us recognized. 'If it begins to rain, I will go into the stable.'

And so we left him there, sitting like a Buddha, his legs drawn up, he was thoroughly self-absorbed, immersed in thought, even before we began our downward climb. This was certainly the most peculiar man I had ever met, a rare and difficult one. It seemed improbable that we would make it to Spain together, but at this point, turning back was not a likely option.

Let me tell you about my study, here in Berlin. It is not yet fully equipped, yet it remains beautiful and livable. My books are all here, and even in these harsh times they have increased over the years from twelve hundred to more than two thousand – and I have not kept many old ones. The room has its peculiarities, I will admit. For one thing, it has no desk; in the course of time, and partly because of circumstances – not only my habit of working a good deal in cafés but also various associations that haunt my memory of the old writing-desk ways – I have reached the point of writing only while lying down. From my predecessor in this flat, I have inherited a sofa that is wonderfully adequate for my purposes, although for sleeping it seems useless.

10

Having decided impulsively to spend this night in the foothills of the Pyrenees, Benjamin saw he was ill-equipped to make it through until morning. He had no provisions, no water or food, no blankets. Yet it was too late. The others, much to his surprise, had not argued with him; indeed, they were gone – Frau Fittko, Henny Gurland, and her son; they had left him alone here, higher in the world than he liked, exposed, in a ruined stable.

It was already colder than he had banked on. The sun had dropped like a bomber going down in flames, and night nested on the world, spreading its icy black wing over the mountains. The moon rose swiftly, and the stars came out in clusters, inventing legends overhead: a bold anthology of giants and heroes, demons, mythical beasts. Searching the sky from the window of the stable, Benjamin imagined what a shepherd in ancient Greece might have felt, tormented each night by so many incoherent, flickering signs, an unreadable script. People needed the gods and heroes, the myths, to gather and display meaning. The mind and the world must join forces to create consciousness. Benjamin began to consider death as simply the end of signification, the removal of signifiers from the passing facts they signed.

He could feel the blunt and irrevocable separation of words and things beginning: a slight shift of the ground he occupied. It was accompanied by the lonely hiss of wind in the high grass, the smell of decay in the stable's rotting struts, and the dying light. And he felt afraid for the first time, realizing that his rumpled suit would never keep him warm; his tie seemed absurd in this context, an obsolete object of clothing, a vestigial organ of a civilized world that had vanished forever. It dangled from his neck like a speechless tongue. What would it say if it could talk? he wondered, then shouted, 'Quack! Quack! Quack!' and dissolved in giggles.

The giggles echoed back from the mountains.

'I am going mad,' he whispered.

His heart fluttered queerly, a wasp in a jar, and his arms tingled. He decided to step outside, to get air. He could not breathe in the stable.

The clearing, its broad field of wiry grass, delighted him. Wrapping himself in his own arms to keep warm, he leaned forward into the sharp wind. His breath puffed ahead of him, a faint diaphanous balloon; his shoes cracked, and he could feel the blister that had formed this afternoon growing steadily more painful on his left toe, where it tingled and burned; another seemed to have developed on his right heel. These abrasions would only make his journey even more of an ordeal.

But he found it hard to think about tomorrow as the temperature plunged and a circle of pain widened in his chest. *I'll be lucky enough to make it through the night*, he said to himself, a faint sardonic smile gathering on his lips. It would shock them all, would it not, if he simply died here, in the stable? They would have to bury him in a shallow pit nearby. The ground was not yet frozen, and there was plenty of dirt around to kick over his corpse. 'He'd have slowed us down anyway,' Henny Gurland would say. He knew Henny.

But who would say Kaddish? Scholem, perhaps? He might organize this.

Yes, Gerhard Scholem would find him, eventually. It might take him twenty years, but he would find him. This was just the sort of absurd, sentimental journey he would adore.

Scholem would be good company tonight if, miraculously, he were to descend from a cloud. They would lie together in the hay talking about Isaac Luria and his school of Kabbalism, or some such thing. Scholem never tired of these recondite conversations.

It had been almost silly, back in the old days, when he and Dora were fighting tooth and nail, the way Scholem would enter the room and begin a discourse on some abstruse topic; his conversations began *in medias res*, with never a preamble, not even a warm-up. Once, when he and Dora were about to make love, Scholem stepped into the bedroom without knocking and began to chatter away about the deficiency of Kantian epistomology. Benjamin was hesitant to interrupt him, but Dora was never shy; holding a sheet around herself, she pushed the astonished scholar from the room, crying, 'Let us fuck in peace, dear Gerhard. We can discuss Kant *after* I've had a good orgasm!'

Kaddish. Benjamin wondered if these ceremonies had any effect on the living or the dead. Yes, he believed in God, most certainly, but he could not visualize a God so personal that one particular fate, among so many, mattered. God was the energy of the universe, and he represented only a small portion of that energy. It would not surprise him if, after his demise, he returned to earth as an animal, perhaps a hedgehog. He would like to be a hedgehog, since hedgehogs were not overly troubled by niceties; they did not, like the jesuitical fox, require a multitude of options. He recalled the famous line from Archilochus: 'The fox knows many things, but the hedgehog knows one big thing.' He guessed that those who knew one big thing were happier in life.

He had himself been a fox, darting among ideas, shape-shifting, trying out this ideology or that dogma. Brecht was a hedgehog, of course; he knew one big thing: that the workers must get control over the means of production. Scholem was another hedgehog: He knew that God was hidden in the world, and that only the best would ever find Him after patient searching through a wilderness of signs. Benjamin, alas, distrusted both of these Big Things, although he understood the truth of both. It made him dizzy just to know he could see so much, so many sides, with options galore. Even here, tonight, he could see many choices.

Life and death were the crude fork in the path before him, but there were countless branches of each, and alternatives to alternatives. He could stumble in the dark, dragging himself back to Banyuls or Port-Vendres, where he could wait in hiding for the war to end. There were Jews in every village along the border, stowed in attics, lofts, cellars, barns; indeed, there was hardly a forest anywhere in southern France that did not contain a clutch of Jews. 'The Jews are everywhere, hanging like fruit from the trees,' his grandmother used to say, citing a Yiddish proverb. The Jews would certainly outlast Hitler.

The Führer was doomed, Benjamin was sure of it. Nothing so inhuman, so lifeless, so essentially dull, could survive for very long. The puzzling thing was how Nazism had managed this well so far.

It doubtless appealed to a certain class of people, mostly the uninformed. For bizarre reasons, it had also attracted a handful of bright people, such as Heidegger, that monster and egomaniac, who perhaps saw Hitler as a projection of his own will to absolute intellectual power. As long as Hitler remained out of reach, in Berlin or perched on some distant yodeling hilltop in Austria, he was unthreatening. One could almost imagine him letting Heidegger, the presumed heir of Nietzsche, run the University of Freiburg in his own way.

But this was implausible. Heidegger had taken over as Rector at Freiburg in April 1933 only because the Nazis would not let the gentle Professor von Möllendorf, a Social Democrat, assume that position. To his credit, Heidegger resigned the following February, having refused to capitulate to Nazi mandates on every point. (They had insisted, for instance, that he fire two deans, including von Möllendorf.) This moment of grace notwithstanding, Heidegger had made some horrific speeches during his tenure in that post, once declaring it the 'supreme privilege' of the academic community to serve the national will. He had practically wept at the revival of the German *Volk*, which had 'won back the truth of its will-to-be.' Hitler himself represented, to him, 'the triumph of hard clarity over rootless and impotent thinking.' Heidegger had gone so far as to publish, in the *Freiburger Studenten Zeitung*, the following sentence: 'The

Führer himself is the only present embodiment and future embodiment of German action and its law.'

This article had been sent to Benjamin in Paris by a friend in the philosophy department at Freiburg, who scribbled in the margins: 'Was this man not the lover of your cousin, Hannah Arendt?' It was true, and impossible. The world was topsy-turvy. Poor Hannah, he thought. She did not have her wits about her when it came to men.

Hannah had last been seen in Paris, before the invasion, and he did not know if she was alive or dead. She was but one of thousands of intellectuals whom the Nazi machine had mangled in its iron teeth. 'And the fools crush what they will not, cannot know,' Goethe had written, and it seemed truer now than ever.

Benjamin had been defeated as an intellectual force in the world, but he had no fear of death as such. Death was simply one more among so many mysteries. As a child, he had once questioned his mother about death, and she – in her inimitable way – explained to him calmly that upon dying, a magic carpet would take him to Jerusalem, where all Jews would eventually gather at the feet of the Messiah. That was the sort of thing Sabbatai Zevi would have preached in the seventeenth century. Or Nathan of Gaza, his rapt disciple, who did even more than Zevi to spread all manner of fantastic teachings, many of which still lingered in certain quarters in asinine, watered-down versions.

Despite his antiliteralism, Benjamin believed in heaven. It was not a *place*, which is to say it was neither up nor down, neither here nor there. It was a dimension, and transported to this dimension he, Walter Benjamin, would find himself the master of his own experience for the first time. What had made this earthly life for him such an imperfect paradise was a feeling of fraudulence that secretly governed every performance of every text he had written.

He had once turned this ambivalence to his advantage in a story, his only good story: '*Rastelli erzählt*.' In that tale, he conjured a conjurer: the fabulous Rastelli, a famous juggler whose genius lay in his unbelievable ability to manipulate a single ball. Whoever saw Rastelli perform came away with the impression that his ball was a living creature. It would leap into the air at the juggler's slightest command, electric, independent of gravity. It could loop and spin, dip and veer. One moment it whirled on Rastelli's scalp, and the next it popped from his vest pocket.

But Rastelli did not practice an honest form of sorcery. His secret was that the mystifying ball contained a minuscule dwarf who controlled its motion though a network of invisible strings.

In Benjamin's story, the juggler is invited to perform before a famously cruel and temperamental sultan. Should the performance fail, Rastelli would be instantly beheaded or shackled forever to a damp wall in some dark chamber below the earth. He is at his best, however, on the night of this command performance; the ball, it seems, has never been more responsive, rising and falling, springing to life so uncannily that the sultan is stunned into admiration and gratitude.

As Rastelli leaves the theater, an urgent note from his dwarf is pressed into his hand. 'Dear Master,' it says, 'You will please forgive me. I am ill today and cannot possibly assist you in your performance before the sultan.' In this way Rastelli is himself deceived in the midst of his own deception; he becomes, unwittingly, authentic for the first time.

The moon was high now, eerily bright though not quite full, orange-colored, pillaring through a scrim of clouds; it seemed, absurdly, to be eavesdropping on Benjamin's thoughts, and he stepped into the shadow of a tall pine. This kind of audience he did not need.

Standing with his back to the tree, he pressed the rough bark to his spine; he was hiding from the moonlight, much as God in the tradition of Kabbalah withdrew from the world. It was Isaac Luria, writing in the sixteenth century, who characterized God's self-exile, *tzimtzum*, so vividly. To make room for the expanding universe, God had hidden himself, sending holy light into the world to buoy it up. The world, alas, could not bear so much glory; it shattered, and the cornerstones of the world – in the shape of vessels – shattered, too. Evil now permeated the world, having found a point of entry.

The expansion of the universe had given evil the space it required to live and grow, and it was everywhere now, spoiling what was once good. To humankind was left the agonizing yet essential work of restitution, *Tikkun olam*, the repair of the world.

Benjamin spoke the lovely phrase aloud: '*Tikkun olam*.' He drew himself up, feeling a surge of defiance. Having struggled to get here, within sight of the summit, he must not give in, slip back, die. He must repair the world.

Listing slightly to one side, like a drunk, Benjamin crossed the clearing. His feet seemed to weigh a hundred pounds each as he dragged them through the wiry grass. The moonlight flooded the valley below, giving it an otherworldly tinge, and it sparkled on the sea, dazzling to behold. The wind, less intense than before and somewhat softer, was fragrant, smelling of pine and salt; it felt cool but not bitter on his cheeks.

Suddenly, a voice startled him. Instinctively, he fell to the ground, digging his face into the coarse grass. Not fifty yards away a small patrol passed, chatting freely among themselves. Benjamin listened tensely, hoping they would not see him. His heart seemed to throb loudly in his chest, like a kettledrum. There was no hiding on this bright night, but the path was well below him, and they would have to crane their necks to see where he lay.

They spoke in French, not German, and this was reassuring. They were probably just local boys pressed into service by the border police. For so many of the younger men in service, the war was fun, a boy's adventure; they would look back on these years later in life with nostalgia, with a vague but unmistakable sense that something important and interesting had once happened to them and was gone. The sad truth was there was no war at all; there were thousands of little wars, in thousands of different places. One could not comprehend such diversity.

When several of the guards broke into loud laughter, Benjamin could not resist lifting his head. They were shockingly close, the moonlight glinting off their helmets and bayonets. Benjamin watched as they filed into the distance, disappearing around a bend in the path, their voices gradually diminishing. He waited for half an hour before lifting himself to his feet to confirm that they were gone.

Afraid that another patrol might be near, he bent low as he walked toward the stable. If they caught him, he would surely be sent to a holding camp, then transported by cattle car to Germany, where he would die. He did not doubt that he would die there; his heart was weak, and he lacked the will to survive in appalling circumstances. Even Georg, his willful brother, was probably dead by now; at least that was his sister-in-law's opinion.

Benjamin entered the stable and stood for a long time, waiting for his eyes to adjust to the dark. At last, he could see a pile of straw in the corner, its sulfurous silver gleam. He did not care if it was moldy or filled with rats and merds, and he burrowed under it; the straw formed a blanket of sorts, and within ten minutes he felt much warmer. What he missed was a glass of brandy, its prickly heat at the back of his throat, the aftertaste of sweetness. But there was, of course, nothing to drink here, and he must not think about it. One of the few things he learned in exile was that you must not dwell on what you do not have.

At least he had a few cigarettes. For comfort and warmth, he lit one, letting the smoke stay in his mouth, in his throat, in his nasal passages; he filled his head with smoke and let his mind float. It surprised him that he felt no need to exhale; he was, perhaps, closer to death than he realized. Death as stillness at the center, a divine breathlessness, suspension of desire.

He had wanted so much in his life, a good deal of it unobtainable: coveted editions of favorite writers, oil paintings, exotic toys, objets d'art. And women. He often found it pleasant to think about women before he fell asleep; the force of eros was such that it took one's mind off everything else. Self-consciously, he let his mind drift to Asja, then to Jula Cohn. An erotic dream would be lovely at this moment, the perfect escape.

The fire of his love for Jula had dimmed, but the coals might still be fanned by fantasy. He had met her for the first time in 1912, in

Berlin. She was a puppy then, full-breasted though still in her teens. Her silky black hair was cut short, daringly so; when she brushed it back, it gave her a boyish look that Benjamin found irresistible. The puffiness around her eyes was merely part of her adolescent charm, as was her moodiness. But mostly, he adored her gaze, its way of attaching itself firmly to his own. She did not have to utter a word to communicate desire.

Benjamin met her secretly many times in obscure cafés, and they would talk into the morning hours, sometimes holding hands beneath a small table. Once, in an isolated section of a park near the river, they kissed deeply; it was a smoky dusk, with a mist floating above the water, swirling around them like a stage set from Wagner. Geese paddled by, snorting, honking, sometimes whirling in rings overhead. Passively, Jula opened her lips for him, letting him dig into her mouth with his tongue, his watery affection drooling into her throat. Another time, nearby, in a grove of copper beeches (he could still see their trunks rising, the bark smooth as steel), she had touched him where no woman had dared to touch him before, unbuttoning his trousers with delicate, moist fingers.

He tried to conjure that time again. It was midsummer, and they had taken a picnic into the park; as the sun dropped behind the high trees, she had casually, unexpectedly, reached for him. He had fallen, weak-kneed as a calf, to the ground, and she sat on top of him, taking the full length of him into her hands. He came too quickly, much to his embarrassment, but she said, 'It is all right, my little Walter. This is natural. It is really quite nice, in fact.'

Not long after this incident in the park, Jula left Berlin with her father (her mother was dead); they moved to Heidelberg, where Benjamin visited her on several occasions, even after his marriage to Dora in 1917.

It had been so awkward: loving Jula, living with Dora. The birth of Stefan only made things worse, tying him to the marriage in a most insidious way. But he continued to dream about Jula, to write and visit her. The distance between them, and the physical and moral obstacles to their union, only inflamed him. He often pondered the question of love. Why was it so difficult for him to love what was accessible? He thought of Dante, who merely glimpsed Beatrice on a bridge one afternoon in Florence, yet this image was enough to fuel a life's work. The beloved is perhaps best captured, possessed, in a text, in lines that writhe on the page, that smolder and burn.

Benjamin wished his marriage to Dora had been better. He had made a bad husband, although this had never been his intention. He had wanted to worship her, to make her happy; he had wanted to be a sympathetic father to Stefan, unlike his own father, who had never listened when he spoke. Benjamin always listened well: It was a cardinal trait, and Dora admitted as much. 'You listen, Walter, but you hear things that have not been said,' she used to scold. It was funny at first, then rueful; at last, it was nothing short of tragic. Whenever his wife spoke, he heard other voices; when she looked at him, he averted his gaze. Her hand on his grew colder, day by day.

Why was he such an enigma to himself? Why had self-knowledge of the most rudimentary kind eluded him?

He sank deeper into the loose straw, the musty odor of mulch permeating his clothes. Bat wings flickered above in the rafters, and he did not like bats. Nor was he fond of spiders; he imagined dozens of them around him now, invisible, crawling into his trousers, under his shirt. His back itched terribly, but when he tried to reach under his shirt to scratch, a sharp pain rippled through his right shoulder and he groaned.

I will soon be skull and bones, he thought. Fleshless. Bleached. Empty. But he did not mind. There was, in fact, a little comfort in this notion of emptiness, of cessation. This terrible running would soon be over. Looking up, he saw the moon breaking through tiny cracks in the ceiling, as through a rib cage. This reminded him that the world was his body, and that he would shine beyond the point of fleshlessness; he would shine like the moon, and his horizons would be infinitely broader.

'Dora!' he said aloud. It startled him to hear the name, embodied, floating in the dark. Yet, why was he calling *her* of all people? How could he expect her to help, when he had not helped her in the least, when he had made her life so frantic? He deeply regretted that he had allowed Jula to share their apartment in Berlin. What madness was that? How could he have been so crazy? Dora had begged him to send Jula away. 'What do you want with her?' she cried. 'Do you sleep with her when I'm not here? Is that it? When I go shopping, you seduce her in my own house? I hope the two of you burn in Gehenna!'

Gehenna. Benjamin began to understand the meaning of hell as a concept. Hell was not something reserved for *after* death; it was part of life itself, some inversion of life. He had burned in Gehenna throughout those months in Berlin when Jula slept in the room beside his, so close he could often hear her breathing through the wall. He often made love with Dora while imagining it was Jula throbbing beneath him, wrapping her long, smooth legs around him, pressing her breasts tightly against his chest. Once, at orgasm, he had actually cried her name, and Dora, startled, rose from the bed, put on her nightgown, and went into the sitting room, where she warmed her hands by the embers of the fire. Benjamin, as if temporarily seized by wisdom, did not try to console her. He could say nothing. It would have been offensive to her if he had tried. For some things, there is no excuse.

Day after day, he had tried to negotiate the impossible. How to live with two women was the issue – the mad, irresolvable issue. Benjamin had studied the matter in the mirroring, mediating shield of Perseus held to his eyes by Goethe in his overwhelming novel *Elective Affinities*. Benjamin's first triumph as a critic had been his essay on that novel, which meant so much because he saw in that painful, perfect text the uncanny reflection of his own contradictory life. Goethe's characters – Eduard, Ottilie, and Charlotte – reeled before him now. Goethe had understood that love is never fully consummated in this earthly incarnation; it requires translation unto death. Benjamin had written in this essay: 'Death, like love, has the power to make us naked.' In sexual congress, one is divinely naked; in death, too, one enters the divine presence without the guilty pretense of clothes.

He wanted nothing more than to lie in a crypt beside Jula or Asja. Or both! Were they not, in a strange way, the same woman? Or was he so contemptuous of the other sex that he considered them all mere manifestations of the Eternal Female? This Jungian nonsense irritated him as he thought about it. Indeed, he had frequently inveighed, in his letters to Adorno, about 'bourgeois psychologizing,' believing Jung even worse than Freud in this regard. At least Freud did not wrap himself in a cloak of facile mysticism.

Benjamin had in fact loved many women, and each he had loved singly, finding some instance of the Divine in every one of them. Each breath, each caress, each point of laughter or tears was unique. But he could not deny that nature – as embodied by the attraction of men to women – had him fully in its febrile grip, and only death could free him. The ideal of married love, as conceived by Goethe, was achievable only through escape – the leap from nature to whatever lies beyond. Perhaps before the face of God, love and marriage were possible. But never here. Life was only missed connections, sleights of affection, approximate words.

The face of Goethe, not God, floated before him as an actual vision. He studied the long, arrogant nose, the massive brow, which was larger on one side than the other, a distortion that drew every eye toward him. He saw the feminine lips that curled in a wry smile, the eyes that coolly observed everything and gave away nothing. What was this attraction to Goethe? This fanatical dependence on the image of genius captured in one man? Was it merely a dream of total competence? Goethe had indeed perfected his life, as Benjamin had not. The master, whose life was founded on concealments, appealed to him in ways he could barely explain.

As a very young man, Benjamin had read the well-known biographies by Gundolf (which he disliked) and Baumgartner, and he had fixed a vision of perfection in life. Having conceived of Goethe in such a fashion, was there nothing left for him but failure? How does one emulate a god?

Benjamin's own poetry had come to nothing but mere fragments, echoes of Goethe, Heine, and Georg. His stories were mostly unrealized, however ingenious. He did not possess the sheer coldness of heart required of a major artist. Even as a critic, he had not yet published an important book. His doctoral thesis at Bern, on Romantic art criticism, had remained deservedly unpublished. His postdoctoral study of the origins of German tragedic drama of the Baroque period was decidedly a botch; indeed, his assessors in Frankfurt (among them the pretentious and dull-witted aesthetician Hans Cornelis) had rejected it, and him, describing the treatise as 'obscurantist, willful, convoluted.' It was no wonder his academic career had skittered to a halt.

Benjamin had tried to write a major exposition of Goethe's life and work for the *New Soviet Encyclopedia*, but that, too, came to nothing: aimless, endless notes, a draft of an essay too rough to seem worth fixing. Even his masterwork on the Parisian arcades had exploded in his hands like a loose pack of cards. The final version, which he clutched to his cheek as a makeshift pillow, would need considerable work. But ultimately, ultimately, it would justify his labors. Here was the sign and signal of his genius.

Even it, however, was finally a book of fragments. His life was composed of fragments, quotations from other, better writers. His days were lived between quotation marks, and the high points of his existence merely italicized and familiar phrases. When he was working on his treatise on German drama, he had gathered more than six hundred quotations, had pinned them to the wall of his room: one index card for each quotation in his tiny hand. A compulsive collector of phrases, bits of poetry, aphorisms, he had lately come to believe the ideal critic was merely a gifted assembler of quotations. 'The great book of the future,' he had written to Adorno, 'will consist of fragments torn from the body of other work; it is a reassembly, a patchwork quilt of meanings already accomplished. The great critic of the future will remain silent, gesturing firmly but himself unable, or unwilling, to speak.'

The face of Jula flashed before him again, replacing Goethe. She was much prettier than Goethe, he thought, laughing softly to himself. 'I love you, Jula,' he whispered, reaching involuntarily toward his trousers. Was it possible that erotic motions could stir in this, the bleakest night of his life? Were sex and death so prone to mingle?

He remembered only too well that terrible stay with Jula on the Côte d'Azur. He was by then a 'free' man, was he not? The marriage to Dora had dissolved, and Jula was traveling with him. On the train, she had put her head affectionately on his shoulder, and he had been pleased when an elderly gentleman looked at them jealously. Jula was his now, he had thought. She had seemed quietly eager for his love for some time, although (despite what Dora had charged) they had never actually had full intercourse. Jula had always withdrawn from his advances at the last moment, whispering, 'Another time.' How many 'other times' were there?

He had come to the Côte d'Azur to pursue this relationship to its natural climax. It was like a ball tossed into the air: One had to hear it, even see it, land. They had taken a room in a boardinghouse by the sea called the Mariposa, a clean, crisp room with a high, vaulted ceiling and white, virginal walls. The room smelled of plaster, and daffodils were bunched in a vase beside their bed – a sign of early spring. The elderly landlady winked at him coyly as she handed him the key to their room, which she knew had only one bed. '*Pour monsieur et madame*,' she said, aware that neither of them boasted a matrimonial ring.

The butterflies in Benjamin's stomach turned to wasps in a glass jar as he watched Jula undress, her back against him as she sat on a low stool before an unframed mirror. The bare room somehow added to her nakedness as she sat, quietly, before the mirror and contemplated her own body: the alabaster skin, the dark pubic hair, the taut, expansive breasts. Her stomach protruded ever so slightly.

Benjamin undressed, his damp clothes pooling on the floor. He crossed the room, utterly naked, erect, his feet cold on the blue ceramic tiles. He pressed himself into the hollow of her spine.

'I cannot make love with you,' she said, flatly.

'I love you, Jula,' he said.

'There's something wrong between us,' she insisted.

'My darling Jula.'

'Forgive me, Walter. I would do this, were it possible. You must believe me.'

He pressed against her harder now, swollen to a point of exquisite pain.

'Please, Walter, don't.' She dangled her black hair before her face like a curtain, and the vertebrae at the back of her neck glistened like an ivory chain. 'I don't want this.'

It was too late, however, for him to stop. He could not control himself.

Jula did not move but let him finish.

Benjamin wiped her back clean with a white towel, saying, 'I'm so sorry, my darling. I am ashamed of myself.'

She was sobbing now, her shoulders shaking.

Benjamin led her gently to the bed. He tucked her into the cool sheets and smoothed her hair on the pillow. Her back was turned to him, but she had stopped sobbing. It was possible, he told himself, that he had broken the ice, and that tomorrow their relations would improve. But he also knew better. Something had always been slightly amiss between himself and Jula. They were like radios tuned to different channels.

It was the same with Asja. Those brief, hideous months when she stayed with him in Berlin under false pretenses still puzzled and enraged him. What was her point? She had let him make love to her, but without reciprocal enthusiasm; it was as if she were fulfilling some grim duty. 'This is not love,' he said to her one time, in the midst of intercourse, 'it is hydraulics.'

She had sat up abruptly in bed. 'It is what you wanted, isn't it?' she said. 'To fuck.'

'Why do you torment me, Asja? I love you,' he had responded.

'You love yourself,' she said.

'Please, dearest. You know that from the first time I saw you – in the little shop in Capri – I have thought about you again and again. I . . . I . . .' The limitations of his expression, so mired in cliché, were agony, and he stuttered toward silence.

Asja raised her eyebrows and lit a cigarette, blowing the smoke into his face. After a while, she said, 'You've been thinking about a lot of things, Walter. Has it ever occurred to you that perhaps you think too much?'

'You are mocking me,' he said, getting out of bed. 'This is not lovemaking. I don't know what to call it.'

Asja sighed. She had left Bernhard Reich back in Moscow, alone and unhappy, for no good reason. To annoy him, perhaps. They had been feuding ever since that dread winter when Benjamin came to stay with them. Reich had, with some justice, considered himself abused by them both, although he blamed Asja for the way she flirted with Benjamin right under his nose. He had seen her, on two or three occasions, put a hand on the poor man's knee. If only he had known the worst: the way she seized him on several occasions and kissed him, voraciously. Once, during their kissing, she had let him reach under her blouse and cup her small breasts in his hands. 'I want to fuck you,' he had said to her. She replied, coyly, 'Not now. Perhaps another time.'

Benjamin could not understand the way she had unexpectedly marched into Berlin that spring and weirdly, even cruelly, offered herself to him like a fillet on a platter. He recalled their first time in bed together, drawing his legs up to his chest now in the musty straw, shivering. She had undressed him first, a peculiarly sexy move, then stood kissing him for a very long time, melting around him. Floor after floor tumbled through the burning house of his body. At last, she pushed him onto the bed and consumed him.

Her lust had been distracting, upsetting. It was not followed by the tenderness he expected; indeed, she dressed quickly and went into the kitchen to make herself a drink. She sat alone by the window of his small room, staring at the rain, which made traceries on the glass. Her cheeks were wet with tears.

Benjamin could not comfort her. 'What is wrong, my Asja?' he asked, stroking her hair.

'It has nothing to do with you, Walter,' she said.

'I wish it had. I could help you.'

'I must return to Moscow.'

'There is nothing for you there. I am here. You must stay with me. We can work out whatever problems you may have. I can help you, if you will let me.'

'I must go,' she said.

He would have let her go willingly, if that would have cured her sadness. But he knew it wouldn't, and she knew it, too. So she stayed, and for two months he lived in complete agony beside the woman he loved more than life itself. The nonsense of this horrified him.

Asja, like a vast foreign city, remained inaccessible yet alluring; he could follow her down labyrinthine ways and hope, foolishly, that satisfaction would occur, that they would meet, embrace, commingle. But without her genuine assent, that sacred commingling could never occur. Even while sharing his bed, she had proved the most difficult text he had ever tried to read, a site of contradictory signs. She demanded his complete attention, like a poem, but she did not reward his attention with a reciprocal gaze. Often, she mocked him, as in Moscow one day when he sat beside her bed in the pale green room of the sanatorium for hours; instead of thanking him, she wondered aloud if he would soon 'be sitting beside some Red general with a fawning gaze.' Then her whip cracked again, more loudly: 'That is, if the general is as stupid as Reich and won't toss you out.'

Reich had stoically put up with Benjamin, aware that Asja was toying with him as a cat would with a helpless mouse before eating it alive. Reich had indeed pitied him, and offered brotherly advice. They were both, after all, fighting the same battle. 'If you were to attend cell meetings in Berlin, you would find many women like Asja, real firebrands,' he said. Benjamin had wondered how Reich could have been so foolish. You cannot substitute, in love, one body for another. He could fall in love with a million other women, but they would not be Asja, just as Asja was not Jula. Nevertheless, it intrigued him that each woman was Woman, too: a piece of the Platonic form.

Leaving Moscow with a battered suitcase on his knees, his eyes wet, his heart contracting painfully, he had decided that erotic love was impossible, at least for him. If he learned one thing in the past few years, it was that he must move beyond the inanity of possession; the lust for women was all part of an outmoded bourgeois desire for property. His desire to own Asja, or Jula, had been retrograde. He would, from this point on, focus on his writing.

For years he hovered between the apparently opposite poles of the aesthetic and the political. He worshiped writers like Goethe and Proust as the embodiment of the aesthetic, then swerved toward the position that Asja occupied: the Party position. Now, in the foothills of the Pyrenees, on this terrifying border, he knew that if he should survive this war, he would argue that only in the convergence of the aesthetic and the political was the art of the future going to find a new life. '*Una vita nuova*,' he muttered aloud, savoring the phrase.

He fell asleep wondering what this art of the future might look like. Somehow, he sensed that reading as he had known it was coming to an end; works of art, too, were doomed by their very reproducibility. How could one put a value on something multiplied into infinity? Then again, one could hardly deny the profound effect of films and photography; the cinematic image held massive sway throughout the Third Reich, for example. Hitler's propagandist, Leni Riefenstahl, had created something completely unreal and yet monstrously effective: The Führer would not be as thoroughly embedded in the public mind without her and her ilk.

Benjamin imagined a future in the West when capital controlled the film industry so thoroughly that every image became a product, with each film itself creating a further line of products. Clothes, furniture, architecture, family constructs, love relations, tastes in art, music, even literature, would be mastered by men like Cecil B. DeMille. Morality would rest with them – the Masters of the Image. Eventually, reality would exist on film or have no credibility; people would work to make enough money to have their lives filmed, and they would be considered successful only if the image they could find on their private monitor matched some elusive archetype. The boundaries between art and life would be obliterated, and the job of the emperor (or prime minister, president, or king) would be to decide which was which, but even he (or she) would be so constructed by cinematic images that nobody would know what to believe; the ontological crises of the future were dazzling to contemplate.

Benjamin opened his eyes with a start, aware that he had been drifting in the no-man's-land between sleep and waking. Disoriented at first, he looked through the window at the cold sky, which had turned slate gray but was tinged with violet. The hushed moments before dawn were a time of day he always treasured. The moon had by now dropped over the far horizon, yet the sun had not begun its rampant charioteering as he groped his way out of the straw pile, desperate to pee.

Standing in the entrance to the stable, he relieved himself on stones that cobbled the entrance; the dark urine hissed and stank, misting the stones. The stars had been thoroughly absorbed by night, digested; a rosy hue was beginning to appear over the mountains, and Benjamin could see the peak that would be his to climb. In the valley below, faintly, he could hear a cock crow.

Feeling groggy, his joints stiff and swollen, hungry and wild with thirst, he limped to a mound behind the stable, dragging his briefcase. The dirt formed a kind of easy chair, with a back of moss; he settled into the seat to watch the sun rise. His mind returned – a tongue to a broken tooth – to Asja Lacis.

He had tried to resign himself in Moscow to life without eros, but this was impossible. He continued to think of Asja almost daily, sometimes removing photographs of her from his wallet and studying them like Rembrandts, trying to conjure her presence, to hear her voice. Mysteriously, he found her in the green eyes of a dozen other women, some of whom he followed through the streets like a pathological lecher. He had paid for the services of dozens of whores, squeezing his eyes tight at the moment of orgasm, inventing Asja over and over. He had missed her so badly. His life, without her, was empty.

And he missed Jula, too, though not so badly. Asja meant more to him. She was brighter, quicker, meaner. She had exacted more from him than anybody else, even his mother, the exhausting Pauline, who had dogged him emotionally for decades. She had never understood his spiritual side, his desire to lift himself above the commercial world of his father. She had supported him, covertly, by sending money, but she had withheld the essential thing: that uncomplicated affection he craved so badly, even today.

In his briefcase, tucked in a pouch behind his manuscript, was a small book of verse by Goethe. He flipped the pages to a favorite poem:

> *Heart, why now this rude insistence?*
> *What is it that makes you grow*
> *so alien inside me, strangely tense?*
> *Heart, I scarcely know you now.*
>
> *Gone are the things I once held dear,*
> *and the pangs that I fear;*
> *gone is your ardor and your rest.*
> *Dear heart, what makes you feel unblessed?*
>
> *It is just the way her youth entrances,*
> *and her form as well, its perfect flower.*
> *And the kindness of her sidelong glances,*
> *each of which displays her power.*
> *When I try to stay, or to withstand*
> *her sweet barrage, I'm helpless. Hand*
> *in hand we go. Her slight command*
> *is more than I can ever stand.*
>
> *She holds me by some silver thread*
> *that's from a magic spindle spun.*
> *I gaze upon her dear, wild head*
> *and know that I am thus undone.*
> *The sorcery is strong that holds me,*

binds me, my desire, molds me.
Where is the man I used to be?
Oh, tyrant love, please set me free!

Once again, serendipity had led him to the perfect text. 'Oh, tyrant love, please set me free!' He found himself weeping as he read.

When he looked up, the whole valley was bathed in a soft, vermilion glow, and Benjamin could see in the distance a scattering of vineyard workers; the wind carried aloft the distant gong of the Church of St Simon, which poised on a hillock overlooking Banyuls. Soon, he thought, the world will blaze with daylight, the sea and sky mirroring the darkest blue, and the vineyards sloping greenly toward the village, flecked with gold. The mountains above him would loom, a wall of purple, jagged, thrilling. And the sun, climbing high at last, would scatter a million spears of light in all directions, and not even death could kill so much glory.

I found myself in a labyrinth of staircases. This labyrinth was open to the sky in places. I climbed up; other stairs led downward. On one landing I realized I was standing on a kind of summit, with a wide view across open country. I noticed that others stood on other peaks. One of these people was suddenly seized by vertigo and began falling. A feeling of light-headedness spread; others toppled from other summits into the depths. Everyone was laughing. When I, too, was overwhelmed by this giddiness, I woke up.

11 LISA FITTKO

The local cocks had long finished crowing by the time Henny Gurland finally tried to wake her son, who kept rolling over and drifting off. I suppose he wanted to return to the dreamworld shattered only a few months ago, when his father was taken away, never to return. In some ways he reminded me of my own brother, Hans, at that age: a beautiful, dreamy boy whose curiosity about the world was self-defining. I wondered if that curiosity could survive the brutal facts he wrestled with now. Certainly he was not ready to face the daylight that lay before him. He wanted to roll back, to plunge into soft dreams, to get away from here.

'He used to wake up so quick and alert,' his mother said. She leaned over him, her prematurely silver hair hanging forward in bangs, and kneaded the muscles of his neck, trying to ease his waking. 'His father used to say José could circle the world in the time it took the rest of us to brush our teeth.'

'His father has just died,' I said.

'José is very strong,' she said, ignoring me. 'When we had to leave Spain, he was so cheerful. You should have seen him, Frau Fittko.'

Henny Gurland puzzled me. She was herself a dignified, highly intelligent, well-educated woman, but she seemed not to recognize that her world had been turned topsy-turvy by the war, and that she was struggling with her own sadness and anger. Under everything she said, I could see a running superscript that read: *I should not be in this situation! I do not deserve it!*

I sat on a small cane chair and studied the map that Mayor Azéma had drawn for us. 'We should try to get away before sunrise,' I said firmly. 'We can't afford to take the risk of—'

'I know, I know!' said Henny. Her cheeks were apple red and wrinkled.

I bit my tongue, reminding myself to remain patient. She couldn't help it that the Nazis wanted to kill her and her son or that her husband was dead. In a better world, she would be letting José sleep till noon in their villa in Bavaria, and he would be fed milk and honey for breakfast.

'Forgive me,' she said. 'Will you have a glass of juice, Frau Fittko?'

I saw that nothing would hurry them, so I accepted.

At five-thirty, half an hour later, we left the Pension Lumise in a powdery pink light. The pastel houses, with their jagged rooflines, were still tightly shuttered for the night; they stumbled on their knees up the hillside, led by a trail of pencil-thin cypress trees. The narrow streets of the village were empty, but one could hear a child's voice calling for its mother, and the ancient cackle of geese and chickens in backyards.

We followed a cobbled road beside an iron railing, then cut across open pastureland toward the path that rose into the foothills. The bulk of vineyard workers had already left Banyuls, but there were plenty of stragglers for us to hide among – dozens of hulking ghosts in thick sweaters, carrying buckets. Nobody spoke, keeping to the habit of all early-morning voyagers en route to work. I had noticed this habit on the early-morning trams in Paris and Berlin – men and women filled with a deep nostalgia for the dreams they have left behind and, like José Gurland, hesitant to plunge into the daylight world.

I carried a rucksack filled with provisions and a canteen with fresh water: Old Benjamin would certainly be thirsty and hungry. He was not the sort of man who would miss his daily feed with good humor. Men of his class and generation were notoriously insistent upon regularity in meals, merely assuming that food would somehow be produced by the hands of women and brought to their tables, hot and tasty.

I had tried my best to get Benjamin to return with us to Banyuls, but he believed passionately that his feet possessed only so many steps per day and that he had already used up his quota in getting to that first plateau. I only hoped his quota wouldn't run out before I delivered him over the mountains. He assured me he would spend the night in a stable and be fit as a bull to charge over the Pyrenees this morning, and I decided not to argue with him. What was the point? Here was a man who suffered racking chest pains when he walked more than ten or fifteen minutes without stopping. 'There is a tiny man in my chest,' he said, 'who keeps squeezing my heart. A cute little fellow. He works my lungs like a bellows. I would banish him, but he's good company.'

I never knew how to take remarks like this; there was something vaguely mad about Benjamin, something impossibly childlike. And for all his commitment to reason, he could be quite unreasonable. Should I have suggested he turn back, he would have simply laughed and marched ahead, with or without me. I had no doubt about this.

Before beginning the day's climb, I spoke frankly to the Gurlands. 'We were a little cavalier yesterday, and we got lucky. Let's take no chances today. On the path itself, you must not speak. Voices carry in the country. Walk steadily, slowly, and silently. Avoid eye contact with anyone you pass.'

I was mildly alarmed that José carried a knife in his belt, and my first impulse was to ask him to abandon it; then again, why spoil his fun? His boyhood was not one to remember with pleasure in later years. If he felt like a bit of swashbuckling today, what harm was there?

We picked our way among chunky stones, with linden trees at either side, some already gold with autumn; broad slopes of marram grass dropped all the way to the sea. It was too bad we'd lingered in the boardinghouse; the sky was brightening quickly along the east rim of the horizon, and the high crooked outline of the mountains loomed. It seemed impossible that we would cross them today.

Less than a few miles from the village we found a sentry posted in the path. He leaned against a large rock, his head tilting forward on his chest, though he seemed awake. A rifle lay across his lap.

'Don't look at him,' I whispered to the Gurlands, who walked behind me.

He never even acknowledged us as we passed, which was just fine with me; he stared dumbly at the ground in front of him as if he could not believe his bad luck in being posted here, in the middle of nowhere, at this hour. Poor boy, I thought. He was hardly a year or two older than José.

The path grew steeper, and in one spot we had to climb with our hands as well as our feet, looping our soles in damp, black roots that stuck through the red clay. Because it had rained steadily for three days the week before, one had to avoid the wettest places.

Old Benjamin had taken a good hour to ascend this particular patch the day before, so I knew it would take longer to cross the Pyrenees than Mayor Azéma predicted. 'Ah, you'll be there before dinner,' he had said, blithely. 'Give or take thirty minutes.' I wanted to add, 'Give or take Old Benjamin.'

The three of us made good time, but as we approached the clearing where Benjamin supposedly waited, I began to fret. What if he had wandered off, then lost himself in the woods? What if the border police had discovered him already? Would he have told them about us? My fantasies ran wild, and I half expected to find the stable full of laughing Nazis, with Benjamin swinging from the rafters. 'Lisa, you always imagine the worst,' my husband, Hans, often said. 'Which is not necessarily a bad thing, because anything you can think of will never happen. That's the way it works. So always try to envision the most hideous possibilities . . . as a way of eliminating them.'

I began to long for Hans and wonder where he could be. If he'd made it to Tangiers, he would probably cool his heels till I arrived. That was our last plan. I would go from Portugal to Tangiers, an easy crossing, and we would go together to Cuba or New York on a freighter. 'I'll be staying at the Hotel Larouche,' he said. How did he know the name of every hotel in the world? Why did he trust me to get to these exotic places by myself? Was he testing me? From the beginning, I'd sensed his pride in my independence, and this forced me to live up to his expectations. Now I must not allow myself to feel weak inside or become afraid that the world could not be managed. This was no time for second thoughts or self-consciousness. The thing was to get the job done. These people had put themselves into my hands, and I must not fail them.

The sun warmed my face, with a few pink clouds moving swiftly across the sky. The slopes in the distance were studded with boulders, but the field beside the ruined stable was deep in grass. I took in slow, meditative breaths and looked back at the valley, the sea, the windy, reeling sky, while José ran ahead to fetch Old Benjamin. There was a catch in his long stride, as if something were holding him back.

He entered the stable and reappeared. 'He's not here!' he shouted.

Henny and I ran to see for ourselves.

'How could he do this to us?' she said, her voice pinched. 'He knew we were coming for him.'

'He's probably nearby,' I said. 'I don't think he'd just walk away.'

'Why did you let him sleep here?' she complained. 'He's inept at this sort of thing.'

'There will be an explanation.'

'Why don't you give it to us, then?' José said, like a little brat. 'You seem to have all the answers.'

'Please be respectful to Frau Fittko,' said his mother. 'She is trying to help us.'

'She's always helpful, isn't she?'

Henny Gurland turned apologetic eyes toward me, but I brushed aside the look. I was not about to let this boy upset me. There was work to be done.

Sure enough, we found Benjamin asleep nearby with a book of poetry on his chest. He might have been dozing on a sandy beach somewhere, with a glass of wine on a table beside him, the waves lapping at his feet. Our voices and footsteps did not wake him. Dark, wiry hair seemed to have grown on his hands overnight.

José squatted and shook him gently, breathing close to his face.

His fingers played across Old Benjamin's chest. Seeing the patch of milky skin exposed above José's socks, I thought of a boy I'd known in Germany, a boy whom I had once kissed by a bridge. It's funny how you suddenly remember these things.

'Ah, you have come for me, dear boy!' said Benjamin, opening one eye first, then the other. 'It is good to see you again!'

José shook his platinum hair into place.

'I see you've found yourself a pleasant spot,' I said. 'Is there any chance that you might come with us?'

'Indeed,' he said. 'A little walk into Spain might do me some good.'

We smiled, but he looked terribly unwell.

'Something has happened to your eyes,' Henny Gurland said, referring to the huge dark spots, reddish-purple in color, circling his eyes.

He took off his glasses and, with a handkerchief, wiped them off. 'The dew, you see. The color rubs off on my face.'

Perhaps it was merely a stain, but I remembered seeing rings like that around my father's eyes in the month before his death. My father also had the sallow skin, like old parchment, and the chest pains and tingling hands. He died just after taking me ice skating on the river near our house, and the strain may have hastened his death – at least that's what my mother always said. 'What did you do that for, Lisa, take an old man skating like that?' I can still hear her voice.

'Have you anything to drink, Frau Fittko? I'm afraid my thirst is prodigious.'

Prodigious? I handed him my canteen, and he drank in huge gulps.

'Please, no more!' I warned. 'It will make you sick.' I was also conscious of having to conserve; we had barely enough water for the three of us today. I broke off a crust of bread for him and cut a piece of cheese with my army knife. 'Eat something. You must have been cold last night. It was freezing in Banyuls.'

'In fact, it was quite lovely in the stable. I should have been a farm animal, you see. I love to sleep in loose straw.'

'You're more adaptable than I imagined,' I said. His formality put a stiffness into my own speech.

'I would make a good soldier,' he said, 'if only my heart were stronger.'

Henny Gurland looked at him sternly from under the silver helmet of her hair. 'Are you absolutely sure about this trek, Walter? It may be wiser for us to return to Banyuls. The route along the coast is bound to open again. This isn't the only way out of France, you know.'

'The situation for Jews is getting worse,' I said. 'I can't really recommend we go back.'

'Are you Jewish?' José asked.

'Yes, I am,' I said. 'But not Hans, my husband.'

'He's a Leftist,' said Benjamin. 'That's worse than a Jew.'

'So what does that make me?' I asked.

'A Jewish Leftist,' he said, 'like my brother, Georg . . . if he's alive.'

'I still think we should reconsider,' said Henny. 'That is, if Dr Benjamin is—'

'We will cross the Pyrenees,' Benjamin cut in loudly. 'You must not worry about me, Frau Gurland. I'm much more durable than I look.'

'Enough conversation,' I said, holding up my hands. I had never imagined that a group of refugees could be so unconscious of the danger they were in. They constantly made me feel as if I were interrupting their afternoon tea.

The path ahead ran parallel to a more accessible and widely known route that traced a ridgeline and was actually tucked beneath the ridge in critical places, making it fairly safe from the border police. Elsewhere, the two parallel routes almost met, so one had to be utterly silent. Mayor Azéma had marked the dangerous spots on the map with large blue Xs.

Benjamin walked swiftly at first but was soon forced to stop for a rest. He squatted to the ground, leaning his back against a rock. His breathing was coarse and erratic. 'If I stop every ten or fifteen minutes, I'll be able to maintain the pace,' he said apologetically. 'I find I must stop before the pain begins. I waited too long just now.'

I asked to take his pulse.

He said, 'Fast or slow, what does it matter? We must get to Spain.'

'Spain is a rotten place,' said José. 'I used to live there.'

Frau Gurland sighed. 'Please, dear. You don't mean that.'

'How do you know what I mean, Mother?'

'You should think about what you're going to say before you speak.'

'Father used to say that about you,' he said.

I decided to keep out of this. These were not, thank goodness, my relatives.

Finally Old Benjamin said, 'I think I am ready now.'

'Let me carry your briefcase for a while,' I said. I could hardly fathom his motives in lugging the old briefcase. He was like a child with his favorite blanket or stuffed animal.

'You will forgive an old man his tedious obsession. It's all I have, you see. I prefer to carry it myself.'

'It's lighter than a case of wine,' José said, 'but not as much fun.'

Dr Benjamin smiled. 'A sense of humor in dire circumstances is always a good thing to possess, José.' It amazed me how the boy never seemed to rankle him.

In a short while, we passed through a wood composed mainly of cypress trees, several of them uprooted, with black mud dripping from the clumps. They made me think of human corpses, the bare branches splayed on the bank, their fingers clutching at air. I shivered. Old Benjamin was a bad influence. Normally I never allowed myself such peculiar thoughts.

It was with some relief that we started along the main trunk of the Lister, which rose through vineyards thickened by the blue-black, swollen Banyuls grapes, just about ripe for picking. There were deep channels where storms had washed down from above, and the ground was still wet, with branching rivulets in places. The tiny streams sputtered and seeped.

Benjamin picked a handful of grapes and tested them. 'They are so sweet!' he said. 'The sugar will give me strength.'

On the edge of the vineyard, we gathered for a late breakfast in the bright sun. Young Gurland sat beside Benjamin, the sun on their backs, while he lit a cigarette. Benjamin made me smile; crooked and pale in his rumpled suit, still panting from our journey, he nevertheless preserved both his dignity and a buoyancy of spirit. José slouched beside him, his posture echoing Benjamin's stoop, but his biscuity brown skin and shining hair proclaimed youth and good health. In another time they might have seemed a funny pair – Weary Adolescence sitting next to Old Before His Time – except that in José I sensed a genuine despair beneath the rude veneer. I saw that he never sniped at Old Benjamin the way he did at his mother. Perhaps some inner code of honor prevented his attacking the nearly dead.

Henny Gurland and I went to pick some grapes. We tore off silver-coated clusters at the edge of the vineyard and dropped them into Henny's bag.

'I hope you will excuse my son,' said Henny, breaking our pleasant silence.

I shrugged. 'He's young. Anyway, it doesn't matter.'

'Young is nothing. I can tell you, he was never like this before.'

'He's like my brother,' I said. 'He used to cross swords with my mother. It went on for years.'

'But this is unlike José. There was never a boy more hopeful. He enjoyed his schoolwork, was always building things with Arkady. They talked every night about machines. And they took walks together and learned about the trees, the animals – I can't do that, you see. I don't know about anything that interests him.'

Of course she was right that the problem was not José's youth. He was not 'young' but angry, which, given the circumstances, was an honest response. Henny Gurland wanted me to say, 'José will be all right.' Maybe he would be, who knows? If so, he was one of the fortunate ones.

When we joined the others, Benjamin was telling José not to worry about the Spanish police. 'They are a different breed,' he was saying. 'They are not anti-Semitic.'

'Franco is a bully,' Henny Gurland muttered.

'He doesn't control everyone in Spain,' I said.

'Believe me, the Spanish are worse than the French,' Frau Gurland continued. 'They hate foreigners, and they make no bones about it. The French, as you know, at least pretend to admire foreigners.'

'They hated us,' said José. 'The teachers especially. They told me not to speak in class because of my accent. The bitches were afraid I would corrupt the ears of the other children.'

Old Benjamin spoke loudly: 'They are too proud, the French, but I have always adored them. Paris, you know, was the capital of the nineteenth century. In this century, of course, New York is the capital.'

'But you are a Berliner,' I said. 'Berliners are the most sophisticated people in the world.'

'There are no Berliners,' he said. 'You are thinking of the Jews in Berlin, or the Russians. The Russians are well-educated and tolerant. The White Russians, that is. There is more Russian literature than German literature coming out of Berlin. It is a great pity, you know. Moscow should have been the capital of the twentieth century.'

It seemed that afternoon tea-chat had resumed. 'Have you been to Moscow, Dr Benjamin?' I asked.

He seemed to blush when I said this. 'I visited there once, yes. An intolerable place, I'm afraid. The Bolsheviks have ruined everything, including their own revolution.'

'You are not a Marxist, I gather.'

'I am nothing.'

'You are a writer,' Henny Gurland said, 'a famous critic.'

'There is no such thing as a famous critic,' he replied. 'I am a critic, yes. Rather, I *was* a critic. Now I am, well – a Jew in flight.'

Toward noon, we arrived at a plateau with startling views of the Pyrenees, range after range in darkening shades of blue. The precipitous drop behind us plunged toward the valley, with villages along the French border clustering among the vineyards and dry stubble-fields.

A falcon hung in the wind above us, with a steady eye.

'Don't worry,' I said to Benjamin, who studied the bird rather anxiously. 'It's not a vulture.'

'Any carrion will do in a pinch,' he said. 'You see why the ancient Greeks placed such a high premium on burial. One does not want to be picked apart by birds.'

'The Indians in Mexico want that to happen,' said José. 'The old men climb a hill and expose themselves to the elements. They let the birds dismember their bodies. I wouldn't mind that.'

'I hope they're dead when the birds begin,' I said.

'Very dead,' José said.

'Where did you hear about that, José?' his mother asked.

'Father told me.' He said it as if to imply, *How else would I know anything?*

Old Benjamin said, 'I used to be very keen on Aztec culture when I was a boy.'

'The Aztec priests used to kill a thousand people a week,' said José. 'They used knives with stone blades to dig out the hearts, and then they offered them to Huitzilopochtli. That was their sun god.'

'They were trying to keep the world from coming to an end,' said Benjamin. 'They believed their god required this terrible sacrifice.'

'They were crazy,' said Henny Gurland.

'They were no more misguided than many other cultures,' Old Benjamin maintained.

Everyone sat in silence as I broke off bits of the bread I had purchased two days before with counterfeit food stamps. I smeared the bread with a soft cheese Mayor Azéma had given me, and passed it around. Each of us had one small tomato as well.

'May I serve myself, Frau Fittko?' asked Benjamin.

I nodded. His courtliness was so profoundly out of step with the times.

'We have a long way to go, don't we?' he asked.

'You will be in Spain today,' I said, 'if we press on.'

'If we're not caught by the Nazis, you mean,' José said.

'It is a good day for climbing, José,' Benjamin said. 'And we are lucky to have one another for company, wouldn't you say?'

José merely grunted. He obviously did not feel lucky to have our company. 'It's going to rain,' he said. 'I can smell it.'

'The wind is strong,' I said, 'and it may just keep the clouds from covering us.'

'Climbers in the Alps are often trapped by snowstorms, even in late spring,' he said.

'He is so encouraging,' said his mother.

This prompted in Old Benjamin a long reminiscence of a walking tour he'd taken in Switzerland some decades before with a woman who later became his fiancée. He told us some hilarious story about how he had accidentally got himself engaged to this woman he barely knew.

José, who had been listening to Old Benjamin with rapt attention, wondered, 'But you did marry someone?'

'Yes, and that was a mistake, too.'

José smiled wryly, and Benjamin explained that his former wife and son were now safely in London, and that he hoped to see them again after the war. 'The boy is about your age,' he said to José.

The sky was growing darker by the second. 'We must move on now,' I said.

We would have to climb through steep, rough terrain in the next hour or so. The map showed a sharp turn ahead along a ridge, with a sheer drop on one side; to make things worse, the main route ran perilously close to the Lister at just this point, so absolute silence must be maintained.

On subsequent trips, when I knew this route by heart, I could slip across the Pyrenees in half a day. But this was my first time, and I was coaxing along a very sick man. Sometimes Old Benjamin had to climb on all fours, digging his absurdly inappropriate shoes into the sides of the mountain, the tail of his jacket flapping.

'How are the blisters?' I asked.

'They've burst,' he said. 'My stockings are soaked, but my feet are more comfortable now. Not a bad trade-off.'

We'd been climbing again for about twenty minutes when it began to hail: white pellets thrashing the side of the mountain, popping in the path and melting, making the way slippery. I watched Benjamin duck forward, as if trying to avoid the pelting, teetering on the brink of the path.

'Be careful,' I whispered, just as Benjamin lost his footing. His feet pawed at the ground before he fell into the mud. José and I rushed to help him.

'I quite like the mud,' Benjamin said.

'We will rest for a few minutes,' I said, 'until the hail stops.'

We pressed together beneath an overhanging ledge, and Benjamin began to chatter. At the slightest provocation, vast histories would spill from his lips. Now he said, 'When I was a boy, my parents sent me to a country boarding school called Haubinda, in Thüringen – a lovely place. There was a meadow behind the school, and in April it was always mud, mud, mud. The masters were strict but sensible. They understood that a boy and a puddle are two halves of some Platonic whole.'

I pointed to the ledge above us. 'If the map is accurate, the route passes just overhead. Please be quiet now.'

Benjamin looked at me gravely. We sat for about ten minutes until the hailing was over, and the sun came out so intensely I had to shield my eyes.

We continued through a grassy stretch where the bleached bones of some large animal, probably a goat, lay strewn in the path. The eye-holes in the skull stared out, horrendous. I feared Old Benjamin would launch into a soliloquy about poor Yorick, but he restrained himself.

When the path curved toward the cliffside again, voices sounded above us. We flattened our backs against the wall and waited. Fifteen minutes passed. Then Benjamin stooped to his briefcase, and my heart quickened. Was he feeling faint? Was he going to get us caught by rooting for his medicine? To my astonishment, Benjamin, unfazed, slipped a book of Goethe's poems from his briefcase. He leaned back against the limestone to read until the voices passed, fifteen minutes later; at one point, his lips moved silently. José watched him with fascination. He had doubtless never encountered anyone like Old Benjamin before.

We now hiked in single file, clinging to the side of the cliff. According to the map, one circled this convex wall of limestone for perhaps half an hour, then ascended through relatively easy terrain before making a final sharp ascent to the summit. I let Benjamin go first, with Henny Gurland and her son behind me. It seemed only right for him to set the pace, given the circumstances, though I planned to switch into the lead when we got safely through this particular stretch. We kept perhaps ten or twenty paces between us.

The accident happened in garish color. Benjamin suddenly began to lose his footing and veer away from the cliff. I watched in horror as he began to teeter toward the precipice, sway on the lip of the cavern, regain his balance, then waver again. Instinctively I lurched toward him, but I was too late. I was just in time to watch him skid down the steep cliffside, rolling and turning, upright part of the way, grabbing with his free hand for roots and branches.

He dropped about thirty yards and landed hard on a lower ledge, hitting a pine shrub that stopped him from pitching into the ravine. Had he missed that shrub, he'd still be falling now.

I didn't dare call down to him, but I waved, and he – after a dreadful minute – lifted a hand in response.

'I'm going down,' I said.

José followed me.

Frau Gurland did not want her son to help, but she had no choice. I could not possibly rescue Benjamin without his assistance. We picked our way down the slope. Once, I caught my foot on a root and stumbled, skittering off the path. Only another root, which I caught in my hand, saved me from toppling à la Benjamin to the ledge below. José was a mountain goat, surefooted, taking my hand and pulling me back into the gully.

It took half an hour to reach Old Benjamin, who lay on his back, clutching his briefcase, staring at the sky. I could see a gash near one temple and blood dribbling to his jawbone. His jacket was torn, but he seemed otherwise undamaged.

'Dr Benjamin, I presume,' I said.

A rueful smile dawned. 'Thank you so much for risking your lives on my behalf,' he said. I guessed that he had spent the last twenty minutes or so thinking up that sentence. 'But I must tell you at once that there is no point in trying to help me. I cannot go on.'

'That's nonsense,' I said.

'It's simply the truth. You see, my leg is badly damaged,' he said, reaching for his left knee.

'Is it broken?'

He groaned, his face contorted by the pain.

'Let me see it.' I felt his knee carefully, where he said it hurt. There did not seem to be a break. 'It's probably a ligament,' I said. 'Let's see if you can stand.'

'There is no point,' he said. 'As you well know, I have a weak heart. My life is behind me. But you must take the manuscript, my book . . . It is much more important than I. Do you understand?' He saw that I did not understand. No manuscript could possibly be worth a human life. 'I have friends in New York – you must send it on . . .' His breath seemed to run out, and he lay back exhausted.

'I'll carry the book,' José said.

'Yes, we'll take the book,' I said, 'but we're taking you, too.' There was no time to argue, with the sky darkening overhead and the light waning. We had to reach the summit within two hours for them to have a chance of crossing the border by nightfall.

Benjamin allowed us to raise him to his feet. 'Ach!' he cried, not quite vertical on wobbly knees. 'I'm afraid it's no use. My left knee . . .'

I felt around the knee again, to make sure no bones were sticking out. 'Can you put any weight on it?'

'No.'

'Please try, Dr Benjamin!' I looked up toward the path, and Henny Gurland waved. I tried vainly to see if there were border guards on the cliffs above her.

Gradually, Benjamin let some weight settle onto his bad knee. He took one or two steps, then more.

'That's good!' I said. 'It's not broken or you couldn't possibly walk. You've probably twisted it.'

Old Benjamin squeezed his face into something that resembled a smile. 'You are a remarkable woman, Frau Fittko,' he said, pulling a handkerchief from his jacket to wipe his brow, now covered with mud and sweat. He had scratched his left ear, and there was still some blood dripping onto his collar.

Suddenly, a flash on the high cliff caught my eye. A bayonet? A soldier's helmet?

'Anyone can see us here,' I said.

José and I shouldered Benjamin along the gully with extreme caution; to slip and tumble now, the three of us, into the abyss, would be too awful. At first, he leaned hard on us, but before long he was able to shift more weight onto the bad knee, which suggested to me that it could not have been hurt as badly as he imagined.

It took the better part of an hour to push, lift, and drag our reluctant cargo up the rain-soaked gully. By the time we reached the path, his knee had recovered much of its former stability. Though he walked from this point on with a limp and needed help on the roughest slopes, he was able to continue, stopping for a short breather whenever his chest tightened. As we approached the summit, his concentration became steadily more fiendish, his eyes plowing ahead, his breathing slow, methodical, calculated.

After what felt like an interminable climb along a bank thickened with ferns, we arrived at a small plateau – an island of high red pines with no underbrush. The trunks were mauve-colored, straight up and down, with the feathery branches interlocking overhead to cast a shadow on the ground.

Benjamin insisted that we sit for a moment. 'I like it here so very much,' he said. 'One almost expects Druids to come rushing through these trees!' His lips had turned a faint purple. I did not think it was to watch for Druids that he had stopped.

'The last ascent is just ahead,' I said. 'We could have a bite to eat here, I suppose.'

'I'm hungry,' said José.

Henny Gurland said, 'Remember, José, that you are only one person among four.'

'He is perfectly right to be hungry,' Old Benjamin said.

'Nobody asked you, for God's sake,' Henny said. 'Mind your business, for once.'

'I am sorry, but José is still growing. His body will be crying out for nourishment.'

'It's all right, Mother,' José said, going toward her.

'Stay away from me,' she said, turning her back.

'We're almost there, Henny,' I said.

José settled back onto his haunches.

'Yes, we'll be free in Spain before dark,' said Benjamin. 'It will be worth every dreadful step!'

I was relieved that this latest firestorm had passed so quickly, and I handed around the last crusts of bread and a bit of chocolate. There was one small, bruised tomato, which I gave to José. Only Henny Gurland refused to take any food.

'I don't know why food tastes so good when it is scarce,' said Old Benjamin. 'I used to notice this in the Alps, on walking tours. We would take a little cheese and bread, and it tasted so wonderful.'

It felt oddly safe in this wood, even cozy, especially when a stiff rain drew its curtain across the sky. Even Henny began to thaw, nibbling on a crust of bread.

'It's not going to last,' I said, pointing to the sunlight in the distance behind us. 'Just a sun shower.' I lay back on the pine floor, resting my head on my rucksack, enjoying the soft spray that moistened my face.

Unexpectedly, Benjamin began to sing an old Jewish song, or mumbled more than sang it. I had heard this song as a child, and now it sounded through the rain with a forgotten strength, a forgotten understanding and tenderness. It evoked the horror of what we were all fleeing from and gave a new life to something that had perished long ago. His chanting absorbed the tension in the air around us and created a shelter where we could rest and gather strength. Soon Henny Gurland's lips began to move with his.

The rain, as I predicted, swept over the crest of the mountain and left a wake of brilliant late-afternoon light that glazed the elephant-colored rocks. Benjamin stopped singing. The air smelled fresh and clean and free.

We began our last ascent. The ridge was slippery and steep, and there was loose gravel everywhere amid clumps of jack pine. 'One step at a time,' I said to the old man, who pulled with both hands on shrubs where that was possible. I stayed close to him. If he fell off the path here, it was all over. The drop was sheer, with no convenient ledges to catch a fall. Indeed, several times small boulders were dislodged by one or another of us, and we would all pause to watch and listen as they dropped loose strings of debris into the vast ravine.

Benjamin did not ask for a rest during the last quarter hour or so of our ascent. He was in a rage of some kind, hurling himself toward the top, his fists clenched, his chin jutting forward as if in defiance of gravity itself and the protestations of his ailing body.

We reached the summit in surprisingly good shape, and Benjamin collapsed to his knees. He put his forehead on the ground and spread his arms forward to balance.

'You made it, Dr Benjamin,' I said. I pointed to a cluster of houses not five miles in the distance – a toylike village. 'That's Port-Bou.'

Port-Bou overlooked the sea, with its twilight crimson burn. The Vermilion Coast of Catalonia glittered, dark cliffs, shoaling up the water. By now, a pink sword of light jabbed through clouds on the western horizon, as if the God of Abraham and Moses were signaling His approval. I looked for a rainbow, but none was visible.

'It's so *pretty*,' said Henny Gurland.

'Too bad such a beautiful country is full of fascists,' said José.

'Your father loved Spain,' said his mother. Her cheeks were glistening.

I should have let them continue on their own from here, but somehow I did not want to let go. I decided to take them down another mile, to a point where the mountain path gave way to an actual road.

We stopped to rest at one point beside a fetid pool where the water, with its froth of green foam, gave off a larval odor.

'I'm very thirsty,' Benjamin said. 'You will please excuse me while I drink.'

My canteen was dry, so I could not help him, but the prospect of his drinking this water appalled me. 'You'll be in Port-Bou within the hour,' I said. 'There will be plenty of fresh water there.'

'I must drink,' he said. 'There is no choice.'

I found myself getting angry. 'Dr Benjamin, please. We have come all this way together. You must act sensibly. This slop is dangerous. Do you want to get typhoid?'

'I'm afraid I cannot do otherwise, *gnädige Frau*,' he said. 'I apologize.' He crawled on all fours toward the pool and cupped several handfuls into his mouth, gagging and swallowing. Henny Gurland and her son turned away.

When he returned, I told them I must turn back. As it was, I would be hiking a good deal of the way by moonlight.

'We must thank you, Frau Fittko,' Old Benjamin said, taking my hands in his. I let him kiss me on both cheeks.

I did not want their thanks. I was not doing this only for them. It was also for my uncles, my aunts, my cousins, and so many friends in the Nazi camps. This was a small gesture of defiance, a way to lash out against something too awful and inhuman to imagine.

WALTER BENJAMIN

'If a man possesses character,' says Nietzsche, 'he will have the same experience over and over again.' Whether or not this may be the case on a grand scale, on a smaller one it seems obviously true. There are paths that lead us repeatedly into the hands of people who serve the same function for us, over and over: passageways that always, in the most diverse periods of life, direct us to the friend, the betrayer, the beloved, the pupil, or the master.

12

Benjamin was almost afraid to look back. He had looked back too many times in his life already and had turned to salt on more than one occasion. With Dora, his wife, he had made an inefficient, unkind practice of reunion; years after they had decided between themselves to end the relationship, he had insisted on seeing her, and she had often acquiesced. It was perhaps difficult to say no to a man who meant no harm, who seemed always on the point of reforming himself and making amends for past failures as a husband or father.

Now he recalled a time in Paris, with Dora. It was mid-May of 1927, and the pear trees along the river blossomed, making the air fragrant, sensuous. The affairs with Jula and Asja, and miscellaneous other adventures of the heart, had come between him and his wife; quite properly, she was fed up with him. They had been living apart for several years, and yet there they were now, at his invitation, in Paris, drinking glasses of Pernod at La Coupole on Montparnasse like any respectable bourgeois couple.

He rarely drank alcohol in quantity, but the anxiety caused by seeing Dora drew him toward the bottle, and he teetered on the brink of inebriation. 'This café,' he said portentously, 'is the center of the center.' Indeed, the restaurant overflowed with famous artists and infamous artists manqués, with motley bohemians from all parts of the globe, with poets and poetasters, philosophers and pseudophilosophers, magicians and mountebanks.

'The French are so very peculiar,' said Dora.

'I doubt more than half of the people here are French,' he told her. 'Look around you: Czechs, Poles, Americans, Spaniards.'

'And Germans,' she said.

Benjamin lifted his eyebrows. 'Our friend Scholem would say that we are Jews.'

'We are Germans,' she insisted. 'Germany has many religions.'

Benjamin simply agreed with her. The subject of Jews and Germany had ceased to interest him. He considered himself a voluntary exile, at home among these odd, artistic types, listening and talking, drowsing over an inexpensive glass of something while scribbling in his notebook, an eye cocked to the crowd. He had heard some astonishing conversations, and many of them had found their way into his journals, verbatim. He called them 'found poetry.'

He spent a delicious week with Dora, courting her as if for the first time. The idea that he might return to her, that their marriage might blaze forth again, remained a tantalizing, hope-engendering possibility. He was not, as his sister maintained, 'using Dora.' Indeed, Dora had been through this with him before, so it was not his fault that she was seduced. At least this is what he told himself in the uncountable hours after midnight, when, like a mysterious visitor in a black cape, Conscience called.

As he and Dora whispered over cognac into the early-morning hours about religion, politics, literature, and philosophy, Benjamin remembered why he had married her in the first place; he even forgot (temporarily) why their coupling had come undone. One night, after sitting under starry skies for hours on a bench overlooking the Seine from the Île St-Louis, they returned to his shabby room in the Hôtel du Midi, on the nondescript avenue du Parc Montsouris, and made love as if for the first time.

As they lay naked beside each other in their damp, scented sheets, their postcoital conversation became an isolate of their marriage, reminding them both that what they had just been doing was a bad idea from the start.

'Do you love me, Walter?' she had asked in a small voice, afraid.

'Yes,' he said. 'I have always loved you. You should know that.'

'How can you say such a thing, when you sleep with other women all the time?'

'That is an overstatement. In any case, I must answer honestly to my feelings.'

'What about *my* feelings? Do they matter to you?'

'I regret the pain I have caused you, Dora.'

'And our son!'

'Our son, yes. I feel particularly bad about Stefan. He does not deserve me for a father.'

'You are a good father when you choose to be. Or you were.'

'I am unreliable.'

'That's right.'

'And irresolute.'

'Completely.'

'And I do not know how to improve upon things.'

'This is frustrating. The whole subject is frustrating.'

'Why did you marry me, Dora?'

'Your good looks, perhaps? I doubt it . . .'

'You mustn't tease me. Tell me the truth.'

'I married you because you say all the right things.'

'At the wrong time?'

'Of course.'

'But you know I love you.'

'That is just a sentence you appear to enjoy saying. It tastes good in your mouth.'

'You have just had sex with me.'

'I have certain animal needs, and so do you.'

'Do other men satisfy these needs when I'm not with you?'

'This is not your business, Walter.'

'I suppose not, but I'm curious.'

'You have a wonderful imagination. Use it.'

'I wish you wouldn't adopt such an attitude . . .'

'You want me to build you up, is that it? To make you feel masculine?'

'I cannot respond when you talk like this.'

'You are a shit, Walter.'

'I know.'

'You are poison for women.'

'Do you think so?'

'I know so.'

'Will you come to see me another time, Dora? If I ask politely?'

'Probably.'

'I am glad to hear this. I don't want to lose you.'

'You are mad, darling.'

'Is the world any saner?'

'Not this world.'

'But I love this world.'

'I know you do.'

'And I hate this world.'

'I know, I know. I know every goddamn thing about you.'

'What will become of us, Dora?'

'We will die.'

'And then?'

'We must wait for that,' she said, 'and grow patient.'

That particular conversation echoed in his head, and he smiled to himself. It was obvious now that his incessant looking back was itself a big problem: with Dora and Jula, with Asja, with the dozen or so other women he had loved. But how could one not turn around, reconsider? Wasn't he naturally drawn to History, which keeps piling up behind us, wrecked and unruly, demanding our backward glance or reappraisal? Wasn't History – this amalgam of stories and sighs, lumps and hunches – always threatening to reinvade the present and to become the future?

He sighed, recalling that he had looked back with nostalgia so many times on his youth in Wilhelminian Germany, on his father's darkly paneled study on Koch Street in Berlin. That house came back to him, too: room after room filled with sumptuous pictures and Persian rugs. He remembered the day, in 1904, when his family got their first telephone, in those days a status symbol of huge magnitude. And he thought of those velvet summer nights in the

Old Western Quarter of Berlin, near the Landwehr Canal, where he gathered with friends in the tremulous, sepia-tinted hours before the Great War began, and they would debate aesthetic and moral questions until the last of them was drained of wakefulness and intellectual energy. He could even recall with humor his first fiancée, the blimplike Grete Radt. What a disaster!

The tragedy of Fritz Heinle, whose suicide had prevented him from becoming the great German poet of his generation, also returned, and the pain was only a little less now. That single death had changed everything, especially his attitude toward the war. Nothing could ever be the same after Heinle was gone. He had killed himself but had taken the youth of a dozen people with him; the corpses, like stains on the floor, lay there and would not fade.

Mostly, he remembered the elusive, impossible genius of Gerhard Scholem, whose big ears and quivering eyes loomed in Benjamin's dream life. That summer of 1918, in Switzerland, had been so pristine, so perfect; afterward, they had tried without success to reinvent that golden time, to rekindle the fires of absolute intellectual kinship by pumping the bellows of their correspondence. But there was always something missing, something a little sad and unsaid.

This past decade in France had been hard, so any nostalgia put there would be misplaced. Benjamin wanted the future now, a world redeemed by moral victory, by a new dialectic. He would perhaps return to Paris one day, after a spell in Manhattan, resuming those long afternoons at the Café Dôme, at La Coupole, at the Lipp. He would watch for the fourth or fifth time every film starring Adolphe Menjou – Menjou the Marvelous. He would visit the Grand Guignol and attempt the impossible – to read everything Simenon published as fast as he actually wrote it. He would also repair his stamp collection, his toy collection, his library of old books and autographs. Everything would be different, but nothing would change. That would be bliss.

His arcades book would appear after the war, too, transforming the way history is written. People would say, 'Are you *the* Walter Benjamin?' and he would look askance at them for putting forward such an embarrassing question, bored by their inquiry and (slightly) irritated by their blunt intrusion. 'Walter Benjamin?' he would say, raising a thick, dark eyebrow. 'Who is Walter Benjamin?'

A sharp voice pierced the veil of his reverie. 'Dr Benjamin, are you all right?'

It was José Gurland, the man who provided a crutch, as needed, for his descent into Spain.

'Yes, I'm well, José. Thank you for asking.'

José was a fine, if troubled, boy. The fact that he sulked, and chafed, was not important. Who wouldn't in his shoes? Benjamin did not himself find Frau Gurland easy. She had married Arkady Gurland, a socialist who had worked in Spain as an administrator for the Republicans during the Civil War. He was gone, dead at the hands of the Nazis, and now his wife and son were in flight. Getting them over the border became a kind of private mission for him, and it pleased him that he had apparently succeeded – if only they could make it through Spanish customs.

Thank goodness for Lisa Fittko. He could still hear the voice of Hans: 'Lisa will take care of you.' After the war, he must somehow contrive to meet them both, to thank them.

The plan, as formulated by Lisa, was for Benjamin and the Gurlands to spend the night at the only hotel in Port-Bou, the Fonda Franca. Mayor Azéma had mentioned it, saying, 'Beware the woman who runs the hotel. She is unreliable.' He did not suggest in what way she was unreliable, but his expression spoke volumes.

Benjamin limped beside José, who carried the briefcase, as Frau Gurland led the way over stony ground, through runnels gouged by the sudden rains. Nearing the bottom slopes, they had to push through a field of waist-high coppery grass toward the trunk road into Port-Bou. In the midst of it, Benjamin stopped, and his legs would not move. He bent his chin upward, amazed by the ultra-marine blue dome, with fragments of peachy cloud-spume pinned high in the corners of the sky. He took long, slow breaths.

'We must keep the pace,' Frau Gurland said, frowning. 'The sun will be gone in an hour or so. If we're too late, the border police will suspect us.'

'They will suspect us in any case,' Benjamin said. 'It is their duty.'

Her countenance did not unfrown. 'You must not argue with everything I say, it is tedious.'

Her abrupt manner, bordering on discourtesy, was inexcusable in these circumstances. If his legs were capable of moving quickly, he would do it.

'You shouldn't talk to him that way,' said José.

'I've had enough of your impertinence for one day,' she said. 'If your father were here . . .'

'I am quite all right,' Benjamin interrupted, trying to hurl water on these sudden flames. 'We must push on, you're quite right about that, Frau Gurland.' His conciliatory tone seemed to give vent to her wrath.

The paved road into Port-Bou glistened wetly just beyond the grassy field, and Benjamin was relieved to feel it underfoot at last. From here on, the going would be easy. He did not even worry about customs, having heard that the border police in Spain were notoriously lax. In any case, most travelers in time of war had bogus papers.

José walked close to Benjamin. 'Were you a teacher, Dr Benjamin?' he asked.

'I am a writer,' he said. 'I write critical essays, you could say.'

'They pay you for this?'

'Sometimes.' He suppressed a laugh. It still appalled him that so much effort had yielded so little money.

'Don't plague him with questions,' Henny Gurland said to José. 'It's not a good idea to talk anyway. Remember that somebody could hear you.'

'We're miles from town, Mother,' said José.

'The questions are wonderful,' Benjamin said to him. 'But your mother has a good point. We should not arouse undue suspicion.'

Benjamin looked at José closely. He liked the blond hair cut across his forehead in a straight line, platinum with streaks of darker blond, and the sharp, straight nose. There was an almost invisible fuzz on his upper lip, and his skin had a biscuity brown color. After a day's hard climbing, he exuded a sharp but almost poignant odor. His unselfconsciousness only added to his beauty.

They walked briskly now, aware that the end of their exhausting day was in view. A quick breeze, tangy with salt, rolled off the sea, refreshing them. It rattled the high weeds on either side of the road. A large bird crossed the sky and flew straight into the sun, dissolving on contact.

'Did you see that amazing bird?' asked Benjamin.

'It's a tern,' said the boy. He explained that his father had once given him a catalog of European birds. On weekends, they had made frequent excursions into the French countryside to look for examples.

'So what do you hope to be one day, José? When you are a grown man?' he asked. The stilted nature of his question bothered him, but he could think of no other way to address the boy. The same difficulty beset him whenever he tried to talk to Stefan. There was perhaps an inevitable distance between a father and a son, as if both understood the impossible ontological difficulty of their situation. As a father, how does one address one's double, one's successor, one's executioner? As a son, how does one begin to comprehend the vast, stupid ongoingness of life itself, and the unique manner devised by nature for replicating itself? Who is this creature who made me and would presume therefore to know me?

'I'm going to be a scientist,' José declared, 'or an engineer.'

'He is a bright boy,' Frau Gurland said, 'with the highest marks in his mathematical exams at the lycée. Tell him about your exams, José.'

The boy blanched at his mother's request, and Benjamin covered for him. 'I was always weak in mathematics,' he said. 'I still am.'

'How is the knee?' Frau Gurland asked. 'You seem to be limping rather badly again.'

'It's perfectly awful, if you must know. I hope you don't mind if I complain?'

'Somebody has to do it,' said Henny Gurland, with a slight smile.

Thirst, hunger, and the prospect of a clean bed now drew them forward, even though they ached inside. Within half an hour, the path turned into a pink-pebbled road, and suddenly Port-Bou glistened like a mirage in the middle distance, a single church spire rising above the red-tiled roofs of houses. The sea wrestled with itself beneath the cliffs, its blood-bright sheen coloring the horizon.

'I smell the sea,' said José.

'Me, too,' said Benjamin, thinking how he loved the sea, even though it suddenly reminded him of a glorious but sad summer on Ibiza in 1933; until then, he had entertained hopes of returning to Berlin, the only place in the world where he was not a foreigner. But Gretel Karplus, his childhood friend, had urged him to stay away from Germany. 'It is no place for Jews,' she had written. 'You must certainly wait until Hitler is gone.'

Exile did not seem awful in those days. He had lived amply enough in an unfinished brick house near the beach. His friend Jean Selz lived nearby, and the idea was that they would work together on French translations of Benjamin's work. Another friend who was still in Berlin managed to sell his autograph collection for enough money to pay for his rent and food, and Benjamin discovered that by submitting articles and reviews to German newspapers under a pseudonym, he could eke out a living.

During his second week on Ibiza he met an elusive young woman from Nancy on the beach one afternoon, and she flirted with him shamelessly. She was a dancer, and they spent long days beside the water on the hot, clean sand. Her tanned legs glistened with sweat as they lay, side by side, under a white sky. Their fingers would crawl toward each other like spiders, meet, and tangle. Sometimes she would run her palm along his arms, thrilling him, or – maddeningly – touch his thigh. Once or twice, her salty lips grazed his. Evening after evening, in the succulent orange grove behind his house, he begged her to come into his bedroom; but she resisted. She was a Catholic, she said, raised in a convent. She would say this while sitting on his lap, toying with his earlobes, rubbing her hand along his thighs. He was paralyzed by desire, breathless, groaning. One day she disappeared without notice, leaving no address. And Benjamin could not even recall her name now, only her salty lips, her opal-escent knees.

Port-Bou arrived in small doses, the usual huddle of mud and stone houses, its streets a tangle of dirt or cobbled alleys. A few dusty palms turned lazily in the sea breezes, and runted junipers grew in random clusters. There was none of the neatness of most French villages. Indeed, it surprised him how untidy the landscape seemed as he stepped to avoid a yellow bit of unripe orange peel in the road.

A small, black-eyed boy in billowy trousers leading a goat was the first human being they encountered, though he showed no interest in them. He did not even turn his head in their direction. Minutes later, a leather-jacketed man on a motorbike passed, yet he, too, did not acknowledge the strangers.

'Remember what Frau Fittko said,' Henny Gurland whispered, 'the less said, the better. Pretend you are out for a leisurely stroll – just taking in the air.'

Benjamin agreed that it was best to speak to no one and maintain an aura of leisure – a welcome idea, since his feet were badly blistered, and every step was agony; his injured knee had swollen so badly that he could bend it only slightly; shooting pains spread like a grass fire along his femur, and his left hip felt tight, as if rusted in place. In his head a hot wire threaded from temple to temple, and he noticed a lump at the back of his skull where he must have hit a rock when he fell off the path a few hours before. His breathing was shallow, raspy, and difficult. A line from Goethe sounded in his ear: 'And I arrived, an old man in a strange city, wearing my suit of pain.'

They entered Port-Bou from the south, stopping at a checkpoint. The brick shed with instructions in Spanish and French on the door was deserted, although a few cats prowled the narrow streets like visitors from another world, wide-eyed and wary. Pigeons settled on the clay rooftops, cooing and billing. One could hear conversations in loud Catalan voices behind closed doors.

'We should wait here for the customs officer,' said Benjamin. 'He is probably having his dinner.'

Henny Gurland shook her head. 'We've been lucky again,

Walter,' she said. 'There's nobody here, so too bad for them. Let's just find our hotel.'

Benjamin could not believe it when they stepped, even glided, past the barrier.

An elderly woman in a black shawl appeared, shouting in Catalan. With her dark eyes and sharp nose, she seemed to Benjamin like a human bat, swishing around their heads with her wings outspread. Frau Gurland stared at her, and she withdrew into a dark doorway and watched, suspiciously, as they passed.

Benjamin felt an unfamiliar shudder in his stomach, and his heart began to thump and stutter. He turned pale and stopped, bending at the waist, exhaling slowly through clenched teeth.

'Are you all right, Dr Benjamin?' asked Henny Gurland.

'Quite,' he said, drawing a long, slow breath. 'I will perhaps need a moment to compose myself.'

'Have you got the map?'

Benjamin nodded, and eventually withdrew from his briefcase the mayor's crude likeness in pencil of the town of Port-Bou, with an X marking the Fonda Franca.

They followed these instructions carefully, threading the labyrinth of small streets, empty now because everyone in town was having dinner. Their voices, muffled but loud, and the clatter of dishes mingled with the smell of garlic, fried fish, and onions.

'You will soon have your dinner, José,' Benjamin said, jolly in spite of his physical distress.

It surprised all of them that, within ten minutes, they stood at the gates of their hotel, the Fonda Franca – a pale pink villa on a cliff-side overlooking the sea. It stood by itself at the end of a road lined with cypress trees. Well-kept gardens surrounded the main building.

The garden entranced Benjamin, and his eye went to a stone bench beside a mimosa.

'You stay here, Dr Benjamin,' said Henny Gurland. 'I will register for all of us.'

'That would be lovely,' said Benjamin. 'I'll come in soon. I would like to rest here for a few minutes.' He limped toward the bench and sat down while Frau Gurland and her son went inside.

The smell of the sea was strong, wafting up from below the nearby cliffs, and it brought Ibiza to mind again. Indeed, Benjamin found that he could not get his mind off Ibiza, or the young woman from Nancy, the lovely Catholic dancer. What was her name? Bella? Bernice? Belinda?

'Beatrice!' he said, aloud. The name seemed to echo in the garden.

He rose, on painful feet, and wandered to the edge of the garden, to where it dropped off steeply to the sea, a massive inky shadow welling up from below. The surf shattered against black rocks, and for a second, Benjamin thought of hurling himself over, into the blue-black water; it would not be a bad way to die. It surprised him that, somehow, he was ready to die now. Having made it to Spain, with the prospect of many years in America or Portugal ahead of him, he felt a certain weariness. His book, after all, was done, or nearly done. But he still had so many unfinished projects, including the book on Baudelaire, the one on Brecht, and the other about the effects of film on writing. Ideas for books and articles seemed to line up daily, like children in a poorhouse, undernourished, eager for attention.

'Are you sleeping?'

He turned to see José, who smiled sheepishly.

'Is everything all right, at the hotel?'

'It's OK.'

'As long as the beds are clean and we can have hot baths, I'll be happy.'

'My mother is lying down,' José said. 'Her head is aching.'

'Ah,' Benjamin said. 'I can understand this.' José sat beside Benjamin, who put his hand on the boy's wrist.

The mimosa rustled, and the breeze was cool.

After a long pause, José said, 'Sometimes I miss my father.'

'I'm sure you do. He must have been a lovely person.'

José nodded and began to cry. At first it was just a whimper, distant, stirred in a faraway depth, but soon enough the tears flowed freely, and the boy sobbed. His bony shoulders shook, and his lips trembled.

Benjamin pulled José close to him, his hand at the back of his warm neck. 'The world is a dark place,' he said. 'It is always in disrepair. But we – you and I, José – we have a little chance, an opportunity. If we try very, very hard, we can imagine goodness. We can think of ways to repair the damage, piece by piece.'

WALTER BENJAMIN

The power of a path through the mountains is different when one is strolling along it than when flying over in a plane. Similarly, the power of a text is different when it is read from when it is copied out by hand. The passenger in a plane observes only how the path pushes through the landscape, unfolding in accordance with the laws of the terrain. Only he who trudges the path on foot comes to understand the power it commands, and how, what for the flier is just unfurled terrain, for the walker calls forth distances, belvederes, clearings, prospects at each of its turns like a commander deploying soldiers at the front.

13 MADAME RUIZ

It is quite impossible, the way these vagabonds take my hospitality for granted. Day after day they troop through my hotel, assuming I owe them a holiday; that I, the mere proprietress of the Fonda Franca, was born to serve them. The situation has grown worse lately, although the police assure me that sooner or later they will put an end to this. Sergeant Consuelo stopped by recently to say he was coming to grips with the 'refugee situation,' as he calls it, although I am less than convinced of his sincerity. (His breath was heavy with alcohol, and he kept forgetting my name.)

The rudeness of these people is miraculous to behold. I try to tell myself that they do not know any better. It is all a matter of breeding. They don't know – or care – that my father was a member of the city council in Nice or that he was trained in law and accountancy at the University of Paris. I can still see him, the dear man, in his navy pinstriped waistcoat (unbuttoned), his collar staves (undone), his stocking feet propped on a velvet ottoman while he read the newspaper or the novels of Anatole France. There are few men around these days of my father's caliber. The new men have no sense of civic pride, and duty means nothing to them. They sneer and scoff. It is not their fault, perhaps, given the general state of our culture. But whose fault is it? The blame must lie somewhere.

We had a large, sunny flat on the avenue Victor Hugo, with two bedrooms for servants. Huge plane trees shaded the building in summer, and one could buy warm chestnuts from a nearby vendor as the leaves turned yellow and swirled in small clouds along the curbside. My sisters and I wore dresses from Paris – almost all of them from Chanteque, where my mother had an account; we ate chocolates from Switzerland and learned how to play the viola and to dance. On two occasions we spent extended holidays with a distant relative in Besançon. The citadel in that jewel of a city stays with me, its image of impregnability.

My father's fortunes dwindled in the late twenties, which was sad. Once I tried to get him to explain what was wrong, and he said, 'Little girls know nothing of finance.' He had no gift for politics, I'm afraid, which is a bad thing for a politician. Nice was rife in those days with the worst sort of maneuvering and backbiting, and there were deceptive types in all branches of government. Someone accused my father of embezzling money, and he was put on trial. One of his so-called friends said the worst things about him, but the case was ultimately dismissed. It was groundless, of course. But my father never recovered from the shame (the local newspapers carried the story on the front page). Even worse, his investments on the Bourse were shortly thereafter sucked into a vortex by the collapse of the world economy; indeed, they were utterly worthless by 1930.

Mother could not weather the vicissitudes of life, and she died of a broken heart in 1933, but not before she and Father were forced to abandon the apartment where they had spent their married life together. They exchanged it for something infinitely smaller and less substantial, in a district where I as a young child had been forbidden to play. It was too frightful and humiliating. My lessons in art and music ground to a halt. All the goodness seemed to disappear from my life.

I met my husband, Claudio Ruiz, in a hotel in Nice. I had become desk manager at the Clarion, a pleasant hotel right on the water, and he was staying there on holiday. Like my father, he was a man of some distinction and education. He joined the Civil Guards during the war in Spain, when we were living in Barcelona, and soon rose to the rank of captain. General Franco himself once pinned a ribbon to his chest in Madrid, he was that heroic. But heroes have a way of dying young. Claudio was killed by a stray sniper bullet while crossing a square in Lérida, in Catalonia. If what they told me is true, he was assassinated by the POUM or some such group. I could never keep all the factions straight in that war, nor could Claudio. What he really preferred was a strong monarchy. Kings and queens, nobility and a tradition of honor. 'You cannot have an ordered world without kings and queens,' he used to say. 'Anarchy does not exist in the natural world. Look around you. Do you see the ants scattering a million different ways? Do the lakes try to rise above the mountains?'

My life became more difficult after Claudio's death. Our daughter, Suzanne, was an infant, and I had to fight with his family to get my inheritance. It was quite humiliating. There is nothing worse than a family squabble over money. Two years ago, as part of the settlement, I was offered the Fonda Franca by Claudio's great-aunt, an eighty-year-old crone who had obviously grown tired of Port-Bou. I saw here my opportunity and seized it. While not a lavish place, the Fonda Franca has its charms.

The thought of returning to Nice occurred, but I take some comfort in the distance that exists between my family and myself. My sisters, who have never seen the Fonda Franca, are apparently fond of bragging that I own a grand hotel on the Spanish Riviera. The Spanish Riviera!

If I were to speak objectively, I would call Port-Bou a dump. Its meager clutch of houses offers nothing in the way of social life. There is no gracious living, no supportive community of like-minded people. I quite enjoy the mayor, Señor López, who is radiantly senile, but the village physician, Dr Ortega, grumbles about everything. Our priest, Father Murillo, is rumored to have a degree in philosophy from the university in Salamanca – an ancient and respectable institution – but one would never guess it from his conversation. He plays cards all day in the Café Moka, drinking *vino con gas* and making rude jokes about women. One hears terrible stories about him, but they are probably not true, or not completely true. (I dislike going to confession, nevertheless. One can smell the wine on his breath in the dark little cubicle, and one does not trust his penances.)

There is an elderly English duchess who lives in a spacious white villa just along the coast, though she never deigns to associate with people of the village. In her mind, we are all peasants, the hoi polloi, even savages. (You know what the English are like!) She has a shiny black Hispano and a Maltese chauffeur. General Franco will, I suspect, take care of her in good time. The English are not welcome here.

I am glad to say that life has not been devoid of color. My classmate and dear friend, Valerie Frunot, once had an apartment overlooking the old harbor in Antibes, and I spent many weekends there in summer as a young girl. It was lovely to see the yachts, with their crisp white sails skittering along the horizon. Valerie was later sent to a lycée in Paris, where she met and married an international banker. For reasons I cannot fathom, she does not respond to my occasional letters. I suspect she was troubled by my father's declining fortunes. Bad luck rubs off.

It goes without saying that I have dined in many well-known restaurants in Paris, including Chez Lumiet and the St-Jacques. My mother's second cousin by marriage, Madame Felice de Cluny, once lived on the place des Vosges in a house with a frontal view of the King's Pavilion – not far from where Victor Hugo himself used to live. She was driven into poverty, as it were, by a sudden change in her husband's fortunes and is now living with her sister-in-law in Rouen. How the mighty have fallen!

Suzanne is seven now, with dark Spanish eyes like her father's. Her chestnut-colored hair droops in ringlets over her collar, rather fetchingly. She is a wonderful girl, but it has not been easy to raise a child in this meager village; there is no one for her to play with, nowhere for her to go. I sometimes worry about her future, but that will have to wait.

When our material conditions improve, and the war is over, I will take her to Paris for a proper season. I must introduce her to her great-uncle, Dr Maurice Berlot, who has a lucrative medical practice on the rue St-Denis. (His wife, I must confess, has never been welcoming. I tried to visit them once, several years ago, but she complained of headaches and refused to let me stay with them. It was excruciating, especially since I had Claudio with me. I had to invent the most appalling stories to protect Claudio from Madame Berlot's utter failure of courtesy.)

Suzanne attends the local school, but she does not like it. The teacher, Señor Rodriguez, seems to lack the power to inspire his pupils. Though he has been teaching here for thirty-five years, he was never properly certified. 'Señor Rodriguez is foolish,' Suzanne has told me. 'His hands are always shaking, and he smells bad. The other children are hooligans.' I quite agree with her about the other children, but what is one to do?

I feel quite lucky to be in Spain, since France is crumbling: Revolutionaries clog the streets, and riffraff wander the back roads. A former schoolmate of mine who lives in Tours wrote to me only last week to say there is no end of trouble. 'The trains are full of Gypsies and Jews,' she says. 'No one is safe anymore.' You pay more for a loaf of bread today than you paid for a decent loin of beef in my childhood.

The world appears to hate the Germans, but they only want to restore order. Hitler and the National Socialists have tried to encourage in the citizens of Poland, Belgium, and France a sense of civic responsibility, which is always a good thing. General Franco holds many of the same goals for Spain, and one sees the improvements (although they occur slowly in a backward country such as this one). The streets of Madrid sparkle for the first time in decades, the train service is reliable and inexpensive, and most of the anarchists have been put in graveyards or jails, where they belong. The general has campaigned against drunkenness, and it has largely worked; at least one no longer stumbles over bodies on the sidewalks of the capital! A new spirit of vigilance is alive in Spain, and it will soon waken in France and elsewhere. It may even come to Port-Bou in time.

I do not like Hitler himself, not as a man. From what they say, he is a megalomaniac. This absurd goose-stepping of his troops is surely a bad sign: Pomp is one thing, preening another. In the newsreels, one sees a glint of insanity in the man's eyes, and his little mustache twitches when he speaks. I am told that his accent is atrocious. But sometimes one has to endure a rude display of egotism, and petty vanities, in a politician, especially when times are bad. Hitler has surely done a lot of good for the Germans, and they seem to appreciate his efforts.

One day (if all goes well) I will sell the Fonda Franca and move back to the Riviera. It would be pleasant to end my days in a small hotel by the sea: a whitewashed cosmos, with gilded mirrors and nut-brown parquet floors. I'd fling open the tall wooden shutters of my bedroom each morning in summer to address the water, the bluest of skies, the orange sun. Flowers would droop and dangle from dozens of clay pots lined up like soldiers along the ivy-clad walls of my garden, and I would drink café au lait with a ruined Russian princess all morning on the terrace until it was too hot to stay outside a moment longer. For relief, I might swim in the sea or retreat to my library, where books and pictures would delight me throughout the afternoon. Later, after a deep siesta, I'd dine with a handful of distinguished guests, who would invite me to their houses in Paris, in Milano, in Munich. 'I'm afraid I don't have time,' I'd be forced to say. 'I almost never leave the coast anymore. But you are so kind to ask.'

The Fonda Franca sits in the oldest garden in the village, on a limestone cliff, with sea views that rival those of Amalfi, where Claudio and I spent our honeymoon at the Hotel Luna. (The *padrone* told us that Richard Wagner lived in this hotel some years before and wrote *Parsifal* there. It is so peculiar how little details like this will stick in one's brain like a fly in toffee.) As in Amalfi, the air is scented with lavender and thyme, and there are clusters of lemon and olive trees mixing with tall cypresses. The local wines are surprisingly good, especially the whites, which are dry and fragrant. I try to keep a small cellar well stocked, but it is not easy – everything is so expensive.

I occasionally play *Parsifal* on the gramophone these days. The music reminds me of a world elsewhere, a larger and grander place, where dignity and aspiration are respected, even revered, and where the mysterious elements of life are simply taken for granted. There is so little else to bank on, to lure one into the future.

I pity my poor Suzanne. She will inherit an indecent and impoverished world, unless some drastic cleansing occurs; this war may well provide such a cleansing, yet somehow I doubt it. The Great War did nothing of the kind.

The Fonda Franca was badly in need of repair when I took it over. It was dismaying at first, though I did the best I could with the small amount of capital at my disposal for refurbishing. There are two main floors, with four rooms to rent on each. Suzanne and I occupy a small flat on the ground floor, at the back, with French doors in our sitting room that open onto a small pool, which attracts wonderful birds.

The high ceilings in the public rooms give the hotel a certain elegance, although the plaster is cracked in many places; in one bedroom, a vast chunk has broken off, and the joists have been exposed. In another, the chandelier has recently come crashing to the floor; fortunately, it was occupied at the time by a soporific gentleman from Romania, who seemed not to notice. The crash woke everyone but him!

There is a toilet at the end of the corridor on each floor, and only in the past few months have they been brought up to standard. One sits in relative comfort on the wooden seats, which were made in England, and pulls a tasseled green rope to flush. The gurgle and sump is lovely to hear when the mechanism is working properly. 'A good toilet is the beginning of prosperity,' my father used to say. He made sure that the Hôtel de Ville in Nice, where he worked, had toilets in perfect working order. (He would have hated most of the toilets in Spain, where the Arab tradition of a hole in the floor has prevailed, even at some of the good hotels in Madrid.)

The dining room still needs work. The table linen is shabby, and the room is far too dark, largely because it faces northwest. A southern exposure is crucial in a good dining room. The floor has been lacquered brownish black, and that poses a small problem: No matter how bright the day, the floor exudes a lugubriousness in keeping with itself. I fight back with potted plants, with flowers in season, and with colorful paintings, but there is only so much one can do about a dark room. A proper crystal chandelier would help, perhaps a Bavarian one, but I cannot afford one now, since fewer and fewer of my guests seem willing or able to pay their bills. It has become quite maddening, the way they all take advantage of me! My establishment should be called Madame's Poorhouse.

My hospitality is often noted, but I have had it with scroungers and misfits, bohemians and wanderers. They flee France in droves, hiding in hay carts, tunneling like moles through the filthy dirt, scaling mountains like Alpine goats, tiptoeing like thieves past the Spanish customs, who cannot possibly cope with the numbers. Sergeant Consuelo has said he would like the people of Port-Bou to assist in small ways. 'How can we do everything by ourselves?' he has said. 'Our law-abiding citizens must cooperate!'

He could certainly do more than he does, but I will help when I can, as I can. Last week, I told him of the presence in my hotel of a man who was obviously destined for the hangman's noose. He had apparently crossed the border on foot, although he reeked of fuel. His snarled beard and gap-toothed smile alerted me to the problem, and though he paid in cash upon arrival (as I insisted), I had good reason to suspect him. His papers did not seem in order, his French was foul, his Spanish nonexistent. I believe he spoke Hungarian or some such thing. 'He is obviously a Bolshevik spy,' said Consuelo, after questioning him for twenty minutes or so in his room at the hotel. The man was turned over to the French border police, who have become less bungling in the past year or so.

A number of army officers from León made reservations this morning by telephone: four men for four nights. I am looking forward to their arrival, this weekend, since one of them knew my husband at the military academy. He has promised to bring a photograph of Claudio, aged twenty or so. It is a shame I never took pictures myself, but I just didn't. The result is that Suzanne has virtually no idea of what her father looked like, so any photograph is welcome.

I must clear out the hotel before they get here. It will not please them to consort with the types who now seem my only clientele.

Three days ago, a couple of silly French girls arrived. They are only eighteen or nineteen, and I saw no need to question their stories. The papers they showed me were in order. I suppose they simply want to get away from France at this time, and I can understand their motives; nevertheless, one cannot be too careful. The girls plan to stay here until tomorrow or the next day, before continuing on to Portugal – where everyone is headed. One of them has a sister who will arrive soon, perhaps tomorrow.

Another suspicious guest is an elderly gentleman from Belgium, Professor Lott. He has been staying here for the past week. If one can believe his story, he taught history in Brussels for some years. I quite like his manner, which is discreet, but there is something evasive about him. 'This is certainly true, madame,' he says repeatedly, even when I have not asked him to verify a statement. I would distrust him were he any younger, but he is probably seventy-five or eighty. A man of that age deserves some credit and respect. Moreover, one cannot expect perfection in one's guests. This is the wrong sort of business for a purist.

Three Germans stumbled into the hotel this evening. They are obviously Jews: a mother and her son, who say very little, and a rumpled little man called Dr Benjamin, who appears to have injured his leg along the way. He hobbles about, groaning and wincing, with a briefcase that never leaves his sight. I do not think he has shaved properly in several days, and his rancid odor will be unwelcome in my dining room.

The evening buffet had just finished for the night by the time they got here, but they seemed terribly hungry, so I took pity. What else can one do? A human being is a human being, despite his or her passport, or lack thereof. I put out a plate of cold meat, olives, and cheese, with a loaf of bread, then tried not to look as they devoured everything within ten minutes. The boy, who is called José, ate like a pig, as boys of his age invariably do. I kept Suzanne well away from these people.

They grew quite talkative after a few bites of food, and produced an exotic array of travel documents. That they are forgeries is not in question: The color of the paper is all wrong, and the stamps are ludicrous. Even the photographs are blurred. But these people do not seem like criminals or spies. Just more Jews on the run. The world is overwhelmed by Jews, as usual. Hitler has sent many of them to work camps or deported them, and the French will soon follow suit. But where will they go? Spain does not want them now any more than it did in the fifteenth century. America will absorb them, perhaps; the Americans have a way of absorbing everything like a great putrid sponge. One will soon be able to smell them across the Atlantic.

Dr Benjamin claims French citizenship, and he speaks the language well enough, with only the slightest rustle of an accent. I heard him whispering in the parlor with Professor Lott a while ago, and I wondered if this was a secret rendezvous of some kind. Why else the camaraderie? It would be too awful if the Fonda Franca became a well-known watering hole for spies, the sort of thing one reads about in cheap thrillers.

I have put Dr Benjamin in the worst room, the one with the hole in the ceiling. His friends, the Gurlands, will stay in the next room, which has two beds. They are apparently intent upon leaving in the morning on the Madrid train, and this is all well and good. It would be dreadful if they were here when the officers from Madrid arrived. It would make no sense to them that I, the widow of Claudio Ruiz, should be harboring such people.

WALTER BENJAMIN

Warmth is ebbing from the things of this world. The objects of daily use gently but insistently repel us, push us away. Day by day, in attempting to overcome our secret resistances to these objects, we are compelled to perform an immense, peculiar labor. We must compensate for the coldness of things with our own warmth if they are not to freeze us to death, to kill us with their alienation; we must handle their spines with infinite patience and care if we do not want to bleed to death.

'Where do you come from?' the little girl asked, the pupils of her eyes like opal beads. She wore a white blouse and a black skirt and spoke in strangely accented French. 'You are not French, are you? You don't sound French.'

'I've been living in Paris for many years,' Benjamin said.

'And before that? Where did you come from?'

It worried him that this girl, the daughter of the proprietress of the hotel, should be so inquisitive. There was something unnerving about her. She had crept up to him in the garden and begun her interrogation.

In his younger days, in Berlin, children did not speak directly to their elders; they rarely spoke at all, except among themselves. He still shuddered to recall an occasion in Berlin when he interrupted his parents while they were entertaining friends at a dinner party. The glare of displeasure in his father's eyes was punishment enough, and he never made the mistake again.

Benjamin wished he could tell the girl where he came from. It would be lovely to tell her about Berlin: the smell of the clay soil in the parks, the dry grass beside the pavement, the tinsel clatter of the wind in dying trees; everything reminded him of his childhood walks to the Tiergarten, over the Herkules Bridge with its gently sloping embankment. After school, in early autumn, he would stagger down the slope and sit under a birch tree or lie on a mossy bank with a view across the stream; it was not unlike the atmosphere in this garden at the Fonda Franca.

The insistent nature of the girl, which masked a deeply ingrained petulance, brought back to him an image of his old schoolmate, Luise von Landau. The sassy, black-eyed daughter of a wealthy Berlin family, she had been the ringleader at this first school, where an energetic young schoolmistress, Fräulein Pufahl, presided over a feisty little group of bourgeois children. The tug-of-war for control of that classroom was epic, with Fräulein Pufahl caving in, always, to Luise, the indomitable Luise.

She lived in an elegant house of pink granite by the Zoological Garden, near the Lichtenstein Bridge, and on weekends he would be taken by his nanny into the garden itself, entering that terrifying world of gnus and zebras, of bare trees where vultures and condors nested, of reeking pens replete with wolves and bears. The wildness of the zoo and his memories of Luise blended in a peculiar, exhilarating way tonight. They had never been close friends, but Luise would nonetheless send him postcards throughout the summer holidays from exotic places like Tabarz, Brindisi, or Madonna di Campiglio. He could still visualize the postcards, their pale pastels evoking the steeply wooded slopes of Tabarz, with ferny undergrowth and blood-bright berries strewn along the way; he could see the yellow-and-white quays of Brindisi, even smell the salt spray as it turned to mist in the hot air below the pier; he could visualize the cupolas of Madonna di Campiglio, blue on blue. The world before the Great War was an anthology of these images, each lovely and remote, alluring.

'Why did you come to Port-Bou?' the girl asked. 'My mother doesn't like everyone who comes here.'

'Indeed,' he said, wiping his forehead with a damp handkerchief. He felt decidedly weak this evening, for good reasons. His bad knee was throbbing, and he had already felt several spasms of intense chest and neck pain: a sign he could read only too clearly. Even the veins in his wrists seemed to be swollen.

'She says that vagabonds are not good for the hotel,' the girl continued, chatting blithely.

'Does this establishment not require paying guests?' he asked so firmly that it surprised him.

'What do you mean by that?'

'This hotel . . . surely your mother needs paying guests.' It seemed odd, talking to a little child as though she were twenty. But this girl was eerily mature. He remembered a Latvian folktale about a race of demons who inhabited the bodies of small children; they could wreak massive psychological damage on susceptible adults, who refused to acknowledge their malevolence. He leaned forward to stare into her dark blue eyes.

'We have too many disreputable guests,' she said flatly. 'My mother likes some of them, but I don't.'

'Ah, it's your opinion then! Your mother does not necessarily agree with everything you say.'

'My mother says you are smelly.'

Benjamin was alarmed by this imputation. 'Me, in particular? I am . . . smelly?'

'You and your friends. Have you been climbing mountains in those clothes? She says you have. It's silly, you know. You should wear proper clothes.'

Benjamin did not know where to begin. 'We have been walking in the country, yes.'

Suzanne's cheeks seemed to implode, became prunelike. She said, 'I wish you would all go away.'

Benjamin watched in dismay as she skipped along the gravel path to the hotel. Her hair was so pretty, so luxurious, and her eyes so devastating. She would grow into a beautiful woman of the sort who could destroy a passing stranger's day with a single, solitary glance. He had lost many days to such women.

Benjamin felt panicky now about his smell and went up to his room to have a bath. He paused briefly in the doorway of the parlor, where the Gurlands were eating, then went upstairs. His body was so fatigued, it seemed impossible that he should be able to find the energy to digest food.

As he lay in the tub, dribbling hot water on his badly bruised kneecap, which had turned greenish-blue, he began to float in memory; a strong smell of disinfectant had triggered, for inexplicable reasons, a string of images. He and his family moved out of their Berlin apartment every summer to a house 'with butterflies and grass,' as his father always said. They would go to Potsdam or Neubabelsberg or – best of all – to Lake Griebnitz. He especially enjoyed Lake Griebnitz, with its pellucid, emerald-green water and the willows that dipped their long braids into the shallows. There was a pine-tufted scarf of land in the middle of the lake, eponymously called Peacock Island, and it had afforded Benjamin the first great disappointment of his life. He had wanted badly to see the peacocks, so his father hired a rowboat and took Walter, Georg, and Dora to see them. 'Even if they fly away, you will find their feathers in the grass,' Émile had said. They combed the island for a glimpse of the famous birds, but there were no peacocks to be found, and no feathers in the grass. When Benjamin complained about this, his father rounded on him: 'You must not have expectations! It can only lead to unhappiness!'

He had since learned not to have expectations. Even now, with the horizon amazingly clear, he did not dare hope that he would make it to New York. Nevertheless, he now recalled what a former acquaintance from Berlin told him about the universities in America and their need for teachers. They were apparently thirsting for scholars with German doctorates, and the salaries were stupendous. He had jotted down the names of several institutions: New York University, City College of New York, Colorado University, the University of Delaware. He would send letters to all of them from Lisbon, if he ever got there, proposing a course of lectures on the development of French culture in the nineteenth century. On the train from Marseilles to Port-Vendres, he had filled his notebook with possible courses he might offer. With almost no preparation, he could lecture on Goethe, Proust, Kafka, Baudelaire, and a dozen other authors. He could teach philosophy, German history, cultural politics. Surely some university would want such a man?

This would be especially true after his book on the Parisian arcades was published; indeed, he might well be lured back to Paris. Or perhaps Berlin was a better choice. There would be obvious satisfactions in returning to his native city as a mature man, a man of culture and attainment. His father had more than once declared, 'You will never succeed at anything, Walter. You are too indecisive.' If he became a professor in Berlin, this would be the ultimate response to his father. He would stand over Émile's grave and say, calmly, without resentment, 'So I am indecisive, father? Is that what you said?'

He would give anything now for a single fresh morning in Berlin in early May, when the flowers spilled from stone pots along the path to the covered market – always his favorite destination as a boy. The compulsive buying and selling, and the atmosphere of controlled frenzy, lured him forward through the big wooden doors hinged on whipping springs; once inside the forecourt, he was in thrall to the female vendors, those high priestesses of Ceres who stood behind their bins and purveyed all manner of edible goods: fruits of the field, pickings of the orchard, wild birds and beasts, some of which hung threateningly from hooks, their eyes filled with the blank gaze of eternity. The flagstone floor was always slippery with fish swill, with scraps of lettuce or banana skins, and he could still see the hunch-backed little man who hosed off the scum, his red cap bobbing up and down as he worked. 'Step aside, ladies!' he would shout.

A steady supply of housewives and old family retainers carrying wicker baskets and cloth bags filled the forecourt. He had often gone there with plump Gretel, their cook; he would follow her at a slight distance, amazed by her skill at bargaining. Tough-minded, quick to reject a bruised piece of fruit, an inferior cut of meat, or a head of lettuce going brown at the edges, she stood up to each and every vendor, thrusting her substantial breasts forward like cannons. 'This will not do!' she would bark. He admired Gretel, even now, as he contemplated the prospect of escaping the Fonda Franca by eluding the guard. Even if he made it free of Port-Bou, there were many difficult passages to thread, and he wished Gretel were here to make rapid, intelligent decisions.

The pink sky framed in the big, open window of the bathroom was darkening with thunderclouds. Suddenly, a flock of geese crossed the windowpane, heading south toward the horizon in a *V* formation; the eerie cries of the long-necked birds trailed behind their perfect wedge like a kite's tail. Benjamin could hear the birds long after they had crossed the window, and he listened keenly, trying not to think about his knee, his shortness of breath, and the pain rippling up and down his arms. He wanted to go south with those birds, and farther.

The bath had soaked away the nervous energy that had kept him going for hour upon hour since before dawn, in what now seemed another life. Exhaustion suddenly piled its dark shadows into every crevice of his body; his lungs filled with its black soot; his joints locked. It was as though his body itself, his sheer corporeality, had evaporated, and he lay there limp, invisible, as the water turned cool and the stain of evening covered the bathroom ceiling. He became, in effect, the dwindling light, the rising wind, the clatter of dishes in the room below, and the distant pulse of sea.

Professor Lott read his newspaper in a dilapidated leather armchair in the shabbily ornate parlor of the hotel; Benjamin, newly washed and combed, sat on the other side of the room by an oblong mahogany table, a plate of cold meat on his lap. A small Bechstein piano was pushed against the wall beside him, an exact replica of the one his mother used to play in their house on Nettlebeck Street, in Berlin. The mere sight of this particular piano was comforting as thunder sounded in the distance, echoing across the bay, and the chandelier flickered overhead. For a moment, the room went dark, then the lights came on, even brighter than before.

'A storm at sea,' said Lott, in German.

Benjamin looked across the room without expression. It was difficult, with his myopia, to see clearly at such a distance. 'I rather like a good storm, don't you?' he said.

'It depends.' The gentleman folded his newspaper and removed his glasses. 'You are a German, sir? I think I hear a trace of Berlin in your accent.'

Benjamin instinctively trusted this man. He was obviously a benign creature or he would not have been so blunt.

'Yes, that is right.'

Lott nodded eagerly. 'Madame Ruiz told me you crossed the border this afternoon.'

'Madame Ruiz has not lied to you.'

Exhaustion and shyness combined to make Benjamin more laconic than usual, and Lott could not pry open the conversation. 'I don't mean to frighten you,' he said. 'I am myself a refugee. My mother was actually from Düsseldorf. Her name was Eva Blum.'

Benjamin visibly relaxed at this confession. Here was another Jew, with German connections.

'I'm a Belgian,' Lott said. 'My passport, I should say, allows me to boast of Belgian citizenship.' He paused. 'If you get sent back, go to the Belgian consulate in Marseilles. It is still possible to get a passport there, I am told. The staff understands our predicament. Ask for Monsieur Peurot.'

'I will remember this. Thank you,' Benjamin said. Shakily, he crossed the room toward Lott. 'I am Dr Walter Benjamin,' he said, bowing slightly.

'Alphonse Lott,' he said, dipping his head forward. 'Have you by chance written essays for some journals, Dr Benjamin? Your name is familiar.'

Benjamin settled into a wicker chair that had seen better days, delighted to have found a reader. It was, for him, the rarest of rare experiences. 'Yes, but mostly for German periodicals.'

'The *Literarische Welt*?'

Benjamin brightened. 'And a few others. For a while, I made my living as a freelance reviewer. It was, at best, a precarious life.'

Lott explained that he had been a professor in Brussels and was something of a writer himself. His reviews appeared in several well-known Belgian papers, although not in the last fifteen years.

The two gentlemen sat for some while, talking about books. Professor Lott, like Benjamin, was a fan of Simenon, but he had read Proust as well. It was a relief for Benjamin to find someone who shared his interest in literature and ideas. It was indeed quite exhausting to be around people who did not share his interests; he was forced to feign enthusiasm for things that truly bored him to death. Ever since leaving Paris, he had felt lonely for real conversation.

'And what are you reading now, Professor Lott?' he asked, leaning toward him eagerly, his eyebrows lifted. 'I can hardly remember when I last browsed in a bookstore.'

Having bid good-night to Professor Lott, Benjamin climbed the stairs to bed, taking each step slowly. Because his knee kept locking, he was forced to rest on each landing. When he finally got to his room, a severe pain in his chest caught him unawares, hitting him like a sledgehammer behind the rib cage. He crumpled to the floor, falling face-forward, and lay there for some time, unable to breathe, his nose digging into the filthy brown hemp of the rug. He tried to call out to Henny Gurland, whose room was only across the hall, but no sound emerged. At last, he managed to roll over onto his back.

I am dying, he said to himself. *This is the end, and I am not sad.*

Half an hour passed, the crunch in his chest eased, and soon he was able to sit up, then stand. His hands groped his body like a blind man feeling a page of poetry in Braille; he was really there, alive, himself. And he was not in pain. Despite his relief that the acute discomfort was over, he felt disappointed by this miraculous recovery. He had been ready, even eager, to die. The end had seemed to come, and he was not sad or afraid. He was even a little happy.

He spent a long time getting into his nightgown, crawling into bed, sitting with his back against the oak headboard, and staring ahead, breathing methodically, listening to the fat tick of an old clock on the dresser. An eternity seemed to hang between each tick: the time before and after life, the brightness at either side of this dark passageway he had been nosing along for nearly half a century.

The ceiling, disfigured by a gaping hole in the middle, intermittently rained plaster, dropping chalky bits on his pillow and into his face. In his head, he called it Spanish snow and laughed quietly to himself. He was still pleased that sadness or regret had not been part of the experience when he fell to the floor; death was benign, a kind of physical forgetfulness. It was not the end but the beginning. The body simply forgot its daily, rueful existence, and the soul fluttered away, found a new life elsewhere, a tangible kingdom beyond mourning and petty discomforts, beyond (as Nietzsche said) good and evil. He was all for it now, whatever it was that lay ahead: the fabled infinite, the pure abstract of heaven. He would hold hands there with his Beloved, with Asja Lacis, hold hands forever.

It was clearly Asja, not Jula, who came to him as he looked up, her face a numinous sheen. Time had done its proper job of winnowing.

Outside, thunder rolled across the bay, and a fine rain picked at the window of his room. The wind whipped off the sea, penetrating the walls of the Fonda Franca as if they were mere lattice. It was cold in the room, and Benjamin wished for a fire in the grate. When earlier in the evening he had asked for one, Madame Ruiz had lifted her eyebrows and left the room abruptly. One apparently did not ask for fires in decent Spanish hotels. To wish to be warm was déclassé.

In the house on Nettlebeck Street, every room boasted a fire on a frosty winter evening, and in the morning a servant would steal into Benjamin's bedroom just before dawn to light a fire. As the flame transfigured the high ceiling, he would wake slowly, letting the room gradually absorb and radiate the heat. On school days, when he had to get up before the room was properly warm, he would leap from bed to dress quickly, huddling so close to the flames that his shins would sting. But it was a good pain, the pain of abundance.

The weight of memories pressed on his chest like thick marble, and he recalled a famous Brechtian maxim: *Do not build on the good old days, but on the bad new ones.*

He found himself missing Brecht, his sly temperament and breathtaking egotism. That last day at his house in Denmark, two years ago, had been a perfect coda to their friendship; a hot summery day, with the sky hard and blue. Benjamin sat all afternoon in the garden under a weeping birch, reading *Kapital*, which he had abandoned several times before. A floppy white hat protected him from the sun.

Brecht came to him with a cup of tea and said, 'Ah, Marx! He is rather old hat, you know. Nobody reads him now, especially the Marxists.'

'I prefer not to read books when they're in fashion,' Benjamin said. 'It's somehow degrading.'

Brecht spat into the grass. 'You are quite right, Walter. When a book is popular, I like to hold it, perhaps smell the pages. But I never read it. Not till the author, or his reputation, dies.'

The night before, Brecht had showed Benjamin a new poem called 'The Farmer to His Oxen.' It was obliquely about Stalin, although Benjamin had found it hard to discern his friend's attitude toward this vicious and megalomaniac leader. Brecht was clearly not in favor of the dictator, nor was he wholly against him; he seemed to hedge his bets.

Benjamin, like his host, still retained a whimsical hope that something good might come of world socialism, but he could never forgive Stalin for his crimes of the past decade. Millions had been murdered or tortured and imprisoned. Reports of the recent show trials in Moscow, and the purge of the intelligentsia, had demoralized Benjamin and most Western socialists. Even worse, he had not heard a word from Asja, who was still living in Moscow. He feared the worst, though he could hardly bear to let his mind rest on the possibility that she was dead.

The attitude toward literature that seemed to emanate from the Kremlin disturbed Benjamin and Brecht alike. As always, Brecht had a theory. 'Literary writers make the Reds uncomfortable,' he said. 'They hate to see genuine artistic production. It is unstable, unpredictable. You can't tell where anything will come out – or how the people will react. And they themselves do not want to produce anything. God forbid! They must play the *apparatchik*.'

Benjamin had shifted the conversation to the familiar ground of Goethe's novels, although Brecht seemed at a loss midway through their discussion; when Benjamin pressed for a response, Brecht said, 'I am sorry, Walter, but I have read only *Elective Affinities*.'

Benjamin concealed his amazement. Brecht usually knew a little about everything, and he rarely admitted to gaps in his own knowledge. On the other hand, he adored finding these gaps in other people.

'*Elective Affinities* is certainly a perfect novel,' Brecht continued, unable to resist a pronouncement. 'This is surprising, given that Goethe wrote it when he was young.'

'He was sixty,' Benjamin said with a slight note of superiority in his voice. 'That was young for Goethe, perhaps, given that he lived into his mid-eighties. But it makes me feel rather like a babe in swaddling clothes.'

Brecht sniffed. 'You are teasing me, Walter. Good for you.' He folded his arms, raising his elbows like wings. 'What I like about Goethe's novel is that it shows no trace of Philistinism. The Germans, even at their best, are horrid Philistines.'

'The novel was not well received, you know.'

'I didn't know this, but it hardly surprises me. In fact, I'm glad to hear it. The Germans are dreadful people. It isn't true that you cannot draw conclusions about the Germans from Adolf Hitler. He is quite typical, I'm afraid. My teachers at the gymnasium in Augsburg were all like Hitler.'

'But what about you, Bertolt? You are German!'

Brecht arched his back, and the sunlight formed a white ring around his head. 'Let me confess something, Walter. What is dreadful in my work is the German element. And don't look surprised! There's a great deal that is truly dreadful in everything I do. You know it's true!'

Benjamin insisted otherwise, but Brecht silenced him with a wave of the hand. 'What makes the Germans intolerable is their narrow-minded self-sufficiency. Nothing like our free imperial cities ever existed anywhere else but on German soil. Lyons was never a free city; the independent cities of the Renaissance were city-states, but they were very different. They had a sense of community. The Germans do not understand that word.'

Benjamin could hear Brecht's voice so clearly now, as he lay in bed at the Fonda Franca; he scrambled for his notebook, which he'd left on the table beside the oil lamp. He wanted to record these conversations exactly as he remembered them. There was so much to record, to remember. 'Art is simply memory organized,' Goethe had once said – and the line popped into Benjamin's head as he began to scribble his recollections of the conversation with Brecht.

The oil lamp wavered as Benjamin wrote, and the letters blurred. The nib of his pen seemed to stick on the page. The exertions and aggravations of the day had ruined his nerves, and his hand was shaking. He could not write or read.

He closed his eyes now, letting the past flood in like surf breaking the seawall, eating the land. It seemed that his ear had been pressed for decades to a conch, and he could hear the sea only in the pearl of distance; tonight it was strangely close. He could smell the water, and the salt stung his eyes. The marine breeze whistled in his face. The light on the water dazzled him. And a beatific figure seemed to float toward him on the water, skidding on the waves like Botticelli's Venus: a divine yet thoroughly embodied presence.

It was Asja again, his own Venus. His mind turned naturally toward her, and he smiled. She was really there, and he could see Brecht standing behind her, putting a hand on her shoulder; the juxtaposition made no sense until he recalled that she had once worked with him as assistant director, in Munich, on a performance of *Edward II*. The battle scene at the center of that play must hold the stage for nearly three-quarters of an hour – an impossible feat for most directors. During one rehearsal, Brecht had turned to Asja and asked: 'What is wrong with these soldiers? What is their dilemma?' With care, she replied, 'They are pale and afraid of dying.' Brecht thought for a moment. 'Yes, and they are thoroughly exhausted,' he said. 'We must make them look ghostly.' Each soldier's face was, at his bidding, covered with a thick layer of chalk. As Asja later said to

Benjamin, 'The epic theater was suddenly born that day – Athena sprung fully grown from the head of Zeus.'

A knock at the door brought him back to the present, and the ghosts of Brecht, of Asja Lacis, fled through the ceiling.

'Just a moment, please,' he said, annoyed, lifting himself to his feet with difficulty. He put on his shirt and crossed the room slowly, sucking in deep breaths.

The knock came again, this time louder.

'Another minute, if you please!' he cried. 'I am coming.'

WALTER BENJAMIN

All close relationships are lit up by an almost intolerable, piercing clarity in which they are barely able to survive. For on the one hand, money stands ruinously at the core of every vital interest, but on the other, this is the very barrier before which almost all relationships halt; so, more and more, in the natural as in the moral sphere, trust, calm, and health are quickly disappearing.

15   MADAME RUIZ

This loneliness is hard to describe, hard even to confess. I often feel like a cloud, translucent, blown sideways across the high, purple skies of history. I feel the wind of time rushing in my hair and hear it in the tops of trees that sway and sometimes snap: the rustle of days, the clatter of branches falling. Always, I fly above the tumult; I am not really a participant in life, but one of life's perpetual observers.

I see the other mothers in the village as they pass through the square before dinner, especially on Sundays after mass, with their children perfectly dressed and scattering pigeons ahead of them like dirty snow. They are not alone, like me; they go home to the fathers of those children who shadow them, bolster them, buoy them up. It is not their duty to act as mother and father, as nurturer and disciplinarian.

I notice the strain on Suzanne at times. She cries easily, sits alone in the garden for long periods, refuses to speak for days on end. Today, for example, she became horribly petulant. She has obviously been disturbed by these Germans, who emerged from nowhere, gritty and exhausted. They are no different from the last ones, or the ones before that I don't understand. In particular, she is obsessed by the 'old man,' as she calls him, this Dr Benjamin.

He is not fifty, but the coloring of his skin, its texture – like old cardboard that has been soaked by rain and dried many times – is telling. It shows in his eyes that he has suffered, and suffering affects the quality of one's skin; it advertises to the world that one has not had an easy life. From what I gather, he has lived in Paris for many years, doing research of some kind, literary or philosophical. The woman who travels with him, Frau Gurland, took some trouble to boast of his accomplishments and connections when I checked them in. She said, 'He is a very important man in the literary world, a contributor to journals and newspapers in several countries.'

Once I saw him, I took pity; I have a soft heart, and he reminded me, in a most disturbing way, of my father: the same formality of gesture, the exaggerated manners, the sorrow in his eyes. The whole world rested, invisibly, on his shoulders, making him slump. Dr Benjamin has not been destroyed by life, but he is crumbling, like one of those Roman structures near Paestum that my husband and I once visited, in southern Italy: a relic, a reminder of the glory that was, and that cannot be restored.

Upon his arrival this evening, Dr Benjamin sat by himself for an hour in the garden, then limped into the villa. He was quite a sight, with a cut on his face, his suit rumpled and torn, his shoes scuffed; his hair was greasy, unkempt. His glasses fogged as soon as he stepped indoors, but he stared straight at me, seeing nothing.

'Your daughter,' he said, 'she is quite beautiful, her dark eyes.'

'Yes, her eyes are lovely.' I did not, of course, have to add that Suzanne's eyes are eerily like my own.

'She reminds me of a girl I once knew,' he said, 'in childhood.'

'Ah,' I said.

'A peculiar, resolute girl.'

I said nothing. My daughter is neither peculiar nor resolute. Determined, perhaps, like me; insistent at times. I would have accepted insistent. But resolute?

'I will come down in a little while,' he said, just before a swirl of coughing disabled him.

'As you like,' I said. 'Can I get you some water?'

'No, thank you.'

When he looked up at me again, I noticed that his lips were a sickly blue, and his cheeks reddish-purple. This is not a sign of health. My father, before he died of heart failure, assumed a similar coloring.

Dr Benjamin hobbled down the hall, favoring one leg, then climbed, stair by stair, to the next floor. He carried a battered briefcase, which (as I learned from Frau Gurland) contained an important manuscript. It took perhaps ten or fifteen minutes for him to ascend only a dozen steps, and I fully expected him to topple over backward at several points. One of our maids, Lucia, stood at the bottom of the staircase and watched nervously.

'The old man smells,' my daughter said, squeezing my hand for reassurance.

'Please, darling. We do not talk about smells in this house. It is vulgar.' I brushed her hair – a way of tending to her that she always found soothing. 'The poor man is not well. His coloring is all wrong. And the way he coughs and limps. It is very sad.'

'I don't care. He smells.'

It is distressing to see Suzanne in this state, so fiercely common in her manners. The village mentality has been stealing upon her, and their grotesque, Catalonian way of speaking has even affected her French. Her verbs are all present tense now, and she pays no attention to grammar. When she wants something, she tends to grunt or mewl. I wish I could find a private school for her, perhaps in Madrid: a nice convent school, run by Carmelite nuns. They are strict with children and do not permit crudeness. There is only so much I can do for her at home.

Frau Gurland came to see me in the kitchen, wild-eyed. Her hair is like a bush, wiry and flecked with gray. She has that guttural, Germanic way of speaking French that one encountered often in Nice. The Riviera was full of German visitors in the twenties, and several of them bought hotels along the coast.

'May I help?' I asked, maintaining perfect neutrality of tone.

'My son is hungry,' she said. 'He has not eaten in a very long time.'

I simply nodded, refusing to give her the satisfaction of a straightforward answer. I had already cleared the buffet table, in fact.

'Will there be more food in the parlor?'

'You'll have to give me a few minutes,' I said. 'We're understaffed at the moment, as you can see.'

Her behaviour was outrageous. The woman is utterly devoid of sensitivity or culture. Her son, though pretty in the way of adolescent boys, has a loutishness about him. I saw him standing in the parlor, looking out the window with his finger in his nose. If he were my son, I would have slapped him for this. You must rein in children at this age, when their natural instincts are all wrong. If the work of discipline is neglected in early childhood, it must be corrected later, when everything is twice as difficult.

It had been a long day, and my ankles were swollen from standing, but I replenished the buffet, then cleared and cleaned most of the dishes, with Lucia's help. Later, I discussed with Suzanne her schoolwork, saw that she had a bath, then let her come into my bedroom to read. The storm made her nervous, as well it might. The rain continued to beat on the windows, the wind howled in the trees, and lightning flashed across the water. The shutters came loose somewhere and banged.

'What is that?' Suzanne asked.

'You mustn't be frightened by the storm,' I said.

'I'm not frightened.'

'You might have had dreams tonight, darling. When I was a child, we had terrible storms coming off the sea, especially in winter. Atlantic storms are the worst, of course.

'I never dream.'

'This is untrue, Suzanne. How many times have you woken up crying? You've had many nightmares. We all do.'

'I don't,' she said.

It was so frustrating. I began to wonder if, when she reached twelve or thirteen, she would become utterly impossible. If that happened without a father in the house to control her impulses, I could be forced to endure a hideous decade. It was the sort of thing my own mother, the poor woman, could not tolerate. The pressures of life were too much for her. She would simply take to her bed, feigning a headache. It was left to the maids to raise us, and after the collapse of my father's investments, we were left to ourselves.

I went outside to see what shutters were banging while Suzanne read, an oil lamp burning beside the bed for comfort as much as light. It was exhilarating to stand in the garden, with the ground steaming, the sea roiling; the surf spit and tangled, booming on the shingle below. I let the rain lash my face and did not flinch. It was tingling, but not too cold.

The offending shutters were on the first floor, just above the parlor, in the room occupied by the mysterious Professor Lott. I had become more and more convinced that he was an agent of the French government, even though his visa was apparently in order. The fact that his room was littered with books by Simenon and Maugham had begun to worry me. Maugham had a house some miles from Nice, and my father said he was an English spy. Simenon, of course, was a scoundrel. One must be careful to note what books are read by one's guests. It is always an indication of character.

I woke Professor Lott, insisting that he latch his shutters. He seemed quite taken aback, but complied. Then I went back into the kitchen for a glass of milk. Its warm wood was softly lit by a lamp beside the sink, and the clean surfaces were soothing. Milk is good to drink before bed, so I poured a glass for Suzanne as well. As I was standing at the sink, I saw shadows in the garden – of men ducking and weaving. My heart began to thump, and I wondered if there were prowlers. Then I saw the huge cedar sway, and I realized it was probably just that.

On a sudden impulse, I decided to call Sergeant Consuelo about the new guests. He had asked me only yesterday to alert him to any irregularities, and one can never be too careful where legal matters are concerned. In a foreign country, it is important to comply with local regulations. One must even intuit regulations that do not yet exist and prepare to satisfy their demands.

Of course almost all refugees coming through Port-Bou will stay at the Fonda Franca. Where else would they go? I daresay a few of them, those without money, sleep in surrounding fields, in haylofts or cow barns. There is a small tavern, El Faro, seven miles south of the village. I believe the proprietor there has leftist leanings and is said to have sympathized with the loyalists during the Civil War. I do not know, nor do I care. I keep my nose well out of politics, probably because of my father. I know the pitfalls.

But I want to help where I can. These are difficult times for Spain. Sergeant Consuelo understands and appreciates my concerns, and he welcomed my call. Within twenty minutes, he arrived with a young man called Rubio, who has just been hired as a policeman. I served them a glass of wine in the kitchen.

'You say they are Germans?'

'They have false passports,' I explained. 'The man – a gentleman, I must say – speaks French extremely well, with a Parisian accent, but he is certainly a German. His visa was so water-stained I could barely read it.'

'And the women?'

'There is only one woman, a woman and her son. He is apparently Spanish. I don't understand it, really. They have Czech passports.'

'Czech?'

'What else?' A Czech passport was worthless, of course. They are sold cheaply on the black market in France and Germany. Virtually everyone who is *sans nationalité* can claim Czech citizenship, although none of them speak the language and few of them could even find their supposed mother country on a map of Europe.

'And when did they arrive?'

'This evening . . . having crossed the mountains.'

'We have no record of this.'

'I'm sure you do not.'

Sergeant Consuelo sipped his wine and smoked a cigar. He is a heavy man, with a large black mustache and darting eyes like a fox terrier's. He combs his oily hair straight back, like the straking on a ship's hull. He is perhaps thirty-five, although the lines of his face make him look older: deep grooves, multiplied when he smiles like the folds of a curtain pulled open. I find him a cheerful man, but like many people in this village, he lacks an appropriate dignity. A person in his position should behave with rectitude, yet he is often seen in a drunken state in one of the local bars. Were his daughter and Suzanne not good friends, and were he not in charge of the police for this district, I doubt that I would have befriended him. As it was, I have had no choice in the matter.

'You see what problems we have, Madame Ruiz,' he said. 'Anyone may cross our borders! Spain is filling up with vagabonds.'

'Spies and criminals,' said Rubio.

'You must eat something,' I said, pushing a plate of sliced pork in front of them.

'Thank you, madame. I don't mind,' he said, snuffing out his cigar in a glass. As he ate, he talked rapidly, the food dribbling on his chin: 'They have just changed the laws. A letter came from Madrid on Monday. Nobody is allowed to pass through Spain without papers. We are cracking down.' He wiped his mouth with his sleeve.

Rubio said, 'The sergeant might be promoted.'

'Is this true?' I asked.

Sergeant Consuelo demurred, but he was obviously pleased to have me think this was a possibility.

'It's important to crack down,' he said, once again. 'Don't you think?'

'Indeed,' I said, 'and not a minute too early.' I explained to him that many of the refugees did not pay their bills. 'This war will bankrupt me,' I said, 'if something isn't done quickly.' I reminded him that I employed several women from the town as maids, and one gardener – the sergeant's cousin, in fact.

'You have a wonderful establishment,' the sergeant said.

I watched him eating and drinking with mild disgust. It is no wonder I have not been tempted to remarry.

We talked briefly, boringly, about his wife and children, about the school, and – passingly – about the war. He seemed to think it likely that Spain would enter the war on the side of Germany, and soon; I suspected that General Franco, who is no fool, would attempt to remain neutral as long as possible, while leaning toward Germany in every other respect. There was no possibility that Spain would give much in the way of material help to Hitler; this is a poor country, decades (if not centuries) behind Germany in its habits; it is a medieval country, too. The modern world has not attracted its attention. Even the Spanish Communists seem to care little about Stalin, and they have certainly not read Marx or Lenin.

'Now tell me about these guests, the suspicious ones,' the sergeant said. 'We must have a good look at their papers.'

Rubio smiled, a prominent gold tooth glinting. I realized at once that he was a rogue, entirely unfit for public duty.

We knocked on Dr Benjamin's door first, partly because his light was on. After an interminable delay, during which time he was apparently dressing, he let us in. His face was expressionless, and the room smelled of stale clothing. The bed was unmade, and the doors of the wardrobe were swung wide. A few books lay scattered on the floor.

'Good evening, Dr Benjamin,' I said, stepping into the room. 'This is Sergeant Consuelo, from the police in Port-Bou.'

'How do you do, sir,' he said. He bowed slightly, his right hand touching his chest. It was strange.

I quite liked this formality, the sense of composure. Here was a man of considerable breeding. A man unbowed by circumstances. Indeed, the contrast with the police sergeant and his lackey was such that I immediately regretted having called them, but I had, and there was no turning back now.

Since Dr Benjamin did not speak Catalan, I was forced to act as interpreter.

'He would like to see your papers,' I said.

'Most certainly. They will see, I think, that everything is in order.'

'Did you check in with a customs officer?'

'The booth was empty,' he said. 'We assumed it did not matter.'

Rubio grinned at him, nodding eagerly, his gold tooth wet and long.

We waited, shifting from foot to foot, while Dr Benjamin searched through his briefcase for a clutch of documents. It was difficult to tell if he was purposely delaying, but it seemed to take forever.

He moved slowly, deliberately, pausing to cough or blow his nose several times.

He walked toward the sergeant with trembling hands, limping and wheezing as usual. The papers that he handed over were blue and pink, miserably faded, tied in a packet with a piece of string. Sergeant Consuelo sat at the table and scrutinized them under the light of one anemic bulb, which hung from the ceiling without a shade. I felt quite embarrassed, but one does not have the money these days to meet acceptable standards for a hotel. This room, in particular, I have let fall.

'What is his country of origin?' the sergeant wondered, assuming a bureaucratic tone. It was a tone my father often adopted on the telephone when underlings called.

Dr Benjamin seemed to understand the question. 'I am a French citizen,' he said. 'I have an apartment in Paris, you see. My address is valid. My sister and I, we live there.' He fumbled in his pocket, producing a library card from the Bibliothèque Nationale. 'I am doing some research, for a book. I've been living in Paris for many years.'

'He is German, no?' the sergeant asked, looking at me.

'Are you a German?' I asked him.

'I consider myself French,' he said. 'That is my point. I no longer recognize my own country.' He blew his nose into a white handkerchief. 'I have disowned Germany.'

'He is Jewish,' said Rubio.

The sergeant glared at his assistant. It was not his place to comment.

Dr Benjamin, however, understood the remark and nodded.

The sergeant ran his fingers through his slick hair. He was obviously uncomfortable. 'I'm afraid that, as far as Spanish law is concerned, this man is *sans nationalite*.' He went on to explain to me that people without specific national affiliation and proper entry visas were no longer permitted to travel in Spain. There was no choice but to turn him over to the border police in the morning, 'after breakfast, of course.'

As I explained this to Dr Benjamin, the color drained from the man's cheeks, which turned livid, ghostly. He staggered backward.

'Rubio will spend the night. He will escort this man to the station in the morning.'

In effect, Dr Benjamin was under house arrest: a point he obviously understood.

'The border police are responsible people,' I said. 'You needn't be afraid of them.'

'They are murderers,' Dr Benjamin said.

The sergeant offered only a rueful laugh. What else could he do? 'Where are the others?' he asked.

'Frau Gurland and her son are across the hall. I will take you there.'

Consuelo rubbed his hands together, as if anguished.

'Good night, Dr Benjamin,' I said.

Dr Benjamin bowed again. He was remarkably composed now, even dignified. But you could see that, from his viewpoint, his long journey had come to an abrupt and unsatisfactory halt. We left him standing there in the middle of the room, wizened and small, one of the loneliest men I have ever seen.

WALTER BENJAMIN

Death is what sanctions everything the storyteller can tell. Indeed, he borrows his authority from death.

16

José craned his neck, looking around the room. 'What's wrong, Mother?'

'Nothing, darling. Go back to sleep.'

'I heard voices.'

'It was nothing. Just the storm, some shutters banging.'

The police had left an hour ago, and though there would be no sleep for her, she hoped José might rest. The poor boy was exhausted. He had managed well thus far, but she knew he had reached his limit.

His father would have been proud of him, she thought. Arkady Gurland had been famously durable: indifferent to fatigue, unworried about his next meal. 'I'll sleep when there is nothing to do, and eat when there is food,' he would say.

Thunder shook the room, and lightning transformed the shutters into a grid of light whenever it struck. The rain swept along the walls and roof, alternately gaining and losing force.

'Arkady,' Henny Gurland whispered to herself, summoning his brave spirit. All she had now was José, in whom she could find remote echoes of Arkady: in the way he tilted his head before answering a question, in smirks and stifled laughs. He had his father's way of throwing his head back in the wind, and sleeping with his knees pulled up to his chin.

A knock came at the door. 'Frau Gurland, please! Open the door!' The voice sounding through the oak panel was disembodied but familiar.

At first her muscles simply refused the summons of her brain. She had finally allowed herself to relax and had begun to sink into the deep, desperate trance that precedes real sleep.

'Frau Gurland, I beg of you!'

José rose in his nightdress, long-legged, shivering. He opened the door only a crack at first, as his mother instructed.

'Who is there?' Henny Gurland whispered.

'It's Dr Benjamin.'

'Let him in!'

Benjamin lurched forward, then leaned against the doorjamb, his eyes like dark scoops in his skull, his hair frenzied. The omnipresent briefcase dropped from one hand, and he was breathing coarsely. His face twitched.

'My dear God, Walter, my dear,' she said. 'Whatever has happened to you?'

Benjamin moved toward her, unbalanced, as if walking on stilts. 'You will forgive, please. This intrusion . . .' His voice could only just be heard.

'What is wrong, Dr Benjamin?' she asked, frightened by the sight of him.

'I – I,' he stuttered, toppling forward to his knees, supporting himself by gripping the bedpost.

José helped him, with difficulty, into a wing chair by the bed, and his mother eased his feet onto the mattress and removed his shoes.

'We'll call a doctor at once!' she said, mopping a glaze of sweat from his forehead.

'No doctor,' he whispered. 'There is no point.'

'We must do something!'

'Nothing,' he said. 'It's too late. I took some pills, you see . . .' He began to swoon, then caught himself.

'What are you talking about? What pills?' She battered him with questions, wishing she could take him by the collar. 'Tell me what you have done to yourself, Dr Benjamin!'

He motioned for her to come close, but she seemed not to understand. Her panic created an impasse that neither could surmount.

'Please, try to listen to him, Mother,' José said. 'He wants to tell us something.'

The words fell from his lips with a muffled thud, unintelligible, spinning across the floor like coins and disappearing through the grates of silence.

Frau Gurland propped him up in the chair, then slapped him on either cheek. 'You must talk to us, Walter! What have you done to yourself?'

Benjamin's head slumped to one side.

José gasped. 'He's dead!'

'He's not dead,' his mother said, 'but he is dying.'

'Frau Gurland,' Benjamin cried, suddenly waking. 'I . . . I—' The two of them bent close to listen, surprised by the clarity and volume of his speech. But he could not continue, the words stuck in his throat before reaching his lips.

José rubbed his eyes now. He could not believe this was happening. Henny Gurland put a comforting hand on his shoulder as he knelt close to the dying man.

'He's trying to talk,' José said.

Benjamin began to mutter, his words just audible. 'My heart, you see . . . And my leg. How could I walk? You must get to the train . . . by six. The guard won't stop you.' He looked toward the door. 'You must go . . . both of you, quickly.'

'We're not going anywhere without you,' Henny Gurland said.

He lurched forward, his eyes wide. 'I will be dead in a short while. You must save yourselves.' This talking seemed to revive him. 'My book,' he continued, 'you must send it to Adorno . . . in New York.' He gestured lamely toward the briefcase. 'Everything is in those pages . . . Teddy will be surprised, you see, he . . .'

The Gurlands bent forward to hear the end of the sentence, but he merely closed his eyes; his head tipped back against the top of the chair.

Frau Gurland glanced at the clock and saw that it was nearly four in the morning. 'Pack up your things,' she said to José. 'We must leave quickly.'

'Not without him,' said her son.'

'I'm afraid so,' she said, already putting things into her own rucksack.

An unfamiliar voice startled them. 'Is something wrong?'

It was Professor Lott. He stood in the doorway in his nightdress, and his white hair formed a thick cap. He held a candle in his hands, which shook.

'Please, come in, *professeur*.' She motioned for him to shut the door. 'Dr Benjamin has taken some pills,' she said.

Lott understood at once. 'I will stay with him,' he said. 'But you and the boy must go.'

Frau Gurland was glad for this confirmation and cast a pleading look at José, who could see for himself now that Walter Benjamin was beyond assistance.

'Are you sure?' she asked.

'Quite sure. You must catch the first train. Before the guard awakens.'

Benjamin opened his eyes again, but he could not speak or raise his head.

'God bless you, Walter,' Frau Gurland said, bending close to whisper into his ear.

'No,' said José. 'This isn't right.'

'Please, darling,' his mother said, trying to pull him away.

'I want to stay with him. We've got to help him!'

'You don't understand,' she said. 'He would not want us to stay.'

The boy began to sob, standing there, too tall to cry, too old, but sobbing like a child. His mother put her cheek against his chest, and he put his hands on her shoulders.

Professor Lott finally intervened. 'You must go quickly,' he said, 'while you can. I will take care of Dr Benjamin; you needn't worry.'

'You are kind, sir,' said Benjamin, trying to sit up. A quickness in Professor Lott's eyes reminded him of Scholem, and this was comforting. It was a sign of intelligence and self-confidence.

'Lie still,' said Lott, firmly. He held Benjamin's hand tightly, as a mother might do for a sick and frightened child.

'I should not have done this, do you think?'

Lott hesitated. The empty bottle of morphine lay on the floor of Benjamin's room, and it amazed him that the man could speak at all.

'I couldn't go on, you know. My heart . . .' But it was not just his heart. It was the world itself. He could no longer attach himself willingly to its bleak trajectory.

As a young man, he put his faith in good sense and in deep learning. He and Scholem, in their imaginary University of Muri, had gobbled up every morsel of information about the world that they could find, consuming knowledge like air and water. One could feed happily, indefinitely, on Plato and Kant, Frege, Goethe, Heine. Kafka would sit on one's shoulder like a sooty crow, providing the appropriately grim music, with the dark laughter of Karl Krause sounding in the woods.

Benjamin had loved so many books: not just the texts, but the physical objects that contained them. Beloved editions had traveled with him from house to house, country to country, but they had all disappeared in the sad shuffle of works and days, and now the only eternity Benjamin could envisage was the eternity of the text, a world in which one never stopped reading, the last word becoming the first word, ad infinitum. The final labyrinth.

'Reality as text, as marginalia,' Benjamin muttered to himself. He felt perfectly awake now, even though he could not speak clearly to Professor Lott; indeed, he could hardly speak at all. Floating, as it were, in darkness, he could visualize heaven as a vast canopy, a planetarium. The luminous bodies that filled his life shone above him: Dora and Stefan, bobbing on the horizon like Mars and Venus, inescapable and distinct. And there was Asja, herself a sun, with votary planets circling. And Jula, Beatrice, and others – those match tips who inflamed his heart. And Scholem, so dear and complex, so fatally selfish, but loving, too. And Brecht, equally selfish, equally loving. Everyone convinced that his or her path was the only way.

So many faces to acknowledge, thought Benjamin as the sky snowed stars.

'Can you hear me, Walter?'

'Yes,' he said, distinctly.

'How do you feel?'

'Like a dying man.' A fractured smile crossed his lips. 'Otherwise, not so bad.'

'Do you believe in God, Walter?'

'No,' Benjamin said, closing his eyes. 'I've been trying to explain this to Him for many years, you see. He doesn't listen to me.'

Professor Lott bent forward, 'What did you say?'

Benjamin lifted his eyelids wearily. 'Gerhard, I knew it . . .'

'Gerhard?'

'You found me, I see . . .'

Professor Lott wondered who Gerhard might be. 'You are not afraid, Walter?'

'Afraid?'

Benjamin seemed to chuckle to himself. 'Jerusalem,' he said. 'Yes, I will come, if you insist.'

Benjamin could hear himself talking but felt curiously detached from the words. The sound of his voice was like someone talking in the next room, heard through a thin wall; he could almost understand what was being said, but not quite.

'Is there anyone I should contact, Walter?'

Benjamin stared at the gentle professor, who spoke slowly and loudly, as one might to a toddler just entering language. He contorted his lips as he spoke to emphasize certain words.

'Tell Dora . . . my wife,' Benjamin said. The words came hard, each one thrust between his teeth like a swollen tongue.

Lott nodded eagerly, pleased to have understood something. 'I will write to her, I assure you.' He seemed to come alive in this crisis, looking monkish in his nightgown, with his hair like a skullcap.

'I have not been a good man, Gerhard,' Benjamin said. 'Your work, I see, is important. The Kabbalah . . .'

The professor wiped the dribble from Benjamin's chin.

'I have completed so little.' The hot tears of contrition lay in pools on his cheeks. His stomach was queasy, his eyelids heavy. A kind of bile seemed to rise in his throat, burning and sour. The face of Gershom Scholem bobbed above him, and he tried to reach it, to touch the bright cheeks and kind eyes.

'You are in good hands, Walter,' Professor Lott said.

Benjamin stared up like a sick animal. The bad new days were no good at all. He wanted the old ones back, and the city of his childhood, where trolley cars slurred by on glistening tracks, their bells clanging, and horses galloped over wet cobbles. He wanted a city where smoke rose comfortingly from a thousand chimneys along each street. He wanted to walk those streets again, tracing their familiar but endlessly rediscoverable patterns. He wanted a world in which there was so much time, and so little to do with it.

Scenes flickered before his eyes: the morning when he had stumbled on a slaughterhouse near the river. A boy of nine or ten, he had stood aghast, watching a stout man in a blood-spattered apron hack away at hens, roosters, geese, ducks. The feathers flew in the midst of terrible quacking, screaming, gabbling; the boy's mouth filled with a bitter froth. It was his first taste of death. And that taste filled his mouth again, green and metallic.

He spat to one side. 'The Jews!' he shouted. 'Why the Jews?'

Professor Lott urged him to rest.

'The Jews,' he mumbled. 'You were right, Gerhard.'

He could see them in Hitler's camps now, their slumping shoulders, rank-and-file; his brother, Georg, was among them, thin and wan, and his cousins Fritz and Artur, and the little girl, Elise, whom he had taken to the park in Munich, and Gustav Hugenberg, Johanna Hochman, Felix Kiepenheuer, Hermann Jessner. Names on a list, and he did not doubt that most of them were dead. Hacked and shredded. Blood on the sawdust floor. No shrieking or gabbling but the mute glare of the damned-without-reason. He had not believed all the stories at first, but he believed them now.

He thought about the difference, or lack thereof, between Jews and Gentiles. Scholem had passionately maintained a belief in difference. Gentiles, he argued, are the opposite of Jews. Their God is, after all, a human being, terrestrial man – an incarnation. The

God of the Jews is beyond mortality, not inhuman but definitely nonhuman. *Totaliter aliter* – Wholly Other. Neither man nor woman, but utterly sexless and beyond reproduction. Because, for Christians, God can be man, therefore, men can be as gods; they can do superhuman things. Thus greatness of any kind appeals to them; tyrants and destroyers are revered as well as heroic painters, poets, and musicians. Rulers of magnitude are celebrated, and magnificent rebels, too. Saints are coveted, even whores if they are extraordinary in their lust. Thrift is admired, but so is vast prodigality: A man who would give away everything is put on a pedestal. The Jews do not worship greatness, nor revere leaders, even their own. They complained about Moses; they killed Zacharias; Jeremiah was left by the side of the road to die. Even Samuel was spurned.

Professor Lott was talking, softly. He seemed to be weeping. 'I had a wife, Elena. She stayed in Berlin when I moved to Belgium. We had been fighting, you see. It was silly of her. Of me, too.' He told Benjamin everything he could remember about Elena, and explained that he could not be sure if she was alive or dead now. His letters urging her to move to Belgium had not been answered. And now, he suspected, she might well be gone.

Benjamin either waved or thought he waved his hand. He caught a sentence or two, and felt sorry for this man. Was it Scholem? Had Scholem's wife stayed in Germany? It seemed impossible.

'We must go to Jerusalem, all of us,' Benjamin whispered.

Professor Lott seemed to understand. 'Jerusalem!' he said.

Benjamin nodded, or tried to, recalling a text from the Kabbalah that Scholem had sent from Jerusalem only a few months ago:

> When you attend the voice of God in all things, you become fully human. Usually the mind hides the Divine by forcing you to believe there is a separate power that causes all mental images, and voices, to arise; but this is false thinking. By listening to the voice of God in every-thing, you comprehend the Eternal. It becomes your mind, flows through your mind. Revelation is yours.

He was listening, alert as a dog on the night of a full moon. In being fully human, he discovered the Divine.

How thin the membrane separating the living from the dead, he thought, mouthing the words. Pressed close to this membrane, he could almost see through its translucent barrier, could almost visualize the pale shapes and shadows on the other side; they would soon have faces, features, concrete particulars.

Professor Lott closed his eyes, recalling a night many years ago in Berlin when his father, a silk merchant, died at home with his four children around him; they waited through a long, wintry night for the end. When it came, everyone stood and kissed one another, and a peculiar happiness settled over the room. They knew their own lives had been sharpened forever, given a contour, a keen edge, palpability.

Benjamin tried to say his friend's name, Scholem. Such a beautiful name, he thought. He had certainly been lucky in his friends. The fact that so many benevolent creatures appeared at one's elbow in a moment of struggle was a sign of repair. *Tikkun olam*.

'You must not worry, Walter,' Professor Lott said, leaning close to Benjamin's face. 'I will arrange everything.'

Benjamin heard this, but worrying and not-worrying were altogether beside the point. Listening was the issue, and becoming receptive; there was music in the distance, unheard; there were colors to see beyond the physical spectrum he could know. He had not realized that, near death, he would feel so calm, so happy. He did not know that everything would point forward so boldly.

'The Gurlands have escaped,' Professor Lott explained, sowing his words like seeds in the soft loam of Benjamin's unconscious mind.

Benjamin looked up and saw Alphonse Lott before him, and a warm feeling spread over his body, like entering a bath. He wanted to speak loudly and clearly, to tell Professor Lott that the work of repair is endless, is never-ending. He had so much to say, and so few words at his disposal.

'*Tikkun olam*,' he whispered. The repair of the world. '*Tikkun olam*.'

Professor Lott heard these odd syllables, but he did not understand them. He watched in awe, with reverence, as a stillness gradually overtook Benjamin. In a while, he put a hesitant ear to his chest, reached for his throat, then his wrist, searching for a pulse. Finally, with a sense of loss beyond explanation, he pulled the sheets up to the sagging chin, smoothed the woolen blankets around him, and tiptoed back to his room. There was nothing more he could do for him now. Walter Benjamin was dead.

WALTER BENJAMIN

A person listening to a story is in the company of the storyteller; even somebody reading a story aloud shares this companionship. The reader of a novel, however, is isolated, more so than any other reader. In this solitude, readers of novels seize upon their material more jealously than anyone else. They are ready to make it completely their own, to devour it, as it were. Indeed, they destroy and swallow up the material presented to them as a fire devours logs in a fireplace. The suspense that permeates a good novel is akin to the draft that fans the flame in the fireplace and enlivens its play.

17

'Is there something to eat?' José wondered.

'I'll get something when we stop. Can you wait?'

José nodded, determined to behave as well as possible. It was not his mother's fault that they were here, in flight, hungry. His head throbbed as the sun beat in hard, searing through the smudged window of the railway car. Outside, the sky had that scraped look that comes after a serious storm: blue beyond blue, and not a cloud anywhere in sight. A perfect morning.

But it had been a hideous night: the lashing rain, thunder across the bay, and then, as if God had suddenly peeled back the lid, this sun too bright to imagine. It sprayed its light everywhere and seemed to blaze from no specific center.

The railway tracks followed the coast, and the sea was gold-flecked, expansive on the left side of the car; on the right were stubble-fields of autumn, haystacks like sentries. Windmills appeared now and then, and cattle in disorganized clusters. Peasant villages scuttled by, nameless, the stone houses huddled together, the orange tiles of their roofs shimmering as the daytime moon kept stubbornly abreast of the window. Signs of life were minimal: a woman lugging water from a well, a boy herding goats up a small hillock, an old man sitting by a tree, smoking.

Henny Gurland and her son had the compartment to themselves, but they said little to each other. The events of the past day and night were beyond articulation. Indeed, they would hardly mention their crossing over the Pyrenees or the events that occurred in Port-Bou for several weeks, and then (in later years) would almost never refer to them again. It was better to leave such things untouched by speech. Language only warps the shapes and forms of attention, reduces them to a caricature. A story is always a lie, since so much is left out.

In the rush to leave the Fonda Franca before the guard woke, José had not had time to wash or brush his teeth. He had simply jumped into the same clothes he had worn the day before, however filthy. His shirt had deep stains around the armpits, and the stench was intolerable, even to him.

He yawned repeatedly, leaning on Benjamin's briefcase, which he kept beside him on the seat, under his arm. He was tempted to open it, to examine the manuscript inside, but he didn't dare. It was too much like prying into a casket.

The village of Girona appeared in the middle distance, and the train began to slow.

'If anyone questions us, remember to say nothing,' Frau Gurland warned as the brakes squealed. 'We are going to Salamanca, to meet your father. That is all you know. Do you understand?'

'I do.'

'Good. The less said the better. That is always the best way.' She added: 'You needn't worry, darling. I will do the talking.'

José was glad to let her speak for him. The strut of independence exercised in the climb over the Pyrenees had worn him out, and he wanted to relapse, to let her take care of him. He understood now that his mother was doing her best in the circumstances and that he must offer sympathy, must try to help in whatever ways he could to see that they did, indeed, make it safely to Portugal.

He put his hand on Benjamin's rough leather briefcase. It was miraculous that the responsibility for getting this manuscript to New York should be his and his mother's. Setting out from the Fonda Franca, he had begged his mother to let him carry it. It was heavy, of course, and she seemed slightly to resent it. 'We can't let anything slow us down,' she said, staring at the briefcase. José tightened his grip on the handle, steeled himself to protect this piece of Walter Benjamin still in their possession. He could almost hear the dear man's voice: 'There is so much of me in the book, José. Everything of me is somewhere in its pages.'

The train stuttered to a halt in the tiny station, which consisted of a single platform and a small, painted shed. After picking up two or three passengers, the train pulled away jerkily, gassing and wheezing. Soon they were rolling smoothly, and José leaned his head against his mother's shoulder.

Frau Gurland found herself tearing up. José had been so difficult on the trek. He had tried to swallow his childhood and become, in one day, an adult, and this meant rejecting her. Now, of course, he needed her again. The soft head against her shoulder confirmed it. Soon he slumped into her lap, and she cradled him like a tiny boy whom she was determined to protect somehow. Arkady had said to her, just before they took him away, 'Take care of him, Henny.' *I will*, she said now. *I will take care of him*.

The train sped south along the coast toward Barcelona, the sun pooling in José's face while he slept. He didn't wake until moments before their arrival in Barcelona.

'We must change trains,' his mother whispered in his ear.

'We're here?'

'Yes, in Barcelona.'

José reached for the briefcase while his mother lifted their rucksacks from the overhead rack.

It was a big, vaulting station, with well-dressed businessmen standing in groups of three or four and talking loudly. Frau Gurland stopped at a kiosk to buy a loaf of bread and some soft cheese, but there was no time to eat it. The express for Madrid was leaving in ten minutes, and they boarded the train with only seconds to spare, finding a seat beside a portly gentleman in a chalk-striped suit.

It was an impressive train, with blue upholstery and embossed leather lining along the walls of each compartment. Tulip-shaped reading lamps were unlit over the head of each passenger. A collapsible table was still pushed up against the wall below the broad, clean window.

The portly gentleman glanced toward Frau Gurland as if to acknowledge her presence. His copious flesh was like swaddling, puffy and white, and his big knuckles seemed to be closing in the skin like dents in dough. His steam-pressed suit and brightly polished shoes, even the flowery smell of cologne, were signs of affluence if not gentility. Henny Gurland guessed that he was a lawyer or businessman of some kind, perhaps a politician.

He puffed a thick, reddish cigar while reading a newspaper intently, sometimes grimacing. The news seemed to upset him visibly. Once, however, he erupted into sharp laughter, spooking José, who looked to his mother for reassurance. Smoke hung above the Spaniard's slick bald head, and soon the air in the compartment became unbreathable. Frau Gurland began to cough, but she did not complain; that would be foolish in these circumstances.

At one point, the man turned to José with a curious look and seemed about to ask a question, but he didn't. Henny Gurland consciously avoided the man's eyes, since that might arouse his interest. Above all, she did not want to enter into a conversation. That could be dangerous. What, for example, if he were a police supervisor or government official?

The train pulled slowly out of the station, skirting the city, which Frau Gurland remembered well from the Civil War: its broad avenues, the rows of linden trees, the toylike trolleys, the bakeries and bars. These images flickered in the big window of the compartment, more like memories than real pictures. It was with some relief that she saw the city give way to dense woodland, to closely cropped villages, or meadows opening fanwise in the window.

An hour or so after the train left the station, the conductor arrived to punch their tickets. A short fellow with a well-trimmed beard, he observed the Gurlands without expression, asking to see their tickets in such guttural Spanish that Frau Gurland became confused.

'You are Spanish?' he wondered.

She merely nodded, holding up two tickets.

The conductor did not bother to examine the tickets closely. Nor did he press for conversation, much to her relief. Her Spanish was moderately good (she had, after all, spent several years in Barcelona with her husband), but her accent and fragile grammar would have given her away.

'Thank you, señora,' the conductor said, handing her both tickets.

Frau Gurland offered a slight smile, then turned her head to look out the window.

The gentleman beside her dropped his newspaper when the conductor was gone. 'Did you say you were Spanish?' he asked. He smiled, and his teeth appeared, as if marionettes onstage, ready for a small, impromptu performance. They were fiercely white but uneven.

Frau Gurland hesitated, then said, 'My husband is Spanish.'

'Ah, you are Colombian, perhaps?'

'No, I'm not.'

'Your accent . . . it reminded me of a Colombian woman I once knew.'

José sat up, anxious, wondering why this man was questioning his mother. His own Spanish was too weak to follow the conversation, but it reassured him that his mother seemed unperturbed.

'Do you like Spain, then?' the man continued.

Frau Gurland shifted in her seat.

'You must not be afraid of me,' he said. 'I'm sorry if my questions are unwelcome. I mean no harm.'

Though she could not guess at his motives, Henny Gurland took him at his word. There was a welcome kindliness in his expression, and she found his voice reassuring. That he meant no harm seemed plausible.

She apologized for her reticence. 'We are both very tired, my son and I. We've been traveling for several days.'

'Of course,' he said, turning his gaze to the newspaper.

José relaxed now, pressing Benjamin's briefcase between his ankles, thinking about an unlikely fellow who had befriended them in Marseilles. He had offered them a meal, even though he apparently had little money to spare. That same night he offered to accompany them to the Spanish border, and to introduce them to Lisa Fittko. Without him (and her), they would almost certainly still be in France, probably in Nazi hands.

Benjamin's deep learning had impressed José; he seemed to know even more than the boy's father. José wondered if he himself could ever know as much. He had not read many books in their entirety. Novels, in particular, remained a puzzle; it simply made no sense to read a book that declared itself untrue from the outset. Why make up stories when the world supplied each day more spectacular ones than anyone could hope to invent? Surely Adolf Hitler was beyond the power of anyone's invention? (He could see Hitler's face staring from the back of the Spanish gentleman's paper, his eyes like holes cut into the page.)

What José preferred to books were bridges and dikes, electrical systems, and complex machinery. He planned to study engineering one day, and to learn how the various parts of the world connected and how energy was transferred. Matter was, to him, the greatest mystery of all. Although everything was chemistry, the complexity of the material world was unfathomable; if only one little atom in his body shifted, he would not be himself, José Gurland. He would be another person – perhaps trapped in the same circumstances, but a different person nonetheless, and therefore able to respond in significantly different ways to these circumstances.

The train rounded a curve, and José was jolted from his daydreaming. 'Could I have a little of that bread, Mother?' he asked.

It frightened his mother that he spoke in French, but the gentleman continued to read his newspaper and puff his cigar, grunting approval or scoffing with raised eyebrows as he turned the pages. She broke off a piece of bread from the small loaf and cut a strip of the yellow, waxy cheese. 'Here,' she said, 'but this will have to do.'

The portly man peered over his newspaper as José ate, barely suppressing a smile.

Late in the afternoon, the train pulled into Torrabla, some

distance north of Madrid. As they approached the station, Henny Gurland noticed a cluster of drab military vehicles beside the tracks, and her scalp prickled with fear. The Spanish army always terrified her. A dozen or more soldiers in black berets had grouped together on the platform, some of them brandishing rifles; an officer barked instructions, though she couldn't hear his voice. He was pointing ominously to their train.

José, who was busily pressing the cheese into his bread, had not seen the soldiers. Like a child, he was humming a tune to himself, more loudly than he realized.

The gentleman in the chalk stripes set aside his newspaper and rose, pulling down the window to peer outside. When he saw the soldiers boarding the train at the front, he turned to Frau Gurland. 'Quickly, madame. You must get off the train.'

Henny Gurland felt her eyebrows lifting.

'Your papers, I assume they are questionable?' he asked.

She stared at him, giving nothing away. Her stomach was clenched, and she wanted only to be far away from this horrible place, the war, this danger, with José safe and happy.

'I will tell them I was alone in this compartment,' the gentleman said. 'I've been traveling by myself since Barcelona. Do you understand?'

Frau Gurland's head spun now. Could she trust this man? Could he possibly be saying this to frighten her? To get her into deeper trouble?

'You must do as I say,' he said, urgently.

She saw in his eyes what could only be genuine concern. 'I'm very grateful to you, sir.'

They heard shouts in the next car, and the slamming of doors.

'Please,' he said, 'don't thank me. Go!'

She and José stepped into the aisle, which was still clear. They heard voices rising loudly in the next car as they leapt from the train and lost themselves in a crowd of onlookers.

José clung to his mother's hand. 'What's going on?' he asked. 'Were those Nazis?'

'I don't think so,' she said. 'Franco's troops. But one can't take a chance. The Gestapo is everywhere. We've been lucky so far.'

'Who was that man, the one on the train?'

'I don't know.'

They stood at the back of the crowd and watched as the whistle blew, leaving a ghost in air, and the wheels engaged. A breath of ashes lingered on the platform as it disappeared slowly around the bend.

'The soldiers stayed on the train,' said José. 'They were looking for someone.'

His mother agreed. 'It was an express, too. It wasn't scheduled to stop here.'

'We'll be stuck here, won't we?'

Frau Gurland shook her head. 'There are plenty of trains, I'm sure. All roads lead to Madrid.' She suggested that they find a café, and they settled in the railway bar, in a corner of a room filled with blue cigarette smoke and loud Spanish voices.

'Would you like another piece of cheese?' Frau Gurland asked.

José reached for the offering, sure that no amount of food would cure the ache in his stomach, this emptiness he had been carrying for months now.

'Eat slowly,' his mother said. 'It will help.'

Suddenly a small fire seemed to light in the back of his eyes, and his lips came apart. He began to rub his hands as if he were cold.

'What is it, darling? Is something wrong?'

José could not find words, though his lips moved slightly.

His mother stood now, hovering. 'Are you all right, José?'

'The briefcase!' he said, in a whisper.

Henny Gurland felt her hands turning to ice.

'We've got to get it!' José said, loudly, standing.

'Please, sit down,' his mother said, noticing that faces had turned in their direction. This was not a moment in their flight to call attention to themselves.

José saw her panic and sat down. He dug one fist into an open palm, grinding it, wincing. He wanted to pound the table, to shout, to throw a jar of salt across the room.

'It's okay,' his mother said.

'It's not,' he said. 'How can you say that?'

'There was nothing you could do.'

'I left the goddamned briefcase on the train!'

'It was an accident,' she said. 'We were in a hurry. The soldiers were coming.'

'I don't care,' he said.

'Please, darling, don't—'

'We've got to find it,' he broke in. The hot tears of self-directed rage filled his eyes.

'Of course we do,' she said, locating a soothing note. 'We'll check with the porters in Madrid. That nice gentleman will know what to do.'

'How do you know?'

'I don't,' she said. 'But in any case, there was an address inside. He will send it along to the man in New York if we don't find it. I feel sure of that.' She surprised herself with her confident tone, but even as she spoke she knew better. They would be lucky enough as it was to get to Fuentes de Onoro, in Portugal, by nightfall.

José looked at his mother angrily, hurt. Her assurance meant nothing to him. He put his big hands on the marble tabletop, studying the long fingers and dirty nails, the fine web of blue veins beneath the skin. The hands seemed detached from him, from José Gurland; they had a life of their own, and he felt he could not control them.

Frau Gurland reached over the table to touch those hands. 'Dr Benjamin wanted us to get to Portugal.'

José shook his head, letting the tears fall unabashedly now. It didn't matter what his mother said or what anyone thought. That manuscript had meant so much to him; indeed, it probably contained everything he had ever thought about, the ultimate formation of his experience as a man. He remembered that Benjamin had asked Frau Fittko to take the manuscript and leave him there, dangling on the precipice, in the Pyrenees. And he was not joking. 'It is more important than I am,' he had said. More important than life.

And he had lost it.

'Don't blame yourself, José,' Henny Gurland said. 'You know he would understand.'

José looked up, recalling how Benjamin had reached for him suddenly, awkwardly, and had pulled him close. It seemed that José could actually smell his presence now, feel the coarse wool of his jacket against his cheek, and the stubby fingers kneading his neck. He could hear that low voice, guttural, keyed and pitched like no other. 'The world is a dark place,' he was saying. 'It is always in disrepair. But we – you and I, José – we have a little chance, an opportunity. If we try very, very hard, we can imagine goodness. We can think of ways to repair the damage, piece by piece.'

In a remote Hasidic village, so the story goes, some Jews were huddled together in a shabby inn one Sabbath evening beside a log fire. They were local people, all of them, with the exception of one person whom nobody could identify. He was obviously poor, a ragged man who squatted silently on all fours in a shadowy corner at the back of the room.

A number of topics were discussed, and then it was suggested that everybody should say what he would ask for if only one wish were granted him. One man wanted money; another would have a faithful son-in-law; a third imagined a brand-new carpenter's bench, with shining tools. Everybody spoke in turn, and when they had finished, only the beggar had said nothing.

They prodded him, of course, and – with reluctance – he said, 'I wish I were the powerful king of a large, important country. Then, one night while I slept in my palace, an enemy would invade my kingdom, and by dawn his horsemen would penetrate my castle, and they would meet with no resistance from my guards. Awakened from a deep sleep, I would have no time to dress; I would have to escape in my nightshirt. Fleeing over hill and dale, through forests day and night, I would arrive at last right here in this despicable inn, and I would be found squatting here in this corner, right now. This is my wish.'

The others looked around the room, deeply confused. 'And what good would that do you?' asked one man.

After a pause, the beggar said: 'At least I'd have a nightshirt.'

Being a rational person, I like to understand why I do things. It is not enough simply to act; animals can do that, the beasts of the field. What separates human beings from such beasts is self-consciousness, however weak this may be. So what exactly brought me here, to Port-Bou, a full decade after Benjamin's death? Was it merely guilt – surely the most boring of motivations?

I must resist this interpretation. I did everything within my powers to help Benjamin get to Palestine, and none of it was exactly easy. What could I say to people in his defense? What evidence would convince them that Walter Benjamin might actually perform a useful service? He had no teaching experience and would probably dissolve in front of a class, pooling on the floor before their very eyes. He could surely never be counted on for regular journalistic writing: Even his book reviews were inscrutable, and he did not have the habits of production necessary to keep up with such pressures.

So how would he live? Who would pay him? There was little money for anyone in those days. Indeed, I lived on air myself when I first came to Palestine, sustained mostly by the vision of Eretz Yisrael that we all shared. I hardly noticed the essential poverty of my people: We survived happily on dust and sunlight, and the parched earth was a blank tablet awaiting our inscription. I remember fingering the dirt: It might have been gold for all anyone who saw me on my knees could tell. God was everywhere, in the stubborn fruit that bloomed in the Negev, in the shimmer of

Galilee's bright surface, in the amber glint of Jerusalem's old city walls. Once I stood mutely before the Wailing Wall, wanting to pray, but could utter nothing. Every moment there was an answered prayer.

Alas, poor Benjamin! What could he do to justify his presence in Palestine? I fretted, month after month, in the late twenties, when I saw that unless something was done soon, he would come to ruin quickly. Some people do not care for themselves very well; they take no pity on their own hearts. Fortunately, the Institute for Social Research in Frankfurt came to the rescue, offering him a small but regular income in return for 'research.' But even there, problems quickly arose. Benjamin resented their assignment, which he found irrelevant to the main strands of his research. 'Why should I write what interests Adorno or Horkheimer? Who are they to insist upon these command performances?' he would ask, full of indignation. He complained bitterly about this work, even when the money was good. As this income began to dwindle, in the mid-thirties, he became frantic, as anyone would. The Institute seemed to demand more and more time for less and less money. 'They treat me like a schoolboy,' he wrote to me from Paris. 'It is reprehensible. *Non serviam.*'

The income they offered, however paltry, was still desperately needed. It was pathetic to see a man of his exquisite learning and originality living in such conditions, half starved and writing essays of little interest to himself. On the other hand, without these assignments from Adorno and Horkheimer, there is no telling what he would have written. I remember asking him once, 'What do you expect to produce in the next decade, Walter?' He turned to me with those baleful eyes, vaguely twinkling, and said, 'Less than in the previous decade, I suspect.' Another time, when I was begging him to write more, for his own sake as well as for his admirers, he said, 'All art aspires to the condition of silence.'

When, in the late thirties, I began to realize the full extent of his financial – and spiritual – problems, I tried to convince my publisher, Salman Schocken (who was deeply enamored of my own work, much to my surprise and delight), to commission a book on Kafka from Benjamin. He had, however, read some of the essays I'd sent him, and he said, 'Your friend Walter Benjamin is a tedious writer. I can't stay awake when I read him. In fact, I have no idea what he's trying to say most of the time.' And that was that. (Of course, I protected Benjamin from the full brunt of this criticism, telling him that Schocken had too many books on Kafka in the works.)

Benjamin was a depressive by nature, which doubtless made it difficult for him to work. Gloom was part of his visage: The hooded eyes seemed to grow darker year by year, slipping deeper into the skull, and the black mustache and hair added to the effect. The sorrowful mouth (which he frequently covered with his right hand, muffling his speech) only made things worse. Especially in the later years, he did not trouble to groom himself, although he was fastidious in other ways, even dandyish in his choice of clothing. I could never reconcile the lack of attention to ordinary hygiene with the overlay of formal white shirts, distinguished ties, and striped waistcoats. The style of clothing he preferred was, of course, antiquarian: a way of broadcasting his affinities with an earlier time, when reading and (more generally) culture mattered. But the sordidness, the soiled effect, somehow ironized the presentation. 'Yes,' he seemed to be saying, 'there are good things in the world, but they are badly tarnished. Look! Even I am badly tarnished!'

In Paris, in the midst of hideously degrading circumstances, he surrounded himself with fragments of an earlier life, the life of an educated, bourgeois gentleman. Old books, in their crumbling buckram covers, would be propped beside assorted ceramics and porcelain bric-a-brac, with small pencil drawings and favorite pictures hung on the walls. Once, when he complained of poverty, I suggested that he sell a particular drawing by Max Unold that held some monetary value. He said, rather fiercely, 'I would rather kill myself.'

Benjamin talked openly, and often, of suicide, so it did not surprise me when I heard about what happened. I always supposed that, sooner or later, he would die by his own hand. In Nice, in the stifling summer of 1932, he went so far as to draw up his will, leaving everything of any material value to Stefan, his son; his manuscripts were to go to me. This sad document arrived in the mail with a note saying that by the time I got it he would certainly be dead. It was almost embarrassing to get his next letter, which made no mention of the previous communication. Being tactful, I did not raise the subject again. Suicide, like masturbation, is a private matter.

Benjamin's misery was evident in his correspondence. In one letter of that time, he spoke of the 'small victories' achieved in his writing, and how little compensation they offered, given the 'great defeats' that life had dealt him. But they were not so great as he imagined. He had obviously not attained everything in his powers; perhaps only Goethe, or Shakespeare, managed to squeeze out everything that was in them. Genius on that scale is sublime, and rare. Benjamin was not of this kind, or anything like it, yet the quality of his mind was undeniable. It was best witnessed in his letters, I think: I treasured each one of them, although his hand was so small and cramped that I resorted often to reading his letters with a magnifying glass, poring over the smudged pages (he invariably spilled coffee on them, or wine) as if I were trying to piece together the marks on some ancient scroll. But what marks they were!

It seems odd, you know, that someone of Benjamin's rarefied and idiosyncratic temperament should suffer from the same ambitions and anxieties that beset even the most commercial of writers. However quixotic, he passionately hoped to acquire a readership large enough to make it possible for him to earn a living from his pen. In the twentieth century, this is no longer possible, not for poets and philosophers. The circle of readers has narrowed, almost vanished. I, for instance, expect to find only a few responsible readers for my work, 'fit company though few.' Benjamin understood this abstractly but continued to struggle in vain for two decades to wrest a small income from his Herculean labors. 'The position from which I approach things,' he wrote to me, in a sad moment of self-awareness, 'is far too advanced still to fall within the purview of a public readership.' Indeed.

Even I, who spent decades in dialogue with this man, could only partially grasp his most difficult and original work, such as the early book on German tragic drama, or his late essay called 'Theses on the Philosophy of History' – a magnificent piece of aphoristic prose, if somewhat strange in its obliqueness and inwardness. Benjamin's highly personal manner of building an argument often eluded me, although I never found a word he wrote less than suggestive. I would hate to think how many times he sent me darting this way or that, frequently into thick briars. I came away scraped and bleeding too many times! Nevertheless, through his essays and letters, I came to know Proust, Kafka, Leskov, Baudelaire, Krause, and so many others as if I had never really read them before. Only the beastly Brecht defeated me, and still defeats me. I will never see the attractions of that man, an obvious charlatan.

It was puzzling, even disquieting, that Benjamin should grow Janus-faced when it came to Brecht, saying one thing to him and another to me. Brecht complained about his 'mysticism' and his 'Judaisms,' writing to him in 1938: 'You must forget these dark gleanings, this almost Oriental aspiration to find the one. The one does not exist. There are only people and their problems, and the point of writing is to annoy the people so badly that they solve – or wish to solve – their problems.' Such humbug!

The mystical and Judaic aspects of Benjamin's thought were precisely what attracted me in the first place. What he saw of value in Brecht is another matter. I had read a number of the playwright's early scenarios without interest, but at Benjamin's urging I went to see a performance of *The Threepenny Opera* in 1932. It had been playing to full houses for two years, and I assumed it must have some power. People do not throw their money away for nothing. So I was truly stunned to witness a middle-class audience cheering a play in which the author spat vengefully upon them. This self-loathing, and mostly Jewish, audience was indeed more shocking to behold than the play. In three months, of course, Hitler would assume total control of Germany; this, in retrospect, makes the attitude of that audience seem all the more baffling and terrifying. (I am almost tempted to say that it explained a little of what followed.)

Apart from Brecht, Benjamin would have nothing to do with 'famous' or 'important' writers of the day like Lion Feuchtwanger or Emil Ludwig. Heinrich Mann was the exception: Those witty, deft, sardonic novels pleased him, and he urged them upon me (I did not care for their flippant cynicism, but I understood what was admirable in the craftsmanship). Heinrich's brother, Thomas, meant nothing to Benjamin until *The Magic Mountain* appeared. Suddenly a missive full of praises arrived: 'What is unmistakably characteristic of this novel is something that moves me and has always moved me; it speaks to me in a way I can evaluate and acknowledge and that I must, in many respects, greatly admire. However charmless such analyses are, I can only imagine that an internal change must have taken place in the author while he was writing. Indeed, I am certain this was the case.'

It saddens me to think what I have lost. But it was already lost. We had ceased, perhaps earlier than I care to admit, to share our intellectual life in a way that followed from what began, in Berlin, so long ago. That trouble started in the late summer of 1928, when he was again beset, besotted by Asja Lacis, who despised me and did everything she could to keep us apart. She tantalized and tormented him; ultimately, she drove him away from his deepest concerns, prompting him to waste his time on dialectical thinking of the crudest sort. Hegel is bad enough, but pseudo-Hegelianism! The Benjamin I knew in 1918 would never have dined happily with the Benjamin of 1928.

It was obvious to me, and (I think) to Benjamin, that his life in Berlin was hopeless. The marriage to Dora had dissolved, and Asja was not going to live with him, except intermittently and falsely. It was clear to anyone who could see with open eyes that Germany was no place for Jews. Jews had been demonized, cast as Other: Hitler and his friends understood only too well that one needs to construct an enemy to advance an ideology, and we were once again the chosen people.

I urged Benjamin, once again, to come to Jerusalem, and he

agreed. 'What I must do is, at last, clear to me,' he wrote. First, however, he would have to learn Hebrew, and I put him in touch with my old friend Max Mayer, from an assimilated family, one of the few Zionists left in Berlin, who knew Hebrew well enough to teach it. Benjamin applied himself vigorously to his studies for about two months, but it soon became obvious from his letters to me that his project was doomed. Benjamin's interests lay elsewhere just now.

As I later surmised, he was wasting his time with a long article on Goethe for some bogus encyclopedia spawned in the Kremlin. This counted as another success for Asja Lacis, who had by now managed to permeate his mind as well as his senses. I wrote a blistering letter, upbraiding him for his failure to pursue Hebrew and further his plans for emigration to Palestine, and he replied with characteristic rue: 'Unfortunately I cannot counter your reproaches with anything at all; they are thoroughly justified, and in this matter I have encountered a pathological vacillation which, I am sorry to admit, I have already witnessed in myself from time to time.' From time to time!

Our sad, last meeting in Paris, a couple of years before the war, stays with me. It had been a decade since I had actually seen him, and his physical degeneration was unsettling to behold. He had grown heavier, with a paunch that tilted upward when he stood; a double chin rippled into existence whenever he dipped his head forward. Even the knuckles on his hands had acquired a faint puffiness: a sign of heart trouble, I guessed. His skin had taken on the aura of old newspaper, and strands of silver mingled with his otherwise jet-black hair; the mustache seemed more copious than before, unkempt, almost decadent. His eyesight, always bad, had grown worse, and he would take my arm like an old man as we walked the city streets. Quick steps or a few stairs inevitably brought on a bout of wheezing, and he would cry, 'You are killing me, Gerhard! You are a young man! Take pity!'

We had been arguing about Marxist theories of language for many years, and I confronted him now more purposefully. 'You want to take away the magical aspects of language,' I said. 'Linguistics is not a science.'

'You are wrong, Gerhard. You have not been listening to me, as usual.'

How many times in my life had those sentences been uttered by my dear friend Benjamin? A thousand times? I used to love to hear them. 'You are wrong, Gerhard. You have not been listening to me.' Always, it was said with affection, with a slight bemusement. But years of reading that Marxist gibberish had taken their toll, and the ironic bite was missing. 'You are wrong, Gerhard' meant, unequivocally, that I was indeed wrong. I was wrong!

Still, whenever we argued about language he continued to make a distinction between God's words and human words. This was, he maintained, the foundation of all linguistic theory. The difference between word and name remained alive in him, although he struggled with himself to keep his terms within the boundaries of Marxist, or pseudo-Marxist, thought. It was painful to listen to him, to watch him shift and squirm: the inevitable product of his disingenuous position.

After a particularly tortuous discussion, I took his hands in mine, and I said, 'Come, Walter. To Jerusalem.'

His eyes, sequestered behind thick lenses, turned watery. 'I cannot come with you, Gerhard,' he said. 'But I would, were it possible. You must believe me.'

We had been sitting on a bench beneath a tulip tree, talking and watching the pedestrians stroll by. There was a bookstore behind us, and I led Benjamin to the broad window, now filled with a hundred copies of Céline's new book, *Bagatelles pour un massacre*, a wild, anti-Semitic rant of six hundred pages. The book had seized the imagination of French intellectuals, and it was much respected, despite its vulgarity and racism.

'What do your friends say about this?' I asked him. 'Do they think Céline means no harm?'

'They say, "But it's a joke."'

'Do you think it's a joke, Walter?'

Benjamin shook his head. It was obviously not a joke. And it would never be a joke. The *trahison des clercs* that led to millions incinerated in the camps had only just begun.

We spent that evening in an obscure café on the Left Bank with Benjamin's quarrelsome relative Hannah Arendt and the even more trying Heinrich Blücher, whom Hannah later married. Arendt was much obsessed with the show trials of Stalin and denounced them volubly. 'Stalin is a monster!' she cried, drawing attention our way.

Benjamin said, 'You overstate the case, Hannah. That is just like you.'

Blücher said, 'Surely, Walter, you cannot defend what is happening in Russia!'

'The Soviet Union is a bold experiment,' he said. 'It is perhaps a failed experiment . . . I will grant this.'

I began to laugh. 'You take away my breath, Walter. How can you call it a failed experiment?' I considered the Stalinist regime a model of barbarism.

'It is sad, you know,' said Benjamin. 'What began as such a noble attempt to make life better . . . has degenerated.' After a heavy pause, he continued: 'Capitalism will not work, not ultimately. There is too much emphasis on short-term gain. It is bad economics, and bad for people.' He cracked his knuckles, then added: 'The world will become a glittering trash heap, then blow away.'

Arendt was contemptuous of this attitude, although she managed to show considerable respect for Benjamin. She adored him, really. You could see it in her eyes.

And I adored him, too, despite his irritating stubbornness, and his way of clinging to a worn-out ideology. He suffered the obsessive desire of many intellectuals to make the world whole by applying intelligent pressure of a specific kind, but human intelligence cannot make the world whole. Unchecked by compassion, humility, and a deep skepticism of its own virility, it can only destroy.

'He was a remarkable man,' said Madame Ruiz. She agreed to show me his 'real grave,' as she put it.

The cemetery attendant, Pablo, had taken me down a gravel path to an unmarked grave the evening before. He claimed he had buried

Benjamin himself in that particular place, and that Sergeant Consuelo, a local police officer, had personally overseen the burial. I can't say why, but I doubted him. His eyes avoided mine: the mark of a liar.

'Pablo cannot be trusted,' Madame Ruiz said. 'He is like the rest of them, thoroughly unreliable.' She took me to another site, although this grave was unmarked as well. 'I am certain that this is the one,' she said. 'I attended the funeral. It was very moving. There were no clouds in the sky, and a seagull landed right there, beside the stone.'

She was lying, too. Nobody would remember a seagull. There were seagulls all over the place, on every gravestone. But I decided it didn't matter. He was here somewhere, in this cemetery, and it was an arresting place, one of the most beautiful I have ever seen. Fragrant smells drifted down the hillside, a mingling of floral scents and the faint odor of moss and mint. The cemetery grove itself hovered precipitously over the Mediterranean, its lawn like a flying carpet suspended in ice-blue air. The coffins were tucked neatly into stone walls, which seemed to defy gravity.

Madame Ruiz was clearly an intelligent, cultivated woman, however unreliable. Apparently she had done what she could to prevent this tragedy, but it was hopeless. Benjamin, for reasons of his own, had decided it was better to take his own life that day, ten years ago, than to push forward into Spain and Portugal with Frau Gurland and her son.

'Did you know him well, professor?' she asked.

'We met in Berlin, before the war . . . the Great War,' I said. I wanted her to know the length of our acquaintance, if not the depth. One cannot really suggest the depth of such a friendship. It is beyond description.

'Ah, the Great War,' she said. 'My father was in that war.' After a long and boring bout of remembrance focused on her father, a minor official of Nice, she asked me about Benjamin. 'Was he some kind of writer? A famous writer?'

I explained to her that his work was not well known but that I admired it. 'One day he will be recognized as an important voice,' I said. 'His philosophical viewpoint was . . .' I could not continue in this fashion, and lapsed into silence.

'Should I read one of his books?' she asked.

'There is only one book, a treatise on German drama,' I explained. 'It is quite unreadable. And a collection of essays and fragments. Tantalizing but inadequate.'

I was tempted to launch into a critique of Benjamin's life and work, but it seemed futile. Standing here, beside his grave, I realized that what is lost is lost. Madame Ruiz was simply pandering to me. I was a customer, nothing more. The longer I remained in Port-Bou, in mourning, the more cash I would spend at her hotel.

In spite of having come so far, I did not wish to remain at his grave for long. The guilty feelings that overwhelmed me there were unwelcome and baseless. It was not my fault that he was dead, after all. Benjamin was killed by Hitler, and by Karl Marx. He was killed by Asja Lacis, who never really loved him, and yes, by Dora, his wife, who had never learned how to love him properly. He was killed most certainly by the Angel of History, whom he could never satisfy. Most obviously, he was killed by Time, which often waits teasingly in the wings, but which always appears onstage at last, claiming full authorship of everything that has gone before, each mincing step and wince, each flicker of the eye, each heartfelt line and random gesture.

I keep thinking of that essay of his, the intractable yet provocative 'Theses on the Philosophy of History.' Benjamin wrote: 'The messianic world is the world of all-sided and integral immediacy. Only there is universal history possible.' These words, written as Hitler's troops moved darkly across the national boundaries of France, hung in memory with a strange white light. 'It would not be written history,' Benjamin continued, 'but a festively enacted history. This feast is purified of all solemnity. It knows no festival hymns. Its language is integrated prose, which has broken the shackles of writing and is understood by all human beings.'

The myth of Babel obsessed him, as it does me. Thick walls of unintelligibility loom between each of us who would lay claim to some measure of humanity, and we are unable to address one another except in crude signs and abstract gestures, in tongues far too idiosyncratic and private to be understood. This point is made often, and beautifully, in the Zohar.

'One day,' Benjamin wrote, 'the confusion of tongues will end. And storytelling will come to an end, too, absorbed in the one integral prose.'

'Are you all right, professor?' Madame Ruiz asked, practically shouting in my face. 'You are preoccupied.'

I shook my head. No, I was not all right. Walter Benjamin was dead, and his words had scattered like so many spores in the black winds that swept Europe in 1940. No, I was not all right, and I would never be all right again. Unless his words, invisible, were somehow to land in hospitable soil, find nourishment, break into roots, tremble, and flush with life.

There was truth in those words, and truth is one thing that cannot be murdered, though it must often be disguised, hidden craftily in places where nobody would care to look.

AUTHOR'S NOTE

This is a work of fiction. As such, it lays no claim to the kinds of truth one expects to find in works of literary scholarship or conventional biography. Nevertheless, I have stuck close to the bare facts of Walter Benjamin's life, which is to say that names, dates, and localities are accurately presented, and that the events described in this novel happened pretty much as described.

I began reading Benjamin in 1969, when a friend passed me a copy of *Illuminations*, which had just been published in the United States. The voice in these unimaginably compressed, enigmatic, suggestive essays stayed with me for years, and I eagerly read most of Benjamin throughout the 1970s, when his work became popular in academic circles. In the mid-1980s, in Italy, I came across a review of Lisa Fittko's memoir of her wartime experiences in France, and her adventures in leading Benjamin and the Gurlands across the Pyrenees. Almost simultaneously, I discovered Gershom Scholem's affecting memoir, *Walter Benjamin: The Story of a Friendship*. From that point on, this novel seemed inevitable.

In 1989, in Jerusalem, I interviewed many friends and former students of Scholem's, and began making notes for this novel. I was also lucky enough to meet and interview Lisa Fittko, who has been consistently friendly and helpful throughout the writing of this book; without her sympathy I would not have undertaken this project. Nevertheless, she made me promise that I would say boldly in this afterword that the 'Lisa Fittko' who appears in my novel, while based on a real person, is a fictional character, the product of my imagination.

A few secondary sources were of special importance to me in the writing of this book, especially the memoirs of Asja Lacis as well as Benjamin's own letters (as collected in *The Correspondence of Walter Benjamin, 1910–1940*, edited by Gershom Scholem and Theodore W. Adorno, 1978) and his *Moscow Diary* (edited by Gary Smith, 1986). I am also grateful for the critical work on Benjamin by Susan Sontag, Hannah Arendt, Gary Smith, Richard Wolin, Leo Lowenthal, Robert Alter, John McCole, Susan Buck-Morrs, Jeffrey Mehlman, and Bernd Witte.

All passages by Walter Benjamin that are quoted in this novel have been translated by me, in part to give a unity to his voice in English.

Finally, I would like to thank my wife, Devon Jersild, for her endless encouragement and intellectual companionship, and to express gratitude to Amos Oz and Sir Isaiah Berlin for many friendly conversations, which helped to shape my vision of Walter Benjamin and his world. I am also grateful to the staff of the Bibliothèque Nationale in Paris for making my time in their library productive and satisfying.